Sisters of the Night

THE ANGRY ANGEL

Sisters of the Night
THE ANGRY ANGEL

CHELSEA QUINN YARBRO

ILLUSTRATED BY CHRISTOPHER H. BING

AVON BOOKS ◆ NEW YORK

AVON BOOKS, INC.
1350 Avenue of the Americas
New York, New York 10019

Copyright © 1998 by Swordsmith Productions and Chelsea Quinn Yarbro
Cover art and interior illustrations copyright © 1998 by Christopher H. Bing
A Swordsmith Production
Edited by Leigh Grossman; Associate editor: Lesley McBain; Consulting editor: Jeanne Cavelos
Illustrated by Christopher H. Bing
Interior design by Kellan Peck
Copyedited by Nancy C. Hanger
Special thanks to Tom Colgan, Lou Aronica, Mark James, and Don Maass
Published by arrangement with the author
ISBN: 0-380-78984-1
www.avonbooks.com

Library of Congress Cataloging in Publication Data:
Yarbro, Chelsea Quinn, 1942-
   The angry angel / Chelsea Quinn Yarbro : illustrated by Christopher H. Bing.
      p.   cm.—(Sisters of the night)
   I. Title. II. Series: Yarbro, Chelsea Quinn, 1942—   Sisters of the night.
PS3575.A7A82   1998   97-27457
813'.54—dc21   CIP

First Avon Books Trade Paperback Printing: April 1999
First Avon Books Hardcover Printing: April 1998

Printed in the U.S.A.

OPM 10 9 8 7 6 5 4 3 2 1

For
Nigel Bennet
because the hero is only as good
as the villain is bad

— ACKNOWLEDGMENTS —

When I was in Oxford in 1967, I found a small bookshop near Magdlene College which had a number of books on Eastern European history, one of which was what appeared to be a thesis: *Folk Lyrics of the Balkan Region, 1200–1700.* I bought it as a souvenir and put it away on my reference shelves for nearly thirty years. When I undertook this trilogy, I went to this book as a source for the epigraphs in this first novel.

As always, there are thanks due to Dave Nee for yet another extensive bibliography; to Maureen Kelly, Scott Winfield, and Jane Morris, who read the manuscript for clarity and at whose suggestions I point out that Kelene is pronounced Keh-LEE-nee; to Leigh Grossman of Swordsmith Productions, who approached me about the project and who shepherded it through the rocky publishing terrain; to my agent, Donald Maass, for his hard work; and to Alice Horst and her horses for all those hours in the saddle.

Berkeley, California, 1997

⇥ PROLOGUE ⇤

Salonika, 1500

Let any who can withstand the flesh,
Whose honied promises are poison . . .
—Romanian love lyric, 15th century

"No. No. I won't listen anymore!" Kelene clapped her hands to her ears and walked as far away from her great-great-aunt Iocasta as the small room would let her. The slanting light from the open door turned her fair hair to a burnished halo. The old woman never did anything but predict trouble. Just because She never got visions anymore, and Kelene's grew stronger every day. The young girl looked up at Iocasta and tried again, "My visions are—"

"You will listen or you will be ruined by your own folly, and your father's pride." The old woman cut her off. Iocasta's frost-blighted eyes burned with cold determination. She clutched her carved walking-staff tightly. "The Militant Angels will abandon you to others, who will not use you kindly."

"And you will not be found wanting, staying here when the Turks have ordered all Christian merchants to leave or embrace Islam?" It was a sharp challenge for a twelve-year-old girl, but Kelene made no apology for her outburst. Instead, she stared toward the window where the courtyard gate stood open, revealing the curve of the bay below. Salonika was a beautiful place, with long, honorable traditions, and it was the home she hated to leave, no matter what warnings the Militant Angels gave her. The crosses were already taken down from the roof, and the ikons were removed from over the door, as the Sultan had ordered. In the yard below, her brothers struggled to move heavy barrels of olive oil and the family's bundled possessions, helping to load the four wagons.

To Kelene's astonishment, Iocasta laughed. "What can they do to me that God has not already done? Take my life? I am well over fifty, my time is certainly ending. What matter if a Turkish sword or a winter cough is the tool?" She held out her hand to Kelene. "I want you to listen to me, child. I have no desire to hurt or shame you. If only you would believe this. I know the burden of visions, far better and longer than you, and—"

"I know what you're going to say," Kelene told her, going on as if

1

reciting a lesson by rote. "You have said it before, often. You think I cannot recognize the voices of the angels, that I will be deceived, that I will be confused by demons of the air who will try to bring us to damnation, presenting their lures in the guise of angels. You believe that the Militant Angels will find me wanting and withdraw their protection. You think I am too weak and compliant to be their messenger. Well, I have not been led astray yet; you have admitted it yourself."

"And you have refused to listen to me." Iocasta responded with unusual gentleness. "You are too willing to feed your father's pride, revealing only what will please or help him. You think of him before you consider the angels. But it is not your father you will answer to if you fail to reveal all that your visions show you. You are not prepared for the demands the Militant Angels will make of you."

"Not this again," Kelene said, trying to break away from Iocasta. She leaned forward. "They are angels. Angels. They won't hurt me."

"And how can you be certain they want your good? They are Militant Angels—warriors fighting the Evil One. Soldiers. They are not always friendly to blond-haired little children like you. Do you really presume to know their purpose? Do you deny they fill you with fever when they come? Or that you are left weak and trembling after their visitation? Aren't they more awe-inspiring than earthquakes? Than the thunder of armies? Do you not fear their presence?" asked Iocasta.

"What if they demand a sacrifice—a real one, not the tokens the popes give—instead of deliverance? Flesh and blood, flesh and blood. That is what the angels seek for God; it is what the popes offer Him. We are no different." The hearth where the old woman sat was almost cold, and the room around her empty of everything but a single chair and a table; the rest had already been put into the wagons. "I am not jealous of your gift, child. I know the Militant Angels too well for that."

"They protect all true Christians," Kelene responded indignantly. "You have said so yourself when you were the one the angels spoke through. They will preserve us in our faith so long as we heed them. They have saved us thus far; why should they not continue in our time of need?" Her visions had been right, no matter what her great-great aunt said.

"If that is truly who they are, you are right. I will not dispute that." She squared her stooped shoulders. "But not all angels stand at the Throne of God to do His bidding. There are those who . . ."

Iocasta did not continue. Kelene realized that she was hearing heresy— the heresy of Rome, that preached damnation as well as salvation. She drew back and crossed herself. "God is not false with His people," she said forcefully, and turned to see her father and mother standing in the open doorway. "Tell her. Tell her that the Militant Angels do not deceive us."

Diogenes drew his fair-haired daughter close to him as he addressed Iocasta. His mellifluous voice rang in the nearly-empty room, "Why do you demand we part with hard words? It is not what I would wish. You have decided to stay here, although the Militant Angels have said that to remain is death. Yet you question this gifted child, who has never done anything to bring harm upon us." He sighed once; this argument was becoming more ritual than substance. "Honored Aunt, can you not realize that there is someone in the family more truly blessed than you are?"

His wife, Melantha, her dark-gold eyes averted, stood behind him, holding her youngest child, the year-old son Phaon, tightly. She kept resolutely silent as her husband confronted his great-aunt one last time.

With a shrug, Iocasta turned away. "If that is what you think, may God send you wisdom. Follow it and have destruction."

"How can that happen? God has favored us with Kelene. He imparts His wisdom to us through her. The Militant Angels have chosen her as their own. As long as we are guided by her visions, we will be in God's sight. Wherever we go, we will be in the protection of the Militant Angels, as we have been before now." Diogenes started to turn away, taking his daughter and his wife with him. Just before crossing the threshold, he turned back. "You do not have to stay here, Aunt Iocasta. You may change your mind and come with us. There is still a chance. The bribe I paid will let us take you and your things. One more wagon will not mean too much."

At this, Kelene spoke up. "Yes, Great-great-aunt. Do not stay here. I know what will come here." In the girl's mind, Salonika was already lost to the Turks, a fading dream of a city. When they were gone from it, she knew she would remember it with the hazy sheen of fantasy.

"Because the Militant Angels have shown you?" Iocasta scoffed. "And did they wrap you in their wings, speaking as if you were their child? Did they praise you?"

"Of course they did," said Diogenes before Kelene could answer. "She is their chosen messenger to us. They always watch over her."

It was a lie, one she had told so often that Kelene realized she could not now deny it; her father would not accept her abjuration if she offered one. The family wanted to think the Militant Angels protected them, not that they gave their pronouncements with the austerity of monks, and imparted visions of salvation and destruction with equal indifference. She looked up at her father, and said, "Yes. They do stand guard over us, keeping us from harm. All of us, Great-great-aunt."

Iocasta made a single, impatient gesture with her hand. "It does not matter."

"There is room for you," said Melantha, knowing her handsome, per-suasive husband expected it of her.

"Go." She turned away from them with great finality. "You will want as many hours of sunlight as you can have to go north. If that is the way the Militant Angels are telling you to go." This last was filled with disgust.

"I do not like to leave you here," Diogenes persisted, releasing Kelene to extend his hand to his great-aunt.

"Go, I tell you," Iocasta ordered in sudden anger. "Go with your family and your daughter and her angels!"

Defeated, Diogenes did as he was told.

PART

I

SUMMONING

February 1501—December 1502

— I —

Kelene lay prostrate before the tremendous figure of the angel, her body aching with the force of his presence. The voice she heard shook the air and bore down upon her, saying, "North, you must go north and then strike to the west. No other way is safe." She tried to plead with the angel, but no words would form. Trembling, she held up her hands in supplication and felt them seized in a grip of tremendous force. She had a fleeting glance of a strong-visaged head, a full, hard mouth and eyes like lambent coals, then she was flung down. "North," the stern order came again as the angel stepped aside and she saw a track through the mountains under a murky sky. Then the sight was blotted out by the angel's wings. She woke with a start, a cry stifled in her throat and a racing pulse that made her head and neck ache. It was the second night of their travels. Lying under the lead wagon with her mother and sisters where they slept close together for warmth, she began by apologizing. "I did not know I had—"

"Hush," Melantha said by way of comfort. "It isn't your fault when the angels visit you." The older woman could not sit upright, so she propped herself on her elbow. "What did you see that caused you such distress?"

"I don't know," said Kelene, and realized her mother would not accept such an answer. "I have not known the angels to visit me in this way before, not in all the years I have had visions. This was more . . . powerful."

"We are traveling. That must change what they do," said Melantha, leaning forward to touch Kelene. Kelene's hands felt cold as death.

"Yes," said Kelene, gratefully taking on the notion. "Yes. It is the unknown road that makes them . . . as they are. Perhaps we are pursued, and the Militant Angels want to keep us from danger. It may be that they are urging us to run from the Turks."

"Perhaps?" Thalia said with skepticism and a yawn. She looked around

7

the darkness; her voice sharpened. "It is still deep night. Why are we awake?" She drew her blanket up to her chin, prepared to be annoyed by her younger sister.

"I had a dream, a vision. It troubled me," Kelene said, trying not to sound proud of her gifts. "Now that I am awake, its meaning . . . perplexes me." She could not bring herself to admit that what her vision had offered frightened her, that the angel had frightened her as well, that some part of her wanted to hide from the angel.

"Where is the oddity in that?" asked Thalia, prepared to go back to sleep. Since their flight had ended her marriage arrangements, she had been alternately waspish and lethargic, blaming her family for what the Turks had caused; without a dowry she could not hope for a husband. That the family who had made the offer for her to wed their third son was as badly off as her own gave Thalia no consolation.

"I think . . ." Kelene began, then faltered; the dream had been so oppressive that it was an effort to find a way to tell what she had seen. She swallowed hard and said more firmly, "I think the Militant Angels wish to show us the way to safety. But this country is strange to me, and I do not recognize what I have seen."

Thalia sighed. "And our father is looking to you to guide us." She made no effort to hide her disgust. "Well, if your Militant Angels are willing to reveal roads and landmarks, inform us of it, won't you? So we may profit from your visions." With that she rolled onto her side and closed her eyes.

"Do not mind her, Kelene," Melantha said. "She is tired and she had to sacrifice her wedding. If you were a little older, you would understand." She touched Kelene's bright hair with her free hand. "But what she tells you is well taken. We will need landmarks to follow."

"I know," said Kelene in a small voice, saying what her mother wished to hear. "I wish I could see them. If only they would show me what to watch for."

"Pray to your angels, and they will give you peace," said her mother as gently as she could. Her pregnancy was in its early stages, disrupting her eating and making sleep a luxury. She lay back and fixed her eyes on the underside of the wagon, hoping the darkness would lure her into dreams.

"Mother?" Kelene ventured a short while later. "Mother? What if I can't find the way the angels show me?"

Whether Melantha slept or not, she did not answer.

She could see the angel more clearly now—an imposing figure, as tall as those on the ikons behind the altar of the church they had left behind, one that would be frightening if it were not so holy—and she sought to cling to it, to take in all its splendor so that the warnings it gave would not be lacking. If only she dared to ask for more. If only the angel were not so forbidding in aspect. She remembered seeing Christian warriors in Salonika, their armor shining, their weapons bristling, and they were not so awe-inspiring as this figure in her dreams, who spoke of danger while revealing hillsides laden with the bodies of the slain. Was that what lay ahead? Was this what they had left behind? The message was not as clear as the figure she saw, and she strove to bring the words into her mind. It was as if she had been enveloped in thunder. Her whole body shook with the presence of the angel, and she feared the shock of it would waken her, ending the visitation before the message was complete. She strove to hold onto the angel, to keep him with her a little longer, to discover what the dire feelings meant. If she could learn more from the angel, she would be prepared. Then she might comprehend what it wanted to impart. . . .

"Kelene. Kelene!" She heard her father's voice as if from a vast distance; it drowned out the angel's warning as the figure faded into nothing behind her closed eyes.

"The angel was with me," she murmured as she came awake.

"Yes, yes," said Diogenes urgently as he pulled his child into his arms. "You were taken with a palsy."

"That was the might of the angel," whispered Kelene. She was inside the second wagon with the rest of the family, lying on a narrow improvised bunk that made her back ache. Their household goods were stacked around them like fortifications, giving an illusion of privacy as well. The rain the night before had driven them into the wagon and now they were all lying on small, makeshift beds. Blinking in the darkness, she had a last, fleeting sense of the Militant Angels, and then it was gone. She saw her mother frowning behind her father's shoulder, and she strove to regain her composure. "We must continue north."

"North?" said Diogenes. "The winter is closing in. The mules can manage the snow, but the oxen might not, not if it is deep or the wind is severe." Oxen pulled the two most heavily laden wagons, containing their stores of food and spices and olive oil, the most valuable of their possessions and the only portion of their wealth they had been able to salvage. "Perhaps we should go to the west, and travel along the shore. The weather will be less severe." He was looking around the wagon now, as if he expected to have to hide there all winter long.

"The angel said north," Kelene insisted, somewhat more confidently. She was almost positive that the word in the tremendous presence was north. "He warned that the Turks will be coming by sea as well as land, and those seeking to find safety to the west will also find battle." She made herself sit up without his help. "I am awake now."

"Yes," Melantha agreed. "The roads in the mountains are dangerous, if they can be found at all after the snows come." This last was said to Diogenes in an undervoice, but Kelene heard it, as she heard one of her brothers strike flint to steel to light the lamp.

"Bandits are not so dangerous as Turks, or starvation," she said, her voice growing sharp. "The angel is stern in his warning." She realized as she spoke that for the first time she was thinking of the Militant Angels— and this one in particular—as male; until now they had seemed too exalted to be defined in earthly terms. Suddenly, she wanted to shake off the lingering presence of the vision, which clung like the brush of wings, or of hands.

"If the Turks are claiming the coast," said Diogenes, "we cannot expect the Venetians to save us." He nodded emphatically. "We thank you, Kelene, for keeping us from harm through the good offices of the Militant Angels." He crossed himself and made certain with his steady gaze that the rest of his family did the same.

Kelene hitched her shoulders up as if to guard herself against the irritation of her family; again she fought the urge to hide. She sensed their dismay at her announcement, and for that reason she kept the more troublesome part of her vision to herself: that she had seen tragedy ahead of them, no matter which way they went. The angel had revealed no easy path, no sure protection. She had chosen to tell of the lesser danger; it would spare them the greatest horrors her dreams had shown before the angel. . . .

"What is it, Kelene?" asked her father, staring at her in the pale lamplight.

"Nothing," she said, a shade too quickly. "Dawn must be coming."

Thalia, who was nearest the door, pulled the blanket-flap aside and looked out. "The sky is lightening. We should rise."

The others grudgingly agreed, although only Alexander got up without complaint. Travel was hard on all of them, and now that they had been without meat for four days, it was difficult to summon the strength to go on.

"We will have eggs shortly," said Pallas, Kelene's younger sister, who had taken on the task of cooking for them all. "The chickens have laid something."

"Pray God we do not lose them while we journey," said Melantha.

"Foxes and lynxes do not attack wagons," scoffed Achilles.

"Foxes and lynxes are the least of our worries," said Thalia sharply as she rose from her bed and began folding her blanket. "It is men we must fear, and the cold. Do the Militant Angels have something to tell us of either?"

"Only that the north is safe," said Kelene just above a whisper.

The others heard this with sober silence until Diogenes managed a bluff smile. "Well, then we should be underway, so as to discourage anyone looking for food." He began to shoo his family into their outer garments and out into the misty morning.

"Six eggs only," said Achilles, bringing these to Pallas in a basket. He shrugged to show he was not bothered by hunger, and volunteered to fetch the cheese.

Alexander, busy trying to get a spark to flare in the damp wood he had gathered last night, peered up at the gray sky, where the sun was like a pale, puckered scar. "We'll have more rain today."

"And wind," said Thalia in a tone of such resignation that the others stared at her. "Listen to the trees," she said to justify her gloomy prediction. "We will have a gale upon us before nightfall."

"The wind will die down," Kelene said suddenly. She was holding her shawl tightly around her shoulders as if to keep out more than the morning cold. "By afternoon, the wind will go."

"Is that what the Militant Angels said?" asked Orien, who sounded genuinely curious.

"Yes," she told them, her head coming up. "We will have clear weather for two days and three nights, and then there will be more rain." She was not certain how she knew this, but the words were out of her mouth before she could think about them.

"Then we will make excellent progress," said Diogenes, cutting short any show of doubt from the rest of his children.

Achilles and Hector went to fetch the four hobbled donkeys and four oxen that had grazed through the night; it was time to check the animals' hooves before hitching them once again to the wagons. It would not help the family if any of the animals went lame, so tending to the hooves had become a necessary ritual, one undertaken faithfully each day.

Melantha gave a wedge of cheese to her husband, then tended to her sons before seeing her daughters were fed. She moved slowly, the queasiness of her early pregnancy taking its toll on her.

Finally there was a fire, and shortly thereafter Pallas had scrambled the eggs with olive oil and garlic in place of precious salt. Diogenes handed around the wine for warmth, and then it was time to be underway again.

As Kelene took her place beside the donkeys pulling the second wagon, she shivered; a specter crossed her vision, the wing of her angel. She tried not to flinch at his touch.

With the rain—which arrived just as Kelene said it would—came mud, and with the mud their wagons slowed in the endless mire the road quickly became, slowing their progress with each passing day. One of the wheels broke beyond repair and they were held up for two days while Diogenes and Alexander made another. Achilles busied himself hunting for rabbits for their evening meal, and succeeded in bringing two for the pot. The others grew restive as they waited to resume their traveling. Only Diogenes' continued heartiness kept them all from becoming outwardly sullen.

"If we had gone toward the sea, we would not have so much mud," said Thalia toward the end of the second day as they huddled around the fire, sharing misery instead of food. It was cold, and the wind smelled of pine and fire.

"Or we might have had more; Kelene's Militant Angels are helping," said Achilles as he jointed the second rabbit, tossing the scraps to their two dogs. "There are more people on the road to the west than the one going north."

His good sense was not satisfactory to Pallas, who said, "Only fools would go north when winter is near."

"Let us hope the Turks think the same thing," said Alexander as he used his hatchet to balance the new wheel.

"Perhaps the angels were wrong," said Hector, and was slapped for his audacity.

"*The Militant Angels are not wrong,*" said Diogenes hotly, his arm raised to strike again. "They have us in their care. We may be sure of it. They have given us their guidance and protection and it is poor gratitude for their favor to carp at their aid, or to question their meaning so closely. The messengers of God do not lie." He sweated in spite of the cold, and his big hands were grimy.

"Then it is possible Kelene is wrong," said Thalia, pursuing the matter. "Great-great-aunt Iocasta said she was not ready to do the bidding of the angels. Why must you think everything she says is right?" She punctuated her misery by bursting into tears.

Kelene was the first to reach her side. She put her arms around Thalia and refused to be shrugged off. "You must not despair," she said, trying to give her sister some comfort. "You will not remain unmarried forever. You may have lost one husband, but you will be wife to a better one." She was by no means certain of her pronouncements, but she knew it was what Thalia longed to hear, and she wanted to help Thalia muster her courage to face their questionable future.

"How is that possible now?" Thalia asked bitterly, trying to wipe the tears from her face. "There are Turks around us, and all of us are in danger. Where is a Christian woman safe in this world?"

"We will be protected in Sarajevo," said Melantha. She walked over and put an arm around Thalia. "We will have family to take us in, and a place to set up the business once again. When we have made a place for ourselves, you will not be so unhappy. Then your father will find you a good husband, and a home you can keep."

Thalia's weeping increased. "If we reach Sarajevo ahead of the Turks. If there is anything left," she finally blurted out. "If we do not—"

"The Militant Angels will guide us and keep us from harm," Diogenes insisted, his manner impatient as he approached his wife and daughters. "Leave off weeping and pray instead." He laid his hand on Kelene's head; she flinched at its weight. "We thank God for blessing us with you, my child. Never doubt that."

Kelene felt herself set apart once again, and knew that the awe of her father was not without ambition, and that her brothers and sisters resented her. She bowed her head and asked for mercy.

Shortly before dawn the next day, as Diogenes' family was preparing once again to travel, Kelene was seized by a curt warning. *Darkness and a constant thunder consumed the world; everything shook as billows of dust rose to blacken everything. The angel rose above the devastation, head bowed in mourning. Then he pointed to their wagons in the same camp they now occupied. He bent down from his impossible height and reached to turn Kelene's face toward him, away from the catastrophe in his tremendous shadow. She felt more than heard him speak: "Do not travel today." His finger touched the corner of her mouth.* She woke at once, crying out that they would have to remain where they were if they were to avoid disaster. Her vision was very clear. This time the danger was specific and the angel had spoken without ambiguity: there was destruction ahead on the road if they traveled it now. If they set out in the morning, nothing could save them.

"Surely there is no reason to waste another day," said Alexander. "All it will do is delay our arrival."

Kelene stared at him. "No. If we depart now, we will come to ruin."

Thalia laughed without amusement. "What will happen that can be worse than this?"

"I don't know," Kelene admitted softly. "But if we go onto the road today, we will have reason to be sorry for it." She crossed herself, wishing she had the sense of the angel's dark wings above her, as she had in sleep, protecting and concealing her.

Achilles folded his arms. "I say we listen to Kelene. She is the one with the visions. She has not misspoken before now. If the Militant Angels advise we wait, then it is best that we do."

Diogenes beamed at the boy, and his splendid voice became warm with approval. "It is good of you to defend Kelene's visions. Yes," he went on, making the decision for all of them, "it will be best if we do as the angels advise. If another day passes, we will not have lost much."

"We would be leagues closer to Sarajevo, if the weather holds. Once the storms come, who knows how far we can go?" said Alexander, glaring at Kelene. "If you do not know what the danger is, then it may be that there is none, and it is your own fear and not the warning of the angels you hear."

"Girls don't understand danger, anyway," said Thalia.

"It is the angel's warning," Kelene insisted, her jaw set stubbornly. "I know when I hear the voice of the angel." She was not sure she had heard everything the angel had said, but she remained firm. What she had seen was specific. "I know we must remain here if we are to be safe."

"We will wait one day," Diogenes declared. "If there is no other warning, we will resume our journey." He went to Melantha's side. "Besides, a little rest will do the baby good, and you will be stronger for it."

The two men who staggered into their camp that evening were more exhausted than injured, although both were bruised and one of them bled from a severe cut on his scalp.

"God and the saints!" Diogenes burst out as the two men reached the firelight. "What has happened?"

Alexander jumped to his feet, knife in hand in case these men should be in the company of robbers. "Who are you?" he asked curtly.

"Where do you come from? What happened?" Diogenes persisted.

"We are drayers," said one, his accent that of Hungary; his voice was harsh. "We were part of a small merchants' caravan over the pass . . ." He fell to his knees. "Help us, in the name of the Christ. We have been walking since midday. We cannot go farther."

"But what happened?" Diogenes repeated forcefully, hesitating to approach the two.

The second man sighed. "It was horrible. Our wagons were carried away, and our . . . our cousins with them." He crossed himself and turned his face away.

Kelene moved toward the two strangers, making herself speak. "It was an avalanche, wasn't it?"

The Hungarian stared at her, his face blank with astonishment. "Yes," he said softly after a moment. "It took the road and everything on it, just half a league this side of the pass. It was worse than anything I have ever seen. Everyone and everything just swept away in all that rock." His tone was distant, as if the event had happened long ago and not just a few hours since; he lifted the saint's medal he wore to his lips, then crossed himself Roman style. "Through God's grace, we were not killed with the others."

"And you say this happened about midday?" Diogenes asked, his voice rich with vindication.

"Shortly before, yes," said the Hungarian. He sank onto the ground and put his face in his hands. "Eight wagons, twenty-six mules, nine men. All gone."

Alexander was staring at Kelene, a strange expression on his face. "This is what you meant." He turned his attention to Pallas. "We planned to reach the pass by midday."

Hector abandoned his playing with a small, roughly carved wooden cannon and listened intently, his eyes widening in astonishment.

"Then we might . . ." Achilles' words trailed off as the full implication struck him. "If we had been traveling, we would have died with the others."

"We might have died," said Hector, as if he could not believe what he heard unless he spoke the words himself.

"And we would have lost everything, including our lives. Let us give thanks, and help these Hungarians. Do not pester them with questions; they have endured enough without you addling them," added Diogenes, and belatedly signaled to his wife. "See the poor men have something to eat. They must be famished."

"And thirsty," said Kelene, whose own mouth was dry.

As Pallas began to stir up the fire to resume cooking, she regarded Kelene with new admiration. "You were right. Your angels guided us through you."

"And saved us from hurt," added Achilles. He shot a single, intense look at Thalia as if daring her to contradict him.

"What are you saying?" asked the second drayer. He glanced at Diogenes and then at Kelene, alarm and confusion in his face. "What do you mean?"

"Our child is gifted, gifted by Heaven," said Diogenes with excusable pride as he held out a waterskin to the stranger; he lowered his eyes and his voice to show his respect and reverence. "The Militant Angels speak to her to guide us. Had they not warned us, we would have suffered as you have suffered."

"She had a vision that saved us," said Hector proudly.

Kelene had a moment of wishing she had never been visited by the angels, never received their gift; and then she lifted her head, saying, "I do not know why I have been chosen, but I am filled with gratitude that it is so."

Diogenes smiled at her and she basked in her newfound approval.

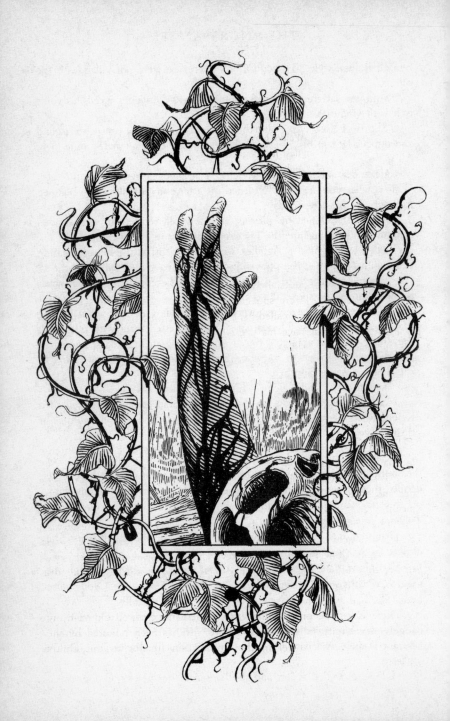

Wolves prowl around the flock!
Alas! for the cruel winter
And the cruelty of men!
　　　—Romanian song, 15th century

⊢ II ⊣

There were no more doubts about Kelene's gifts, or the importance of her visions—or none that were spoken aloud. As Diogenes put his sons to aiding the two drayers, he called his fair-haired daughter to his side, telling her loudly enough to have his words carry to all his family, "Let us be glad. If you had not told us to wait here, we would have been killed in the avalanche, and all our goods lost. God and the Militant Angels be thanked for the visions He has given you. And may He forgive those who doubted you."

It was high praise, and Kelene could not keep from blushing because of it. "I do only what the angel instructs," she said, knowing it was what her father wanted to hear.

Melantha came to Kelene and laid her hand atop her husband's. "For the souls of us all, we thank you for telling us the warning. If there were doubts, they are now answered. Let those who question your visions think on this day, and remember these two drayers." She looked directly at Thalia as she spoke.

Thalia colored and looked away, her dark eyes filling with tears. She crossed herself and moved nearer the fire.

The Hungarian drayer stared at them, curiosity cutting through his shock. "What do you mean? Why has she been favored, that you praise her?"

There was pride in his smile as Diogenes answered, "I told you: my daughter has a gift. It is as my son said. She has been honored by the Militant Angels. We travel in their protection, thanks to this child's visions."

Kelene was gripped by a shyness as intense as it was sudden; she bowed over her hands as if in prayer.

Alexander added, "Our great-great-aunt had visions, too."

This mention of Iocasta silenced Diogenes, who had been about to praise Kelene further. "Yes," he said at last. "But she ignored them."

"She said there would be an avalanche? that girl of yours?" the other drayer asked. His face was white under the smears of mud and his breathing was not quite right.

"She said there was danger and we would be harmed if we set out on the road this morning," Diogenes explained with an unavoidable hint of smugness. "You have revealed to us what that danger was."

"We have lost a day but that has saved us; without the warning we would have pressed on," said Melantha, indicating to Pallas that she was to be careful with the food she was stirring in the cooking pot. "Bring the bread and salt for these men." This traditional show of hospitality removed the last awkwardness between Diogenes' family and the two drayers.

"And give some to our father and mother as well," said Thalia, to make herself feel less excluded from the rest.

"Of course," said Pallas. The softness of childhood made her vapidly pretty in contrast to her sensible and pragmatic demeanor; brown ringlets were confined by a headband without regard to flattering her face. She went about her work with the ease of one long used to it, paying scant attention to the flurry of activity around her. As soon as the bread and salt had been ceremonially consumed, she went back to her cooking pots.

"Our daughter has shown remarkable gifts since she was very young," said Diogenes, his voice hypnotic in its intensity. "There have been other women in my family who have had such gifts, but none so greatly as she."

Kelene listened to her father as he recounted the history of her visions; in spite of herself, she shivered, and tried to account for it as a sudden chill. The day was cold enough to make such an explanation acceptable. But she knew it was the presence of the angel of her visions—the dark wings hovered over her, leaving her trembling. She said nothing, but took satisfaction in the moment, pleased to have the angel to herself.

"They say Selim the Grim is going to burn Venice," the Hungarian drayer announced suddenly. "What do her angels make of that?"

"What in the name—" began Alexander, his brow darkening.

Melantha stopped him. "The man has escaped death, my son. He is not yet sure he is alive." She glanced at Kelene with the same sort of expectancy that Diogenes wore.

Much as she disliked being challenged in this way when the thrill of success was so fresh, Kelene answered, "The Ottoman Emperor will not reach Venice. The Turks will be defeated at sea." Where had that come from? she wondered. Had the angel imparted it with his touch?

"Cyprus is in Turkish hands," said the Hungarian, unwilling to believe her. "The Venetians could not hold it."

"Cyprus is not Venice," said Diogenes, who nonetheless could not wholly disguise his alarm at such a prospect. "Selim will find that out if he attempts to conquer it."

Kelene wished she could silence her father; instead she turned away from him.

"Selim will exact a price from Christians everywhere if Venice does not fall," the Hungarian persisted. "They are saying that none of us will be safe in a year or so."

"The Militant Angels will guard us," Diogenes declared in a tone that brooked no opposition.

"Through your daughter," said the Hungarian, nodding once. "Why should God keep you from danger while so many good Christians are dead? What have you done to deserve such a daughter?"

"It is not our part to question God," said Melantha abruptly. "It is for us to thank Him for His mercy."

This seemed to satisfy the Hungarian drayer, for he stopped asking questions and gave his full attention to the thick soup Pallas ladled into bowls and held out to the two men. "We are bound to the south, to Athens," he told Diogenes' family before he ate. "We want to see it one last time before it falls."

When Diogenes' family departed the next morning, they took a small, less-frequented track that led to the northwest. The road was narrow, leading through groves of oak and laurel and larch, shadowed by higher peaks, so that the light was muted and the wind cutting; her vision had not shown her how lonely the road would be. At first the way was so remote that it seemed impossible that anyone lived along it, but by the following day, the family had passed through two farming hamlets, both of them filled with suspicious and fearful peasants who refused to provide food or shelter to the travelers.

"There are Turks about," one peasant told them, begrudging them so much information. "They have not come here yet, but if we take in travelers, they will."

"But we are Christians," protested Alexander.

"Why should the Turks care that you help us?" asked Diogenes, his question evoking nothing more than a shrug from the peasant.

The local pope was no more helpful. He stood in the door of his little church and made a gesture of resignation. "It is not possible. We will pray for you."

"What good is that?" Alexander demanded, making no apology after he had glanced at his father to be certain he would not be punished for his outburst.

"We have not been able to worship since we left Salonika, not in a church," said Melantha suddenly. "Will you have a service today?"

The pope shook his head. "The Turks will attack us if I do that."

Diogenes gave the pope a hard stare. "You will not permit us the comforts of our faith? You are pope here, and you will not give us the solace of—"

"Will you stay with us to fight the Turks, because we, too, are Christians?" the village pope asked, and was not surprised at the silence that answered him. "So you see." He gave the family his blessing. "Go peacefully. God will watch over you."

"He has done so thus far," said Diogenes, crossing himself by way of apology. "And for that we praise Him."

The pope relented a bit. "Be careful whom you speak to. There are those who are not so willing to give God back the sacrifice He has made already."

"What are you saying?" Diogenes asked sharply. "Are there those who give their fellow-Christians to the Turks to spare themselves? We have seen this before." His face was grim. "I would not like to answer to God or the Militant Angels." He put his hand on Kelene's shoulder. "Those would be hard visions to see, would they not?"

"I hope never to see them," said Kelene devoutly.

The pope did not truly smile, but his expression changed enough to show that he had a similar hope. "There is a village, along that road. They have crosses on their roofs and crescents in their hearts."

"What do you think, Kelene?" her father demanded.

Kelene had not been paying much attention, her mind on the dismaying things the angel had shown her of the road ahead, and the fate of those who betrayed their faith. Achilles whispered the remarks of the pope to her, and she answered without thinking, "I think this place spawns human jackals. The pope is a clever man."

Diogenes thanked the pope. Once they were beyond the village, he instructed his sons to arm themselves.

The next day they had to hide from bandits. Kelene wakened with the words, "There will be danger on the road. Men with swords and pistols. They will pursue us." She could not remember the angel showing her this, but the words came as her eyes opened. "We will have to . . . to conceal ourselves."

By now Diogenes tolerated no questions with regard to her pronouncements. The family fretted at the delay, but when the dogs began to whine, the matter was settled.

"We will go there, and wait until the danger passes. Better that than to fight desperate men," he said as soon as Kelene suggested that they get away from the road. "There is no shame in hiding from thieves and murderers." He ignored the impatient gesture Alexander offered him.

The trees provided a thick screen from the road; Diogenes told his sons to hold the noses of their mules, so they would not bray when horses came near. His wife gathered her daughters with her in the family sleeping wagon and gave each of them a knife. "If you cannot save yourselves, save your honor," she said, and held up a knife of her own.

Thalia held the handle with grim determination. "God will not mind if we die to save ourselves," she said to her younger sisters. "God will not withhold grace from us if we die to keep from being raped."

"Kill ourselves?" Pallas was stunned by the order. "Shouldn't we save you, Mother? If they take us, they may leave you alone. The sacrifice would be acceptable to God, wouldn't it? It would not matter how we died."

"If they take me, they will rip open my belly and kill the child there, and then they will ruin my soul with their bodies," said Melantha. "And that will not save you from them; you will all—"

"God will not save us from the Turks so we may die here at the hands of outlaws," said Kelene distantly as she gazed at the knife. How easy it would be, she thought, to press this up under her ribs and stop her visions. . . . She all but dropped the knife when she realized what she was considering. Crossing herself to eradicate her sin, she wondered if the angel was aware of her error, or, more terrible still, had put the idea in her along with the knowledge of the bandits.

Outside, Hector and Alexander busied themselves concealing the evidence of their passing, using branches to rub the tracks of the mules and oxen from the road.

"Do not be too hasty," Diogenes admonished them. "They are not easily misled, men of that kind."

Kelene listened intently, the knife clutched in her hands. If the angel forgave her for her thoughts of suicide, she would know when the outlaws passed them by; if they were discovered, then she was lost for eternity.

Not long after they had hidden themselves they heard the approach of several horses, and a harsh curse. "That peasant didn't know what he was saying. Four wagons, mules and oxen!"

"Should we scour the woods?" asked one man among them.

"No," the leader declared. "If they're in the woods, they're prepared for us."

Another voice cursed as the horses thundered on.

When they could hear nothing but the slicing wind and the sounds of animals in the underbrush, Diogenes called Kelene out of the wagon to his side. "Without your guidance, those men would surely have robbed us of everything," he said to her. "A company of so many men might have killed us all."

"We would have been on a different road, were it not for Kelene, one that soldiers patrol," Thalia said, without her customary sharpness.

"That road is no longer there, or it is not safe to travel," said Achilles, springing to his sister's defense with alacrity. "Kelene has protected us once more."

Although their gratitude weighed heavily upon her, Kelene answered as she knew they wanted. "Thanks should be given to God and His Militant Angels." As long as her visions continued, she added inwardly. She could not wholly keep from thinking that the day her guidance failed would be the day that all the blame would be on her, for none of her family would ever hold God accountable for such misfortune. And worst of all, she dreaded that their condemnation would be right.

Darkly glorious, the angel rose before her, his wings outspread like a cloak, his head refulgently haloed. His mightiness was like a god of the times before salvation. He commanded veneration. In one hand he held a shining sword, in the other a chalice. There was majesty in his stance. He embodied the ineffable, his splendor filling Kelene with such wonder that she felt suspended by it, hardly able to breathe, her pulse loud in her own ears. "Guide them," he said. All she could see was his burning eyes; the rest of his face was shadowed by his wings.

"Where?" she murmured, not sure she had spoken at all.

"Guide them," the angel repeated, and moved aside.

But this time instead of showing her a scene, he reached out to her and dragged her into the vision; she felt her knees strike rocks hidden under the snow and grow hot with her own blood. She whimpered but made no other protest.

The road became wilder, more remote, with crosses set beside it. Then it was less than a road, more of a path forest animals might follow. The whole region was desolate and empty, as if it had been savaged and abandoned. She wanted to bless herself as she saw them, but the angel had too strong a grip upon her.

Then, abruptly, she was once again alone with the angel on a distant mountain peak, her injuries gone. The angel bent down above her and held out a chalice. "Drink," he ordered her, and put the golden cup to her lips.

The wine was warm and oddly thick, metallic and heavy. She tasted it and all but gagged. Horrified that she could so profane a sacred thing, she fell to her knees before him. "Forgive me."

"Forgive you?" The angel bent down and pressed his full, hard mouth to her forehead; his kiss burned there as she stared up into his aquiline features. She wondered if she could fall into his eyes, or be transfixed by them. Once again he said, "Guide them." Then he drew back from her, spread his enormous, dark wings and left her, alone and shivering, on the crest of the mountain with only his kiss to warm her.

A few days later, as the first flakes of snow came drifting down from a leaden sky, Alexander—walking ahead of the wagons on the narrow, rutted road—caught sight of an inn. It was a tumbledown affair, with few windows and thatch in need of repair, but smoke came from the chimney and there were pigs in the barnyard. The smoke smelled of pine and boiling cabbage.

"We can sleep in real beds," he cried as he reported his discovery with enthusiasm. "We can eat at a table."

"And be taken by the innkeeper and sold into slavery to the Turks," Kelene responded at once, again sensing the angel's nearness. She had spoken without thought or any guidance she recognized; there had been no dream that she remembered the night before and now she felt strangely disoriented, without direction.

"They would not dare to take so many," Alexander protested. "We have knives and I can charge the pistol." He looked pleadingly at his father. "I'm so *cold*. I want to get inside. I want to be *warm*."

Pallas and Orien took up his supplication, both speaking at once, both begging to be allowed to stay at the inn.

"No." Diogenes held up his hand for silence. "If the inn is dangerous, we must not stay there." He put his hand protectively on Kelene's shoulder. "You are certain about the danger?"

"I only know that the angel tells me that they have sold other travelers to the Turks as slaves in return for being left alone." She felt her father's approval with pride mixed with apprehension. "I would not feel safe in such a place. If they put a sleeping potion in their cheese or—"

"That is enough," Diogenes ordered. "We will pass the inn by and thank the Militant Angels for saving us again."

Melantha sighed. "It would be good to be warm again. And to eat real food." She drew her shawl over the face of her youngest child, holding him against her shoulder to lend him the heat of her body. "Hush, Phaon," she murmured as he whimpered.

"But we all are cold and tired," said Hector, his young voice roughened from coughing. "We all want to go to the inn."

"That is what the innkeeper must count on," said Diogenes. "If the

Militant Angels warn us of danger, we would be worse than fools to go against them. God is showing us how to keep alive and remain together."

"If Turks come to the inn, wouldn't we see them?" asked Alexander, inspiration lighting his face.

"Yes," said Achilles, his young face shining at the chance to do battle. "We would be ready for them."

"It is the innkeeper who goes to the Turks," said Kelene flatly, wondering if the angel or something else spoke through her. "If he waited for them to come to him he would no longer have an inn."

"But we are cold," said Pallas. "One night would not mean we would be captives, would it?"

Kelene went on in the same uninflected way, "I will not sleep there. I will stay in the wagon." She blinked once as if coming out of a daze.

Hector sniffled and squinted back tears. "It does not matter. A warm bed isn't worth being a slave for." He stopped a cough.

"Hector is right," said Melantha unexpectedly. "Better to pass the inn by than take such a risk."

"But we could take turns watching," Achilles insisted. "We would not have to sleep at the same time. We could. I'd stay awake."

"There is too much risk," said Thalia. "If I must lose a chance to marry, I will not become a slave instead of a wife." It was as close to an apology as she had ever offered her blond sister. "We must go on."

Diogenes saw the disappointment in his children's faces. "There will be other inns, less isolated, where we may rest and be safe. Pray for those travelers who did not have the warning of the Militant Angels."

"I want to find a place the Militant Angels will approve," said Alexander, his annoyance making his voice harsh. "Do you think you can persuade them to guide us to such a place, Kelene?"

"I wish I could ask them such things," she said wistfully, "but they reveal themselves only in visions, not at my desire."

The following evening as they made their way into a high, narrow valley, they came upon a small village that had been raided—whether by outlaws or Turks they could not tell. The buildings were rubble, charred and broken, and the pens where livestock had lived were destroyed, the animals taken. A number of bodies lay on the frozen ground, blood making dark halos around them. Every corpse had had its throat cut; a few had been more hideously desecrated. Only the cold kept the smell from becoming unbearable.

Kelene saw half a dozen women, their clothes torn off them, their bodies obscenely exposed, their flesh bruised and bloody; she had to clamp her jaw against the nausea that stung her mouth. One of the women had

had her arms cut off. Perhaps, Kelene thought, she had tried to fight her murderers.

"I hope he was dead when that happened," said Achilles, looking away from one of the slaughtered men, whose severed genitals lay next to his head.

"God welcome them." Kelene shuddered. No angels had protected these people and she wondered again why it was that she should be given warnings and guidance when others suffered such terrible fates. What were they being saved for, and why? The questions echoed in her mind as she stared at the hideous carnage. The ferocity of what had happened in this village staggered her; she steadied herself against the flank of the ox she walked beside, and felt the warmth of his hide. It was somehow reassuring to feel that stolid animal amid the disaster around them.

Melantha kept her shawl over Phaon's face.

"We cannot remain here," said Diogenes. "We will have to press on."

"To where?" asked Alexander, his brown eyes enormous with horror.

"But it is getting dark," protested Thalia, shuddering. "And we can have shelter behind the barn. It isn't too badly burned. We won't have to . . . look at . . . this." She glanced at her mother. "We're all tired, and she is the most tired of us all."

Kelene was appalled that her sister could be so indifferent to what she saw around them, and she said, "This is worse than a graveyard. How can you suggest—"

"Thalia's right. We would be safe," said Alexander. "After this, who would return? If we go into the barn, we will not be discovered or—"

"But *look* at them!" Kelene cried out. "How can we stay here?"

Diogenes scowled unhappily. "We press on. It cannot be helped. It would be sacrilegious to remain here since we cannot bury the dead."

The children exchanged worried looks, and finally Hector spoke for them all. "What does Kelene say?"

She had dreaded the question. The angel did not speak to her no matter how ardently she sought him. She responded to her surroundings with her own emotion. "It would be better to move on. There will be shelter further on." She shrugged in the direction of the road, hoping it was so.

"What if the marauders are still in the area?" asked Alexander. "They are not likely to come back here. Mightn't it be wisest to do as Thalia suggests and set up the wagons on the other side of the barn?"

Achilles settled the matter. "If the killers do not come tonight, others will—wolves and other hungry creatures."

Diogenes let his family consider this before he said, "We must get underway, and pray for the souls of the slain as we go."

Kelene sighed gratefully, and took her place beside the ox. She carefully averted her eyes from the bodies they would have to leave behind.

The images had been worse than what she had seen in the village: corpses and parts of corpses strewn over a blood-soaked plain amid broken and discarded weapons; kites circling overhead, ready to feast. Occasionally a dying cry arose from the carnage, or a savaged body would move, and the birds would rise higher. A few slaughtered horses, bloating in death, turned stiffened legs toward the kites. A stench permeated everything, cloying and vile. The angel carried her over the battlefield, unwilling to spare her the hideous sight, or to comfort her. She strove to hide in the shelter of his wings.

Again the angel offered her the chalice, and again she found it difficult to drink the dark red wine. She knew she must accept this token of sacrifice, for as a Christian, to do anything else was apostasy. Her hands shook as she took the chalice from the angel and drank, crossing herself as she gave it back.

"Good," purred the angel. And when he kissed her this time, it was on the mouth.

In the morning, Kelene drifted out of sleep. She tried to remember the images of her dream, but all she could bring to mind was the kiss. Confused by all it had evoked in her, she said nothing of the dream to anyone, afraid of what it might portend. What would her mother say, or her sisters? How would her father react? But surely, she thought, a kiss from an angel is a blessing. What else could it be but an honor?

"Poor Kelene," Melantha said, smoothing her fair hair back from her brow. "You're catching the same cough your brothers have. It is the cold." She patted the thin mattress. "You just lie back and rest. Pallas will bring you broth. Drink it and be strong." She sighed. "It is always so in winter: an illness passes through a family like water through a field."

"I don't feel ill, Mama, just . . . strange," said Kelene, wanting to tell her about the dream and afraid to speak of it.

Again Melantha patted the mattress. "Rest, child. You have carried a heavier burden than the rest of us." She got to her feet and rubbed the small of her back with both hands. "I hope we do not have all of you down with it at the same time. It is hard enough in a house, but traveling—"

"But Mama," Kelene tried to protest.

"Not now, Kelene. You must rest until the fever is gone." She explained this as if Kelene were no older than Phaon. "We depend on you for our safety. Without the guidance of the Militant Angels, we are at the mercy of the Turks. If you are not well, how can the Militant Angels speak through you?" She bent down and kissed Kelene's shining hair. "I will see if we can put beds in one of the other wagons. Perhaps then your brothers and sisters will be spared."

The thought that she might have brought infection to her family filled

Kelene with shame. She lowered her head and tried to think of an adequate apology. "I . . . I didn't think, Mama—"

"One of us will watch you," Melantha assured her. "And when you are better, you may nurse the ones who aren't." With that she left the wagon.

Kelene huddled in the blankets. Was it possible? that the wine had brought this about? Or was it that the angel had sought to heal her with his disturbing kiss? Much as she fretted, she could discover no answers. Only new questions came, as tormenting as the embrace of the fever. A short while later the wagon lurched into motion. For the moment all she cared about was the misery that held her flesh in its hot grip.

"It is a blessing that the fever passed so quickly," said Diogenes as he looked in on his sleeping daughter three nights later; even pitched low, his voice was wonderful to hear, sweet and musical. "We may thank God for His continuing protection. Surely the Militant Angels have healed her. They may heal the others as well."

Melantha frowned thoughtfully. "Only two of the others have it. The rest may escape. We may indeed be spared much." She placed her hand on Kelene's forehead. "Why is it that the Militant Angels demand so much of her?"

"It is the price of the gift," said Diogenes softly. He could not conceal his relief that Kelene had recovered so quickly.

"How can a gift have a price?" Melantha asked.

Five days later, as they huddled in the lee of a copse of pine, Diogenes was forced to slaughter one of the oxen. The animal had gone lame two days before and now his whole right front leg was swollen and the infection was spreading.

"At least we can have some meat," said Alexander as he helped to gut the ox.

"Most of it is filled with infection," said Melantha, sniffing at the exposed tissue. "The haunches are still wholesome." She called to Pallas. "If you will make a thick broth, I will give some to Hector." As she said this, she fretted; the boy had been listless and coughing for the last three nights.

"I'll cook as much as I can; we can salt the rest." Pallas watched greedily as three of her brothers set to cutting away the meat Melantha said was still good to eat. "It will be as it was at home, with good food and—"

"And I'll drag the bones and the guts away from the wagons. The wolves and bears can fight over what's left in another place." Achilles did his best to laugh, but the mention of the formidable masters of the forests brought a wariness to his demeanor.

"I'm hungry," said Orien, joining into Pallas' game. "I'll help cook if we can eat sooner."

"Should we keep the hide?" Alexander wondered aloud, "or would its scent bring hunters after it?"

Inside the wagon, Kelene listened to the voices of her brothers; she would not look at Thalia. She put a damp cloth on the boy's face. Her mother had been right: the fever had come upon Achilles, Orien, and Pallas, and they were improving. Hector was the latest to feel its touch.

"Let them have what they can get of that ox, hide and all." Alexander made up his mind. "That way we can keep our other oxen and our mules. Let the beasts fight over the hide and the guts of the dead."

Thalia emerged from the wagon, leaving Kelene to minister to Hector; there were two red spots in her cheeks caused by the freezing wind and the first onset of the illness, and she moved slowly. "At least Hector is not filled with fever," she said. "Kelene is taking good care of him." This last comment was given reluctantly. "We are far from any help, and if there is more sickness, what can Kelene's vision do then?"

"She is devoted to the family," said Melantha, "and the angels know it." She had let Phaon stay near the hobbled mules, but kept looking up to be certain he was not in danger of any kind.

Pallas had gathered wood for a cooking fire, but was unable to get her tinder to light; she struck her flint-and-steel with aggravation, and then burst out in tears. "It isn't going right."

Melantha hurried to her side. "Don't cry, child. We know it is difficult." She put her arm around Pallas' shoulder and pulled her close to comfort her. "We are the fortunate ones. We have remained together and we have not had to sacrifice our faith. God has been good to us." She rocked gently, letting her swelling pregnancy buoy up Pallas.

"Let me try," Orien offered, taking the flint-and-steel from his sister.

"We will all feel better when we have eaten. The ox has not perished in vain," said Diogenes, doing his best to encourage the others. "Look at Achilles. He's up from his bed and doing his chores. He's stout as ever." This was not entirely true, but they all did their best to believe it.

"And meat will strengthen us," said Alexander, with a pointed glance at Pallas.

"And I'm *hungry*," Orien declared again.

"I can't . . . there's no flame . . ." Pallas cried, her hands to her face in shame. "I don't . . ."

"Orien will start the fire," Melantha promised her as she used her shawl to dry her daughter's eyes. "And then you will have a chance to make the broth. Let Thalia tend to the salting."

"Is there enough salt to spare?" asked Thalia. "Should we not cook most of it?"

"There is salt enough," said Diogenes, adding, "We will need the meat later, as winter deepens." This observation brought numb nods from four of his children.

"How long will we remain here?" asked Pallas, looking about uneasily as she regarded their cooking pot. "I will cook more if we will have time to eat again."

"We will be here for tonight, at least," said Diogenes, huddling into his long sheepskin shuba. "If none of the rest of you are taken ill, we will travel soon after dawn."

With the two dogs trailing after him, Achilles returned from his task, his face ruddy, his step brisk.

Pallas nodded dumbly and permitted herself to receive solace from Melantha. "Poor Hector. He's never ill."

"He will be strong again," said Melantha. "And when he has had some of your food, he will get better quickly."

Kelene took the oil lamp and held it above Hector's face, studying him, while she listened to Melantha encourage her family.

Pallas had the impetus she needed. "Not if I do not make broth for him," she said as she got to her feet. "Achilles! Come here. Help Orien. I will need more snow."

If Achilles wondered why Pallas did not perform this minor chore herself, he said nothing of it. Obeying her promptly, he was secretly glad to get away from the bloody carcass of the ox; it spared him for a short while from going deeper into the copse with the remains.

Kelene bowed her head, her blue eyes glistening with the tears she refused to shed; she made the sign of the cross on her brother's forehead.

Outside Orien sang as he brought a basket of fresh-fallen snow to Pallas. He had been out of bed for a day so his voice was still rough. No one told him to stop. There had been so few times any of them felt like singing that his high, piping voice seemed a joyous omen in these dire hours. He sang of home, the olive groves, and the smell of thyme on the wind.

In a short while the cooking pot was filled with chunks of meat and water from the snow, and Pallas was managing to be cheerful again, vowing to make broth every night until Hector recovered completely. "It is almost like eating back home," she declared to support her intentions. "I can almost hear Great Aunt Iocasta saying her prayers by the hearth." The gloom that had possessed them began to lift with the aromas spreading from the pot.

Which made it a far more painful task for Kelene to leave the wagon to tell her family that Hector was dead.

As cedars in Lebanon,
As roses in Jericho,
Most Holy Mother Maria
—Orthodox response, 12th century

⊢ III ⊣

"And the rites?" asked Melantha, her voice breaking with grief as she stared down at the little body wrapped in a thin blanket. "What of the prayers?" The wan sunlight made little headway in the brightening day. Overhead, thickening clouds turned the morning to dusk.

"We will say them ourselves, as God wishes us to do. We do not have to find a priest if our hearts and souls are in our prayers," Diogenes told them, as if his idea was not outrageous. "Not all of them. They take too long."

Melantha clung to Achilles and Orien, weeping steadily; Thalia and Pallas huddled together at the side of the wagon, both pale with shock, little Phaon between them; Alexander paced restlessly, unwilling to look at the swaddled body.

Kelene could not bring herself to move nearer to any of them, certain she was to blame for Hector's death. Her emotions roiled within her, and she sought the protection of her angel in vain.

"But—" Alexander began, only to be interrupted by his mother.

"*No!*" Melantha wailed. "You cannot!" She broke free of her two sons and went to wrap her arms around Hector. "It is bad enough that there is no priest to minister to him, and no holy ground to hold him. But not to give him all the prayers . . ." Whatever else she said was lost in weeping.

"It would take two hours, and that is more than we can spare." Diogenes reached out and gently pulled his wife away from their dead son. "Think, Melantha. Would our child want us to put the whole family in danger for his sake? He was better than that. The Militant Angels will guard him, as they have guarded us."

Kelene wanted to apologize, but the words caught in her throat and all she could do was turn her stricken eyes from one to another in mute appeal for compassion. How much she wished she could reveal something hopeful to them, but last night the angel had not come, and her dreams had been of the house they had left behind, and of Great-great Aunt Iocasta.

"We can bring rocks," Achilles offered suddenly. "We can pile them up. That way we won't have to dig very much."

"I can do that, too," Orien seconded, his expression a mixture of helpfulness and shock. "Achilles and I will bring the rocks. You can say the prayers while we prepare the ground. If Alexander digs . . ." He saw the look in his oldest brother's face and his words trailed off.

"That is a fine idea," said Diogenes, and signaled to Alexander. "Listen to Achilles. He has thought well."

Melantha sobbed wretchedly now, her face turned away from her living children. She leaned on her husband and knotted her hands in her shawl. "We can't. We mustn't," she repeated over and over.

Thalia glared at Kelene. "What do your angels say about this? Look at what they've done!"

Kelene was unable to protest; she shrank back, full of self-condemnation. Was this the price of the angel's kiss? Should she have turned away? Did the kiss bring the fever that had claimed her brother? She sank down to her knees, pleased at the way the cold lanced through her; it would serve to help her expiate her sin of letting her brother die. She began to recite prayers for Hector.

"No!" Thalia shouted, and took several hasty steps toward Kelene.

"Thalia," her father said firmly, halting her advance with her name. "Enough."

Though she went no further, Thalia was not to be so easily mollified. "But, Father, how dare she? It's her fault Hector's dead! She brought us here! Don't let her pray. It's sickening."

"I will say nothing," Kelene called out. "If that is what you want." She would pray silently, trusting that the angel would know what she did.

"It might be best," said Diogenes to her, his voice softer now.

The service they improvised was less than a third the length of the usual rites for the dead. Diogenes intoned the prayers, his voice like musical thunder, while Thalia and Melantha sang the responses accompanied by the steady chop of Alexander's shovel as he strove to hollow out a little of the frozen ground. Achilles and Orien busied themselves carrying rocks, and Pallas stacked them next to the grave, readying them for use.

Watching this, Kelene mourned her brother with a kind of steady misery that eroded her senses so that all she felt was sorrow and the pain of guilt. Every other emotion, all her perceptions, were bludgeoned and numb. In her soul, she knew this death was her fault; she should have been able to prevent it. In vain she remembered that the angel demanded sacrifice for God, as God sacrificed His Son for the world. She remained on her knees, imploring the angel to come to her again, to bring her some glimmer of salvation. Silent tears chapped her face yet she was unaware of them.

Alexander prayed as he made the grave, his recitation a counterpoint to the weeping of his brothers and sisters. His cheeks were slick with freezing tears.

Their two dogs circled the copse unhappily, tails down and movements furtive, as if they had contributed to the tragedy.

The susurrus of the wind in the trees joined the lament of the family, bringing snow to augment their tears.

When the body was laid down for burial, Melantha fainted; as Kelene hurried to her mother's side, Thalia stopped her once again. "No," she said. "I won't let you near her. You have enough to answer for without adding to our mother's anguish with your tales of protection."

Again Diogenes intervened. "Kelene has saved us all from death, Thalia. That she could not spare all of us is not her doing, but the will of God." He held out his hand to Kelene. "You tended Hector faithfully and you have kept us from harm with your visions. No father can ask more of a child."

"If her angels are such guardians, why did Hector die?" Thalia demanded. Her face had darkened with wrath.

"God knows these things, my child, not I. I am only thankful that we have been given the care of the Militant Angels. Without their watchfulness, I am certain we would have buried more than Hector by now." He looked directly at Kelene; she shivered under the weight of his gaze. "I know, if all others forget, that you have preserved us with your visions, my daughter. You have been our one defense. Let no one think you have brought us anything but wisdom and care."

As Kelene hugged him, she wanted to tell him that there would be no more deaths for them before Sarajevo, but she faltered, for she had not known Hector would die until two days after he fell ill. So she clung to him as if he could assuage her distress by touch alone.

Finally Hector's body was protected by stones. The mound seemed strangely small now that it was finished. Alexander took a cross from their first wagon and set it in place at the peak of the grave, saying nothing as he did. The rest of the family paused in their preparations for leaving to witness this act. It was the only farewell they could endure.

Then the oxen were yoked and the mules harnessed to the wagons and they started off again into the storm-swathed mountains, away from the copse and Hector's grave.

When they stopped that evening, Kelene was reluctant to go to sleep. She made herself remain sitting upright, her mind caught up in all the angel had told her. What more might the angel reveal that would mean tragedy for them all?

"My child?" Diogenes said softly as he came to his daughter's side. "Why do you remain awake? We are relying upon you to bring the guidance of the Militant Angels." He laid his hand on her head. "Tell me what troubles you."

"Hector . . . I didn't know it would happen. The angel did not tell me—" She clapped her hand to her mouth.

Diogenes tightened his hand and shook her. "What are you saying?"

"I . . ." Did she dare to tell him? "What if the angel is not the guardian we think? What if God is not showing us mercy, but something else?"

His face darkened. "What do you mean?"

Kelene could not stop herself now, though she began to fear what she saw in her father's eyes. "What if Heaven is angry with us for not defending our faith against the Turks?" It all came out in a rush. "What if the angel is not one of God's creatures, but something else?"

The blow took her by surprise, Diogenes' knuckles colliding with her cheek loudly enough to wake the others, although no one stirred. "Do you mean you question Heaven? You? No wonder Hector died, if you have lost faith. If you do not trust in the Militant Angels, how can we hope to live?" He grabbed her shoulders and all but lifted her from her bed. "How many more of us will pay the price of your apostasy?"

"Father," she protested, unable to raise her hands to defend herself. "I never meant any harm."

His voice was hushed but the accusations cut like cold steel. He struck her twice more. Kelene sobbed, as much from despair as from pain. "The Militant Angels are distraught and Hector is dead because of it." Leaning near her, he said, "Pray to have your faith returned, or have our fate on your conscience." Then he turned away and left Kelene to her private misery, and the sanctuary of the figure in her dreams.

For the next three nights, Kelene's dreams were possessed by the angel. His dark wings blended with the blackness, and his urgings left her wary and exhausted. She reported the messages of the angel each morning, taking solace in the warnings she received. There was something more in her response to the angel now, a stirring she did not understand, that she was reluctant to confide to Melantha or one of her sisters. Her bruises faded, though none of the family mentioned them.

As the storm worsened, Diogenes' family was forced to find a place where they could wait out the developing blizzard; their wagons were not adequate to protect them, and the animals suffered from the cold. The last of the chickens went into the pot, and Alexander could find no small game to furnish meat for their dinners. They used a little of the salt beef, not wanting to deplete their stores any more than absolutely necessary.

Melantha, wan as a ghost, sat silently on the end of her bed, unwilling to do more than pray, while Thalia tended her with the fierce devotion of a nun. She ate only when her mother had completed a meager meal.

"There is an inn at Priboj, in the next high valley," Kelene told the family the morning after they ate the chicken. "We can be there tomorrow." She could not bring herself to look at her father as she added in a soft voice, "The angel showed me."

"Then we must go there," said Diogenes, his tone sharper than Kelene liked, but more forgiving than it had been. "If the Militant Angels have revealed it."

"Real beds," said Achilles. "And food."

"And then what?" asked Thalia, her question filled with sarcasm. She stood between Melantha and the rest as if on guard. "Will the Turks have burned it, or will they want to take us captive?"

"Nothing like that," said Kelene, her face reddening so that the last marks on her cheek were mottled. "The angel told me we would have shelter there and come to no harm. It is a small inn, not costly, and there are barns for our animals. If we spend a day or two there, we would be able to reach Sarajevo in another two or three days." She folded her hands in her lap and looked about the wagon. "Don't you want—"

Alexander interrupted. "What did the angels say about this place? What did they tell you?" He nudged one of the dogs with his foot. "Another few days like this and the dogs will starve, and then the mules and oxen."

Melantha put her hands over her eyes and turned away from her family.

"And then we will starve, as well," Thalia declared with a tinge of satisfaction. "Or will the angels bring us food?"

Kelene directed her plea to her father. "I tell you there is an inn. The village isn't large enough to attract much attention. If we go there, we will . . . we will have warmth and shelter. I saw it clearly."

"There will be more snow tomorrow, and heavier," Diogenes mused. "The Militant Angels will not desert us now, not after all that has transpired." His single glance at Kelene was eloquent.

"Let us go to the inn," said Melantha suddenly. "Before any more of our children become ill. I do not want to lose another, not now. Wasn't Hector enough?" Her voice rose and she put her hand to her mouth.

Hearing this, Kelene felt all her doubts return. How much more would the angel require of them, and how much of the blame for it would be hers?

As the angel pointed out the road his gesture was stern: the family would have to travel this way or suffer for it. He glinted as he moved, as if clad in armor. His dark wings were larger than before, all but blotting out the glory of his halo.

"Is this the road we are traveling now?" Kelene asked, astonished at how brazen she had become.

"There will be a fork; you will take the westward one and be safe, or you will find destruction." The angel was uncompromising, his warning more of a threat now.

Kelene bowed her head in acquiescence. "Thank you," she whispered.

The angel showed her a city spread in a valley, prosperous and thriving. Golden church domes shone in the clear spring light. People, tiny as fleas, hurried about the streets. There were fortifications on the hills around it, but the place itself looked quiet. "You will not remain here, but it will be a respite. Do not remain more than a year, or you will have cause to grieve again."

As was increasingly the case, Kelene wanted to ask why the angel should do this. Why had he chosen her? But she could not bring herself to speak; that would reveal too much of her doubts, and the angel might become angry with her. If her father was willing to beat her for uncertainty of faith, what would the angel do to her? She clasped her hands and held them up to the angel, hoping he would not look too deeply into her soul and see her torment.

The peaceful city of her vision began to burn.

"That will be your legacy if you remain more than a year." The angel reached down to her, dragging her to her feet. "You will tell your family they must not remain at Sarajevo."

"I . . . I don't know if I can," she confessed, self-condemnation coursing through her like a malign current. "If they want to stay."

"You will travel or you will suffer." It was so absolute a statement that Kelene was unable to respond in any way. "You will tell them. Travel or die."

She nodded, the angel's arms all but pressing the breath out of her. As the angel relented, she said, "I will tell them."

"Good."

In the manner of dreams, they again stood on the crag where he had brought her before. The chalice was in his hand; she knelt to drink from it. When he kissed her lips, he held her against him. Releasing her, he admonished her: "Remember."

Kelene was not certain whether he meant his warning or his kiss.

*   *   *

Shortly before noon the next day they found the inn, along the west-ward fork in the road. It was much as Kelene had told them: small, in good repair, an overgrown version of the peasants' houses in the village. The peak of the roof was crowned with a pair of ornate wooden crosses, very like the bulbous steeple of the church at the other end of Priboj.

"This time of year," the saturnine innkeeper said when he had con-cluded haggling the price of room and meals for two days with Diogenes, "we don't see many travelers." He looked over the wagons with ill-dis-guised curiosity.

"The Turks drove us out," said Diogenes bluntly. "We are going to my half-brother in Sarajevo."

"You chose a bad time of year to set out. Not that the Turks gave you much say in the matter, or so we've heard," the innkeeper said, and pointed toward the barn. "You will have to tend your animals yourselves. Use the two rear stalls. I haven't the hands to spare in winter."

Alexander responded at once. "We have done so thus far. We will continue to do it." He called to Achilles to help him as the rest of the family gathered around Diogenes.

"How much longer?" the innkeeper asked as he took note of Melan-tha's pregnancy.

"Three months or so," she answered guardedly, mistrusting the man and his blunt questions. It was not for strangers to mention such things.

"I have a soft bed I keep for women in your condition," the innkeeper said by way of explanation. "My wife will see to it that you have dou-ble servings."

At this suggestion, Diogenes bristled. "We are not wealthy people. If you seek to earn more gold—"

"For your wife we will make no additional charge," said the innkeeper. "In these days, good Christians must look after the welfare of those of us who have felt the hand of the heathen Turks. You are doing God's bidding, bringing another Christian soul into the world." He opened the door to his taproom, indicating the long plank tables. "There is soup and bread and cheese. We will have hot wine for you directly, and for four coppers more, we will make the bathhouse ready for your use."

The temptation of a hot bath was too great to resist. "Very well," Diogenes said after he noticed the slight nod Melantha offered him in encouragement.

"I will set my nephew to stoking the fire. It should be ready by the time your animals are stalled and fed." He turned and led the way inside, all but bowing to Melantha.

The food was simple but plentiful and filling, by far the best meal the family had eaten in more than a week. Baked ewes' cheese and pork cooked with cabbage were augmented by pickles and small, fragrant loaves of bread with cardamom seeds and lemon rind on the crust. The hot red wine warmed them and helped them to shake off the melancholy of their circumstances. With precariously gladdened spirits they went to the bathhouse, males to one side, females to the other, to wash away the sweat and grime of long days of travel. The building, squat and long under a slated roof, had a large stone furnace in the center which heated both compartments of the bath.

"If this is the work of the Militant Angels, then I thank them with more gratitude than I have words to tell," said Thalia as she poured a pailful of water over her hair. "I count myself favored." Her laughter echoed through the steam.

Pallas was not quite so fulsome in her enthusiasm. "I wish we could be certain that the Militant Angels would offer us such relief again." She glanced at Kelene as if expecting reassurance.

"I cannot tell," said Kelene before they could ask her anything; her body felt unusually tender, and she touched herself gingerly, as if expecting bruises from the impact of her palms. "I know only what my visions in dreams reveal, and those are not to be summoned at my whim. I am the servant of the angel, he is not mine." She was sitting in the bath, warm water lapping at her shoulders. The dream that had so troubled her was far off from this place, and little as she wanted to admit it, she was glad. For the first time since Hector's death, she felt herself protected. It was so good to be here, she thought, that it would be tempting to linger for more than two days; perhaps then the angel would show her some other path ahead of them, something that would keep them safe from the things in her visions. It could be that winter would interfere with their journey again. There could be many reasons to remain here, she thought. If there were another blizzard they might be able to keep on here. . . .

"What are you thinking?" Melantha demanded, cutting into Kelene's reverie. "Do you have something to tell us?"

"Only that it would be pleasant to stay here a while." She sighed. "But that isn't possible, is it?"

"No, it is not," said Thalia, regret and practicality mixed in her words. She rose from the bath and reached for the sheets set aside for drying bathers. She had lost flesh during their travels, as they all had, but she resented it the most. "My hips are getting narrow as a boy's. What man will think I can carry sons for him?" The question did not require an answer. "Let us hope we will eat well in Sarajevo."

Melantha and Pallas followed Thalia out of the water at once; Kelene was the last to leave the water. Her wooden comb made slow progress through her long, blond hair, and so she remained in the bathhouse after her mother and sisters had returned along the underground corridor to the inn. The steam sent up spectres to fill the small, dark room. In the light from the single oil lamp, Kelene thought she could make out shapes like wings. She told herself that it was nothing more than her imagination. Then she felt something graze her arm, like an insubstantial hand, or the brush of feathers.

For an instant she could not breathe, and when the feeling passed, she was able to stop herself from screaming. She peered into the warm mists, hoping to see what had touched her, but she could see nothing; the more she redoubled her efforts, the less she was able to discern. Finally she gave up, feeling she had failed the angel—if it was the angel who touched her.

When the angel visited her that night, Kelene sensed a greater command in his presence. He seemed nearer, somehow; his force was more that of a great warrior than a messenger of God. His features, less obscure than previously, were forbidding and imperious: his countenance long and angular, eyes deep-set. As she felt herself drawn more deeply into the vision, her flesh responded more intensely than it had before, as if it still retained the sensitivity she experienced in the bath. In a distant part of her mind she was troubled that an angel should so affect her, for surely Heaven subdued the body, not wakened it. Her vision showed her the safe road to Sarajevo, and she was relieved that she would be able to give her father such sought-for news. Again the angel showed the haven, and again it became an inferno. For now, she thought, she would tell her family the news of Sarajevo. She would keep to herself the rest of what the angel imparted—that their journey would not end there.

Sleep was their only refuge,
Dreams their only joy . . .
—Moravian song, 13th century

⊢ IV ⊣

Markos of Salonika kept a house near the central market of Sarajevo where he sold oil and the fruits from the orchards he owned around the city. He had a good-sized house with a dozen servants to tend to his needs and those of his family. He was a portly man with a mouth that pouted more readily than it smiled. Although he met his half-brother and his family with all the outward signs of hospitality—wine, bread, and salt— Markos could not conceal his dissatisfaction at their arrival.

"We thank God you have been spared, of course, and we mourn for your lost son. But this is not sanctuary. The Turks are strong here as well, my brother," he said to Diogenes once the formalities of greeting were over. "They make many demands of good Christians, and we cannot resist them without bringing terrible calamity to all of us." He signaled his daughters to serve the required sweetmeats and fruit, but his manner was not cordial. "We have other brothers, you and I, and what am I to do for them if I have given all to you?"

Diogenes achieved a smile. "I have no doubt we may be an imposition. God has asked many hard things of us all. Still, we did not come to you as complete paupers, Markos. Two of our wagons have spices and oil. They are of value. And I have a little gold."

At this, Markos' face brightened. "A little gold is good, as are spices. I have my own olive oil to sell." He studied the far wall where a large cabinet stood, as if reading signs in the grain of its wood. "That is useful. If you save the olive oil for part of a dowry, it may still be possible to find husbands for your daughters. Perhaps not great matches, but as reasonable as you may expect in these times. They will at least be taken care of; you will not have that burden to support."

Diogenes took umbrage at this. "My family is not a burden—"

"Not to you, perhaps."

Kelene studied her half-uncle, and found him oddly distressing. There was a hardness in his eyes that did not yield to smiling, and an air of self-satisfaction that did not match his outward signs of piety.

"We have come to you in good faith," said Diogenes, less affably than a moment before. "It is fitting that you, as a Christian and the son of my father, be concerned for our welfare."

"Alas," said Markos with an upward roll of his ruddy-brown eyes, "if the Turks had not made it impossible for an honest Christian to sell his goods without taxation, it might be better for us all. I would be more capable of rendering the charity you need. It was not so long ago that we had great stores of goods and lived well. But we are forever being put upon to deliver money to the Sultan's coffers, and so our pockets are empty and we have little opportunity to keep more than a small part of what we earn."

"We were told that Sarajevo was not so oppressed," said Diogenes, looking directly at Kelene.

Markos waved his hand, unaware of what passed between Diogenes and his daughter. "Well, we are much better off than many other places. We have not had the restrictions plaguing many Christians. The Sultan is not pressing his advantage here, being more threatened by Venice than by us. As long as we do not cause too much trouble and pay the taxes they impose, we manage fairly well. We do not have to give up everything to the Sultan's army. It is not like Salonika. We may keep our houses and our land for ourselves." He poured himself a little more wine, not offering any to his guests. "I regret that there is so little we can do for you. We must be frugal, but we do not have to suffer too badly."

"My children know their duty and they are grateful to you, my brother, for permitting us to live under your roof." Diogenes gave Markos a slight bow from his sitting position and went on. "The question of a dowry is not a difficult one, not yet. My daughters are not much inclined to marry. Only Thalia is of age. Kelene has not shown herself to be a woman. And Pallas will not reach marrying state for four years yet. By that time, I hope God will have delivered us from the Turks."

Once again Markos looked displeased. He fingered the bottle of scent that hung on a chain around his neck. "Let us pray it is so, but a prudent man will prepare for the worst. God tests us all in many ways." He pointed to Orien. "There are many who would find such a young man a treasure in their household, if you cannot restore your fortunes."

Diogenes went white. "Let me understand you, my brother. Are you suggesting we *sell* our son?"

Aware he had overstepped himself, Markos laughed a bit too loudly.

"Certainly not. No. Nothing of the sort. I only meant that if matters become more desperate, a fair-haired boy will fetch far more than a dark-haired one. It is not so desperate now that we must consider such acts. But should it come to that, you ought to know that Christian boys are commanding good prices, and those families without resources have been saved from penury by the timely sacrifice of a child. If it should come to that—not that I think it must," he added hastily, "the fair children are more in demand than dark ones. Your son is well-formed. And he is still young enough to be trained." He saw his retraction had not been sufficient. "I want you to realize that if our situation changes, if the Sultan asks of us what he claimed in Salonika, you must be prepared to consider . . . sacrifices."

Orien moved closer to Achilles, and Pallas took Thalia's hand. Kelene wished she would vanish from the house.

"Selling our son is not a sacrifice, it is an obscenity," said Diogenes, trying to keep his temper. "If Thalia can find a worthy husband, that will be a good enough beginning." His tone was conciliatory; his expression was not.

"I will make a few inquiries. There is a widower, a cooper, who may be interested in remarrying. He will not demand as large a dowry as many another might, being over forty himself. He has three children already, and will want a good, sensible wife." This was clearly an offering of truce, and Diogenes was glad of it.

"Thalia is of a practical turn of mind. She and my wife and I will speak of this. In the meantime, it is time we found our quarters and discovered what duties you will want us to perform for you." He rose and again bowed to his half-brother. "I thank you for extending your hospitality to us in our hour of need," he said as convention required, and was able to keep most of the irony out of his tone.

"I thought Sarajevo would be safe," said Alexander as the family gathered in what was clearly servants' quarters in the house of Diogenes' half-brother. "Isn't that what the Militant Angels said?" The room was plain, whitewashed and neat, but lacking any decoration beyond a single ikon of Saint Spiridion. Five simple chairs and a table completed the furnishing.

"We are much safer than we were," Pallas reminded him; the pinched look she had worn for the last week of their travels had changed, but the wariness remained in her eyes. "They will not take all our belongings and imprison us, as they would have in Salonika." She looked around the small, shabby common room and sighed. "At least the walls are stout and the roof does not leak."

They looked around their quarters and did their best not to be discouraged.

"And there are six rooms to sleep in," added Melantha; that they each contained only a cot and a chest was left unmentioned. "We can have Orien and Phaon share until the baby comes."

"And then what?" asked Thalia, sounding despondent. "I will be its nurse, if you like. To spare your nights."

"If we are fortunate, you will not have to concern yourself for very long." Alexander winked broadly. "You may yet find a husband."

Thalia sighed. "If we do not have to flee the Turks again. If the Militant Angels do not tell us that Sarajevo is no longer protection." She looked once at Kelene as if anticipating information that would bring more misfortune upon her.

Since this was precisely what Kelene feared most from the warnings the angel had given her, she cringed back in her chair. "The angel has not spoken to me since the night before we arrived. At that time he showed me a peaceful place here and good Christians around us. He promised then that we could restore ourselves." It was the truth, but only part of it. No doubt the angel would be angry at her refusal to reveal the whole of what he had imparted, but perhaps she would have a few more nights before the angel visited her once again. Perhaps she could claim then that she had not grasped the angel's intention when the vision was granted her. It was some comfort to realize her family was not happy in the Markos household. She could not help but feel glad now that their sojourn here would not be long; this was not a place she wanted to remain.

Diogenes grinned at what Kelene said. "Think of how well we are served," he exclaimed. "The Militant Angels will guide us if any mischance should come."

"May God continue to watch over us," said Melantha. "If we must rely on the charity of Markos, who knows what will become of us?"

"I wish the Militant Angels had warned us about Markos," said Achilles, glancing once at Orien.

"Why didn't they?" Thalia inquired, staring hard at Kelene.

"I don't know," she answered rather wildly. "I would have liked to know more, myself. If anything had been imparted to me, I would have told you of it." She felt her cheeks darken. What would they say if they knew she had withheld some of the angel's warning? How would they treat her? The memory of her father's fist striking her face reduced her to silence.

Pallas strove to reassure them all. "He probably thinks we will be nothing but burdensome to him. When he finds we are not, he will be less vexed by our presence."

Diogenes beamed his approval on his family and bowed his head to lead them in prayers of thanksgiving for their deliverance.

For the next several days, the family was occupied in learning the ways of Markos' household and the tasks they were to perform; no one noticed that Kelene had no visions to report in the morning when they rose before the sun to make themselves useful. As much as this calmed her family, it made Kelene upset. To her profound distress, she knew she missed the angel, as troubling as his presence and messages had been. She felt as if her very safety were a betrayal of the angel, yet she dared not admit so much to her family, not with the memory of her beating still stark in her mind.

Kelene worked in the kitchen, hanging herbs to dry and sorting them into the appropriate boxes when they were ready to be stored. She and Pallas kept to the kitchen, Pallas making cheese, while Thalia milked and herded the goats Markos kept. Melantha was set to carding goat hair for spinning, and to dying the cloth when it was woven. None of the work was arduous, but it all required their attention and judgment. They were kept separate from the women of Markos' household, so that Diogenes' family could not become too much a part of the domestic organization.

By the time their routine was established, the angel had spoken to Kelene again, this time to warn her that there would be tax collectors in the marketplace in two days and recommending that all gold be hidden. What followed the warning was so overwhelming that Kelene could find no words to express it, had she been able to speak of it without shame and confusion: the angel enveloped her in his wings and so inflamed her senses that she woke trembling, with an unfamiliar pleasure jolting through her like a beating pulse. Nothing she had been told of the nature of angels prepared her for such a reaction. Her certainty that her angel served some master other than God grew stronger. There had been more than one kiss, and her eager response in the dream upset her when she came awake late at night. She knew no prayers that would banish the tingling in her flesh, and so she forced herself to stay awake, in the hope that she would not have to encounter the angel again. She was filled with such turmoil that she did not know if she or the angel had sinned.

By morning, Kelene had decided how much of her vision to tell.

Thalia was smiling when Kelene reported the warning in her vision. "If anything can make Half-uncle Markos pleased we are living here, this should be what will satisfy him the most. It will save him money."

"Is that your opinion, Father?" asked Alexander.

"I think it would be wise to warn him, no matter what he might save," said Melantha, her eyes wary.

"If he is saved from having goods and monies seized, it is possible he would be grateful," said Diogenes.

"Why should the Militant Angels protect him?" asked Achilles reasonably. "He has not shown us much more than the approval he would give servants."

"If he is saved from misfortune, he will be better disposed to us, and will not think of us as impositions, as he does now," said Melantha, studying the faces of her children.

"We can protect what we have left," Alexander pointed out. "It would be prudent to see that our money and goods are hidden."

"Of course," said Diogenes, dismissing the remark as too obvious for serious discussion. "I have already found a good place behind the livestock pens; we will attend to the matter tonight."

"When will you tell him about Kelene's vision?" asked Melantha, her attention distracted by the movements of her unborn child.

"At noon, I think, when we have our meal. You will not dine with him, but I will."

Kelene kept quiet, hoping that her family had not sensed her reticence in what she said about the angel, or if they had, that they would attribute it to something other than the true cause.

"How is it you know these things?" Markos asked his half-brother when Diogenes imparted the warning to him. He was seated at a trestle table, his account books open before him, and a stack of silver coins next to them. Outside the marketplace slumbered in the first warm weather of spring. Trading would commence again at midafternoon, but for now the peasants and merchants rested after their noonday meal.

"It is a gift of the spirit, the chrism. The prophecy she receives is of God, for it has protected us. My daughter Kelene has visions, and what the Militant Angels tell her has served to guide us this far." It was impossible for Diogenes to conceal his pride in his fair-haired daughter. He saw that his half-brother was not convinced. "Without her visions, we would have died coming here, not once but many times."

"That blond child has the chrism?" Markos said, disbelief coloring his tone. "I would not have thought the angels would want so fragile a vessel for their work."

"The gift is in the blood," said Diogenes, becoming more insistent. "My Great-aunt Iocasta has it. Being old, she decided to pass the torch to my daughter. The visions have been with her since she was a child." He lifted his head. "Kelene has proven worthy of the favor of the Militant Angels."

"And they tell of coming tax collectors?" Markos repeated, his small eyes hard as the glint of metal. "In two days? Why does the coming of tax collectors trouble the Militant Angels?"

"We are Christians opposed by the might of Islam. Any act we undertake to confound them is a victory in our faith. So you may heed the warning and prepare; there is time to protect yourself from their demands. It is one of the ways the Militant Angels show their regard for the welfare of our family."

"And your daughter? What does she make of all this?" Markos demanded, his face stiff with indignation. "What sort of fool are you, to put any stock in what a girl of her age says?"

For once, Diogenes refused to be provoked. "She prevented us from using a road on which there came an avalanche which surely would have killed us. Without her visions we would all have perished. She has had many other visions as well. The Militant Angels have kept us safe. She has told us of other dangers on the road—outlaws and other pernicious men—to keep us from harm. She guided us, with the visions of the angel, away from roads where danger waited. Had we not heeded her, we would have lost more than one ox and . . . and Hector. For all our hardships, they would have been much worse if not for the timely warnings we received. All because the Militant Angels speak to her in her dreams."

"You are certain that the Militant Angels are speaking? We know that the Devil found his ally in Eve, and mankind has suffered for her error. What if it is a servant of the Roman Hell?" Markos shook his head. "To listen to your boasting, it would seem to me that you are caught up in pride, which is a sin, or so the pope of our church tells us."

"All popes condemn pride," said Diogenes, doing his best to hold his ire in check. "I would question this myself were it not for the fact that Kelene has had visions since she was young, as did my great-aunt before her."

"It is all foolishness," Markos said. "It will avail you nothing to make such claims here in Sarajevo. You might have impressed the desperate people of Salonika with such tales, but they will not be given credence here. We are not so gullible as you may think." He was eating dried figs, but he paused long enough to wipe his fingers and make a gesture to ward off evil. "Unless what you say is true, and then I would be sacrilegious to allow you to remain beneath my roof."

"You will not speak so about my daughter," Diogenes said evenly. *"You will not speak so, you will not."* He took hold of the front of Markos' garments and now all but lifted him from his seat.

Markos sputtered in shock and fury. "How dare you do this? I took you in! Without me, you'd all be beggars in the street."

"My daughter has given you a warning from the Militant Angels," said

Diogenes. "What harm is there in taking the warning? You will know in two days if she was right. If you do not, you will curse me for your own foolishness." He released his hold and stepped back. He saw he had knocked over the brass ewer in the corner of the room. As he righted this, he said, "I cannot ask your forgiveness, half-brother, because I have not erred. You have been given the benefits of Kelene's gifts. You ignore the message at your peril."

There were two Christian women selling eggs in the shadow of the Church of the Dormition at the far end of the marketplace. They were respectable widows, known to most of the Christians of Sarajevo, and so their first cry of alarm brought the full attention of those farmers and merchants who had come to sell and buy. All business halted.

Four soldiers on glossy horses escorted a large, prosperous-looking eunuch in voluminous white robes, riding a mule. He carried tablets and a scale, and on the mule sat two capacious saddle-baskets, making his purpose plain from the first.

Diogenes nudged Markos in the arm. "Look. The tax collector is here." He indicated the new arrivals with a touch of satisfaction. "It is fitting they should come: Kelene said they would be here."

"I remember; she had a vision," said Markos as he began sorting out jars of salted olives and amphorae of first-pressed oil, moving them to the back of his booth. He did his best not to appear furtive in his movements. "Quick," he snapped at Diogenes. "Put these behind the rest."

The soldiers were making their way down the aisles between the stalls and booths, pausing now and again to issue orders to various of the occupants. The leader had drawn his scimitar.

As Diogenes scrambled to conceal the most valuable portion of their wares, he said, "They will want to see your counting room. Kelene was certain about that."

"They usually do," said Markos. "I would expect nothing less of them, no matter what sort of vision your child has had." He turned to the marketplace again, making himself smile at the Sultan's officers as they approached. "May God bless you, good Ottomites." He bowed in the Turkish manner, exuding goodwill.

"You are the olive merchant, aren't you? Markos; I remember you, do I not?" asked the eunuch in a high, clear voice. "The one who—"

"I have that honor," he answered before the eunuch could insult him. "And what will it be my privilege to do for you today?"

"We must examine your wares," said the eunuch, "and your counting room. You will be assessed for payment to permit the Sultan to maintain his lands. It is fitting that you pay, since it is the Christians who make this advancement necessary." He peered at Diogenes. "And who is this man?"

"He is my half-brother, from Salonika." Markos raised his voice a bit more than respect required. "The Sultan—"

"The Sultan did as Allah, the All-Merciful, gave him to do, as do we all. You Christians do not accept the Will of Allah," said the eunuch. "We will abide by what the Sultan has ordered us to do in the Name of the One God. You will do as you are ordered, or you will suffer for it." He motioned to one of the soldiers, who dismounted. "Markos of Salonika, be warned. Your ways have not gone unnoticed. You have tried to conceal your best goods in the past. This man will examine what you have here, and take what is due the Sultan's men."

"As you have in the past," said Markos, stepping aside to permit the soldier to come into the booth.

Many of the merchants were watching this exchange closely.

"You will show respect," ordered the senior officer, raising his scimitar. "It is fitting that you honor the Sultan's men."

Markos bowed several times, moving as if his spine should moan in protest. "It is my honor to serve." He glanced at Diogenes to see what his half-brother was doing. "And this son-of-my-father is at your service as well."

"No doubt," said the officer without any conviction. He remained where he was as his deputy went through the jars and amphorae, setting out half a dozen for confiscation.

"Your counting room is in your house, isn't it?" the eunuch asked when the wares were safely stowed in his large saddle-baskets. "You will take my soldiers to it. Conceal anything from us, and your hand will be struck off for theft."

With a loud, deliberate sigh, Markos said to Diogenes, "Stay here and guard this place until I return. I know how much they have taken. More must not be missing when I return."

"She was right about the tax collectors," Markos admitted two nights later. "I would have lost much more if you hadn't told me about her vision." He lowered his eyes. "I ask your pardon for my disbelief, but I still cannot be easy in my mind about her visions." This last was abrupt and without any pretext at cordiality.

"The Militant Angels have spoken through her; I have said her visions are true." A dangerous glint showed in Diogenes' eyes. Here in Markos' study, the two men were alone and undisturbed; the counting room beyond the closed door, a silent reminder of the service Kelene had done. The rest of the household was preparing for bed, reciting prayers to keep them from danger in the night. "She has been a visionary since she was very young. The Militant Angels have made her their own."

"So you told me," said Markos, and went on with the semblance of nonchalance. "But I did not realize that God's angels concerned themselves with tax collectors. Or that a girl like that one would be their messenger."

Stung by this observation, Diogenes answered with some heat. "The Militant Angels have the protection of the faithful as their task. You have forgotten that God has given His Angels the task to guard us as well as to correct us in errors. They seek for those who will do their bidding truly, who are humble. They do not look for those who are mightiest, but those whose vision is most clear. They are concerned for the welfare of good Christians. If the followers of Mohammed are the enemies of Christ, then the angels would spare Christians the burdens given them falsely." He sat very straight, his embroidered vest moving with his deepened breath.

"I do not mean that the warning was not useful," said Markos. His voice lowered slightly. "I would not have concealed those two chests under the floor had it not been for the warning, and I am grateful. I admit it. It was very useful, which is what troubles me, for the popes tell us that those things that are of the soul do not often touch the marketplace."

"Because of what Christ told Matthias?" asked Diogenes. "It is well to give Caesar his due, no doubt, and you do not begrudge your Christian rulers the payments they require. That is why your chests must be saved."

"Not that I scorn the aid," said Markos, not quite accurately. He poured out a cup of wine for each of them. "Merchants like us often strive to keep as much of our gain as we can, no matter who attempts to take it."

Diogenes used what advantage he had gained to pursue the matter. "But to advance the cause of Mohammed through paying tribute to his leaders is an act against Christ. The Militant Angels admonish us to persevere in our faith. Why would they not warn us against the depredations of the officers of the Sultan?"

Aware that he could not counter Diogenes' argument, Markos changed tactics. "If word of her . . . gifts should get out, it would bring attention to this house that is unwelcome and unsought. It is all to the good to give warnings, but if I too often anticipate the demands of the Sultan, it could bring a scrutiny to my life that would have unwanted consequences for all of us."

Flushed with success, Diogenes rose and bowed. "If you do not want to know what the Militant Angels say, I will keep their messages to myself."

Markos frowned. "Tell me what the warnings are; I will decide what to do when I receive them. And in the meantime, let no word of her chrism spread, or it will go badly for us all."

When the angel came this time, Kelene could no longer tell herself his purpose was only revelation: she felt wholly possessed by him, her skin hot under his hands, her lips swollen by his kiss. There was no pretext of warning, no implied protection: she drank the dark, rich wine and offered her body to his use without question or resistance, seeking only to be one with him, to bind her soul to him even as she promised her flesh.

It was terrifying to speak to her father of her fears, but after the dream of the previous night it was more terrifying not to, not with so many changes in the manner of the angel, and her doubts gnawing away at her faith. Her father might beat her, she knew—but if she did not speak now, she might never summon up the courage to do it again. She made herself seek him out. Kelene found him in the garden working among the fragrant herbs—rosemary and thyme and the last of the winter savory—a rake in his hand and sweat from the warm spring sun marking his shirt.

"Kelene," said Diogenes in surprise as he caught sight of her. He straightened up. "What is it?"

"I had another dream last night," she said, and shuddered at the memory. "I . . . I have not wanted to speak of it, for it will distress you." This was truthful enough as far as it went, but did not force her to tell him all the reasons for her worry. She was not prepared to reveal the emotions the angel's kisses wrought in her.

"The Turks will want more money?" It was the most obvious threat facing them all and he accepted the inevitability with resignation.

She shrugged. "It is possible. But that is not what troubles me." She saw his face become rigid. "I have not told you all that has been imparted, the things the angel has done." She waited for his castigation, and when none came, she gathered her faltering courage and went on. "He has said that we will not remain here, and that greater losses will befall us." She stopped, searching for what more to tell him.

Diogenes came to her side, his expression filled with sympathy. "I did not think we would not have any demands made of us. God is a stern father to His children." He put his hand on her shoulder, looking down at her with approval. "I suppose the angel says much that is hard to understand. If that is the worst of it, I thank God that along with visions, He has given you good sense. Some things ought not to be told unless it is absolutely necessary. I have come to think you did well to keep your knowledge of Hector's death to yourself. If there are other such warnings, do not reveal them unless you have to. Your mother would not like to hear such things, and with her time coming near, it is best for her thoughts to be for the baby and Heaven, not the troubles we face."

This made what she wanted to say next both easier and more difficult. "It isn't that alone. Not only that. There is something more." She was suddenly weak, as if her sinews had lost all their tautness. It would be easy to leave now, and deal with the rest of it some other time. But there might not be another time, she reminded herself.

Something of her consternation touched Diogenes, and he took her by the shoulders. "What is it? What troubles you so? It isn't the baby, is it?"

"No. Not that. At least, not that I know of." Lowering her eyes, she said, "The angel is . . . making demands of me. Not as prophecy, but for . . . for other matters, ones I . . . it is hard to describe, and I am afraid that what I do then is sinful. But he is the angel and . . . and I cannot control what he does. When he . . . does them, I have no heart to . . . deny him. I feel that in order to continue to serve him, I will have to sin." She could feel the heat in her face and neck, and a tightening lower in her body that added to her confusion. "I am ashamed to tell you what the angel has done, for it is not fitting that I should talk of . . . of . . ."

Diogenes studied her, his eyes troubled, his hands clenched on the handle of the rake. When Kelene straggled into silence, he regarded her somberly. "Is there anything else?"

"Yes," she admitted, hoping he would not become so irate that he struck her again. "I know it is my body that betrays me." She felt tears on her face; she did not wipe them away. "I cannot subdue the flesh as the holy ones do. I am too frail. It . . . overwhelms me, no matter what I do. I . . . I have tried to stop it. When the angel has made me see things that are . . . horrible . . . I do not want to speak of them, and I think that is why I cannot turn away from the flesh. I have not been true to all the angel imparts, and so I am being punished." She dropped to her knees. "My father, I can no longer promise that what the angel tells me is of God. And since it may be born in sin, I want you to . . . exorcise the angel."

"What?" Diogenes thundered. "Exorcise the angel!" He brought his hand back to strike her.

Kelene grabbed his leg and clung to it. "I do not want to be the means by which we all come to ruin. I couldn't bear that." She wiped tears from her face with one hasty swipe of her hand. "But, Father, think! If the angel is not of God, if I am exorcised and my gift remains, then I will be free to have the Militant Angels speak through me once more." She looked up at him, trying to keep from cringing at the play of emotions she read in his features. She had said too much to stop now. With an uneven breath, she implored him, "Let me be exorcised, I beg of you. I've thought it all out, and it is the only way to be certain. Great-great Aunt Iocasta warned me and I would not heed her. I thought she begrudged me this gift. Now I know that she was wise and kind to tell me all she did. Help me guard us from greater harm, Father. Find a pope and rid me of the Militant Angels. For the sake of our family and our faith. Please, Father. *Please!*"

That night she dreamed of angels
As if pursued by demons . . .
—Greek ballad, 14th century

⊢ V ⊣

"What are you talking about? Exorcised? Exorcism is for those caught in the toils of the Serpen—" Diogenes tugged himself free of his daughter's grasp. "Why should you be exorcised?"

She managed to hold onto her fading courage well enough to reply, "I am afraid. I see things, things I've never told you. Terrible things. Fleshly things."

"I will not hear of this. We must continue in the angel's care!" he shouted at her. "Do you think we are so secure here that we no longer require guidance and protection? You know what happened in the market-place with the tax collector. It might not be the same as robbers on the road, but we needed the help of the Militant Angels, nonetheless. How can you shirk your duty this way?"

"Father, it's not that . . . I cannot tell you . . . Do not beat me. Do not. Not again. Listen to me, please. I have tried to do as you wish. But I am afraid, of the angel, of myself. If I continue in his thrall, I will become his creature."

He raised his hand to strike her, but stopped himself. "What sin do you fear you will commit?"

She was astonished at his forbearance, and for a moment could not speak. Then, as she saw the hardness return to his face, she blurted out, "I don't know. Sins of the flesh, I suppose. Sins against chastity."

"Sins of the flesh?" he repeated incredulously. "Sins of the flesh? You? That is ridiculous. What angel demands sin of any kind?" He lowered his arm and stared down at her. "What do you know of sins of the flesh?"

"Nothing," she said quickly. "But I know to fear them."

He reflected for a moment, then cocked his head. "Why should an angel lead you to sins of the flesh?"

"I . . . I don't know," she admitted, her voice trembling. She pressed her forehead against her father's leg once again. "But he stirs me, and I do not know what I ought to do."

Diogenes coughed once; recently he had seen the first changes in Kelene's body, but had not assumed she would feel the weight of the flesh as his other daughters. Perhaps he had been wrong. Perhaps not even the Militant Angels could eradicate the body. Perhaps the Eve in her was awakening, hearing the promises of the Serpent, and the angel was being lost in the lures of promised rapture. He rubbed his chin, and after a short while, he touched Kelene's shining head. "All right. All right, my girl. If I find you an exorcist, and the angel is still with you when the work is done, will you renew your dedication to your visions?"

Kelene raised herself up on her knees and tried to smile. "Oh, yes, Father. Yes. I will gladly consent to your terms." She was a bit startled that he had agreed so readily. "If the priest removes this danger to my soul and my visions remain, I will be the servant of the angel for as long as my service is acceptable to him." Flushed with relief, she kissed her father's hand before she got to her feet. "Thank you. Thank you."

Diogenes stared at her, wondering if she had any notion of what she was doing to him. He had bought himself and his family a little time, but he realized he would have to bring her what she wanted or risk having her withdraw from him altogether: that was more than he was willing to accept. He had staked too much on his golden-haired daughter's gifts to allow her to abandon the Militant Angels now. "I will find an exorcist," he promised her, and decided he would have to find one who would not do too much damage. He owed his child the appearance of concern.

"Soon, Papa," she urged. "I do not want to sin."

"You will not, Kelene." He patted her arm. "And you are good to tell me of your fear. It is fitting that a father should aid and guard his children. As the Militant Angels aid and guide us, through you."

She nodded once, trying not to look so relieved that she would shock her father any more than she already had. "I will pray; if the angel is not trying to . . . do ill, the prayers will give strength to us both." It was what he wanted to hear.

"I will speak to the pope tomorrow. He will know which of the exorcists in Sarajevo will be most capable of—" He did not go on; his face was set and his eyes did not quite meet hers.

Kelene knew how disappointed he was in her, and she did her best to apologize. "I'm very sorry, Papa, but I knew you would not want me to lead the family into sin, all because my gifts had been tainted." She thought his expression lightened a little, and she pressed on, "You are always so willing to hear what my visions tell"—at least, she told herself, as much of them as could be imparted—"that I want to do all that I can to make the visions as reliable as . . ." Words failed her as she stared at Diogenes.

"They have been our salvation. They were from the first." His tone was intent.

"But I did not tell you all. I was warned of death and suffering, much more than I spoke of. It frightened me so much that I told you little of it." Her voice dropped. "And the rest . . . what emotions are roused in me, I can only say they are . . . not what I suppose an angel would impart. If only I could be certain that it is my own failings that have tainted the visions—"

"You are a good girl," said her father, "and I do not want you to think badly of what you have done. Without the Militant Angels, we would be lost. But if you are certain that you cannot continue—" Again he patted her arm, sighing. "Let me arrange everything."

She started to cross herself, then stopped, not convinced that she would gain anything by it; her hand dropped to her side. "I will pray tonight."

"Very good," Diogenes approved.

What she did that night was dream. *In a desolate landscape swept by storms the angel hovered over her, his cloaklike wings extended above her as she huddled beneath him.*

"Ruin is coming: ruin and destruction such as has not been seen since Attila and his Huns blasted the land. If you do not tell your family, they will suffer the same fate as those who were in the path of the Huns. But you—you, my acolyte—will be left alive. I will save you from death so long as you are mine. And you are mine."

She trembled. "But it is not fitting that I should . . . My blood runs at the sight of you. My heart speeds, my skin . . ."

He bent down, his lips brushing her face, his breath on her cheek. "That is your devotion. As you become more a woman, your body will answer the call of the spirit."

"I feel . . . I am not in grace when I am so much a servant of my flesh." Kelene did not have the strength to raise her face to him.

The ferocity of the storm increased. Thunder pursued lightning from horizon to horizon, the jagged, baleful glare leaving afterimages in her dazzled eyes like rent bodies. The angel remained steadfast above her, his eyes like smoldering beacons. "Do you think my grace has no cost?" he demanded, the thunder no more awesome than his voice. "Did you suppose you would not be held to account? You never considered the price of your knowledge, did you?"

She quailed under this onslaught. "No."

"Then listen to me, and learn afresh," the angel said, his gaze hot as the lightning, striking fire in her where it touched. "You are mine. I summoned you, and you will answer my call, though it be from the far side of the grave."

"Amen," she whispered, and trembled at the enormity of her consent.

"Yes, and I say it, too." He reached down and stroked her arm and shoulder; she wondered if there would be burns on her skin from this, like the furrows of claws.

Lightning slithered overhead; thunder drubbed the rioting winds.

She heard herself say, pleading with the angel, "And you will protect us, still? You will not desert us?"

"You will not be rid of me now, my own Kelene, my Dark Star, no matter what you do. Nothing will part us, not in your life, not after it. You have my mark upon your soul and you are mine eternally." Under these crooning promises there was an inexorable vow as binding as vows to the dead, or to God.

"But—" Why should it frighten her so, she wondered, that he knew the meaning of her name? Did angels not know these things?

He touched the tip of his finger to her lips, silencing her, and leaving behind the hot, metallic taste of blood and a sensitivity like that of a raw burn. "I will guide and protect you, never doubt it. The time will come when you will have to move on once again. You have been warned of this before now. You may be certain that I will keep faith with you. If you turn from me, you will stand in the heart of the storm, without refuge. As long as you submit to me, I will shield you from all that is to come. I will reveal signs to you as the day approaches, so that you may be certain of the prophecy."

Lying beneath him, Kelene felt her heart beat erratically, as if his weight were on her and not above her. Sweat slicked her skin, and she told herself that it was her sin, not the presence of the angel, that accounted for it. As much as she wanted to roll away from him, the frenzy of the storm stopped her. How she despised herself for her cowardice.

"Kelene," the angel said somberly, "only the foolish are not afraid of me."

"But the exorcist . . . it has gone too far to stop." She held her breath, waiting for his answer.

"No exorcist can prevail against me as long as you are mine. And you are mine." Abruptly the storm ended and she was standing beside her angel on a high crag with mountains flanking them; the tranquility of the scene, after the storm, ought to have calmed her, but it did not: leached of all color, the whole landscape was rimed with moonlight, long, livid shadows hiding the narrow valleys beneath them, valleys that might contain . . . anything.

"Here," the angel said, holding a chalice out to her. "To seal our pledge." He held it to her mouth while she drank, and then turned the chalice so that his lips touched the metal rim where hers had been.

Kelene licked the rich, warm wine from her lips, doing what she could to ignore the taste, and the odd hunger it summoned up from deep within her soul.

*   *   *

As his family broke their fast the next morning, Diogenes noticed his golden-haired daughter was unusually subdued and heavy-eyed; he took this as an indication that she had spent most of the night praying, and he hoped it had relieved the worst of her fears. A night of calm reflection had convinced him that Kelene needed nothing more than the reassurance that she was not caught in the wiles of the body, which ever toiled to ensnare and corrupt the soul.

"My husband," said Melantha, cutting into his thoughts as she sat down, putting the large, earthenware pot of mint-and-lemon tea into the center of the table. Her dark gold eyes were troubled.

"Yes?" he answered, his tone abrupt. "What is it that disturbs you?"

Melantha was not put off by this; she was used to Diogenes' occasional reveries and no longer hesitated to interrupt them. "Your brother has spoken to me," she said, flushing slightly, looking uncomfortable. "You will not like what he suggests."

"Oh?" Diogenes waited to hear the rest, knowing his children were listening closely. "Why should he address you instead of me? It isn't fitting." He strove to look interested instead of offended, but could not disguise his apprehension.

"He thought I would understand him better. His object in coming to me was to have my support for something he thought you would refuse out of hand." Now she had the full attention of her entire family. "He wants to sell Kelene's visions. He said it would make our circumstances far better if he could report her warnings to other Christians." She made no attempt to conceal her dissatisfaction. "I said that I would speak with you. I have done it."

All the family listened attentively, one or two of them nodding. Pallas grinned.

"Markos insists." Melantha looked away, her face showing no emotion whatsoever. "He will not let us stay here if you will not permit him to sell Kelene's visions."

To Kelene's horror, her father rubbed his chin thoughtfully. "Papa, no; no, I can't," she said. "You promised me you would find an exorcist . . ." She remembered her vow from her dream and the words trailed off.

"Oh, yes," Diogenes said, a bit too heartily. "You do not want anyone complaining that your visions are not from the Militant Angels. We will have the exorcism; I will persuade my brother. And then we will do what we can to comply with his wishes."

"But . . ." Kelene stared at her father, trying to find some way to persuade him to reject what Markos demanded.

"We will look for the exorcist, yes, yes," said Diogenes, dismissing

Kelene's apprehension with a single gesture. "I will explain it all to Markos, and he will see reason in what I tell him." He rubbed his hands vigorously. "If all goes well, we will not have to depend upon the cold hospitality we have here once Kelene's abilities are known."

Only Melantha revealed any unease at the prospect of establishing their fortunes on Kelene's visions. "What if the Militant Angels do not promise benefits, but reveal coming catastrophe? It was thus before."

When Diogenes wished to have his voice as sweet and enveloping as honey, he could; he did so now. "We have no wish to abuse our child's gifts, or to make the words of the Militant Angels the object of trade, but we must look to our safety, and to the safety of all Christians."

Kelene shook her head several times, as if trying to shake her thoughts into sensible order. "Father, I do not know—"

"No, of course you don't," said Diogenes, soothing her. "You must rely on your father to know what is best for you and for the family. We have followed your visions from our home, we have sacrificed willingly to meet the demands of the Militant Angels." He drank a little of the hot mint-and-lemon tea.

"Yes," said Pallas. "We've done what you wanted."

"And now," said Thalia, "you will have to accommodate us. We came here because you said it was necessary. It is time you did something to make amends for what we have endured because of your vision."

"Thalia," said Diogenes, "we are alive, thanks to the Militant Angels and your sister." He turned to Kelene, and the hope that had sprung up in her was dashed as he went on. "Not that it would not be wise to make the most of what you can do. We know the value of your visions. It would be of much use if you were able to tell us more of what you see."

"I tell you . . . what will save us," Kelene said haltingly.

"Exactly," Diogenes approved. "And once the exorcist has shown that your visions are untainted—"

"Papa," Kelene interrupted, "what if the exorcism ends the visions?"

Achilles laughed aloud. "You've been having them for years and years. Why should they stop now?"

There was a noisy babble of agreement, and finally Alexander declared, "If we have been led into error by your visions, then we deserve to be punished."

Melantha took Phaon into her lap. "The exorcist will end the matter, one way or another."

"Yes," said Thalia, her smile showing more smugness than confidence. "We'll know what has been protecting us."

"If you think it is one of the Fallen Angels," said Orien, "you might not like it if Kelene keeps her gifts."

This candid observation was so near the mark that Thalia flushed and mumbled a few words that might be construed as an apology.

"We will have to wait until the exorcism is done," said Diogenes. "Once we have attended to the exorcism, I will talk with my brother." He took one of the dried figs and popped it into his mouth, adding while he chewed, "For now, we all have tasks to do, and Markos expects us to do them."

Thalia glanced at her younger sister. "Until she earns our living for us," she said under her breath.

"Thalia," Melantha said sharply. "The exorcism may end all her visions."

Alexander struck the flat of his hand on the table. "If that happens, then the least of our worries will be making our living, from Kelene or anyone. We will no longer know when we are safe."

"I will have to watch over her for three nights," said the tall, bearded monk, looking at Diogenes instead of Kelene. "Only then will I know if I might be of help. It is hard to know about such cases as hers. She may not need exorcism at all; she may be called of the spirit. You say she has the chrism, and if that is the case, she may seek a cloister." Brother Iraneus had a formidable reputation as a preacher and an inspired teacher of the young. He showed his disdain for the world by fasting often and bathing rarely. When Markos' slaves offered him refreshments, he accepted only water and flat bread, leaving the dates and wine to Diogenes.

"You are the fifth man we have spoken to in regard to my daughter's gift, and our wish to determine its source," said Diogenes, wishing he could learn more from the monk without impugning his dedication to his calling; it was more than a week since Diogenes had promised his daughter to find her an exorcist, and he was growing aggravated with the time-consuming process. "The others wanted large donations to exorcise her. You have not yet asked for one."

"If I agree to undertake to rid her of malign spirits, I will accept whatever you decide is the value of my work, when it is completed," said Brother Iraneus. "You need not fret about payment."

At this welcome news, Diogenes smiled ingratiatingly. "You are certainly a reasonable man for an unworldly monk."

"My brothers and nephews are merchants," said Brother Iraneus, glancing once at Kelene as if to be certain she was listening. "I learned early in life, before I retired from the world, the difference between value and price."

"Yes; they are different," said Diogenes, warming to the monk. "In hard times—and we have certainly had hardships enough—that lesson is brought home in many ways. If her visions are of the Militant Angels, we will have a gift beyond all price."

"Truly," said Brother Iraneus.

Listening to this discussion, Kelene wondered if Brother Iraneus seemed as inane to her father as he did to her. She said nothing more than, "I do not want to lead anyone astray."

Brother Iraneus favored her with a stern nod. "That is a good beginning, child. If you abide in humility, our efforts will be rewarded."

Diogenes' next question required a great measure of tact; he coughed to show his good intentions. "I have not been told much regarding your previous exorcisms?"

"Yes," said Brother Iraneus. "I have cast demonical spirits out of swine, in the Name of the Christ." He crossed himself. "And I have laid hands on one suffering from the bite of a mad dog and he was restored to perfect health."

"Then you do not hesitate to confront a Fallen Angel, if that should prove to be necessary?" Diogenes' expression made it apparent that he thought this would not be necessary.

"Alone, yes, I would hesitate, as all faithful Christians must. But with the power of the Christ as my shield and guide, and in His Light, I would walk into death without fear." Brother Iraneus spoke with complete calm, his gaunt face revealing his determination.

Suddenly Kelene asked, "Why must you watch me for three nights if you have Christ to uphold your purpose?" Her pulse beat loudly in her ears.

"Kelene," her father admonished her.

Brother Iraneus held up his hand. "No, it is a wise question for her to ask." He looked at her from under a thicket of eyebrows. "I do not want to call upon the Christ without good cause. Until I understand the nature of your . . . visitations, I will be unable to know how I am to prepare, and for what."

"You see?" Diogenes said. "The monk is practical enough to want to see for himself. You cannot object to that, can you?" His expression indicated that he would tolerate no protest from her.

"No, Papa," she said softly, staring at the monk's filthy sandals protruding from the ragged hem of his habit.

"Good," said Diogenes, settling the matter. "Are you able to begin tonight?"

"Tomorrow night," said Brother Iraneus, rising from his place on the small wooden bench. "I must fast and pray tonight, in preparation."

"Yes, of course you must. Well, then, until tomorrow at sundown." Diogenes bowed to the monk as if he were a dignitary of high rank. "My family is most grateful to you, Brother."

"I have done nothing yet," said Brother Iraneus, offering a blessing to Diogenes and Kelene. "There will be time enough for thanks when I have done."

Brother Iraneus' first night watching over Kelene was uneventful, and before dawn, the monk snored gently. He departed with many apologies when the family rose, and returned the following evening more full of purpose than before. He did not go into the crowded main room where the family gathered, but remained in the corridor with Diogenes and Kelene.

"You may be certain I will not fail you tonight," he promised Kelene, and showed her a small cluster of spiny burrs he held in his palm. "This will keep me awake and at my devotions."

Kelene said nothing, though she thought the solution unnecessarily severe. Her father made a sign of approval. "Very clever, Brother."

"The pain is a reminder of the suffering of the Christ," said Brother Iraneus. "Whether it is angel or demon I must confront, I will not be caught unprepared." He lowered his voice so that only Diogenes could hear him. "I expect nothing will happen tonight. Usually these powers manifest on the third night, in honor of the Trinity."

"Why should that be, unless she is the instrument of the Militant Angels?" Diogenes asked.

"The Serpent lies, and never more than in perverting the work of the angels," Brother Iraneus declared.

Diogenes nodded. "Then my daughter is right to be . . . uncertain about her visions?"

"It is to her credit that she has asked to be exorcised, for not only is her soul at stake, but so are the souls of you all, who have followed the teaching of her visions." Brother Iraneus put his hands into his sleeves and indicated the door to Kelene's bedroom with a nod of his head.

"By all means, you may wait there." Diogenes plucked at Kelene's sleeve as he went on to the monk. "My daughter will put on her nightshift before she leaves the bath, so as not to compromise you."

"Very kind," murmured Brother Iraneus, and went to begin his rituals.

By the time Kelene retired, Brother Iraneus was on his knees, whispering prayers, watching her closely as she pulled her blanket up to her chin. He continued to stare at her as she did her best to fall asleep under his scrutiny.

Looking up at the ceiling, Kelene tried to persuade herself to ignore the presence of Brother Iraneus, to pay no heed to his susurrus of prayers. At least, she thought, she had done her best. It was all in the hands of the angel now; she had given him her pledge, and if he had strength and will enough, she would have nothing to fear.

"You are mine," the angel said, hovering over her in the dark that went far beyond the limits of the night.

Kelene stirred on the bed, her body responding to the presence of the angel; on the far side of the little room, Brother Iraneus raised his head, alert.

The vastness around them seemed eternal, stretching to encompass the stars. The angel bore her upward, holding her clasped to him with powerful arms; she could feel the armor against her. "You are with me, Kelene. All this is yours."

"But there is nothing," she exclaimed as she stared into the void.

Brother Iraneus strained to hear what she said; when he could not make it out, he moved nearer to her bed.

"There is everything," the angel said. "All of creation is at your disposal. Reach out to it. Take it. Take it."

"I . . . I cannot see it," Kelene muttered, grasping his shoulders with straining hands. "There is nothing but . . . emptiness."

"But no; there is everything you could want, all you can desire," the angel promised her. "Take it."

She began to shiver as if caught in a sudden winter gale. "If I let go of you, I will fall."

"No, you will not. I will hold you," the angel said, his lips near her ear. "So long as you are faithful to me, only to me, I will hold you." He kissed her mouth once more, not as a benediction, or as a promise, but as something far more disturbing.

"Why . . . ?" she breathed as their lips parted.

"Did you like it?" the angel asked, his body pressed the length of hers.

"I . . . yes." An emotion that was not quite shame rushed over her; deep within her something had awakened.

Brother Iraneus began to pray aloud.

The angel's low, seductive voice drowned out the holy invocations. "You will want more, Kelene." How evocative his words were.

"Yes." There was much more than consent in her response.

"I am the sustenance of your spirit." His fingers reached the youthful curve of her breasts.

"Yes," she repeated.

He kissed her urgently, saying when he was done, "This is my dominion. This is my seal." Then he pressed his mouth to her throat instead of her lips. The pain was intense but fleeting, replaced by lassitude and a sensation of falling, though she remained secure in his embrace.

From his place beside her bed, Brother Iraneus gave all his attention to the burrs pressing into his palms. Had Kelene been younger, he would have taken her hand between his own, but with her womanhood coming upon her, he hesitated, unconvinced of her innocence.

As she began to waken, Kelene heard the angel's voice, but could not make out the words.

But what voice is it I hear
Calling in the dead of night?
—Moravian ballad, 15th century

⟜ VI ⟞

When Brother Iraneus arrived the following evening just as supper was ending, he was greeted promptly by Diogenes and his family, all exhibiting an uneasy combination of reverence and anxiety. Kelene had remained, fasting, in her bedroom, as her father had insisted.

"I will perform the rite of exorcism on Kelene tonight, as your father has requested. Be content; if the visitation is a malign one, it will be routed by the power given to me by God, to do His work in His Name," he explained as Diogenes' children listened. "You may hear many things, some of them distasteful, some of them frightening. You must not interrupt, no matter how dire you think the danger may be, for your interference would pose a greater danger than anything I might face otherwise."

"But mightn't it . . . the Serpent, come after us? If it is in Kelene, that is? If the angels are Fallen? Or if it is the Serpent?" asked Achilles.

Brother Iraneus regarded Achilles tenderly. "You are sustained by your innocence. I am protected by my calling, and by the strength of the Christ." He looked from one face to the next, making sure that all of the children were giving him their full attention. "Only your intervention in my work can keep me from completing it, and resolving at last the question of the source of your sister's visions. If the angels are malign, they will be gone by morning, and she will return to grace. If they are of God, they will be stronger for this act of faith." He blessed each of the children in turn. "You have not been the object of the angels' prophesies, but it could happen that if these angels are fallen, they could try to fix on one of you as their tool. You would not like that to happen, would you?" His hand lingered on Achilles' head. "Unspoiled youth is always vulnerable to such corruption, the more so for its purity. Pray that this is not the case with your sister."

"What corruption is that?" asked Achilles, scowling at Brother Iraneus.

"The perversions of the Fallen Angels," said the monk. "They who fled the goodness and majesty of God and His Christ."

"But wouldn't they hurt Kelene?" Achilles' young features were tight with worry. "If they are bad, they could—"

Thalia could not conceal her annoyance. "I don't know what we should fear anyway. We have been at Kelene's beck and call since she announced we would have to leave Salonika. Longer: she was making predictions when she was four."

"Do you think she is protected by her angel, then?" asked Brother Iraneus.

"No. If we were really protected, Hector would still be alive and I would have married. I think that whatever she is answering to, we have been made as much a tool of it as she is. We are as much servants of her . . . angel as she is. Hasn't she drawn us into whatever temptation she has accepted?" She pinched away angry tears in her eyes.

"You must have faith in God, and His care of you," said Brother Iraneus. "You must pray for guidance and protection, for the strengthening of the angel, if it is one of the Militant, and strength for me if it is not."

"And what if He does not? Might God not have left us to fend for ourselves?" Alexander challenged. "Why should God give His protection to ones who have not known His Will?"

"You suppose that God will abandon anyone who calls to Him? That is not so," Brother Iraneus exclaimed. "Christ is the source of salvation, and you deny His redemption at your peril. If you cannot appeal to Him, the Virgin will intercede for you, if you ask it. She will plead for mercy for all who come to her. Salvation is always there for those who seek it." He stood before Orien, turning the youngster's face up. "You are the hope of all Christians, an unblemished innocent, without sin since your baptism. No appeal from such a child as you will go unheeded."

Orien blushed. "I wouldn't know what to say."

"You need say nothing," Brother Iraneus assured him. "Your soul is uncorrupt and it will appeal with its purity."

Pallas was wan with terror. "But we have followed their guidance for so long, and we have lived. We are alive now because we have trusted the angels. Our doubt, after we have been spared through the visions, will not please God, will it? If the Militant Angels become angry, won't they try to punish us for—"

"You are showing your faith, girl," said Brother Iraneus sternly. "No servant of God would punish any true Christian for that."

"I suppose that's true," said Melantha, breaking her silence for the first time.

"Trust in God, my good woman," said Brother Iraneus. "All things happen by His Will, and your summoning me is as much God's intent as anything in the world." He held out his arms to include them all. "Pray for Kelene. God will show Himself in answer to your prayers."

Kelene's knees hurt from kneeling on the stone floor; she was tired of petitioning Heaven to cast out all uncleanliness from her soul. Her little bedchamber seemed even smaller than it was with Brother Iraneus taking up so much room in it. She was becoming hoarse. Her head had started to ache. She wanted to go to sleep, not remain where she was; her whole body was heavy and light at once.

"You are a wilful child," Brother Iraneus declared suddenly. "You ought to humble yourself before God and ask Him to spare you from sin. You should beg Heaven to pardon your offenses, to forgive your pride." He shoved her so that she nearly fell forward onto her face.

"I've *been doing* that for hours; you haven't been listening." She would not prostrate herself to this monk, she vowed silently.

"Your words have been empty, nothing but rote. I can see why your father is worried for your soul. You lack piety. No wonder your family questions the source of your vision." Brother Iraneus gave her a long, reproachful stare. "You are praying not only for yourself, child. There is more at risk here than your soul alone. Your brothers and sisters must be shown—"

"Shown what? That Fallen Angels are as brave as the Militant ones?" Kelene asked. "And I was the one who—" She stopped suddenly, not wanting to admit that she, not her father, had sought this exorcism; she had begged for it. Now she thought she had been foolish to do so, but could not make herself admit it aloud. "If my visions are not true, I do want to be rid of them. I didn't mean to question you, Brother. But I am exhausted and hungry." She wondered if she might be sleepwalking, for everything around her seemed slowed, filmy, and unreal.

"You must pray." Brother Iraneus followed his own instruction, resuming his droning intonation.

Kelene tried to do as she was told, dutifully reciting the Salutation to the Virgin, trying to imbue the words with sincerity, thinking that the sooner Brother Iraneus was satisfied with her devotions, the sooner he would allow her to sleep. She was wrong. As soon as she completed her third repetition of the Salutation, Brother Iraneus ordered her to lie prone, arms stretched out to the sides. Grudgingly, Kelene complied. "I will place ikon medals to protect you." Brother Iraneus drew half a dozen metallic ikons from the leather wallet hanging from his belt. "They are blessed and will save you from any of the Fallen. God has promised it."

"If they are strong enough," Kelene warned. She had to resist the urge to squirm as she lay pressed to the stones.

"Servants of the Fallen are never as strong as God; you are in error to think that they are. They will depart from you if they are unholy." He began to recite blessings as he carefully placed the medals first at her feet, then her outstretched arms, then above and to the sides of her head.

"If it were as simple as you say, the Militant Angels should have prevailed long before now," said Kelene, surprised at her own temerity.

"Then you must hope that all this is unnecessary, or you will answer for it." He took out his pyx. "Father Demetrios gave this to me, when he blessed the ikons. It will keep any Fallen Angel from touching you." He laid the pyx on her back, between her shoulder blades. "Now be silent and still while I pray."

Fatigue and melancholy began to work on Kelene despite her determination to resist them. She was worn out from the exorcism and it was just beginning. She tried again to recall why it had seemed so important to her, and why she had begged her father for it. The sins were hers, she thought, not the angel's. After what the angel had given her in her dream, she knew now that she was his creature. If Saint Agatha could endure her torture, surely, Kelene told herself, she could endure what the angel demanded of her. She strove to be comfortable on the unyielding stone, and tried to set her mind on the angel and not on the cold stone pressing against her face as Brother Iraneus' prayers went on and on.

"You will reveal the truth to me, O Angel: whether you are God's angel still, or among the Fallen," Brother Iraneus cried out.

Kelene was jolted from her doze, her cheek scraping on the stone floor. She winced, blinking back tears. If her family had been sleeping before Brother Iraneus demanded the angel speak, they were assuredly awake now.

"You must not move. You will lose the protection of the ikon medals if you do," he warned her sharply, then resumed his invocation. "You who hold this child, reveal the truth to me. Tell me the Mandate you serve, and the source of your power over her."

The voice that answered came from Kelene's mouth, but was deep, masculine and commanding; she recognized it at once, and it frightened her. It was one thing to hear the angel in her dreams, but quite another to have him use her to speak aloud to others. *"Are you certain you want the truth, Brother?"*

Brother Iraneus had lit incense in a silver censer; this he now lifted into the air, and swung it, the cloyingly sweet smoke drifting to all parts of the little room. "You will answer me in everything I require. You will tell the truth. In the Name of the Christ, I require you to speak."

The angel laughed. *"Then I will tell the truth."* Kelene listened to the pronouncements coming from her mouth in the angel's voice. *"I will tell you all the truth, and more."* Kelene shook.

"Be still," Brother Iraneus told her. "You must not dislodge the pyx."

"I'm *trying*," Kelene said as she felt her cheek start to bleed again.

"Trying is not enough," Brother Iraneus said, with the first hint of fear in his tone. "It must remain secure."

"I'll do my best," Kelene said, forcing herself to lie still. The pyx was hot on her back, as if the silver were melting.

"What is the source of your might? In the Name of the Christ I charge you: answer me." The monk stood over Kelene, his crucifix held high as if he were preparing to dash her brains out with it.

"You touch this girl at your peril, Brother," warned the angel. *"And my power was bestowed upon me long ago. It is beyond your understanding."*

Brother Iraneus kept to the rite. "And are you one with the Militants, or one with the Fallen?"

"I have triumphed in every battle I have entered, those remembered and those forgotten. Death has no hold on me." The angel very nearly laughed. *"You will know me in the deeds I have done."*

"And in whose name have you performed these deeds? Who is your master?" asked Brother Iraneus.

"In his might, Saint George of Armenia slew the dragon, that was mightier than the Serpent. There are those mightier than Saint George," the angel pronounced; Kelene felt the pyx shift on her back.

"Mightier than the Serpent, or than Saint George?" Brother Iraneus did not realize how distracted he was becoming. "Which are you?"

"Why, I am greater than either, as I must be." A sound that might have been laughter came from Kelene in the angel's voice.

"You will answer me!" Brother Iraneus declared, trying to restore the disrupted ritual.

"Yes. I will. I will comply with your demands. Listen well to me, then: you seek to hear the truth." The angel paused; Kelene trembled. *"Very well. Truth you shall have. Until you choke on it. The truth is that you lied when you promised chastity, when you professed your devotion to Christ. Your desires were of the flesh, so wrought in sin that you still contrive to conceal them, excusing yourself with the certainty that you can deny any accusation of wrong. You thought that—"*

Brother Iraneus gasped aloud and nearly dropped his crucifix.

Kelene winced, fearing the crucifix would strike her. She tried to huddle into the stone floor.

"Be careful, Brother. I will protect my servant from all harm. I have done so before." Kelene tried to control her shivering, but she felt the pyx begin to roll down her back, and then drop off her body to lie beside her waist.

"Since you require it, the truth. You are unable to keep your thoughts as pure as you decided your vows would make them. You have allowed yourself to become the tutor of children, rather than avoiding them." The recriminations came relentlessly, without pity. *"You touch them. You fondle them. You caress them. You taste them. You penetrate their soft bodies everywhere you can, and tell yourself that they are blessed by you. You covet them. You dream of them. You pollute them with your flesh and your desire. You have done such things to your charges as will make them suffer until they die, and you believe that because you are a monk, you have done nothing wrong, that God and your vows obviate your sin."*

"I—I have done nothing—" Brother Iraneus began.

"Those children would tell you otherwise. They smell your semen on their breath, they have your skin under their nails, and no sweet herbs or cleaning will take it away."

"It's not like that—" Brother Iraneus protested.

"Are you so lost to your own depravity that you cannot understand what you are doing, or are you trying to excuse in yourself what you would condemn in others?" The angel's contempt made the deep voice rough.

Brother Iraneus renewed his attack "You are not talking of me, you are to tell me what—"

"You have ordered me to speak the truth, and I am doing that. Since it is what you have insisted I tell." The angel paused briefly, and Kelene sensed his nearness. *"You profane the cross you claim to venerate. You make dissolute that which is most sacred. You usurp the authority of your Christ for your own lascivious ends."*

"It's nothing like that," Brother Iraneus cried out.

"When you take their heads in your hands and push yourself into their mouths, do you think they permit this for love of you? What you leave in them, do you reckon it a baptism?" The angel paused. *"You say this is the same love that your Savior gave His apostles, and the children comply. Are you so deluded that you are convinced you are truly showing Christ's love when they struggle and bleed, when they cower in shame, when they gag on your seed?"*

Kelene heard this out, astonished that such words could come from her mouth. She had been told all her life that the seduction of children was something only the Turks did, because they were without the Christ to save them. Brother Iraneus had given himself to a life of service to the Christ, and to the salvation of the world. These things the angel revealed could not possibly be true, she thought. And yet, the angel—her angel—had always revealed the truth.

"Be silent!" Brother Iraneus screamed, and kicked at Kelene's shoulder.

"You will regret that, Brother," the angel promised in a smooth purr. *"Only I may abuse this girl. You have children enough to vent your fury on. Subject them to your will and leave Kelene to me. This one is mine, and I begrudge you every injury, no matter how slight, you inflict upon her."*

Kelene moved, impelled by the angel, dislodging two of the metallic ikons from where they had been placed. She felt as if she had grown suddenly very tall and very strong.

"I command you to reveal if you are one of the Fallen!" Brother Iraneus strove to recover his failed mastery of the angel. He swayed a bit, as if intoxicated; his knuckles were white with straining to hold the crucifix.

"*I told you I have never been beaten in battle,*" said the angel.

Brother Iraneus stepped back, his crucifix held out at arm's length; he was as breathless as if he had run from one end of Sarajevo to the other. "If you are one of the Militant Angels, you will not attack a man sworn to serve God."

"*But you do not serve God; you use God to serve your ends. To dare to invoke God to help you is temerity. To corrupt children is despicable.*" Kelene had risen to her feet as if lifted by strong, invisible hands. She steadied herself.

"I adjure you, depart from this child!" Brother Iraneus' eyes were wild, protruding. A vein throbbed on his forehead.

"*And leave her to you?*" the deep voice mocked as Kelene faced the monk. "*No. I would fail in my protection if I allowed her to be abandoned to your care. The first signs of womanhood are on her, but not so much as to cause you disgust of her. You will not be allowed to violate her. I will not permit you to debauch her. You, who sent a boy from your cell, wailing and swollen with injuries, only yesterday. You, who violated your own brother, before you took your habit? You, who denounced a child as evil because she dared to tell what you had done to her? Were you pleased at her burning? You think you are capable of subduing me? Do you suppose you can summon the Christ with nothing more than words? You, with children's blood on you, with their pain clinging to you like a stench? I will watch over her, for she is mine. If you would rout a Fallen Angel, start with yourself.*"

Brother Iraneus brandished the crucifix as if it were a sword as he backed against the wall. "It is lies! All lies!"

"*Then what have you to fear? Why do you quake?*"

Impelled by the angel, Kelene moved forward in a single, swift lunge, striking Brother Iraneus just above the belt with such force that the breath went out of him in a rush, doubling him over as he dropped the crucifix. Kelene stepped back as the monk dropped to his knees, his body bowed as he struggled to fill his lungs again. She heard a movement in the hall behind her and called out, "Stay away! For your own sakes!"

"You . . . you are monstrous," gasped Brother Iraneus.

"*No more than you are, Brother,*" said the angel. "*I, at least, take only those who answer my call.*" Kelene swayed on her feet.

With a tremendous effort Brother Iraneus strove to get to his feet; he used the wall to support him, pushing himself upward with his thighs and shoulders. "In the Name of God, be gone, Fallen One," he panted.

"*Even if I were of the Fallen, you could not banish me. Could anyone who*" *impregnated his sister and then hid from the consequences in a monk's habit be capable of exorcising anything or anyone? Do you dream of it still? How did it feel, to force your way into her flesh? Was it strange, or was it familiar? Did you want her because you desired her, or because you despised her? Did you hear her cries? Was that why you throttled her—to quiet her? You were brave enough to rape her, but not brave enough to kill her. How do you think she remembers you now, in the brothel where she was sold in her shame? Do you think she prays for the child you gave her?"*

"I didn't . . . she tempted . . ." Brother Iraneus said falteringly.

"Do you believe that? Do you believe you have saved yourself from your sins by wearing a habit and keeping your rituals? I tell you that you are with the Fallen. That everything touched by you falls with you." Kelene was slick with sweat and her hands shook. *"How will you answer for your life, when it has profaned God's gift so entirely? Will you say that you were seduced? That you were weak? That your vocation was false? That you were wrong?"*

Brother Iraneus wrapped his arms over his head as if to ward off blows. He made a thin, keening moan. "Have mercy have mercy have mercy have mercy," he repeated endlessly.

"How can I, when you never did?"

With a howl of despair, Brother Iraneus bolted from the room, pushing his way through Diogenes' family gathered in the corridor, leaving behind his incense and crucifix, pyx, ikon medals, and all hope of salvation.

"We heard what the angel said," Diogenes said to Kelene early the next morning.

Kelene stared down at her bowl of yoghurt, her face flushed. "I . . . I did not know it would be . . ."

"Who would have thought a monk had done such wrongs?" said Melantha. She had Phaon on her lap, and held him more closely.

"If he did them," said Thalia curtly.

"The angel accused him," said Diogenes. "Remember, Brother Iraneus did not deny them. He begged for mercy."

It was windy, making their quarters colder than the day outside.

"It may have been the horror that kept him silent, and his own good soul that wanted mercy from such hideous things," Thalia insisted. "When the monk ordered the angel to depart, he would not go."

"Because he was not Fallen," said Diogenes carefully. "If he had been among the Fallen, Brother Iraneus would have prevailed—"

"Would he?" Alexander demanded. "With such sins on his soul, the angel may have been right: Brother Iraneus could exorcise nothing."

Kelene listened intently while pretending to eat.

"If they were real," Thalia reiterated. "They may have been fabricated to keep the monk from accomplishing his goal."

"That voice," said Pallas quietly. "Who would have thought Kelene could sound like that?" She dipped a slice of plain bread into her yoghurt and chewed slowly, her expression distant.

"If that is what has spoken to you in dreams," said Diogenes heartily, "I can well understand why you do his bidding."

Kelene shook her head. "It is not always so . . . so encompassing," she said carefully. "I have not had such a visitation before." She did not add that she was gratified that her family had at last discovered for themselves the might of the angel. She contented herself with saying, "He said he was not one of the Fallen. That should ease—"

"He did not say he was one of the Militants, either," Thalia cut in sharply. "Only that he called and you answered his call."

"He also said he would protect Kelene," Achilles said. He had slept poorly and his eyes were hollow. "If he protects her, he will protect us all."

It was wrong to be pleased by such support, Kelene knew, but she could not escape a sense of vindication. Her angel had prevailed.

"Yes," said Diogenes with enthusiasm. "Just my thoughts. The angel has shown himself to be our staunch defender. So long as Kelene tells her visions, we will have nothing to fear." He clapped once. "I will explain to Markos that the exorcism is complete, and that the angel was not banished. Kelene will be known for one of the messengers of the Militant Angels, and therefore honorable. The exorcism is over."

"If it is over," said Thalia, and when the rest of the family regarded her with varying degrees of disapproval, she went on, "Well, the rite was never finished. Brother Iraneus fled without completing it. Shouldn't another exorcist be called, to end the rite properly?"

"No," said Kelene hastily.

"The angel had answered the challenge," said Alexander, pausing in his eating. "No true monk or priest would have been able to exorcise such an angel."

"But the rite was not over," Thalia persisted. "The monk did not reclaim any of his things—"

"And why should he?" Achilles asked. "He was unworthy. It means nothing that he left before he finished. He could not have done it." He smiled sunnily. "So now we can let Kelene keep us safe."

Kelene straightened up on her stool. "As long as the angel provides me with visions, I will reveal them to you." She noticed that Thalia did not look pleased.

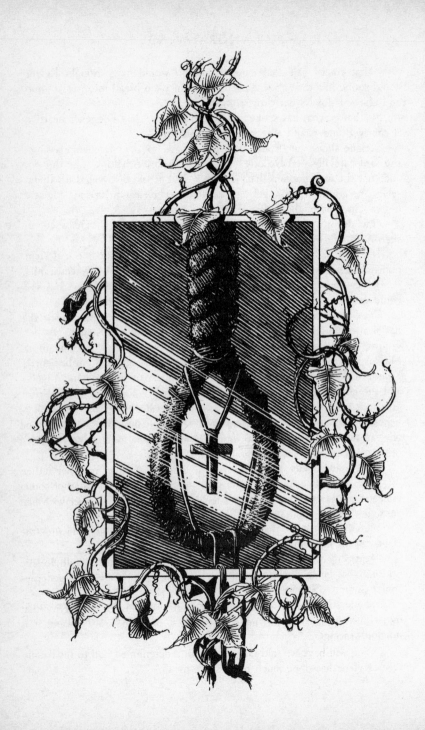

Let us strive anew, you and I,
To mend our wounds and our land.
—Hungarian lyric, 14th century

⸺ VII ⸺

"That warning about the tax collector was useful, very useful; I ought to have paid more attention to it," Markos conceded as he faced Diogenes and Kelene in his counting room later that day. "Any similar information would be very . . . valuable. I count it as part of our arrangement that you will tell me about any prophecy in that regard immediately."

"If the angel gives me such another warning you will know of it." Kelene stood beside her father, her hair braided neatly, her clothing modest and virtuous.

"And such matters as flood and droughts may be used to good turn, and all events that would hamper trade," Markos went on. "As well as anything you might learn of the Ottomites through your angel." He stood up, striding the length of the room. "If you will help me preserve what I have accumulated, I will be grateful; truly, I will."

Taking a chance, and ignoring the sidelong glance from her father, Kelene said, "My sister Thalia wants to marry. Surely you know of someone who is suitable for her, not a feeble old man, or a widower with half a dozen children, but a young merchant or farmer."

"I will consider it," said Markos, pursing his lips as if tasting the proposition, "when you have made it worth my while."

Diogenes smiled ingratiatingly. "You see what a selfless child Kelene is, to think of her sister before herself. She will be similarly generous with you."

Markos cocked his head, his soft features taking on a severity that was as arresting as it was unexpected. "It is not generosity I want, it is timely warning."

"You will have it," said Diogenes with a determined nod to his daughter. "Kelene has done much to preserve us all."

Markos smiled slightly. "I will expect something of use before a month passes."

Kelene held up her hand in alarm. "Uncle . . . I may not . . . the angel cannot be compelled . . . our guardian is not always . . ." Her confusion was made worse by the critical shine in Markos' eyes. "I will try," she promised, hoping she had not said too much.

"That you will," said Markos. "In the meantime, I will give some consideration to finding a husband for . . . is it Thalia?"

Diogenes bowed. "Yes. She is the oldest; it is time she was married."

"And an unwed daughter is a foolish expense," Markos declared as he reached out for one of the sweetmeats in a bowl on his counting table. "Yes, yes. The bargain is a reasonable one, if Kelene can provide what I want." He chewed thoughtfully, then said, "Oh, you might not have heard: that monk—Brother Iraneus?—was found hanging in his cell this morning."

"Hanging?" Kelene repeated, her hands to her mouth as if to call back the accusations the angel had made.

"Used his belt, they said, to make a noose. Put it over the beam in the ceiling. His tongue was swollen out of his mouth, I was told." He swallowed the sweetmeat and took another. "Bad thing, a monk killing himself."

There were words that Kelene knew she ought to speak but they would not come.

"Better dead than discredited and disgraced," said Markos. He brushed his fingertips together to rid them of the sugar that remained from the sweetmeats. "At least we can show that your daughter is not cursed. Any who say so will be disregarded. Those who doubt will do so in silence. And the rest will pay well for what she reveals. Her angel defeated the monk in exorcism, and that should satisfy most Christians."

Kelene tried to tell herself that she had not played a role in Brother Iraneus' suicide, that the angel had revealed the monk's sins, that Brother Iraneus had put the belt around his own neck and not she. Her eyes stung with tears and she tried to wipe them away without being noticed.

"There, Markos, do you see how good this child of mine is?" Diogenes beamed at Kelene. "She knows all that the monk did, and yet she is Christian enough to weep for him."

"Father, no; I—" she began.

"Very noble of her, I'm certain," said Markos, massively disinterested. "I will be glad when the story gets about the town a bit; it will lend credibility to her visions. I will be able to charge more for what she says." He helped himself to another sweetmeat, sighing a little as he bit into it.

"Don't you see what it means," Diogenes urged, moving closer to Markos, his splendid voice at its most persuasive. "She will not be thought to be uncaring, or without compassion. How many girls would have been able to weep for such a monster as Brother Iraneus after what he did?"

"I am convinced, Brother," said Markos, then turned to Kelene. "You work in the kitchen, don't you?"

"Yes, Uncle," she said quietly.

"You do not have to continue there," Markos offered. "If you will have a vision sooner."

"I cannot say when I will have visions, or if I will have them," she admitted, adding dutifully in response to a stern glance from Diogenes, "But I am . . . grateful for—"

"I don't care about your gratitude, girl. Leave that to your father. You will need to tell me something that I can turn to advantage." His cherubic features looked sullen. "I will do what I can to make your visions come more easily, and frequently."

"How frequently?" Kelene asked, her skin going cold.

"Oh, nothing too difficult." He stared out the window as if what he was saying was a brand new notion to him. "Twice a month will do. If you have visions more often than that, they will not be valued; it is more enticing to have the angel's messages in short supply. But if they do not come with regularity, some will be less willing to pay for what you offer."

"You must understand that the angel will not be commanded; rather it is the angel who comes when it suits his purposes," Diogenes said quickly, forestalling any objection Kelene might have.

"Surely the warnings have been regular enough to bring you here," Markos said, his tone sharpening.

"The angel has spoken more frequently than that; occasionally as often as every other day," said Diogenes. "If the vision is—"

Markos interrupted with determination. "You will let me be the judge of how to present what this girl sees. I will decide then how I will make it available, and to whom."

Diogenes continued to grin, although the expression was now more of a rictus mask. "Certainly. It will be as you say."

"Yes. It will," Markos agreed.

After a month and two warnings from Kelene's angel—one of battles to the east that stopped trade, one of more Ottomite soldiers posted to Sarajevo—Markos announced that he had found a likely husband for Thalia.

He made his announcement to Diogenes' family as they gathered for their supper. "He has holdings just outside the city: he is a farmer of some substance, a Christian, twenty-five, of good reputation and enough wealth to keep Thalia in comfort, and to provide well for their children."

Thalia blushed and looked at her mother, as if trying to gauge her response to Melantha's. Finally she said, "You are very good to me, Uncle."

"Well, it is fitting that I deal in good faith," Markos said obliquely as he walked around the crowded room. "There is a proviso to the arrangement."

Diogenes glanced up from his seat, trying not to look too concerned. "What might that be, Brother?"

Markos was enjoying the suspense he had created. "Why, that the man has a farm where he would want you to live—your whole family, sharing in the crops and livestock with the farmer. My obligation to you will be discharged. There are a cottage, a bake- and bathhouse, two barns, a pigsty, a goat pen, an orchard, and some planting plots. The holding is not large, and you would have to work hard to make it profitable, but you would not be wholly without means." He pursed his lips at this reminder of the family's dependent state. "When Thalia gives this farmer an heir, the full title of the land will pass to you; you will owe him nothing more, neither in payment nor in shares."

"Will the Ottomites allow it?" Alexander asked. "Isn't there a tax on the transfer of lands between Christians?"

"In the ordinary way, yes," said Markos with an approving gesture. "You are a most sensible youth. It is true that the Ottomites require large sums when Christians buy and sell land. But among members of the same family, the tax cannot apply." He folded his hands over his paunch.

"That is good news, indeed," said Diogenes. "Isn't it, Thalia?"

Thalia shifted on her stool, nothing in her expression showing emotion of any kind. "I am . . . very pleased."

Kelene recalled that the angel had warned her that they would not stay long in Sarajevo. Perhaps, she thought, this was what he had meant: the family would move outside the city. She wanted to say something encouraging to Thalia, but could not.

"The man is called Bozidar, and I have arranged for him to come here day after tomorrow," Markos informed them, hearing their gasps with contentment.

"Mother, what am I to do?" Thalia whispered, not daring to raise her voice. "I want a husband, but—"

Melantha held up her hand in caution and tried to catch her husband's eye.

Diogenes got to his feet and kissed his half-brother's hand. "We can never thank you enough. You are the salvation of our family."

This was just what Markos wanted to hear. "Well," he allowed, "you have done me a good turn. I am pleased to be of service to you."

*   *   *

Try as she would, Kelene could not stay awake: *When the angel came to her that night, she was unaccountably frightened. As he strode up to her, his armor shining against the night, she wanted to shrink down to nothing, to disappear before him.*

"You need not tell me—I know about your sister and the farm," he said.

"It . . . it is what my family wants," she ventured. Around her the landscape of the dream was beginning to sharpen: burned houses and ruined churches limned by moonlight. Kelene shuddered at the sight.

"Your father believes all is settled," the angel said. "It is not." Light flared around him as if from dying flames.

"But—"

"I have said you must not remain in Sarajevo. The longer you delay leaving, the more you will lose." He bent over her. "Hear me, Kelene. When matters are most hopeless, I will come." His mouth closed on hers, and she clung to him as his wings went around them both.

She castigated herself for the heat that coursed through her flesh, for the pounding of her heart, for the weakness of her devotion that turned zeal to desire. She gathered the courage to push away from him. "You . . . don't know how I . . ."

"Yearn for me?" the angel suggested, the smoothness of his question troubling for its very serenity. "You answered me when you were a child. How can I not know?"

Of course, she told herself, he would have to know. "I'm . . . sorry."

"In time you will understand," said the angel, caressing her shining golden hair and drawing her back against him. "What you see here is coming," he went on in the same tranquil tone. "It will overtake Sarajevo. If you are not gone when it does, you will suffer greatly. The longer you remain here, the greater your losses will be."

That sedate voice, imperturbably telling such ghastliness! Kelene struggled in his arms, but this time could not gain her release. She shook her head repeatedly. "No. No. All will be well."

"For a short time it may appear so." He gave a short, hard sigh. "You will need to offer your uncle a tidbit. Very well: In two days an important Ottomite official will arrive in Sarajevo. Someone will try to kill him, and many Christians will be imprisoned and executed for this. Those who are in the marketplace that day will be most suspect."

"Those who stay away will be safer?" she asked, wanting to be certain that her message did not cause more trouble than it averted.

"Yes." The angel went on stroking her hair and back. "Sarajevo is a dangerous place. Leave now, leave later, but you will leave. All that must be determined is the cost of it." His laughter was low and smooth as water running over round stones. "Oh, you will not perish, Kelene. I protect what is mine."

Then they stood before a stone altar in a stone room, illuminated only by three tall candles. A constant moan of wind, or perhaps of distant chanting, echoed around the chamber. He now held his chalice out to her. "Take it, and drink, Kelene. Of your own free will."

A frisson went through her: Kelene took the chalice and drank the dark, warm liquid. As she returned it to her angel, she said, "I pledge myself to you, now and forever." The angel smiled fiercely. "I know," and drew her to him once more.

Bozidar announced he was satisfied with Thalia, and Markos took care of the rest, making the arrangements for the wedding and Diogenes' family's move to the offered farm with such alacrity that Diogenes could not protest the commission his half-brother demanded for the transaction. Markos was effulgent with praise for Kelene's warning that had kept him away from the marketplace on the day the Turkish Bey had almost been killed, and professed himself eager to show his indebtedness by making Thalia's wedding and dowry as magnificent as he could. "Of course," he added hastily, "in these difficult times, I cannot do as much as I would like; it would draw attention to your family, and that would be unwise."

Diogenes was more willing to be convinced than Melantha, who said in private the night before Thalia's wedding that Markos was already profiting outrageously by his sales of Kelene's angelic messages.

"Do you mean that you do not think Bozidar a good match for Thalia? Do you dislike him?" Diogenes challenged his wife as they went from the bathhouse to their own quarters at the end of the day.

"I think he is well enough," Melantha allowed. "But I think that the marriage settlements could have favored Thalia more than they do. To leave her wholly dependent on her sons for support if her husband dies before her—"

"It is traditional in Sarajevo," Diogenes reminded her.

"Then it is a tradition they would be well rid of," Melantha shot back. "Think of your own family, my husband. May God save you, but if you were to die, how could Alexander provide for us all?" She stretched, trying to ease the ache in her back. Her delivery was five weeks away and she was beginning to worry in earnest about her baby, who was more lethargic than her previous children had been at this stage of pregnancy.

"We will have land of our own again, when Thalia delivers a son," Diogenes said as they reached the door of their quarters, "and we will be able to earn—"

"That puts me in mind of one other thing," said Melantha. "It is unreasonable to require us to purchase our seed and our livestock from what little money we can spare. Bozidar is prosperous. He might well have helped us with some seed and a goat or two. As it is, once we have what we need to farm, we will have almost nothing left to keep us in food until we have—"

"My good wife," Diogenes said gently, "the chickens will give us eggs, the goats will provide milk, the hives will have honey. We are not entirely helpless. We will not starve."

"But will we thrive?" she asked, and got no answer.

Two rooms away, their three daughters were gathered together for the last time. "To think you will be married tomorrow," Pallas marveled as she and Kelene put the finishing embroidery flourishes on Thalia's wedding cape. The flower buds were pale red and gold, the leaves were green.

"Yes," said Thalia, proud and uneasy at once. "We have every reason to be grateful to our uncle all over again."

"He has done so much for us," Pallas said, glancing at Kelene.

Knowing she had to say something, Kelene tried to look pleased. "Yes. He has done a great deal." She stared down at the gold flower she was working on, putting her mind on the tiny stitches, making them uniform. "I am so sorry about the people in the marketplace who . . . who were killed."

"It is not good to speak of them," Thalia said cuttingly.

Kelene could not keep from saying, "But we must remember them."

"Do your angels tell you that?" Thalia's eyes narrowed.

On the table the lamp was guttering; Pallas trimmed it, and the light grew clearer.

"My faith tells me that," Kelene said, and tried to smile at her sister. "That does not mean I do not wish you happy, Thalia. I do, with all my heart."

Thalia frowned studiously, saying, "I should think so, since you will not be married." She heard Pallas gasp, but turned her gaze on Kelene. "Will you?"

"No," said Kelene calmly. "I will not."

"Because of your angels and your visions," said Thalia with a gesture of confirmation. "Father told me."

"Yes. I know," said Kelene, and saw the pitying expression in Thalia's eyes with unconcern. Privately she thought herself far better off pledged to her angel instead of to a farmer who was thick-bodied and smelled of goats and manure.

"It's bad luck on the eve of your wedding, rejoicing in a sister's single state," Pallas said to Thalia. She concentrated on her embroidering, her face deliberately placid.

"Well, Kelene began it. With my wedding so near, I should be thinking of my husband, not unhappy events." She preened again, touching her face in approval. "I will look very nice for him. I will have three servants to command, and a cook. Did you know that?"

In spite of the fact that Thalia had been crowing about her household staff every day since the wedding settlements were agreed upon, Kelene said, "No one is more deserving than you, Thalia."

"Mother has given me many suggestions on how best to govern my servants. I will think of them often, I know." Thalia stood up suddenly and did a slow twirl. "I will never have to worry again."

Two days after Thalia's wedding, as Diogenes and his family prepared to leave Markos' house for the farm Bozidar had provided, Melantha went into labor, and their departure was postponed for a week. Markos complained about the inconvenience.

"The infant will die. He left the womb too early," the angel informed Kelene three nights after Pericles' birth. "In two months at most, he will be gone." They were in the same stone chamber as the last dream, although now the burning candles were black and the indistinct crucifix was hung with what appeared to be black mourning drapes, as if for Lent.

"Just two months?"

"He is too fragile. He will not survive." The angel reached out a hand and turned her face up to his, his long-hewn visage stern. "You will watch over him, Kelene. You will keep vigil so that your mother can rest; she is worn out with giving birth. You have nothing to fear. I will be with you."

Kelene looked confused. "But if he is going to die . . ." Her confusion stopped her words.

"Tell your parents they will be relieved of some of their burden if you will do this." His touch on her cheek was gentle. "You will not watch alone; I will be with you all night long."

"Must he die?" Kelene pleaded, recalling how desolate Melantha was after the death of Hector. "Isn't there a chance he might—"

"The infant is weak. He will let go of life easily. He will hardly miss his breath, or the blood in his veins." The angel held up his hands, but not in supplication; he rested them over her developing breasts.

"I told you there would be losses: the baby is but the first, if your family does not leave Sarajevo behind. He is the easiest. The others will be harder." Again he offered her the chalice. When she gave the chalice back to him, he set it on the altar and put his mouth to hers.

She sighed as her head lolled on his shoulder. "Without you, I am alone. You are my sustenance," she murmured.

"And you are mine," the angel said, bending his lips to her neck.

On the morning of Diogenes' family's departure for their farm, Markos came and pulled Kelene aside with her father. "You understand," he said, his lips pursed, "that I will have to receive news of your dreams as often as possible."

"Yes," said Diogenes, motioning Kelene to silence.

"Yes," Markos seconded, his small eyes glittering. "I have in mind to send my slave Hassan with you, so that you will have a messenger to bring me word of all dreams. He can then bring your share of our money back to you." When Diogenes did not jump at this opportunity, Markos said, "I want to spare you losing the labor of your sons for a day, for surely you would not send either of your daughters, would you?" He let Diogenes consider this possibility for a short while, then pulled at his lower lip with his thumb and forefinger. "If I give you authorization to have the slave, with the assurance that he remains mine, you will have some use of him without having to pay the tax levied on Christians for their slaves. It is advantageous for all of us."

"You have thought it out, haven't you?" Diogenes said, doing his best to hide his annoyance.

"I have considered what would be best for us all," said Markos.

"I might not always have much to tell you, Uncle," said Kelene. "Your slave might not always be needed to carry messages."

Diogenes coughed. "I would need a writ from you, with all this spelled out in it, or the tax collectors might well take your slave as payment of taxes, and that would leave us more deeply in debt to you than before."

"I would do that, of course," said Markos in a reasonable tone of voice, his mouth curved in a smirk. "Hassan is useful to me, and I would not want the Ottomites to claim him."

"Might they not, anyway?" Kelene asked. "Isn't he a Turk? We're Christians: isn't that enough for them to take him?"

"His father was, and he was a slave. His mother was Serbian, I am told, and also a slave," Markos said. "Even if the tax collector tried, he would have no legal claim to Hassan; I made sure of that before I laid out gold for him. The law will not let Christians buy slaves who are fully Turkish." He pulled his voluminous cloak more closely around him.

"I suppose we could use an extra pair of hands," said Diogenes, ignoring the warning look his daughter shot him. "It would make our labors less . . . less extreme."

"I will provide his keeping, you may be sure of it," said Markos, as if aware of Diogenes' reservations. "It will make it apparent that I am not lending him to you in an effort to circumvent the law. The Ottomites will not have good reason to deny you his labor. You are getting the advantage, my brother." With an ingratiating smile, he favored his half-brother with a respectful bow. "I am certain Kelene's warnings will make any slight inconvenience I feel well worth my while."

Night is fleeting; the wings of owls
Become the wings of falcons
With the coming of the sun.
—Greek song, 14th century

⟞ VIII ⟝

"At least they left us the plow," said Alexander as the family, in four laden carts, passed beyond the Ottoman-controlled gates. He was doing his best to make light of the seizure of half their seeds and supplies demanded by the Turks as a condition of allowing them to leave.

"They want us to have a crop to tax," said Kelene, thinking that the Ottomites were very clever to allow them enough to survive, but not so much that they would prosper. "If they take everything, they make us beggars, which is of no use to them."

"They don't think of such things," said Pallas, keeping the two baskets of chickens from sliding by resting her ankles on top of them.

"Only three chickens gone, and one of the cocks; we will have eggs, but no chicken soup for a while," said Kelene, wanting to soften the blow of what she had said before. The rest of the family did not know what they faced; they deserved a little happiness while they could have it.

"Yes. We still have nine chickens and a cock. That's something," agreed Achilles, riding beside his brother in this third wagon. The wagons ahead of them and behind were driven by Bozidar's slaves, who would return them to their master the next day.

"You'd think Bozidar would have come, with Thalia," said Pallas, downcast at her sister's absence.

"She's his wife now," said Alexander. "She must stay where he wishes her to be."

Behind them Melantha held Pericles to her breast, frowning because he made no effort to nurse; beside her, Phaon continued to pluck at her sleeve.

"It doesn't seem the same without Thalia," said Pallas, on the other side of Phaon.

"It doesn't seem the same without Hector, either," remarked Orien, without a trace of condemnation in his voice.

Kelene did her best to change the subject. "It will be nice to have a farm." As she said it, she reminded herself it would not last. "At least we are away from Markos' house. We will have the benefits of our labors."

"Markos. I don't like his mouth—as if he was tasting something that had gone off," said Pallas.

"Or that was too sweet," said Orien.

Alexander snapped the reins to urge the mule to move faster: in the way of mules, this one paid no attention, continuing at a steady walk.

"I didn't realize the farm was on a hillside," said Pallas, trying to sound optimistic as the road began to wind along the river-cut slope. "I hope some of the land is flat enough to keep the crops in the ground."

"We can let the goats out on the steep part," said Achilles. "They won't mind. They like to climb."

"And," Pallas joined in, "it will make for better cheese if they climb."

On the first wagon, Diogenes watched the countryside around him with growing dismay. "What sort of farmland is this? It does not look—"

Hassan, who rode beside him, acting as guide, said, "You will see it shortly. It is in a small defile, where half the ground is flat and the buildings are protected from the winds." He smiled automatically. "You will not need more than two hours to go from my master's house to yours. It is a good distance for market day."

"I suppose so," Diogenes said. "I never thought the tax collectors would demand so much."

"They demand it because they can," said Hassan. "The tax collectors coming to the farms are as bad." He noticed the expression of distaste that crossed Diogenes' features, and added, "It was worse in Salonika, I've heard."

"Yes, it was very bad," said Diogenes, remembering the huge bribe he had paid, and his great-aunt, left behind to endure the Turks. "They gave us less than three days to pack our goods and go. And that was only because of the bribe I paid. We could take only what we could load into four wagons. We did not have an easy journey here." He looked about, and added, "Without the warning from Kelene's angel, we would have fared far worse than we did."

"She is a treasure, that daughter, and not only for her golden hair," said Hassan.

"Because of her, we have been spared much," said Diogenes automatically.

"Then," said Hassan, "you should want to do well here. My master says you cannot afford to go anywhere else."

Diogenes flicked the ends of the reins as if to speed the mule.

"If we must give so much to Markos, and so much to the Turks, how are we to prosper?" Diogenes asked, deciding as he did that if Kelene's visions were to be sold, he would drive a harder bargain for them. "How much further?"

"It is just around that shoulder of the hill," said Hassan, pointing. "You can see how the road turns from here? That will take us to the farm."

Their first sight of the farm was not promising. The buildings all needed repair, the fences were broken in several places, and the well in the middle of the yard seemed covered with green scum.

"No wonder Bozidar wanted someone here," said Alexander as he pulled in the wagon behind the first two. "I hope Thalia will have her first son within the year."

Achilles smiled. "It is nothing too difficult. We need only put our backs into it and we will do very well." He jumped down from the driving box and hurried to where his father stood. "Don't worry, Papa. It will turn out better than we've hoped," he promised as he saw his father's shoulders droop.

Diogenes turned and tried to look cheerful. "Of course it will."

Alexander was repairing the fence nearest the road a week later when a group of Turkish soldiers rode up to the farm, accompanying a hard-eyed official and his two slave-clerks. "Father!" he shouted, running across the pasture toward the house.

In the fields where she was helping Orien and Pallas with planting, Kelene hardly bothered to look up. She had been expecting this for the last two days. She stood up.

"What's happening?" whispered Pallas, coming up beside her.

"Turks," said Kelene. "At least their weapons are sheathed." She lifted her skirt and began to trudge across the newly turned furrows, her thoughts racing ahead of her.

Orien trotted along beside her, with Pallas reluctantly bringing up the rear. "What do you think they want?"

Kelene said nothing at first, then reluctantly conceded. "I think they want to issue orders," she said carefully. "I think they intend to put us on notice."

"Because your angel tells you?" Orien inquired.

"Because I know the Turks. And so do you," Kelene said. They reached the fence and climbed over it and onto the path leading down to the house.

The Ottomites were already in the yard beside the well, drawn up to face the house. Three of the soldiers dismounted and held the horses of the official and his slaves. Hassan had come down the ladder from the roof and was in the process of bowing to the Turks when Diogenes rushed out of the barn, wiping his face with a cloth and calling aloud to his children and his wife.

As Kelene came near enough to hear, she listened closely.

"—from the fortress at the pass," Hassan was saying to Diogenes, pointing vaguely up the hill. "They have claims on all the farms in this area."

"Why did Bozidar say nothing of this?" Diogenes asked Hassan, making sure the Ottomites could hear him so that they would not accuse him of treachery. "We have it down in the marriage settlements. It was my understanding that as long as we were his tenants we would have such claims paid through him." He turned to the official and began to explain his relationship with his son-in-law, only to be cut short.

"These are Christian contracts," said the official in very good Greek. "We are not obligated to honor them."

With a trifle too much respect Diogenes bowed to the official. "The contracts were approved in Sarajevo. They are on record there, with the terms carefully set down and approved." He showed his open hands.

Achilles ran up, the last to arrive; his leggings were smirched with mud and he was out of breath. He halted a short distance behind his father and stared at what was going on in front of the house. He signaled to Orien, who left his sisters and ran to Achilles' side.

"You have fine children," remarked the official. "Is this all of them? Are there others?"

"My wife has recently given birth to a son," said Diogenes. "And, as you must know, my oldest daughter has married Bozidar, who provided us with this farm to work for him."

"Ah, yes," said the official. "We have spoken with Bozidar, and he has assigned us the right to one third of your crops, and one third of the fruit of your orchards. Half of that will come from the share you give to Bozidar, half will come from what you would take to market. We will not take Bozidar's mules, so you can work the land."

Kelene looked up sharply. The sum demanded was well beyond what the soldiers were entitled to—they all knew it, but remained silent. Kelene wanted to scream in frustration. She suspected her mother was watching them from the house; she wanted to go to her, but she could not bring herself to move. "Pallas?" she whispered.

"What?" her sister answered softly.

"Have you seen Mama?"

Pallas sighed impatiently. "She's in the house. With Pericles."

"But she's watching, isn't she?" Kelene realized that Pallas was too frightened to think sensibly about their mother.

"I guess," said Pallas, then asked, "Why?"

"The Turks will want to see Pericles."

"Why?" Pallas asked with more curiosity and less resentment than before.

"They want to know about our brothers," Kelene replied.

"The angel told you?" Pallas spoke so quietly that it was difficult to hear her.

"Yes." Then she heard the official summon Melantha out of the house, with orders to bring her infant with her. She felt Pallas shiver beside her.

Melantha was pale as she came out of the house, her listless baby in her arms. She did not look at the official or the soldiers; all her attention was on Pericles.

"Why do they want to see him?" Pallas breathed.

"They have to decide if they want to take him," Kelene said.

"Take him?" Pallas repeated in a disbelieving squeak. "You mean *take* him? But why?"

Kelene lied, "I don't know." She did not want to frighten her sister by telling her that the Turks often held children hostage in order to guarantee the continued cooperation of their parents.

Pallas sniffed once to keep from crying. "They won't take him, will they?"

"No," said Kelene, "not the Turks."

"Not a promising boy," the official said. "Still, you have other sons, have you not?"

Diogenes bowed again. "God has been good to us."

"Praise Allah," said the official, and indicated Hassan. "Your slave is forfeit."

Diogenes was ready for this. "He is not my slave."

The official's scowl was immediate and fierce. "How can that be?"

"He is one of my half-brother's slaves, loaned to me while we set this farm to rights. My half-brother is a merchant in Sarajevo: Markos of Salonika. He may be known to you." Diogenes made his obeisance so profound it was an affront. "I have the contracts in the house, if you would like to look them over."

Kelene wanted to tell her father to be more careful, that this official would remember all slights and would exact a price for each of them, but she knew her father would never listen.

"No," the official said tersely. "You would not dare to invent so outrageous a falsehood." He gestured to his men, then said to Diogenes as his soldiers remounted. "We will return in a month. You will have eggs for us, and honey. If you do not, it will go badly for you." He looked around, as if taking inventory of what he saw.

"Certainly, you shall have your share, if we have any ourselves," Diogenes said, bowing again.

"Any attempts to hide what is due us will be dealt with severely; any failure to have eggs and honey for us will result in confiscation of goods," the official warned him, then signaled his escort to depart. As he tugged the reins to turn his mount, he added, "Your obligations are established." Then, spurring his horse, the official repeated, "We will return."

One by one, her family turned toward Kelene. She rushed to Melantha's side, only to be shrugged away.

It was twelve days later when the Turks came back, this time demanding water from the well, and obviously surveying what progress there had been with planting. They had noticed that one of the sows was piggy, and complained that they, as Moslems, could not eat pork; one of the soldiers had broadly hinted that when the nanny goats had kids, they would claim the largest as their due.

"Of course, good Ottomites, of course; we will let you have the first choice of the kids," Diogenes had said, so obsequiously that Kelene shuddered to hear him. "As soon as they are weaned, you shall have whichever one—or more—you want."

"See to it," the leader of the Turks had ordered. "Otherwise we will have to make our assessment in a different way."

As she kept watch over Pericles that night, Kelene fumed at her father for accommodating the Turks with such a display of sycophancy. He should have maintained his dignity, she thought, her anger helping her to keep her eyes open. Her thoughts drifted to her angel again, and the contrast between his powerful presence and her father's deference did not favor Diogenes.

Later, in spite of her best efforts, she dozed. In her dream, the angel lifted her far above the earth and praised her for her courage. She was distantly aware of Pericles, crying pitifully.

"Pay no heed," the angel told her as she sank into her dream. "He cannot be saved, whether you watch him or not. Leave him to sleep." He put his hands on her shoulders. *"He is a weight that will soon be gone."*

"But he is my brother," Kelene protested, still distantly aware of his thin wailing. "It will crush my mother to lose—"

"Worry for your brothers whose fates are less certain: Alexander, and Achilles, and Orien, and Phaon are your brothers, as well as Pericles."

"So was Hector," Kelene reminded him. "And I know how it hurt us all to bury him. If another of us dies, my mother—"

His hands moved down her arms, then around her, pulling her close to him.

She let him wrap her more tightly in his arms.

"You cannot save Pericles, can you?" the angel persisted.

Kelene leaned her head on his shoulder. "No," she said, and waited for the chalice to be given her, so she could drink the warm, dark wine he offered her and, in drinking, be closer to him.

When she woke, it was not yet dawn. There was a coppery taste on her mouth; Pericles seemed more pale than ever.

At the front of the little church—the same church in which Thalia had been married to Bozidar seven weeks previously—the pope was concluding the prayers at the foot of the tiny coffin; at the rear of the church Melantha wept wretchedly, tearing at her clothes. "You've had Hector. Isn't that enough?" she demanded, staring at the majestic figure of the Risen Christ worked in mosaics in the dome of the church.

Diogenes put his arm around his wife's shoulder, at the same time making an apologetic gesture to the pope. "You knew he was not strong," he said, trying to make her grief more bearable.

"But it's *spring*," she wailed. "He should not have died in spring."

Pallas, dazed with sorrow, stood behind her mother, holding Phaon in her arms, and with Orien leaning against her leg. She was unable to put into words the sense of impending disaster that had come over her when Pericles began to fail. At the time she had confided her misgivings to Kelene, who had only nodded. Now Pallas tried to avoid her sister, as if her nearness made the danger worse.

Alexander and Achilles were in the churchyard, digging the grave for their youngest brother. They worked silently, with steady effort, as if sore muscles would provide solace. Occasionally they would glance at Kelene, who lingered just outside the narthex, forbidden by Melantha to enter the church.

"I'm hungry," said Achilles, sounding guilt stricken.

"We'll have food at home," Alexander said, weary and stoic at once.

"This is hard work; I wish Hassan were Christian, so he could help us," Achilles said. "This is harder than carrying stones for Hector."

As Melantha emerged from the church, she stepped around Kelene, pulling her skirts aside and muttering to Diogenes that Kelene was not to go near the grave. "He must rest, poor little boy," she said, "and she will rob him of that, as much as she robbed him of breath."

"She saved us," Diogenes said, not quite chiding Melantha as he supported her to where her sons were finishing their work. "Without her, we would face much worse than we have."

"What can be worse than this?" Melantha demanded, glaring at Kelene and motioning to Pallas to come closer.

"Have your third son approach me," said the Turkish official a week later when he came with his escort of soldiers.

Spring was well underway and there was measurable growth in the fields; the orchard was in bud, opening now, and the hives hummed under the blossoms. In the pigpen, the sow nursed her shoats, grunting. There were a number of fluffy chicks among the chickens now, and one of the nanny goats was round as a hassock. Most of the fences were now in good repair, and a ladder leaned against the barn where Alexander had been working on the roof.

Kelene had been banished to the vegetable patch to work alone, and was occupying her time with pulling a few green onions for their supper; she had abandoned her task when the Ottomites had come. Now she waited at the side of the house, reluctant to go in to her mother.

"You are most industrious; I do not want to keep you from your work any longer than I must," the official went on as Orien reluctantly stepped forward. "In a year or so, you will be doing quite well, if you continue as you have begun." He sighed dramatically. "Unfortunately, the eggs and honey you have provided is less than required, and I am not certain that you can produce sufficient quantities for the next taxation. If I thought you might be able to, I would not have to make this decision." He leaned down in his saddle and laid his hand on Orien's bright curls. "Such a beautiful child."

Orien squirmed, biting his tongue to keep from speaking.

"You will make him ready to come with us tomorrow," the official announced. "We ought to take him now, and ordinarily we would, but since you have just buried a son, out of kindness to you, we will allow you a night to say your farewells. We will be back at midmorning. Make sure he is bathed and his garments are clean. He will be a great favorite in the seraglio."

"No!" Diogenes shouted, and would have rushed forward had Achilles and Alexander not restrained him; the soldiers lowered their lances menacingly. "You must not, for the love of God! Not my son!"

In the door of the house Melantha burst into tears, and motioned to Phaon to come to her side, clutching him against her skirts as soon as she could reach him.

Kelene watched with curiosity but little emotion.

"How can you do this?" Diogenes cried out. "I will not permit it!"

The official laughed. "How do you plan to prevent it?" he asked lightly. "Your half-brother has much to lose—do you think he would be willing to forfeit half his wealth for this boy? Your son-in-law could have half his lands seized in lieu of your surrender of this boy. Accept what is coming, and know that your son may rise to a place of influence." He stroked Orien's face. "It would be a shame for such perfect cheeks to be hidden with a beard."

Orien slapped the hand away and ran back to his father where he began to cry; Achilles put his arm around Orien's shoulder and held him close. "I don't want . . . I won't do it," Orien gasped between sobs.

Diogenes shook free of Alexander's restraining arm and went up to the Turk's dish-faced Barb. He did not take his eyes from the ornate iron off-side stirrup and the embroidered boot in it. "I appeal to you, good Ottomite, do not do this."

Kelene knew the answer before she heard it.

"You have other sons," the official pointed out to Diogenes. "We are leaving you the oldest ones, so you will not have to lose too much for labor."

"Each one is precious to me," Diogenes insisted, the words coming numbly in spite of the beauty of his voice, as if his plea were already denied. "God has already made claims on our sons. We have buried two already, good Ottomite. Spare us the children who remain, I beg you."

"Lament his leaving. That is only to be expected. In regard to the others, you are not the only father—Moslem or Christian—ever to bury a son. The boy will live well. Can you promise him as much? Surely you do not begrudge him safety?"

Diogenes made himself look up. "But he will be a *eunuch*."

"If he were your only male child, we would not deprive you of him. Your other sons will give you grandchildren to bear your name; you will not need him," said the official, running out of patience. "Resign yourself, Christian, and do not try to keep him from us or it will go hard for your half-brother and your son-in-law. It will not save the boy." He added this last as an afterthought. "Hide him and we will hunt him down, and take one of your other sons as well."

Kelene could hear her mother weeping, a punctuation to Orien's affronted cries. She wanted to offer solace, but could not bring herself to approach either her mother or her brother.

The official shoved Diogenes away with his foot and rose in the saddle. "You will give us your son or you will sacrifice much more than him. Fail to provide what we demand, and you will give us another child, perhaps one of your daughters, perhaps not." He pointed to Achilles. "He's a sturdy boy. He could be trained for many things."

Achilles turned scarlet with fury but did not move.

"Midmorning tomorrow," the official reiterated. "See to it he is ready!" Then, at his signal, the soldiers raised their lances, wheeled their mounts, and cantered away from the farm, dust rising from the hooves of their horses, obscuring them before the road took them out of sight.

For a short while no one moved. Then Orien broke away, rushing toward the barn, screaming his defiance to the wind. An instant later Achilles pelted after him. Alexander started into the house to comfort his mother. Pallas emerged from the new chicken coop, pale and silent. Diogenes dropped to his knees to vomit. Only Kelene remained still, her thoughts as distant as if she were in the fabled city of Paris, studying events that happened long ago.

The mules were restive at this late disturbance; as Alexander and Diogenes made their way in the gloom holding two small lamps aloft, one brayed out his protest; tack was handled with care, and the largest mule was saddled first by Diogenes while Alexander brought a large number of various-sized sacks into the barn, stacking them by the stalls of the mules designated to carry them. The largest mule fretted as more sacks were strapped to his saddle. The other two stiffened their necks in disapproval, but did nothing to stop the careful preparations. The third mule, the jenny, was the mate of the largest mule.

"Markos will curse you," Alexander whispered to Diogenes. "I am certain the threat was real—the Ottomites will punish him for our flight."

Diogenes paused in his activities. "If I must choose between my half-brother and my son, I will choose my son." He slipped the bit into the mule's mouth and adjusted the headstall.

"And Thalia's husband?" Alexander asked, preparing to lead the mule out of his stall. "Will he not consider her a bad bargain when his lands are taken?"

"What choice do we have? We cannot seek protection from him, so—" Diogenes said for the twentieth time that night. "If they are prepared to take Orien and geld him, none of us is safe."

Alexander moved the small oil-burning lamp to give better light to his efforts. "But Bozidar will have grounds to abjure the marriage contract if we leave."

"He may; I pray he will not," Diogenes said as he went to the next stall, ready to saddle the second mule. "Your mother and Phaon will have to ride. We can put them on the jenny." He jutted his chin in the direction of the third mule, the only female. "Two bags of food and three waterskins will be all she should carry if Melantha and Phaon are on her."

"I'll have Pallas tend to it," Alexander said, going to saddle the jenny.

"How much longer?" Diogenes asked, speaking to the darkness.

"Not very long," Alexander answered.

"If only the moon were not down," Diogenes said.

"Kelene's angel will have to guide us," Alexander said. "Mother will not like it, but—"

"Your mother is melancholy from the death of Pericles. We all grieve for him, but she has taken the brunt of his loss," said Diogenes. "Since she must fault someone, she blames Kelene, whose knowledge could not save him."

"But will she follow the angel now?"

"She has said she will not refuse," Diogenes said. "I have prevailed upon her to accept what Kelene tells us."

"For the sake of the family?" Alexander guessed.

"Yes. Nothing else is sufficient." Diogenes fumbled for the girth on the saddle; he could feel the mule hold his breath against the tightening. Cursing the mule amicably, he kneed the animal's tawny side, and as the air rushed out, Diogenes secured the girth and began to buckle the breast-collar into place. "And we should thank God that we have her, and her angel, or who knows what would become of us. I have prepared a letter for Markos, saying that Kelene's angel has foretold annihilation of our family unless we flee. He may accept it once he learns of the intentions for Orien. Melantha will understand this when she realizes what we have escaped."

"A pity we have so little gold left," said Alexander, bridling the patient jenny.

"We will manage," said Diogenes. "As long as Kelene's angel is with us, we will manage."

"And if he is not?" Alexander made himself ask. "What then?"

Diogenes sighed. "Then we pray that God still has room for martyrs in Heaven."

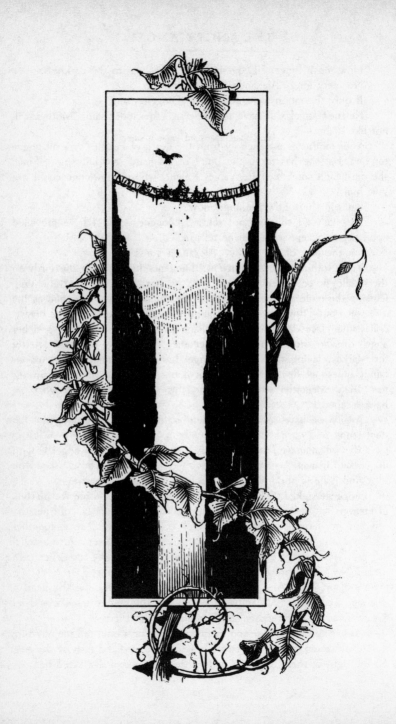

⊢ IX ⊣

"Iocasta said that Kelene was not strong enough to master her gift," Melantha declared on their third day of travel as they made their way along a narrow river defile. "And here is the proof of it—we are lost and the angel has not visited the child for two nights. We should have heeded her."

"We are not so lost as that," Diogenes said, glancing anxiously at Kelene, who was pale with exhaustion. By way of encouragement, he said, "We took a wrong turn, not so far back, where the bridge was washed out, and we must find the road again, so we can continue toward Belgrade."

Kelene stared at the rocky trail leading into the thick forest of larch, oak, and pine. She dreaded what might lie in wait under those trees. It was difficult to think with her legs aching and her feet nearly numb in her wooden shoes. Her voice shook slightly as she said, "We will not be able to get across the river."

"The Ottomites are not in Belgrade yet, are they?" Achilles asked from the other side of the mule he and Kelene were leading.

"No," she said flatly. "They will not be there for a while yet. Years." The angel had assured her of this the night before when he told her that she and her family would have to reach that city or face death together. She had not been able to tell anyone. "Belgrade will remain untouched for more than ten years at least. The angel said so." She lifted her chin, daring any of her brothers or her mother to doubt her.

"Tell me," said Alexander, not turning from his place at the head of the lead mule where Melantha rode, "do you think your angel would tell you if Belgrade came under attack before we got there?"

"Yes," she said, a trifle too loudly. "I think he would tell me anything I . . . we would require to remain alive." She heard the rush of the river to the right of them as a roar in her head; the sound distracted her.

"What about the forest?" asked Diogenes. His determination had long since given way to irritation. "Should we or should we not attempt to go through it?"

To her horror, Kelene began to weep, the tears running down her face; she kept herself from sobbing though her voice shook. "I don't know, I don't know," she said. "If you will let me have time—"

"To consult the angel," finished Melantha spitefully. "If he will come. How can you tell whether he will? Might he not let us wander in these mountains until we starve, or worse?" She had pulled her shawl over her head, swathing herself entirely in black.

"Wife," said Diogenes sharply. "We have buried two children. Surely you do not wish to bury more?"

"How can you be certain that we will not?" she shot back at him. "You rely too much on the angel. He will not spare you any grief. It is the demand of Heaven that Christians welcome martyrdom." She crossed herself reluctantly, as if driven to do it against her will.

Kelene folded her arms, keeping the lead rope firmly clutched in her hand. "If I could sleep, I might learn something. It is late in the day—"

Pallas, riding on the third mule with Phaon, called out, "Yes. Let us stop. No one is chasing us so far as this. I am tired." As if to add his opinion, Phaon sniffed loudly.

"I want to stop," Orien ventured from his place next to the third mule.

"Yes, let's stop," Achilles seconded.

"We have two more hours of daylight left," Alexander said, growing impatient. "It would not be wise to waste it."

"If we are lost in the forest, we will have wasted more than time," said Achilles. "There is a copse over there"—he pointed to a place up the slope where larch and pine stood as if outriders in the van of the forest—"where we could make camp for the night." For additional encouragement, he said, "I will trim the mules' hooves, since there will be light for a while."

Diogenes accepted this offer with alacrity. "Yes. It will not do for the mules to go lame on us." He pointed to the copse. "Let us go up."

The third mule, the jenny, protested, refusing to budge until Achilles improvised a come-along around her rump, pressing the backs of her gaskin, above the hocks, forcing her to walk forward. "We're almost there, girl," he encouraged the animal, tugging lightly on the lead rope as he pulled the come-along. Reluctantly, as if cheated, the mule moved.

"There's light enough to go down to the river and fish," said Alexander. "I can bring back water from the river."

"Oh, very good," Diogenes approved, using his walking stick as a prod for the mule. "I don't blame these poor creatures. They have had two long days, and they are not over."

"We have come as far," said Alexander, scrambling on the stony footing.

"But we carry only small sacks. The mules have much greater burdens." As they approached the copse, they saw the declivity in which it stood was deeper than seemed apparent from the track below. On the far side, a small stream of water flowed into a narrow crevasse that led toward the river behind them.

"There's a spring!" shouted Pallas from her vantage on the jenny.

"The ground may be wet," warned Alexander.

A thought struck Kelene suddenly. "We must remember to string the bells," she warned. "There are bears in the forest. They will be hungry. Our food and the mules will tempt them." Bears were not her only worries, but they were the most obvious, and in spring they were known to have unreliable tempers.

"Oh, God," said Alexander as he was the first to climb the stone lip of the copse. "She's right."

"We should have insisted at Markos' on keeping our dogs," said Achilles, sounding more disheartened than usual. "But bells will have to do."

Pallas recalled her scorn when Alexander had insisted they bring as many as they could, taken from their goats and pigs: space was limited and bells seemed frivolous. Now she called out, "You were right. Bells are necessary."

"Thank you for that," he called back. As he stepped into the shelter of the trees there was a crash, and two hasty breaths later a doe with two fawns bounded away, jumping lightly across the rocks before leaping noisily into the forest.

Melantha watched them go, then turned to Kelene. Although she said nothing, the condemnation in her face was visible to all her family.

There were flames in her dream, towering, loud as a cataract. She tried to flee, but the fire pursued her, plucking at her garments and her golden hair in a deadly flirtation. Terror lent her speed and she rushed with the futility of dreams: nothing she did removed her from the inferno. The fire sought her as surely as if it had eyes and ears, and its relentless hunt for her went furiously on. She prayed for a river, a raincloud, anything that might quench the flames, and all the time her strength was failing. Only when she was certain she could go no further did tremendous dark wings blot out the hellish vision as the angel descended, his dark armor shining red in the firelight.

"Look around you," he ordered as he rose into the air. "This is what you are leaving behind. Look!"

Kelene held onto him with all the strength she could summon up, her eyes fixed on his face. "No," she said. "I've seen enough. The fire—"

The angel laughed. "You defy me?"

"I adore you."

"Yes. And very soon, you will have the chance to prove your adoration. I will come for you," he vowed as one hand slid down her back to her thigh.

She shivered. "I am going to die?"

"All men die," he said curtly, continuing to caress her as their flight went on.

"My brothers are already with you, aren't they?" she asked, holding her breath for the answer.

"They are at peace," the angel answered. "I am at war."

After a short while, she asked, "Will there be other . . . losses?"

"I told you there would be if you remained in Sarajevo too long," he reminded her.

"I tried to explain to my father," she protested, ashamed of her failure.

"He was not wise, and you did not convince him of his danger," said the angel. "Your family will suffer for it."

"Haven't they suffered enough already?"

"What is enough?" the angel countered, hovering now over what appeared to be battlements.

"Well," she said tentatively, "two of the boys are dead."

"Two," the angel marveled, an edge in the number. "What a great loss, to be sure."

Kelene flushed. "There are many others who have lost more, and many who have lost fewer," she allowed. "But my mother is—"

"Your mother is consumed with her misfortunes," said the angel. "In Belgrade she will suffer her final losses, should you but reach that city."

"Belgrade?" Kelene exclaimed in despair. "Belgrade is leagues and leagues and leagues away."

"Then it would be sensible to hasten there; you cannot reach it by wishing." He brought her down to the highest battlement, and looked over to the deep canyon below; he released her and began to stride about, his wings moving around him. "There have been hundreds of thousands who have marched against this fortress since the Huns came. What a battle that was! They fought bravely, without regard for their lives, but we drove them back."

"To preserve our faith," said Kelene, awe in her shining eyes; a surge of fervor gave her strength again, and the blood sang in her veins.

The angel laughed again, and rounded on her. "What is the loss of two children to me? If your mother is despondent, let her think on all those who have fallen since the Romans strode these mountains."

Kelene knelt before him, extending her clasped hands up to him. "But you will protect us, won't you?"

"Come to Belgrade; I will find you in Belgrade. The road is long, but you will make the journey if you truly seek me. If you continue around the flank of the forest, you will find a river crossing near the peak. You can reach it before sundown," the angel said, and began to rise into the air. "In Belgrade you will find what you are seeking."

Bewildered, she watched him go, then called out in confusion, "What have I done? Have I erred?" She held up her hands to him in supplication. "Where is the chalice? Will you not—"

"When you are bound for Belgrade, then you will deserve sustenance." His wings expanded, making him part of the night sky.

Kelene stared upward until he was only a denser black speck against the starless heaven.

The first thing that struck Kelene when she wakened, groggy and saddened, was the anger in her mother's eyes, and the resentment in her voice when she spoke. "Good. You're awake. Now you can tell us why we had to leave that farm and Thalia behind."

"We were not safe," Kelene said, shoving herself onto her elbows. "Orien was not safe."

"But something could have been done," said Melantha, signaling for Diogenes. "She's awake. Finally."

Kelene blinked rapidly, as much from distress as from sleepiness; as Diogenes came up to her roll of blankets, she said, "He told me we must go to Belgrade."

"Belgrade is so far. Belgrade! Lord God deliver us! How are we to get there?" Diogenes pulled his shuba more closely around him, protecting himself from more than cold.

"I suppose we will have to walk, or ride the mules when we can," said Kelene; she looked around at her brothers, but could not meet Melantha's dark gaze; she threw back her blankets and reached for her shawl, shivering. "The angel was very specific. It must be Belgrade."

"What can we do? We cannot go so far," said Alexander. "We haven't enough food or money to go so great a distance. And look where we are. This is a wilderness. We might as well be on the far side of the earth." Mist was rising from the river and the forest was pale with white wraiths winding around the trees. The morning chill was made worse by damp, and all but Orien moved stiffly.

"We reached Sarajevo, didn't we," said Achilles. "If we have to be there, then the angel will help us."

Pallas was boiling millet for their breakfast; she paused in stirring long enough to say, "We cannot remain here. We might as well go to Belgrade as anywhere."

"It is time we found a place where we can settle," said Alexander. "It is not good to be roaming everywhere, not in these times. If the angel approves Belgrade, then we might as well try to go there."

"It can't be worse than Sarajevo," said Pallas, sniffing once.

"At least it is spring," said Diogenes with an attempt at levity. "This will be less arduous than coming to Sarajevo."

Kelene did not smile, but she could not entirely conceal her satisfaction. Her family would make the effort, and the angel would not withhold his benefaction from her. She could see Melantha shake her head and fold her hands to pray. "The angel said we would find what we are searching for in Belgrade." The angel had not extended his assurance to her family, but she was certain it would be correct to do so. She realized that Alexander was watching Melantha as if hoping for some sign. "It was a promise," she said emphatically. "The angel promised."

"Tell me," said Diogenes, addressing Kelene, "what would you do if I refused to go so far?"

"I would have to try to get there myself." She was emboldened by hearing her own words. "I'm sorry, Papa, but I must do what the angel . . . I would have to go there, Papa. I must go there, whether or not the rest of you . . . The angel has revealed what I must do, and if I fail to do as he commands, he may never . . . visit me again." Her voice dropped to a whisper. "That would be worse than anything. I couldn't endure that."

"I would think not," said Diogenes hurriedly. "But you would not go alone, would you?" He tried to chuckle to show his indulgence of his daughter's assertion. "Think of the hazards on the way."

Kelene sat very still. "Yes. I would go alone, and pray that my angel would protect me from danger." She looked over at Melantha, huddled near the fire. "If the family does not want to go so far, so be it: I must."

Melantha's eyes were bruised with fatigue; she made a sign of indifference. "Go. We will manage for ourselves. Your angel can watch over you. He has not done well by the rest of us."

"My good wife—" Diogenes began coaxingly.

She would not permit him to continue. "When will you realize that Kelene's angel seeks only to guard *her*? We are only protected because Kelene needs protection. If she were not here, we would be chaff in the wind to the angel. The rest of us may die horribly and the angel will do nothing to save us so long as Kelene is guarded. It is she he wants; the rest of us are only a convenience." Suddenly she reached out for Phaon and drew him close to her. "I begrudge her angel any harm done on her behalf."

"Melantha, you forget yourself," Diogenes chided her, more severity in his demeanor than he had used with her since Hector died. "Without Kelene we would have perished—all of us—months ago."

"That may be true. We will never know. But we have lived only because the angel wants his Kelene cared for." Melantha turned away.

"Well, you will do just as you like, husband. What I say has no bearing on your decisions. You listen only to Kelene."

"Because the *angel* is our *protector*," Diogenes insisted. "You may not want to believe that, but we have followed Kelene's visions and we are alive. How can you have so little regard for your daughter? She has preserved us." He held up both hands, palms outward. "We have lost two children. I know. I feel it keenly. But think of those who have lost all their children. Think of the orphans, destitute, surviving as wild as foxes. Think, woman. The angel cannot watch after them all while the Ottomites are storming across the land. Some Christians will die, no matter how devout and ardent their faith. Without the warning given by the angel, we must have been dead months ago. Can you say it is chance that has spared us, or the angel, who guides our daughter in her visions?"

"You will think what you wish," said Melantha, and turned away from him.

There was a brief silence, and then Kelene spoke up. "I think it might be better if I did leave you. Mother"—the word caught in her throat—"would prefer it. And I think she is not alone."

Diogenes clapped his hands smartly. "That is ridiculous. You are not some madwoman, to be left to wander. We know your worth." He glanced in Melantha's direction. "It is not easy to accept the losses God sends us, just as not everyone is willing to be guided by the visions granted by angels."

"Papa, what if . . . what if more of us die?" Pallas asked in a soft, still voice. She was preparing to ladle out the millet into bowls, but she did not move as she waited for an answer.

"We will trust this will not happen," said Diogenes. "And if it should come to pass, we will pray for the souls of those who have died, and put our trust in God's Mercy, knowing that they have died as martyrs."

Kelene listened, appalled at her father. "You can't mean that; oh, please, say you do not," she protested. "What purpose is the angel's visitations if not to save us all from . . . death." She began to cross herself, but stopped when Orien jumped up.

"I would die, if it meant the rest of you would not." He beamed at them all, and after a moment sat down again in confusion when no one hurried to approve of his offer.

Belatedly Pallas began filling the bowls with steaming millet, remarking that there were still enough dried figs to put two in each serving. "You should eat while the food is hot. It will lose its virtue if you do not."

Achilles was the first to begin his breakfast, his appetite the heartiest of all. As he sniffed at the millet, he remarked, "If we sold one of the mules, we would have gold enough to keep us in food for a while." He rubbed his chin. "Keep the mated pair, sell the other."

"We would not have to carry so much with us," said Alexander, "if we had a little more money." He looked across at his father. "If we are going to Belgrade, we will have to travel as lightly as we can."

Melantha moaned; beside her Phaon huddled, confused and frightened.

"We must ready ourselves," Diogenes declared. "We have a long way to go."

The bridge across the river was a rickety, swinging affair, hardly more than an arm's length wide. Stretching over the river just where its gray-green water dropped off the rocky highlands in a lacy, thunderous display, into the canyon it had carved for millennia, the bridge was the only crossing point for ten leagues up- or downstream.

"Two gold angels is outrageous!" Diogenes shouted to be heard over the falls.

The bridge keeper shrugged, putting one hand to his ear to indicate he did not understand; years of listening to the waterfall had blunted his hearing. "You will have a long way to go to get to the other side, and you will pay no matter where you cross." He recited this automatically, having received the same complaint many times.

Diogenes scowled; he knew the bridge keeper was in the right. "Two gold angels for all?" he bellowed.

"Yes. For all, including the mules." He ducked his head as if this sum represented a bargain.

The amount would reduce the family's money by a third. There was no help for it, and they all knew it. "Two gold angels," Diogenes agreed, and went to Melantha's side on the jenny, reaching up to receive his wallet from her. Under her disapproving gaze he took out the coins, closed the wallet and handed it back to her. "We have light enough yet to cover another league or two before we stop for the night," he said to her, as if this intelligence would cheer her.

Alexander looked up at his mother and tried to find words of comfort; none came. He glanced away, trying to reckon the number of strides the mules would have to take to get across the bridge.

"I think it's exciting," Achilles told Diogenes as his father passed him on the way back to the barrier.

The bridge keeper accepted the coins without comment, then lifted the barrier to allow the family and their three mules to cross.

The lead mule laid back his long ears as he stepped onto the uncertain footing of the bridge, his head coming up in resistance; Orien clucked approval from his perch on the saddle, but the mule was not about to be cajoled. Behind him, the second mule with Pallas riding him began to pull back, taking his hint from the leader. Achilles snapped the lead rope once and tugged the mule forward. Slowly the mules began to cross, the sway of the bridge magnifying each move they made.

They were at the middle of the rocking span when a large dark bird of prey came plummeting out of the sky, swooping over the family and their mules, a high shriek of frustration accompanying its disappearance in the spray above the waterfalls.

On the bridge, all plunged into disorder. The mules sidled and brayed; their riders clung to the necks of their mounts, and those leading the mules struggled to keep hold of the animals and to maintain their footing at the same time. A large sack containing oats slipped its knots and dropped away into the glassy water below.

"No!" Pallas shouted, bending down in a fruitless effort to retrieve the falling sack.

Achilles grabbed her, steadying her once again on the back of the second mule. "It's gone," he yelled at her in order to be heard. "You can't get it back!"

"But we need it! It's food!"

"Let it go!"

Melantha grasped at the short, spiky mane of the jenny, at the same time trying to keep Phaon tightly against her; her features were white with panic, and she screamed curses and prayers mixed together. Alexander grabbed her leg and held on as he strove to calm the jenny. His own footing was uncertain as the bridge seemed to slither underfoot.

Walking next to the lead mule, Kelene hung onto the hempen guards as she watched Diogenes regain control over the stubborn creature. She dared not act, for fear that any new losses would be blamed on her.

"Let's move on!" Diogenes ordered, making a sweeping gesture with his arm so that the others would know what he wanted; gingerly the family resumed their crossing, arriving on the east side of the river in shaky relief.

Alexander, who was guiding the jenny, was the last to step onto solid ground, and he did it with an expression of gratitude that all but Melantha shared.

From the safe vantage point of the eastern bridge-head Kelene paused and looked back, struck by the thought that the wings of the bird that had caused so much trouble were as glossy and black as the wings of her angel.

Women and the Devil
Know God best.
—Greek aphorism, 14th century

— X —

Their second mule fetched a better price than Diogenes had expected; the market in Osecina did not have a Turkish tax collector to lay claim to a third of all Christian transactions, and so the family pocketed the full amount paid. Diogenes announced himself well-pleased as his family sat at plank tables in the hostelry of a small but prosperous monastery. "We will have gold enough for the rest of the journey."

"And what then?" Melantha asked, making the question a reprimand. She had grown quite gaunt on their travels, and now that she could eat, she was unable to put more than small amounts of food into her body. She gave what she could not consume to Phaon.

"What do you mean, wife?" asked Diogenes, being deliberately obtuse.

"Are you relying on Kelene's angel to provide for us? Once the angel has her within his grasp, there will be no need to care for us." She drank a little of the watered wine the monks served to their guests. "Or have you thought of that?"

Kelene wished she could disappear; just then she hated her mother's scorn almost as much as she hated her mother for showing such contempt for her. She stared down at the small loaf of black bread and wedge of hard cheese that she had not yet touched. "We will be safe," she muttered, not looking up.

"You hear that, Melantha?" Diogenes asked her, his face flushing.

"I hear," she replied, sounding wholly unconvinced.

Achilles had cut into his cheese with his knife and was about to begin the laborious chewing when something occurred to him. "I don't know what the angel tells Kelene, but they were saying in the market that the Turks have not yet taken Belgrade. I was listening to the merchants from the north." He was very pleased with himself.

"If that is true, then well and good; we will not have to suffer as we did in Sarajevo," said Alexander. "We will not have to pay any more Turkish taxes." He coughed to make a point. "But how are we to live? Who will employ us—and we must be employed. I am not willing to be a beggar, not after all we have gone through. What is the use of enduring adversity if it never ceases? We will not be the only Christians in the city who are fleeing the Turks."

Without appearing to, Kelene listened intently.

Diogenes pressed his hands together. "I've been thinking on this. My mother's cousin lives on the east side of Belgrade. The last I heard of her, she was a widow with only two daughters alive. Unless she has sons-in-law who have taken over the property she inherited, she might welcome hardworking relatives."

Pallas looked doubtful, and spoke with more force than usual. "Your half-brother treated us like slaves; why should your mother's cousin receive us any more kindly?"

"Because we have something she will want," answered Diogenes promptly.

"If you say Kelene's visions—" Melantha warned.

Diogenes did not allow her to finish. "We have strong sons, who are used to hard work, who will labor for her for low wages in exchange for a place to live. We have daughters who are not lazy or pampered, who can make themselves useful in a thousand ways." He leaned forward. "It is not so difficult. I have thought it all out. I will locate her while you remain at one of the monasteries. Once she and I have spoken, we will arrange to move to her holding."

"You must assume she will be glad to have us," said Alexander, unpersuaded by his father. "What if she is not?"

"She will know those who need laborers, and I do not think she would withhold such knowledge from us." Diogenes answered in the unconcerned manner that revealed he did not think this would be necessary. "And she will know to whom we must speak to arrange for living accommodations."

Kelene heard this out with growing misgivings as she steeled herself for their long journey. She was not convinced that her father was on as certain ground as he claimed to be, nor did she think that her angel was prepared to guide the family into a comfortable life simply because they had suffered for their faith.

Belgrade was filled with soldiers from all over Europe. The streets rang with a cacophony of languages; the markets were hectic with activity. The inns were filled to capacity and beyond.

"It is warm, Father," said Alexander as they left the eighth inn they had entered with the same refusal they had encountered previously. "We can camp in the fields north of the walls."

"Where we will be set upon by who-knows-how-many scoundrels," said Diogenes, his face set with resolution. "No. It is too great a risk. With half the scaff-and-raff of Europe flocking here, we must be careful."

Kelene had remained silent for most of their traveling, only speaking when the angel had visited her to issue warnings or reprimands or encouragement. She had grown accustomed to her mother's distrust. But now it would not be long before she would have what the angel had promised her, now that she was in Belgrade. She made an effort to conceal her excitement. The backs of her legs were numb from walking.

"And your mother's cousin?" Melantha suggested sarcastically. "Why not seek her out today?"

Diogenes would not be goaded into a sharp reply; he stared up at his wife on the jenny and said, "I have not found her yet. When I do, I will appeal to her to provide us safe lodging until we are ready to establish ourselves." He signaled to Alexander. "That stable ahead: go and see if they will let us sleep in the hayloft tonight. It is getting late. We must find a place soon or—"

Pallas sighed noisily. "I am so tired of traveling. I wouldn't mind sleeping in a creamery if I had to."

"The loft might be reasonable; we can stall the mules beneath us," said Alexander, surrendering his lead rope to his father and striding off in the direction of the stable.

"It will not be long now, wife," said Diogenes. "We have come a long way, but we are at our journey's end."

"Unless Kelene is told to have us move on again," Melantha declared, refusing to be comforted. She looked up at the brassy sky beyond the roofs of the buildings, saying, "It will rain before nightfall."

"All the more reason to find a place now," Diogenes insisted. "We have some money left. We will not have to go hungry for a while yet— nor will the mules."

Achilles noticed some soldiers at the end of the street. He pointed. "Look, Kelene. Their hair is as light as yours."

Before Kelene could speak, Melantha tossed her head. "They're Poles," she said condemningly.

"How do you know?" Achilles asked with unabashed curiosity.

"I've seen Poles before," Melantha said. "Fair-haired, blue-eyed louts who expected every girl to sit on their knees."

Pallas studied the soldiers. "I think they're Germans," she announced suddenly. "They have yellow and black on their badges. That's a German device, isn't it?"

"Prussians, I think," said Diogenes, glad to have something to discuss that did not involve Kelene or their accommodations for the night. "Many of the people in the north are fair."

"As was Great Alexander, like Kelene," said Achilles proudly. He glanced quickly at Kelene as if to be certain she heard him.

"So he was," Diogenes approved. "Blond Greeks are always remarkable." He said this last firmly, and although he did not look at his wife, his observation was clearly intended for her.

Pallas ended the tension. "Alexander's coming back. He's smiling."

Taking care to walk around the group of yellow-haired foreign soldiers, Alexander made his way through the bustle back to his family. "We can sleep in the loft and stall our mules for the next three nights," he announced as he reached them. "After that a Hungarian regiment is coming and they will take over the stable. I got the price down to four silver crowns for the three nights. He would go no lower."

Diogenes shook his head. "Well, we cannot complain too loudly. At least we have found shelter."

"A loft in a stable," said Melantha. "No better than gypsies."

"A stable was good enough for the Christ," said Achilles in his most adult tone. "Who are we to disdain it?"

"Because we, too, have found no room at the inn?" Pallas asked, laughing. Her laughter was contagious; even Melantha could not maintain her attitude of severity for very long.

For the first time Kelene was struck with how much the feathers of her angel's wings looked like scales when light shone full on them. The angel strode toward her as if crossing the Great Market Square in Belgrade, dream-empty, to the platform where slaves were auctioned. His armor shone dully in the late afternoon sun, a luminous black. He came toward her as if he were laying claim to something he owned.

"You said we would meet in Belgrade. Are you with me now?" Kelene asked as the angel seized her arms above the elbows and pulled her to him.

The angel shook her as if chastising a child. "How can I be? This is a dream. You are asleep in a hayloft. I am in your dream, not lying beside you as your sister is." He bent to kiss her forehead. "But it will not be much longer. I am coming to Belgrade. In your darkest hour, you will find me at your side."

"My darkest hour?" she repeated. "Is there worse to come? My mother despises me already. If anything more befalls us, she will probably want to abandon me in the forest."

"Would that be so terrible?" the angel asked. He put his hand into her golden hair. "I would protect you. What would you have to fear that did not fear me more?" He turned her face up to him, lean, hawkish features made stark in the light of the setting sun. "Do not come to rely on this place. You will not remain here."

Kelene trembled. "We will not have to move again," she whispered.

"Your travels are not at an end," the angel told her. "Your family will face at least one more loss before they achieve safety."

"Oh, no," Kelene protested faintly.

The angel stared down into her eyes, inexorable and pitiless. "Your parents will lose one more child."

"Not that. Please. Not that." She shook her head. "If my mother . . . ever since Hector died, she has held me accountable. When Pericles . . . she was certain I had brought it about. Or you had."

The angel was unperturbed by this. He kissed her full on the mouth—it is for comfort, she told herself as her flesh tingled, for comfort, not for passion—and pressed against the length of her body. When he was finished, he spread his wings and carried her into the air with him, rushing through the sky to the east, into the coming night. Belgrade became a smear on the land behind them: beneath their passage shone fires and the distant clamor of battle rang. The angel paid no heed to any of this, continuing his flight without regard for events below. Kelene was not so indifferent.

"It was a hard journey," said Kelene, as if to account for her distress.

The angel said nothing as he rushed into darkness.

They returned to the battlements above the gorge, the fortress forbidding in its isolation. Kelene looked over the crenelation and had to fight off a rush of vertigo. "Where are we? What place is this?"

"This is the castle of the Dragon," said the angel, his voice echoing eerily from the stones around them. "It has never been defeated." He gestured at the dark shapes of the mountains. "All else has fallen; never this."

Kelene tried to summon up the response that would most please her angel. "It is your castle, isn't it?"

"Certainly it is mine," said the angel grandly. "I have kept it by the strength of my right hand and my will." He motioned to her to follow him, leading her along the parapets, past smoking torches, down corridors blackened with centuries of soot. Finally they reached the small stone room that served as the angel's chapel. "Here. Since you seek it." He held out the chalice to her. "And I will take what is mine."

Kelene drank from the chalice with a sense of deliverance. The dark, warm wine was good on her lips.

"Not in life, not in death shall you be free of me," the angel murmured as she drank. "Amen."

"Yes. Amen." Then the angel laid her upon the altar and knelt over her to nuzzle her throat; Kelene was dizzy with pleasure which she would have liked to transmute to holy rapture; in time, she vowed, she would be chaste as a nun. For now, she let herself be ruled by her traitorous flesh.

"She will let us make camp in her fallow field and permit us to take the windfalls from her orchards; a gracious cousin, Galatea," Diogenes reported with disgust when he returned from his meeting with his mother's cousin. "I have asked if we could serve her in any way and make some wherewithal for ourselves. She does not want me or our boys to make too great a claim upon her, in case the courts should want to provide an inheritance for our efforts. Thus she will accept only females from our family. You, wife, and Pallas and Kelene she will permit to use her looms if she is given half of the cloth you weave. Bad as the Turks! Not so much as a loaf of bread or a wedge of cheese did she offer. She says that if we seek more charity, we must go to church to get it. She is not willing to recommend us to anyone she knows: says the world is overfull with poor relations. Heaven does not expect her to care for every single member of her family, for if she did, there would be nothing left to support the armies defending the city and the Christ. She claims that she is unable to show us any favor, for then she would be sought out by every wandering layabout. I am afraid we may have to camp in her fields for a short while, little as I want to." He looked at their sacks and parcels piled at the lip of the hayloft, and shrugged. "There are no more accommodations at the hostelries or in the monasteries outside the city walls. I've already made inquiries." He knew how disappointing this news would be to his family. "The innkeepers are doing well. We may be able to hire out to one or another of them."

Pallas nudged Kelene, whispering, "You'd better tell him."

Diogenes stared at Kelene, the beginning of hope in his eyes. "The Militant Angels have spoken to you again. Now that we are in Belgrade, you have had a vision."

Kelene faltered. "I . . . have been shown certain things." She did not say anything more for a moment. She saw her mother draw away from her, anger making Melantha's face rigid.

"What things are those, child?" Diogenes urged her. "I don't think it will be of use with my mother's cousin, but—"

"The angel has said there will be one more loss for the family," she blurted out, and heard her mother utter a curse.

"Did he say when?" Alexander asked when no one else dared to.

"No," Kelene admitted. "But he said it would be in our darkest hour." She sat up straighter, trying to make herself look optimistic. "If Pallas and I weave for your mother's cousin, Galatea, we might bring in money enough to permit you to find a suitable place for us. Unless the Turks attack, we will not have anything to fear. We will not have dark hours, and there will be no losses." As she spoke, she realized she did not actually believe anything she said.

"Which child?" Melantha demanded.

Kelene sighed. "I don't know. All the angel told me is that one more child would be lost in our darkest hour." She stared down at their two mules. "And that has not come yet."

At the far end of the fallow wheat field Diogenes' family rigged three tents: one for Diogenes and Melantha, one for Alexander, Achilles, Orien, and Phaon, and one for Pallas and Kelene.

Melantha cleared a pit for their fire and set up her cooking pot over it. Achilles, given charge of the mules, improvised a pen for them, keeping them in grass, oats and apples through the long summer, often using them to carry goods into Belgrade on market days.

Pallas and Kelene worked the looms provided by Galatea and tended the goats whose hair provided the yarn for the looms. Alexander hired out as a farmhand wherever he could. Orien and Phaon spent most of their time in the orchards, searching out windfalls, giving the wind a little help when they dared.

The warm days passed pleasantly enough, lulling Diogenes' family into a spurious comfort. The first rains of autumn hit, recalling the family to their predicament with unpleasant suddenness. They huddled in their damp blankets listening to the drip of water where their tents leaked.

"Galatea will not allow us to move into better shelter," Diogenes announced to Melantha the night after the storm ended. Since their arrival, he had continued to try to find jobs and housing for his family at one of the inns near the Belgrade gates, but without avail. "I have offered her money, but she will not take it. She says she has too much at risk to allow us to establish ourselves on her land."

"Then what are we to do?" Melantha demanded.

In the next tent, Kelene rolled closer to the fabric wall, listening closely to what was being said outside. When Pallas started to speak, Kelene motioned her into silence.

"We will have to find a place to stay, and not another patch of field, either," said Diogenes. "Once it turns cold, we will have to have greater protection than tents can provide. We are not gypsies, to live wild. We are going to make our lives here in Belgrade. We have endured much; I know you have borne the brunt of the burden of our troubles. But they will be over soon, and you will be richly rewarded for all that has come before."

"Don't say that. The Militant Angels will punish you for pride."

"The Militant Angels have guided us and saved us from destruction," Diogenes said sternly. "You have told me that you doubt Kelene's visions. But they have never been wrong. We have survived because she has the angel to guide her. How can you doubt this?"

Kelene winced at this.

"I suppose I should not," Melantha allowed, then burst out, "But if that is the case, we have worse to suffer, for the angel told her that we would lose another member of this family in our darkest hour."

"As long as that does not come," said Diogenes with exaggerated patience, "what have we to concern ourselves with? We are doing our utmost to prevent such a misfortune from befalling us."

"Yes," she agreed reluctantly. "But that is not to say that we will escape." Her eyes were haunted: there was more sorrow than defiance in what she said next. "Trust in the Militant Angels if you must, but understand why I will not."

Diogenes scowled in discomfort. In the last year his face had changed: there were lines where he had none before, and where lines had been there were now furrows, as if an invisible sculptor were hewing his history in living stone. Only his voice remained the same, and it rang with the same persuasive beauty as always. "No, Melantha, I do not understand. I wish I did. But I accept that you have come to blame the Militant Angels for your suffering. I do not fault you, but I am saddened."

"Kelene?" Pallas whispered.

"Shush."

"Then I will have to bear with your sorrow, husband, as you bear with mine. You are willing to be guided by Kelene's angel still, well and good. But I will not permit her to sacrifice another of our children in order to pay for her visions."

"Do you think that is what she has done?" Diogenes asked in horror.

"What else can it be?" Melantha asked, her voice choking. "Hector died and the rest of us reached Sarajevo. Pericles died before everything could be taken in taxes, so that we could escape. If we must lose another child for Kelene to keep us safe in Belgrade, I would rather wander the roads for the rest of my life."

"How can you think that God would bargain so with us?" Diogenes demanded. "Or that Kelene would be party to it?"

"She is the servant of the angel. You've said so yourself," Melantha reminded him. "You have praised her for her service. You consider it an honor, that the Militant Angels should find her worthy of their guidance."

Unable to listen to more, Kelene turned over and snuggled into her inadequate blankets.

"What did they say?" Pallas asked in an undervoice.

"They're having an argument," Kelene said, doing her best to make light of it.

"I'm not surprised," said Pallas, becoming very worldly. "Mother does not do well in cold weather. She is worrying about winter already."

"In part," Kelene admitted. "And we must find better quarters soon."

"Yes, we must," Pallas said. "I do not want to be here when the snow comes, do you?"

"No. Go back to sleep. I'm tired."

Pallas tossed her head huffily. "I'm tired, too, you know."

Kelene heard the injury in her sister's voice but could not overcome the ill-defined grief that had taken possession of her. Without wondering why she was doing it, she cried herself to sleep.

Alexander brought good news two nights later when he returned from his hired-farmhand labors to have supper. "I've talked to the innkeeper. He says that if we will serve as porters and cleaners for him, we can have room in his attic for the winter. He will charge us only three silver crowns each for the whole season."

"So little," Melantha marveled ironically. "You could stable a dozen horses for that amount. Not that we have it."

"Wife," Diogenes said, not quite as a reprimand.

Alexander stiffened. "I could find nothing better anywhere. I told him," he went on, his voice a little louder, "that we would come tomorrow, to take up residence. I have paid my full keep to him already."

"If he is not going to pay us, but we are to pay him, how will we earn anything?" Achilles wanted to know.

"Those whom we assist will pay us for our labors," said Alexander, patting the small wallet tied to his belt. "Sometimes they pay very well."

"That is well enough for you, and for Achilles, but what of the younger ones?" Melantha asked. "Or do you intend that all the children should depend upon the labors of their elders?"

"We can do many things; many, many things," said Orien staunchly. "We will not have to beg our bread."

Achilles was following his own thoughts. "If we sell the mules, we may have three silver crowns for each of us now, and enough for food through the winter. No one will have to beg for anything. But when spring comes, won't we be without shelter or means again? And once we sell the mules, we will be without their labor."

"We will also be without their cost," said Pallas. "They can graze in the field for a while longer, but once the snows come, they will need hay."

"But once spring comes, it won't be so hard. We can ask Cousin Galatea for this place in her fields; she wouldn't refuse us," said Orien. "We will make enough to purchase something of our own if we have—"

"And what if Kelene's angel tells us we must travel again?" Melantha cut in. "We will have nothing to pay for our travel, no mules to carry our burdens. We will go on foot, as beggars." She rubbed her face with her rough hands. "What will we do, then?"

"Melantha," Diogenes soothed her. "You do not know that we will—"

"No," she said. "And neither do you." She pointed to Phaon. "Look at him. Do you think he would stand the long hours trudging to the next place the angel tells us we will be safe? Think of Pallas. She is not going to get a husband if she is reduced to penury. You cannot pretend that we will find patronage in another place any more generous than what your mother's cousin has shown us."

"It may be so," said Diogenes. "But would you deny the angel's guardianship for the sake of comfort?"

"I cannot fathom why we must be driven to such a point," said Melantha. "It is not fitting for us to be forced to live so meanly."

"That is not the fault of the Militant Angels," Pallas said. "It is the fault of the Ottomites. We have had the Militant Angels to save us from the worst that the Turks could do, Mama. Think of what has become of so many others. We have much to be thankful for."

Melantha glared at her youngest daughter. "You are as bad as your father," she said, and gave her attention to Alexander. "I can see that you have made up your minds." She sighed and went on with artificial enthusiasm, "Well, since we have so little choice, tell your landlord that we will accept his . . . very kind offer for quarters through the winter in his attic. And Achilles," she added, "you had better go brush the mules. We will want them to look their best when we offer them for sale."

At least, thought Kelene, for the moment Melantha's resentment was not confined to her.

Low ceilings, poor light, strong drafts, and a pervasive odor of boiling onions made the attic a difficult place to stay. The family members found excuses to be of service in the rooms below them. This led to more industry than the innkeeper had expected, and he expressed his thanks by providing one meal a day for those who performed tasks for him.

"You see?" Diogenes said as they prepared for bed on the tenth day of their residence in the attic. "It is not pleasant, but it could be much worse."

"We could be freezing in Cousin Galatea's field," said Pallas, trying to cook a meal on the small hearth.

"We could be the prisoners or slaves of the Turks," said Kelene.

"That we could," said Achilles; he was nursing a bruised shoulder, the result of a minor accident lifting a chest down from the roof of a Kocs carriage. "And we would still have our mules, and might have done some hauling."

"You wanted to sell the mules," said Alexander without rancor.

"Yes, I did, but I still wish we might have kept them," he said, a bit wistfully. "We are so much more *here* without the mules."

"That we are," said Alexander. "And all the more reason for us to make the most of what we have to do." He chuckled, the sound ringing false. "You may yet make your fortune, brother, enough to buy mules of your own."

Kelene tried to imagine Achilles with half a dozen mules, and could not; her lack of such a vision chilled her more than the finger of cold air on her neck.

"I was given a silver crown today," said Orien proudly. "I helped that merchant in the grand carriage to put the bales of fabric in his carriage."

"Very good. Very, very good," Diogenes said, adding, "Let him be an example to you all. I would not want the rest of you to falter when Orien is forging ahead."

There were murmurs of determination as the family prepared to eat; Kelene wished she had sufficient appetite to enjoy the chicken-and-cabbage soup Pallas had made.

Outside the rain was mixed with snowflakes, heralding the arrival of winter.

Distraught, enchanted, seduced,
Love torments my every hour
With visions and dreams . . .
—Hungarian lyric, 15th century

⊢ XI ⊢

At first the wraiths of smoke were hard to see against the blowing snow. Then a shower of sparks erupted from the roof, and one of the ostlers pointed upward with a shout of "Fire!"

From their labors in the yard, Diogenes and Alexander looked upward, their faces stiff with cold and shock. "Fire?" Diogenes repeated, as if he could not possibly have heard correctly.

"In the roof!" the ostler bellowed. "Look!"

As if to make the task easier, a shout of flame appeared at the peak of the inn, questing for more to feed it. In the next moment, two of the cooks stumbled out of the kitchen, one of them coughing and batting at the air with a long-handled spatula. Half a dozen servants were behind them, among them Melantha and Pallas.

Diogenes dropped the harness he had been unbuckling from the two-horse hitch and ran to his wife and daughter. "The others! Where are they?" he demanded as he reached them. "They're not upstairs?"

Melantha all but fell into his arms. "They will be safe," she said, clinging to his shoulders. "Phaon and Orien are with the cooks' children, in the garden." She trembled. "I think they will be guarded. Achilles is still in the city; he will be back . . ."

"Kelene!" Diogenes yelled. "What about Kelene?"

Melantha's answer was vague. "I . . . she must be all right." She did not notice that Pallas had moved farther away from the building.

"But *where is she?*" he screamed. "Is she—?" He gestured to the flaming roof, unable to speak his fears aloud.

"No . . ." Melantha shook her head. "Pallas would know. The cooks' children are in the garden."

"I must find Kelene!" Diogenes broke away from his wife and plunged into the confusion around him.

Alexander was holding his sister in his arms, telling her not to look at the burning inn. He saw Diogenes pushing his way through the milling crowd; he wiped Pallas' eyes with his sleeve. "We'll be fine. You'll see."

"But everything we have is—" she said, and began to sob in earnest.

Diogenes reached their side. "Have you seen Kelene? Phaon and Orien should be safe, and Achilles is still in Belgrade." He noticed the smear of ash on Pallas' face and his demeanor changed. "You were not hurt, were you?"

"No. I am well," said Pallas, striving to control her tears. She looked over her shoulder at the inn; the fire had spread alarmingly, and half the building was aflame. Quite suddenly she buckled at the knees and surely would have collapsed had the press of people around them not held her up.

Alexander kept holding her firmly in his arms so that she could not fall. "She'll be all right," he said to Diogenes.

"The Militant Angels will guard her," said Diogenes with more hope than conviction. "They will not let her come to harm."

"This was a very narrow escape," Alexander said, a note of caution in his tone.

"If we have all escaped," said Diogenes, trying to remain where he was while more and more of those in the innyard pressed toward the gate and the road behind them to get away from the fire. "If Phaon and Orien are with the cooks' children. If Kelene . . . is safe."

Now there were more than seventy people milling about in the innyard—many soot-smeared and coughing from the acrid smoke. Some of them were trying to throw handfuls of snow on the burning building, while others cowered in dread. Smoke billowed upward to the heavens. As the fire spread, eating hungrily at the inn's frame, the crowd continued to increase.

"Papa," said Pallas, holding her tears back as best she could. "What if . . . they die?"

Diogenes had no time to answer her. A rafter gave way inside the inn; sparks and flames exploded in all directions. Baleful orange light suffused the innyard with its malign glow. Those watching ran, many shrieking in fear. Diogenes barely kept his footing as he was tugged away from Alexander and Pallas. An elbow dug into his back; a man in Italian clothes shouted a curse at him as all rushed toward the open gate. Jostled and pummeled, he was helpless against the panic gripping the crowd. Like a leaf caught in a fast-moving river, Diogenes was propelled through the gate, then lost in an eddy on the far side of the timber walls. He took advantage of this, watching for his wife and children in the human mael-strom. He caught sight of Alexander, and assumed Pallas was with him. A few moments later he saw a woman he hoped was Melantha.

It took the inn a bit more than an hour to burn, its old wood proving to be fine, dry tinder for the fire. The stable had been charred, but the ostlers, realizing the inn was lost, had turned the terrified horses into the field behind the inn, then worked to save the stable, packing the roof with snow and tossing water on the walls inside.

Alexander helped the ostlers, laboring beyond exhaustion in the frigid temperatures, while Diogenes began to search for his family among the remaining crowd. The crowd—swollen to over a hundred people—stood in the road, heedless of the weather and of traffic.

Pallas found Diogenes shortly after the crowd shoved her out of the innyard gate; not long after Melantha came up to them, her eyes hollow and ghastly, muttering that she had not seen Phaon or Orien. She began to pray, continuing in the steady, helpless way of one past desperation.

By the time the flames were dying, Orien had dragged Phaon, sullen with fright, to their parents' side. Melantha seized both boys, praying more insistently. Pallas watched Alexander, holding her breath when she could not see him, cheering him when she could.

Gradually the blackened ashes paled as the snow fell, melted, turned to ice which was soon topped with more snow. Only the hearths held enough heat still to remain stark, unconquered by heat and cold alike.

Just as the crowd began to disperse, Achilles rushed up, shouting for his family. When he pushed his way through to them, he started to cry with relief. "I couldn't get out of Belgrade. I kept trying, but the Guard would not let me leave."

"Well, you're here now," said Diogenes, trying to sound satisfied.

Achilles glanced around. "Where's Alexander?"

"There," said Pallas, pointing him out among the ostlers on the sta-ble roof.

"I might have known," Achilles said. "And Kelene? Where is she?"

This question was met with silence. Finally Diogenes said, "I don't know."

"No one's seen her," Melantha added.

Achilles crossed himself. "You don't think she . . . Her angel would not let her . . . would he?"

"Of course not," said Diogenes. "She must be safe."

"Why?" Melantha demanded. As her family stared at her, she went on, "Why must she be safe when none of the rest of us are? Might not her angel call her to Heaven?"

"No," said Diogenes, his denial unconvincing. "To lose everything, and Kelene, the Militant Angels cannot demand so much of us."

"Why not?" Melantha countered. "If Kelene is dead, we have no reason to think the Militant Angels will spare us." She held her two youngest children close to her, her eyes daring Diogenes to argue.

"If Kelene is dead, then we are lost," said Achilles quietly.

Alexander joined them, his clothes charred, his face blackened by soot. He embraced them all in turn, saying finally, "The innkeeper says we can sleep in one of the stalls tonight. I don't know what we are to do tomorrow."

"First we must find Kelene," Diogenes announced. "All the rest can wait until we know what has become of her."

Alexander coughed as he spoke. "She's in the stable. One of the ostlers found her in the pantry. She had fainted from the smoke."

"God and His Angels be thanked," said Diogenes, relief making him weak. He turned his head up to the snowing sky. "Thank you, thank you, thank you."

"The ostler said she had filled four baskets with food," said Alexander. "The innkeeper is giving one of the baskets to us, so we will not starve quite yet."

"So we have food," said Pallas. "The monks at Saint Gregory of Sinaia will have clothing they will give us, seeing that we have lost all through an act of God."

"And I have eight silver crowns, so we are not entirely without money," said Achilles, his optimism somewhat forced. "I will work twice as hard tomorrow."

"We will leave tomorrow in the hands of God," said Diogenes. "For now, let us go to Kelene, and pray the Militant Angels will show her mercy in her visions."

As they made their way back into the innyard, only Melantha lagged behind.

"I should have known," Kelene said the next morning as the family shared dry bread and cheese in the cold stable. "The angel should have warned me."

"Your angel is capricious," said Melantha, making no excuses for her condemnation. "If we are not—"

"Wife," Diogenes warned. "It is not for us to question what the Militant Angels do. If the fire had started an hour later, we might all have died in the blaze. We may have seen the power of the angel to protect us. None of us perished."

"This time," Melantha added. She studied Kelene briefly. "You claim you knew nothing of this?"

"If I had, you would have known of it," Kelene said with a false calm. Her composure was fragile as new ice; she listened as if for the approach of enemies.

Melantha was not satisfied. "If the angel ordered you to say nothing, would you disobey him?"

"My visions are to guide us," Kelene reminded her mother. "What would be the point of keeping them to myself? Why would the angel make such a demand of me?"

"To test you," said Melantha.

"Wife," Diogenes chided her. "The fire was not Kelene's fault."

"So she says," Melantha said harshly. "But we are without food, shelter, clothing, or means, just the same."

"We could ask Cousin Galatea if we might put up tents in her field again," Pallas suggested half-heartedly.

"Tents in winter," Melantha scoffed. "Without food, or blankets."

All of them remained speechless for a short while. Finally Alexander said, "I think the innkeeper will take me on to help him rebuild. I might be able to trade my labor for a place to stay for all of us."

Achilles seconded the idea. "I can work, too. That will help."

"I would like to work a loom again," Kelene offered, only to be ignored. She raised her voice. "I am willing to be bonded, if it will bring money. I will be bonded to a weaver, if that will—"

"I will not allow you to do that," said Diogenes emphatically. The color was high in his face and his marvelous voice had turned raspy. "The Militant Angels do not intend you for menial labor. Do not speak of it again."

"One of us may have to be willing to go," said Melantha, looking directly at her husband. "If Kelene is willing to be bonded, then I would let her."

"Melantha!" Diogenes said indignantly. "If any one of us should become a bondsman, it would better be one of the boys. The innkeeper can advise us how we go about such arrangements here. We don't know enough about them, and this is not Salonika."

"Or Sarajevo," said Alexander.

"At least in Sarajevo we had a place," said Orien wistfully.

"We will have one here," Diogenes declared, tousling Orien's hair. "It will take time, but we will have a place of our own. You'll see."

"There are more immediate troubles, husband, little as you may believe it," said Melantha. "Clothes and shelter and a few belongings—"

"But what about food? The innkeeper doesn't have any to spare, and will not have for some time to come. And Mama is right, we will need more than a single robe to wear. We must get cloth. We must get bedding. We must get combs, and bowls, and hats," Pallas exclaimed, her voice rising. "If your illness worsens—"

"I will be fine in the morning," Diogenes said, waving away her concern. "Let us worry about real troubles, not imagined ones."

"If we get to spring, we will endure," Kelene said.

"But what must we endure?" demanded Melantha. "Have the Militant Angels told you that? Is there more loss coming? Are we reduced to—"

"Melantha," said Diogenes, stopping to cough, "you are too much moved. Kelene has not brought this upon us."

"Hasn't she?" Melantha said, refusing to accept his rebuke. "You have always defended her. You will not look at what she is. You cannot bear to think that the visions she reveals save us, but only for greater suffering. I say this, though she is my daughter: she will be the ruin of this family, if she is not already."

"Mother," Achilles protested.

"No. I will not be silenced again," said Melantha. "You have all shut your eyes to what has become of us, and now we are destitute. I am not willing to make my daughters whores in order to get bread. I will not be parted from my sons."

"Soon," the angel crooned. "It will not be long. I am coming to you, Kelene. You will be mine."

"I am now," she said, and the stone chapel echoed with her words. "I am yours forever."

"Not as you will be," said the angel purposefully. "I am still a vision to you. Soon I will be myself." His hands slid down her body; she was disgusted with herself for the traitorous thrill she felt. "You will know me as I am."

"How will I be worthy?" she asked, her whole demeanor forlorn. "You do not know how your presence moves me. It is not—"

"You will understand all when you are with me," the angel promised her.

"Then I will die?" she asked, pleased that she had so little fear of death.

"Then you will rise," said the angel. He caressed her neck with a fingertip, murmuring, "So sweet, so young."

She wanted to prove her devotion, to ensure that he would not shut himself away from her as her family was doing. So she held him tightly as he bent over her. Kelene welcomed the sharp pain at her throat, the touch of the angel's lips and the tremors that swept over her body in response. Biting back a cry, she knew without question that he was her only salvation in this world and the next.

Later, the angel left her side and strode about the chamber. "You must trust in me as you trust in nothing else. You must obey me without question or hesitation. Do you understand me?"

"Yes," she answered, as if her dream had become a dream. "I will do as you tell me."

"No matter what protestations your family may have? No matter what my orders may be?" He came back to her, looking directly down at her. "You will not falter."

"No, I will not falter," she repeated hazily, not moving from where she lay. If only she knew what he had done to her, she wondered in a distant part of her mind, that required such binding promises.

"You must not despair. I will be with you when you are certain all hope is gone. I will claim you." His laughter disquieted her, and he was quick to soothe her. "I am joyous, my child. At last we will be together."

Kelene rose enough to face him, saying tranquilly, "For I will be dead."

"Dead and risen," said the angel as he bent to press his mouth to hers.

The innkeeper hitched his shoulders apologetically. "I am sorry Diogenes is ill. I am not in any position to help him. You will need a physician to tend to him, and you will have to pay him. I can offer work to Alexander, but only in exchange for shelter." In the four days since the inn had burned, winter had all but overwhelmed Belgrade. "I lost almost everything in the fire, and the cost of rebuilding is demanding every crown I had saved." He crossed himself. "The angels guided me when I put my strongbox in the bathhouse. At least I have almost enough money to rebuild. Without Alexander's labor, given for trade and not money, it would not be possible."

"I will work," Achilles volunteered. "I am stronger than I look. And I am small enough to go into tight places." His smile was fueled by desperation.

Kelene, who had spent the morning digging in the snow for herbs to put in their soup, could not help but remember the angel's as-yet unfulfilled promise to come to her in her darkest hour. She wished she were with Pallas, tending Diogenes in his fever, but Melantha had forbidden her to approach Diogenes because of what had become of Hector. So she remained where she was, dejected and fretful.

"We are living on thin soup," said Melantha dully. "In another few days, we will not have even that and my husband will die." She glowered at the innkeeper. "He was helping you when he became sick."

"The monks will look after him," the innkeeper suggested hesitantly. "Take him to Saint Gregory's. They will know—"

"They will know how to make his death easy," said Melantha scornfully. "And then I will be a widow without any means of keeping my family from ruin." She tossed her head. "We must bond one of the children."

The innkeeper stared down at his feet. "You are not part of a guild

in Belgrade. It is not likely anyone will accept your children as bonded
servants." He put his hand on Alexander's shoulder. "This one is too old,
in any case. Best leave him here with me, so you will have a place to live."

"A place to starve," said Melantha, worry making her look old.

The sound of muffled coughing came from the stall at the rear of the
stable. Everyone listened guiltily, as if Diogenes' illness reproved them all.

"You will have to sell one of the children," said the innkeeper, shame
making him turn away from Melantha. "Even if you were to find some
tradesman to take one of your sons in bond, it would not happen quickly,
and your need is urgent."

Melantha's stern expression did not alter, but something at the back
of her eyes changed. "Yes. You are right," she said slowly.

Kelene realized that none of them was shocked; all of them had
known it would come to this. Diogenes' coughing underscored their plight.

"I'll do it," Achilles said at once, his bravery undiminished by the
tremor in his voice. "I'm quick and I—"

"I'll do it," said Kelene.

"Your father wouldn't like it," Melantha said, her tone making it apparent that she would.

"My father is too ill to make such a decision," said Kelene with a
directness that startled her brothers and gained the full attention of her
mother. "And if what you say is true, and my visions have brought the
family to this state, then it is my duty to relieve your suffering in any
way I can."

Orien started to cry. "I don't want you to go, Kelene. I'll be the one."

"You're just a child," said Melantha uncertainly.

"I know," said Alexander. "We will have to choose from beans. The
one who draws the dark one will go. It's the only way. Otherwise there
will be many recriminations, no matter who is chosen." He stared directly
at Melantha. "What do you say, Mother? Do you agree?"

"How can you talk about this so readily?" asked Orien, his voice high.
"Don't you know what will *happen?* It will be as if one of us died."

"As things are now, all of us may well die," said Kelene quietly.

"What about the monastery?" asked Achilles. "We could become lay
brothers, couldn't we?" Before anyone else could speak, he went on with
resolution, "But there would be no money, would there? And we need
money."

"There must also be a vocation," said Alexander, sadness tingeing his
words.

"Phaon is not to be considered; he's too young," Melantha said
abruptly. "Nor you. Your labor is accounted for."

Alexander glanced at the others. "What do you say? Will you agree that Phaon is too young?"

Kelene spoke up again. "I say that you will need Pallas to look after Papa, and to do the family chores. She should not be included."

"Then it would be you, Achilles, and Orien?" said Alexander.

The innkeeper cleared his throat. "The slave market is on Thursdays. You will have to bribe the auctioneer to ensure that he sells only to Christians, if you want to keep your child in our faith." He did his best to look sympathetic. "Better to sacrifice one than to sacrifice all."

Melantha turned to him; when she spoke her voice was flat. "If you will arrange it, I would be most grateful. You will have a commission from what we receive."

Now the innkeeper was flustered. "I don't . . . No. You need not . . . It wouldn't be right . . ."

"We will discuss it when all is done," said Melantha in that same emotionless tone. Her eyes were like pebbles in her face.

There was an awkward pause while each of them tried to think of what to do next. At last Kelene stood up. "I'll get the beans."

"No," Melantha said. "Let Alexander do it." She got to her feet, steadying herself against a stall wall as the dizziness of hunger gripped her. "I will leave you to your task, Alexander. It is time I saw to my husband."

She is moving as if she were as ancient as great-great aunt Iocasta, thought Kelene as she watched her mother going to the rear of the stable. She has become an old woman. It took only a moment to happen.

"Come," said Alexander gently, a few minutes later. "I have the beans ready. We should all close our eyes." He lined up Kelene, Orien, and Achilles, then stood in front of them, eyes closed, bag held out. "Each of you reach in the bag and take one."

Kelene closed her eyes tightly and fumbled in the rough bag. The beans slid coolly through her fingers. Breathing a silent prayer to her angel, she grasped one and withdrew her hand from the bag. Clenching her fist around the bean, she listened to the rustle as Orien and Achilles drew their lots in turn.

As soon as all had chosen, Alexander opened his eyes. "Now, open your hands."

To Kelene's astonishment, it was Orien who held the dark bean.

PART
II

JOURNEYING

December 1502–March 1503

With saddened heart and full of grief
I turn myself from my mother's door.
—Greek lament, 14th century

⊢ XII ⊣

"He will not bring much," the auctioneer said as he scrutinized Orien. "If he were a little older or a bit stouter, you could get a better price. Still, he is a pretty boy, and fair. That will count for something."

Melantha was pale, but she did not flinch, though the early morning sun slanting into her eyes made her squint. "I have a single gold angel to give you to ensure his owner will be Christian."

The auctioneer, a ruddy-haired Magyar with a paunch and a too-ready smile, took the coin. "It's not much, but I will do my best," he said. "It will depend upon who is buying today. Luckily the weather is clear. That will make your chances of him fetching a reasonable price better; more people will be here to buy. I'll put him up early, that way you will not have to be kept waiting." He nodded in Kelene's direction. "Now, if you were selling her, that golden hair of hers would drive the price very high. I could get you perhaps fifty golden angels for her. She's pretty, too. Of course, it would be better if she wasn't wearing the monks' charity. You might as well wrap her in a sack. Still, it must be warm, and in winter . . ." He shrugged.

"Thank you," said Melantha, her expression distant and anxious. "We will wait." There was a place set aside for that purpose and Melantha went there without another glance at the auctioneer. Once they were off the platform, she swung around to face Kelene. "If your father dies, I will never forgive him." Her shoulders were tense and her hands gathered into fists. "I will see it through. The physician will have his nine golden angels, and we should have enough to get us through the winter, if Orien brings us thirteen or fourteen angels. He should be worth at least that: thirteen angels. Once the physician has his money, we will have four angels left. That will feed and house us until spring, if we are frugal—unless the city is attacked by the Turks. I hope your angel has no more surprises in store for us for a while. I don't think I could stand any more protection just now."

"Do not fear," Kelene said. "The day will come when we can buy him back."

"That isn't another vision, is it?" Anger flared in Melantha's dead eyes.

"No," Kelene admitted. "It is what I pray may happen." She looked toward the platform where the auctioneer was preparing to begin the morning's business. Six Slavs, burly men, their wide faces stoic, were waiting to be sold. None of them were younger than twenty and all had the stringy bodies of men who lived by hard labor. One of the Slavs bore a cross-hatch of scars on his back.

"At least Orien is better looking than those," said Melantha. "He is so young. . . . Someone will pay well for such a handsome boy." The breath caught in her throat, but she would not allow herself to weep. "No one would want to injure him. He's only nine."

"Mama," said Kelene, "I've made up my mind. I am going to find a weaver who will pay me to do piece-work. There are bound to be mercers in Belgrade, and their weavers will have looms needing workers. I am a good weaver and I am quick; someone will take me on. It will not bring in much, but it will make me less of a burden on the family. I will be able to give you a little each week, and you will not have to feed me. You will not have to worry about me." She saw that another few slaves were being brought onto the platform; Orien was among them, doing his best to look indifferent to his surroundings. Kelene caught his eye, then turned away as she realized he was about to cry.

"Worry? About you? You brought us to this!" Melantha grabbed the thick sleeve of Kelene's donated habit. "It was you!"

"Mama!" Kelene protested.

"If we lose any more, you will be the one sold, no matter what your father may say. He may be deceived by your visions, but I am not, not any longer," Melantha went on, her words all the more frightening for being whispered. "You have much to answer for, you and your angel."

"Let them sell me now, and be done with it. Spare Orien," Kelene offered. "I will not mind, Mama. Truly I will not."

As if recalled to a sense of duty, Melantha shook her head. "This was the way it turned out. If your angel had been willing to have you sold, you would have drawn the dark bean. We must live with the Will of God."

"I have a will, too. And if you are convinced that I have brought misfortune on you, then you should be glad to be rid of me."

"So I would, if not for your father," Melantha said. "And the winter." That silenced Kelene. She stood beside her mother toward the rear of the platform and felt that she was as far away from her as if she were on the wharf at Salonika.

Orien was the second offering that day; he was stripped to the waist in spite of the cold, and made to walk, run, and turn around several times before the auctioneer began the bidding.

"I cannot watch this," Melantha muttered, fixing her gaze determinedly on the tower of the church just off the square. "Tell me what happens."

"But—" Kelene said, not wanting to see Orien sold.

"You are the reason this is necessary. You will have to witness what your visions have done. Let your angel answer for the misery he has brought us."

Numbly Kelene gave her attention to the auctioneer.

The first bidding was brisk, but the prices were very low—nothing more than two golden angels—then it slowed as the amount began to rise. Soon, only two men were raising the price, by silver crowns, not golden angels: one of the men was in Swiss military clothing, the other in a merchant's gown of luxurious Venetian silk.

"Eight gold angels, fifteen silver crowns," announced the auctioneer. "Is any more offered?" He glanced over at the military man who had continued the bidding. "Seventeen crowns? Sixteen?"

The soldier considered, then shook his head. "I do not need a servant that badly."

"Sold to Pietro Zarrin, merchant of Trieste, for eight golden angels, fifteen silver crowns." The auctioneer gave a swift look toward Kelene and shrugged as if to say, *What else can I do.* "You have a bargain, Signor Zarrin, if you want my opinion."

"It is a fair price." Zarrin had a strong Venetian accent. "He will be very popular with my clients."

"But the physician wants nine golden angels," Kelene burst out, trying not to sound too desperate. "This isn't enough to pay—"

"Hush!" Melantha ordered sharply. "You shame me." She started toward the platform to claim the coins, her concentration turned inward, her expression detached.

"Mama!" Orien cried out. "I'm sorry!"

Melantha emerged from her dark reverie, jarred by what she heard. "Not even nine golden angels for my son?"

The auctioneer looked abashed, spreading his hands to show he was powerless to change the outcome. "There is nothing I can do. I . . . I cannot force anyone to pay more than the highest bid." His confusion increased Melantha's ire.

"He is worth more than a donkey, isn't he? What donkey costs less

than nine golden angels?" She appeared ready to attack the auctioneer or
Pietro Zarrin. "We must have nine golden angels."

"You would not allow any non-Christian to purchase him," said the
auctioneer with umbrage. "He would have fetched more from one of
them—would he not?" he asked of the men in Turkish garb gathered at
the back of the small crowd.

A few of them called out their agreement. Melantha directed a venom-
ous look at them.

"It is a fair price." Pietro Zarrin had a strong Venetian accent. "He
will be very popular with my clients."

Zarrin approached Melantha cautiously, his manner respectful. "Good
woman, I honor your feelings. What mother wants to have a son sold
away from her? I can only surmise you must have pressing reasons for
doing this." He tapped his chin at the line of his neat beard. "You say
you need nine golden angels?"

"Yes," said Melantha resentfully, unconcerned that she was attracting
whispered attention. "My husband is very ill. We lost all our belongings
in a fire. We have been reduced to this extremity."

"Most unfortunate," said Zarrin, as if he meant it. "I will tell you what
I shall do: I will give you the extra golden angel, if it is so necessary."
His expression was politely inquisitive. "Is it necessary?"

"Yes," Melantha spat. "It is."

"Then you shall have the angel. And you will come to my establishment and work for me until midsummer," said Zarrin, his smile as wide as
it was false. "Those are good wages for simple labor; you would be fed,
of course."

Melantha glowered at him. "Very reasonable," she admitted grudgingly.

"And you will see your son every day; that must make my offer more
acceptable to you," Zarrin went on, as if he were performing an act of
philanthropy. His gaze lighted on Kelene. "Or you could decide to let
me buy two of your children; I would give you thirty golden angels for
the girl."

Kelene winced at the caressing way Zarrin spoke; she despised herself
for being glad this man had not bought her. Her offer to be sold was
genuine, she scolded herself inwardly. How could she now cavil at any
purchaser? She remembered the words of the priest who had come to
bless her father the night before: what use was sacrifice if it did not
entail suffering?

"She is worth more than that," said the auctioneer hastily. "Much
more."

Zarrin shrugged. "As you wish. I will not withdraw my offer for a while, if you should change your mind." He signaled Orien to come nearer. "I have my slaves branded on the shoulder, not the forehead."

"You must not!" Melantha exclaimed.

"Slaves are always branded," said Zarrin reasonably. "But, if you like, I will wait for three days before I do it. In case your fortunes change. You can buy him back before sunrise on Sunday for ten golden angels."

Melantha seized on this postponement as if it were a lifetime reprieve. "I would thank you in my prayers every night."

"You and all your family," said Zarrin. "You will be with him when the brand is made, if you like. You can tend to him." He nodded to Orien. "Come. It is time I got back to my business."

"What business is it?" Melantha asked. "I will have to know where to find you if I am to work for you until midsummer."

"The sign of the Green Dog, in Saint Nicholas Street," replied Pietro Zarrin, laughing at the shocked expression on Melantha's face and the gasp Kelene gave; the Green Dog was the most notorious brothel in Belgrade.

"Mother, you must let me be sold. You must," Kelene insisted as they made their way through the streets to the physician's house. "It is unthinkable that Orien should . . . You cannot permit Orien to . . . to be in that place. I know Papa would agree, if he were not so ill." With every step they took, her guilt burgeoned until it loomed, huge and inescapable in her thoughts.

"If he were not ill, we should not have to come to this pass," Melantha said, more melancholy than angry. "Orien is the price for having him well again."

"But not at the Green Dog, surely," Kelene said, unable to imagine her brother living in a place of such dissipation.

"I will see him," Melantha said grimly. "He will not be lost completely."

Kelene tried again. "But in a place where there is debauchery everywhere . . . Mama, you cannot want—"

Melantha refused to face Kelene as she continued on toward the physician's house. "No. I did not want to leave Salonika, but we did, because your angel told us to go. We lived through it, all of us but Hector. I did not want to leave Sarajevo, but your father would not act against what your visions revealed. This time Thalia was lost, and most of our belongings. I did not want to sell my child—let alone to such a place as the Green Dog—but it is that or have my husband die. It seems we must leave some part of our family here as well, to satisfy the angel who protects us." Finally she halted. "And when the physician is paid, we will be destitute."

"Mama," Kelene began. "Since I am to blame, I ought to be allowed to put our troubles to rights. Let me do what I can to alleviate the hardships you endure. If you would let me be sold, you could buy back Orien, and have shelter and food until summer, perhaps longer than that. You would not have to plead with Cousin Galatea for a place in her fields. Oh, please." She reached out for her mother's hands only to have them snatched away from her. "Let me do this, Mama. Papa will understand when he is well. He will know . . . this is for the best."

Melantha fussed with her shawl so that Kelene could not touch her again. "It would not be suitable for you to be a whore," she said at last.

"My angel would not permit that." Kelene did her best to look haughty. "And if the Venetian merchant will only pay thirty golden angels for me, I have nothing to fear from him. The auctioneer would demand a higher price for me."

"According to your angel?" her mother asked scornfully.

"I . . . No. But if it were against the angel's bidding, he would stop me before now. So I beg of you, Mama, let me do this. God will not let me come to harm."

Melantha's laughter grated on the ear. "That angel has not taught you humility, has he? Well, perhaps it is just as well. If you are to be a slave, you will learn it soon enough." She stared hard at her daughter, speaking quickly, more to herself than her daughter. "If Orien were not in such a place, I would do as your father commands and keep you with us no matter how great the burden. But Orien must not remain at the Green Dog."

"No, he must not," said Kelene. "The angel would not want my brother to be compelled to such sin."

Melantha crossed herself as she made up her mind. "The physician must be paid. Then you and I will return to the auctioneer."

"I did the best I could," the auctioneer declared as Melantha and Kelene approached him through the noonday crowd. "I tried to get the price up."

"I am not blaming you," said Melantha. "You said you could get fifty angels for my daughter?"

The auctioneer's face went crafty, but his glittering eyes gave him away. "Forty, at least," he said. "She is . . . a prize."

Melantha did not try to conceal her disgust. "You are correct, no doubt," she said. "And for that reason, I require you to do everything you can to raise the price as high as possible."

Kelene tried not to listen to them, taking sad consolation in her angel's promise. The trials of this life would be behind her forever.

"Yes, yes," said the auctioneer. "What are her accomplishments? What can she do?" He smiled lasciviously. "Is she a virgin?"

"Of course she is! We have lost our belongings and our money, but we have not lost our honor." Melantha pulled her shawl more closely about her shoulders; the spurious glow of winter sunshine was brilliant, but made little headway against the cold. "She is a good weaver and spinner. She is devout."

"Does she sing, or dance, or play?" the auctioneer asked. "A pity she does not have better clothes, but I will manage."

"She knows the dances of Salonika, as every Christian does," Melantha said huffily. "And she sings pleasantly." This concession was made gracelessly. "Her father does not think that she needed any—"

"Does she read?" the auctioneer interrupted.

Melantha was affronted. "No. Certainly not."

Virtuous women did not read. Kelene knew that as well as anyone, but she had always wanted to. Now she would never have the chance.

"Are we going to bid on that Russian or not?" shouted a man in the crowd, pointing to the short, massive fellow currently being auctioned.

"Yes!" the auctioneer yelled back. "Let me arrange for this morsel first, will you?" He pointed to Kelene and heard whoops of approval.

"I cannot promise her buyer will be a Christian," the auctioneer warned Melantha. "I will do what I can, but in cases like this—" He hitched up his shoulder, a concession to the inevitable.

"You will do as you must," said Melantha. She no longer looked at Kelene. "I will return at sundown. It should be over by then, shouldn't it?"

The auctioneer considered. "I would rather offer her late in the day, to whet the appetites of the buyers for the afternoon." He pulled at his lower lip. "But I expect it would be over by . . . shall we say by Vespers?"

"I will come as soon as my devotions are complete," said Melantha, her voice low and rough, intended for the auctioneer alone.

Kelene started to lift her hand in farewell, then realized that Melantha would not glance her way. Slowly her hand fell to her side.

"Good enough," approved the auctioneer, who then turned to Kelene. "Stand at the edge of the platform—there, toward the front. Let them see you. Modesty is not admired in a slave. Remain there until I tell you to move." With that he resumed the bidding on the Russian.

It will not be like that for me, Kelene thought desperately, not for me. She did her best not to listen as the price on the man rose and many in the crowd made deprecating remarks about the man in the hope of staying in the bidding. She wanted to lean against something; the weight of the eyes on her was intolerable.

When the Russian was led off, the auctioneer strolled over to Kelene. Ignoring her start, he roughly undid her braids, letting her hair fall loosely over her shoulders. Then he ran his hand through her hair and held up a golden tress for the crowd to see. Kelene tried not to shiver as a finger of cold air touched the back of her neck.

"A rose to be plucked by the most fortunate of men," said the auctioneer as he caressed her hip through the heavy fabric of her habit. Forcing herself not to flinch, Kelene stood still.

"Put her up now!" one of the buyers demanded, licking his lips.

"Yes," another called out. "Before the word spreads—"

"No no, not yet," said the auctioneer. "You must savor her, so you will pay well for her. Look." He took Kelene by the shoulders and turned her first one way, then the other. There were murmurs of appreciation—and comments Kelene tried not to hear—from the crowd. She felt cold and hot at once, as if the eyes on her left scorch marks.

"You will have the big fish here if you leave such bait about," called a voice with a Serbian accent.

"Idiot. That's what he's hoping for," said another.

Kelene stared down at her feet. Sunlight streamed across the planks of the slave platform, but did not warm her. She hugged herself in a futile attempt at protection, the donated habit's sleeves rough under her fingertips. The auctioneer roughly pulled her arms down to her sides. "None of that," he said in her ear, then forced her chin up with his finger. "Head up, slave. Let them look."

"Not much width in the belly," said another.

"Surely you would not waste such loveliness on breeding, would you, Arpad?" the auctioneer asked. "Keep her for your own amusement. Let your other female slaves bear your children."

Kelene's skin crawled at the words. Surely her angel would not allow . . .

"Getting her that way will be the best part," shouted a man with a Greek accent. His remark was seconded with encouraging howls and other comments that Kelene—although not entirely sure of their meaning—blushed to hear.

The auctioneer chuckled. "Keep that in mind while I sell some of these Slovaks. You'll find them docile and strong." He added to Kelene, "Lift your habit, slave. To the knees."

Kelene swallowed hard, her gaze pleading with the auctioneer. She saw no pity, no sympathy in his face. She had agreed to this, she thought numbly, for her family's sake. With trembling fingers, she grasped the hem of her habit and slowly drew it up to her knees. Cold air eddied about her legs, making her flesh prickle with goosebumps.

"That gives you more to think of," said the auctioneer.

Hollers of approval and impatience filled the market square, attracting more of the people thronging the aisles between the merchants' stalls.

Many pushed their way over to the auctioneer's platform, drawn by the excitement pulsing through the crowd. The smell of sweat, horses, mules, and dung filled Kelene's nostrils. She took the opportunity to stare down at her feet, trying not to look at her bare legs or at the men crowding and jostling each other at the edges of the platform.

"Over there!" someone cried out. "That's Stavros, isn't it?"

"The girl's as good as sold," another exclaimed.

Kelene continued to stare at her feet. The auctioneer put a hand out and jerked her chin up.

"Not if Karoly Orban, or Wojciech of Tarnow, or Daulo the Cypriot gets here," another suggested.

"Or Lorinc von Rottblum," called out a voice from the edge of the crowd.

The laughter that greeted this name had an ugly sound. The meaning sunk in no matter how she tried to avoid it: hands on her, dirty, grasping hands instead of her angel's touch, hands that would . . . *men* that would . . . like Brother Iraneus had. . . . .

"What about Captain Tolek? Or Pietro Zarrin?" offered another voice, only to be hooted down. Dread ran through Kelene at the sound of the last name, and she shivered. Catcalls greeted her shivering.

"You will find out who the lucky man is at the end of the day," the auctioneer vowed, and signaled one of the Slovaks to step forward.

Shame engulfed Kelene through the next hours as she stood in front of a sea of upturned faces. All for her, a traitorous thought crept into her mind, all looking at *her*. But soon her life would be over. Cold numbed her legs and arms, stiff from standing so long in one position, and her fingers felt cramped from clutching her habit's hem. She did her best to appear serene despite the constant stream of remarks and speculations— some of which she tried desperately not to understand.

As the afternoon wore on, Kelene became less and less surprised that her angel offered her no comfort. This was her own trial, she compre- hended at last: it was her darkest hour and the angel had not come.

How it will end I cannot guess,
But how it begins is madness . . .
—Hungarian ballad, 15th century

⟜ XIII ⟜

"I will start the bidding for this treasure at twenty golden angels," the auctioneer announced at last, holding up both his hands for silence.

The clamor that greeted the amount quickly drove the price up to forty-three golden angels; Kelene listened, filled with chagrin that Orien had not brought ten golden angels. It was so unfair. It was so demeaning to listen to what these men would be willing to pay for the right to own her. As a Christian she knew it was her duty to submit, but her visions had promised her so much more.

"That was amusing," said the auctioneer. "Now let us begin to bid in earnest." He went to Kelene, leading her to the center of the platform; now that the day was fading the cold insinuated itself everywhere. She shivered, but the auctioneer only gestured at her to raise the hem of her habit once more, this time almost as high as her hip.

Slowly, Kelene complied. The crowd shouted its approval.

"This is what your gold will give you, good buyers. I will not show more. Not yet. If the bidding passes one hundred golden angels, I will cut open the neck to her waist."

"How old is she?" one man shouted.

The auctioneer looked at Kelene. "Well? How old are you?"

She lowered her eyes, hating to speak aloud, or reveal anything to these strangers.

"Fourteen."

"And you were born—when?" demanded another voice. "What feast?"

"On Saint Chrysogonus' Day," she replied in a quieter tone. "Two months ago."

"Last week in November," said the auctioneer. He cocked his head. "Do you bleed yet?"

Mutely Kelene nodded her head. She wanted to vanish from the earth.

"So she will give you sons for many years, if you buy her," the auctioneer crowed. "With hair as yellow as the Great Alexander's was!"

Again the market rang with bellows and yowls, out of which came a loud bark: "Fifty golden angels!"

The auctioneer bowed. "How good to have you with us, von Rottblum," he said affably. "You have been expected."

"Who else is here that I should worry about?" von Rottblum asked.

"You are the first to make yourself known," said the auctioneer. "I am certain that you will not be the only one eager for this treasure."

"Which you intend to charge for her, no doubt," von Rottblum shouted back. The crowd laughed.

"With your help," said the auctioneer, smiling. "The bid is fifty golden angels. Who will offer more than that?"

"I," came a voice with a Polish accent. "Fifty-five golden angels. I assume she is a virgin."

"Wojciech of Tarnow. Excellent," said the auctioneer. "Yes, she is."

Whispers and ribald comments went through the crowd; Kelene heard them and bit her lower lip to keep from screaming.

"I'll go sixty," said von Rottblum, holding up a purse. "I admire golden hair."

"And you want to see how much of it there is," said a wag in the crowd; he was rewarded with guffaws.

At that, the auctioneer motioned to Kelene. At first she did not understand his meaning; then a hot blush of shame swept over her as she mutely raised the hem of her habit so that it brushed the tops of her thighs. Her pulse pounded in her ears, and she thought she might faint, or scream.

"Sixty-five," said Wojciech of Tarnow at once.

Another voice bid seventy; von Rottblum bid seventy-two. Then a Greek said, "Let us stop playing this game. Ninety golden angels."

The auctioneer looked out at the men around his platform. "Daub of Cyprus. Welcome. I was afraid we would not see you today."

"Friends summoned me," said the Cypriot. "They told me I would regret not coming. For once you have something worth buying, Magyar."

"Someone bid a hundred," shouted a youth. "We want to see her tits."

This was met by a roar of approval; Kelene's hands knotted in the hem of her habit.

"Very well," said the Pole in a heavy voice. "One hundred golden angels."

As good as his word, the auctioneer stepped up to Kelene and slashed the front of her habit down to the waist before she could flinch away. She felt the chill steel tip of the knife graze her, but it drew no blood.

The auctioneer yanked the ragged flaps of fabric back, exposing her breasts and belly to the crowd. Another roar of approval sounded as the mass of men stared hungrily at her. Some licked their lips; some had glazed expressions on their faces. The youth who had shouted pressed forward to get a better view, but others shoved him back.

Kelene trembled with anger.

The auctioneer's calloused hand reached out to cup one of Kelene's breasts, drawing a hoarse cheer. "There. Small but promising. She is only fourteen, remember." He gave her breast a squeeze before letting it go.

Kelene dropped her hem and tried to pull the slashed halves of her habit together. The auctioneer grabbed her elbows from behind, forcing her hands back and away from her. The flaps gaped open again; the relentless grip of the auctioneer thrust her chest forward.

The men cheered.

"Please," Kelene protested, head bent in an attempt to cover herself with her long blond hair. The tresses swayed in the chill breeze, offering little protection from the men's hot stares. "Don't."

"I'll offer one hundred ten golden angels for the girl," said the Cypriot.

"One hundred twelve," said the Pole.

"I'll make it one hundred twenty," said von Rottblum. "It is time we showed our true colors."

"Gold," said the disgusted, cracked voice of an old man; he earned a few yelps of laughing approval.

"So the German is trying to impress us," said the auctioneer. "Is no one willing to save this girl from him?"

Daub laughed. "All right. One hundred twenty-five golden angels. And one silver crown. To show my determination."

"That leaves you, Wojciech of Tarnow," said the auctioneer, nodding his head over Kelene's shoulder while he maintained his grip on her arms. "Do you wish to continue the bidding?"

"I suppose I must, for a virgin with such hair. One hundred twenty-seven golden angels; and three silver crowns." He did not sound quite so eager now. "How much higher can the bidding go? Stavros isn't here."

At the rear of the crowd, Achilles heard this astonishing sum with near disbelief. The blood rushing to his face, he tried not to look at Kelene as the auctioneer tore open her habit and she futilely attempted to cover herself. He did his helpless best to ignore the laughter and crude jests of the men surrounding him.

As the Cypriot bid one hundred thirty golden angels and Kelene shivered on the auction platform, Achilles sprinted away from the market square, making for the gate that would lead out of Belgrade to the ruin of the inn. The icy wind burned in his lungs, but he did not falter until he arrived at the gates to the innyard, where he staggered and clung to the posts. As soon as he stopped panting, he hurried on to the stable.

"Achilles," said Pallas, lifting a cautioning hand to her lips. She was standing beside their improvised hearth, giving too much attention to the pot that hung over it boiling; the steam smelled of cabbage and stale butter. "Papa is resting." She nodded toward door. "Phaon is with Alexander."

"How is Papa's fever?" asked Achilles bluntly.

"The physician says it will break by morning. He has bled Papa and given him an infusion of herbs to drink." Her lip trembled. "I hope . . . I hope he will—"

"So do I," said Achilles. "Where is Mama?"

"With Papa. She is very worried." Pallas looked at her brother uneasily.

"They are paying more than a hundred golden angels for Kelene!" Achilles blurted out.

Pallas stared at him, her eyes wide. "No! What will they—"

"The last bid I heard before I came away was one hundred thirty golden angels!" He could not stop the smile that spread over his face.

"One hundred thirty," Pallas repeated, slightly dazed. "We could buy back Orien," she added slowly, almost forcing the words out.

"Buy back Orien, and live well for three years, prudently for five." Achilles stopped, remembering Kelene's stricken expression as the auctioneer made her lift the hem of her habit to her thighs.

Pallas' eyes reddened with unshed tears. "Poor Kelene. Will . . . will they treat her well, then?"

"The rest of us can keep together, at least," Achilles said hurriedly. "You will have a real dowry, Pallas, so you can choose your husband to suit yourself." His satisfaction was not as great as he thought it would be. "Who would have known that Kelene would—"

Melantha emerged from the stall where Diogenes lay, at the other end of the stable. "Achilles. You're disturbing your father." She scowled. "How can you smile at this dreadful time?"

"It isn't as dreadful as you thought, Mama," he said. "I've just come from the market. It's Kelene."

Melantha stared at him. "What has she done now?" She did not wait for an answer. "She has run away, hasn't she? She's refused to be sold after all. I knew it. I *knew* it. She will not be content until we are destroyed."

Pallas dropped the spoon into the soup. "Mama. No."

Achilles straightened up. "You will not think so when you hear me out," he said. "When I left the market, the bidding was up to—"

"One hundred thirty golden angels!" Pallas interrupted him.

"It's probably more by now," said Achilles, trying to be nonchalant.

"One hundred thirty golden angels," whispered Melantha. "It's not possible."

The stable door opened, revealing two dark figures in the sunset glow; Alexander came in with Phaon behind him. There was sawdust and soot on Alexander's shuba, and Phaon dragged his feet.

Melantha reached out to her youngest son. "Come here," she said, pulling him close to her side. "I hate to see you so tired, Phaon."

"I don't like it much," the boy whined.

"You will not have to do it much longer," Melantha said, "if what Achilles says is true."

"Tell him that later, Mama," said Achilles. "Come to the market. You must."

She shook her head. "I cannot watch another child of mine sold."

"You won't have to," Achilles said. "By the time we get there, it will all be over." He kicked at the straw near his feet.

Melantha sniffed. "I said I would return after Vespers."

"Mama!" Pallas objected. "You cannot mean to go through with this."

"I mean to stay with my husband. When Vespers are finished, I will go into Belgrade and claim whatever sum the auctioneer has for us." She frowned at Alexander. "Do you dislike my decision?"

Alexander considered his answer carefully. "It is not mine to make."

"Very true," said Melantha. "And very wise." She drew her shawl around her shoulders and averted her eyes.

"Mama," said Achilles, watching Pallas for support, "does Papa know about Kelene?"

Her head came up. "He is much too ill to be bothered with these matters. When he is more himself, I will explain it to him."

"He won't like it," said Pallas quietly.

When the bidding reached one hundred fifty-five golden angels, von Rottblum dropped out, shaking his head and saying that no woman was worth so much. "The two of you are fools," he said to the Cypriot and the Pole. "She is only a woman, and there is just so much you can do to her." He folded his arms and stared at Kelene in disgust.

It began to grow dark as the day rolled into night. Most of the marketplace was obscured by long shadows. The church spire laid a bulbous spike over the center of the platform. The auction would soon be over, for the law required all selling to be ended by nightfall.

"Someone buy her before she freezes," a man toward the front of the crowd said.

Daub the Cypriot rolled his eyes and bid one hundred fifty-seven golden angels. A flurry of new bets as to the eventual winner greeted his bid. The men stamped their feet and shifted position to keep warm, drinking and laughing all the while.

"You are trying to show which of you can afford to pay the most," von Rottblum said in contempt, and was criticized with derisive whistles from the crowd.

"One hundred sixty, and she had better be worth it," said Wojciech of Tarnow. He had given up his air of insouciance when the price had risen past one hundred forty golden angels.

"Is that your last offer? Shall I declare the last bid the final one?" the auctioneer asked, whispering to Kelene's back, "It will not be. He is too proud to let the Cypriot have you. Wait. You'll find out." He pulled her elbows back a little more, exposing her bare breasts further and provoking a round of whistles and cheers.

Kelene looked at the sun smoldering in the western sky and tried to tell herself that it would be over by dark. It was growing steadily colder, but she no longer noticed. This was the first, feathery touch of death and she welcomed it.

The Cypriot pulled at his mustaches to show his indecision. Then he said, as if summoning the dead from their tombs, "One hundred sixty-two golden angels."

"One hundred sixty-three," was the Pole's prompt response.

Most of the market square was in shadow now; the faces in the crowd were becoming indistinct. Kelene gave up looking at them as the bidding rose by single angels to one hundred eighty-two. Nothing would touch her again, not in this life.

"Five hundred forty-six golden angels," said a new voice from the rear of the crowd, resonant, carrying without effort.

"What?" The auctioneer was so astonished that he nearly let go of Kelene. "Repeat that."

Over the susurrus of speculation spreading through the audience at the platform the deep voice rang out again. "Five hundred forty-six golden angels."

"Stavros?" the auctioneer ventured.

"No." The speaker was drawing nearer, making his way through the press of people, who left murmurs of "Draco" and "Dragon" and "Dracul" in his wake; other whispers accompanied his passage, ones delivered with averted eyes and the sign of the cross for protection.

A tall figure in black armor and a long cape that moved on his shoulders like wings strode confidently toward the platform.

Kelene heard him with utter incredulity and dawning exultation. Against all hope, she recognized the man coming toward her.

The auctioneer hastily let go of Kelene as her angel vaulted onto the platform. She stumbled a little, muscles stiff and cramped from being held so long. Her angel swung her up in his arms as if she weighed only a feather, drawing his cloak around her.

"Five hundred forty-six golden angels?" the auctioneer repeated over the increasing clamor.

"Yes," he said as if the sum were nothing. "I have a purse, if you will allow me to—" He lowered Kelene, keeping her next to him. The cold metal of his armor touched her bare arm, and she shivered.

"That is a . . . a fortune: more than a fortune," said the auctioneer.

"The amount is of no concern to me," came the response as the angel reached for a wide wallet secured to his belt. He opened it, removed a handful of golden coins and gave the wallet to the auctioneer. "You had better count it. I would not want you to be cheated."

"You brought six hundred. . . . Of course," the auctioneer interrupted himself as he caught the stern gaze of the stranger. The crowd jammed nearer to the platform to see this fabulous sum for themselves, any apprehension they had in regard to the tall, armored stranger banished by the shining coins. The auctioneer handled the money reverently.

Kelene straightened up, secure in the enveloping folds of her angel's cape. She stood pressed against her angel's side, surveying the crowd with her head held high.

Fascinated by the coins, the auctioneer could not stop himself from asking, "Would you have paid more?"

The smile on the tall man's hawkish face was cold. "Do you doubt I could?"

"I . . . have no . . ." The auctioneer faltered. "My mistake if I have offended you, um—? The weight of so much gold is ponderous. I am . . . surprised you would carry it so . . . Your name, sir?"

"Dracula," said the man, his smile becoming slightly more vulpine as his name was echoed through the crowd.

"The Dragon Prince?" the auctioneer asked, his voice hushed. "From Transylvania?"

"Some have other names for me," said Dracula to the auctioneer as he looked down at Kelene.

For an instant Kelene wanted to flee; she did not want her angel to emerge from her visions into her life.

The auctioneer had put two heaps of fifty coins each aside. "I am sorry. So large an amount cannot be counted in a few minutes," he said by way of apology.

"You may take all night, if it pleases you, and the Watch will allow it," said Dracula, his attention still on Kelene.

"But . . . all that money . . ." She faltered, afraid that if she said anything more, he might change his mind.

"All that money," Dracula repeated, shrugging.

"Am I going to die now?" she asked softly.

"Shortly." He continued to smile with his mouth while his eyes had fire in them. "There are things I must attend to before I can leave here." Dracula readjusted the concealing folds of the cloak around both him and Kelene; as he did, his gloved hand brushed across her breast.

She felt herself go scarlet as awareness of her flesh rushed in on her. Her breast tingled where he had touched it. He loomed over her, his armor cold against her side, his arm now tight around her waist. Her breath quickened. "I . . ."

"Do I trouble you?" The prospect awakened some emotion in him that was not amusement, but pulled the corners of his lips up.

The auctioneer saved Kelene from having to answer. "There are five hundred forty-six golden angels here. The full amount." His attempt to sound unimpressed failed miserably. "It will be dangerous for the family—poor as they have been—to have so . . . so immense an amount to guard."

Dracula swung around, pulling Kelene with him, and addressed both the auctioneer and everyone in the crowd. "If this girl's family receives one silver crown less than the amount due them, or if anyone attempts to take the money from them, I swear he will regret it."

Kelene shuddered. She wanted to lean on him. Yet she held back.

"How will you know, Prince?" The derisive shout was met with silence, then hushed, frightened-sounding whispers.

"I will know," said Dracula. He held up his right hand. "There is no escape from me."

Kelene trembled.

"Tell me," said the auctioneer, speaking with deference, "do you want me to have her branded?"

Dracula looked directly at the auctioneer. "I will put my mark on her."

As repugnant as the thought of branding was to Kelene—as much as it made her knees go weak with fear for a moment—she felt an almost physical rush of pride that her angel would want to single her out in this way. And the pain would punish her for the way she had thought about him, the feelings that stirred in her when she dreamed of him. Her fault would be gone when she was marked by him; all the ignominy of this afternoon would be gone.

"Now?" the auctioneer went on. "It is almost dark. By law we must have the brands hot before last light. It will take time to heat them, and—"

"I will tend to it myself. Later." Dracula pointed westward to the last embers of sunset. "As you say, it is almost dark."

"Where do you want her taken, lord?" asked the auctioneer, bowing almost double. Someone pressed a cloak into his hands and he held it out toward Kelene. She stretched out a hand, looking up at Dracula for permission. He nodded and dropped his arm from around her waist, freeing her for an instant. Hastily, she wrapped the thin cloak around herself.

"I will take her where I want her," said Dracula, as he swung around, his cloak spread. For an instant it appeared he might take flight. Then he wrapped one side of the cloak around Kelene again. "You must stay warm."

"While I live," she said.

Dracula laughed mirthlessly. "There is a long way to go before you rest," he said, then addressed the auctioneer. "You may keep the wallet. Give it to her family when you—"

"Kelene! Kelene!" Achilles shouted from the confusion at the edge of the crowd. He shoved his way through the dispersing mob toward the platform, one hand raised so his sister could mark his progress. "Don't go yet! We're coming. Mama's with Alexander." He was panting and his face was flushed as he reached the edge of the platform.

"Achilles," Kelene said as she started to reach out, then faltered as Dracula glowered at her. She dropped her hand and looked into her brother's eyes. "I've been sold."

"You will not believe the price," said the auctioneer with awed emotion.

"I heard someone saying as I came through the gates that it was more than five hundred golden angels," Achilles said, clearly unconvinced. "That can't be right."

"Five hundred forty-six," snapped the auctioneer, annoyed at having his fun spoiled. "I have the coins right here. My commission is in this pile, leaving you four hundred ninety-two angels, eighteen silver crowns, and three brass lilies." He gave the wallet a proprietary pat. "I have it here for your mother."

Achilles simply stared, and finally blinked as if he expected the wallet to vanish. "So much," he muttered. "Mama may say what she likes, but I know you've saved us once again."

Kelene swallowed hard at the expression on her brother's face. She could feel Dracula's presence hovering over her like dark wings. The auctioneer jingled the wallet impatiently.

Then Achilles turned beseeching eyes on his sister, looking as if he were ready to cry.

"And now we've lost you, Kelene."

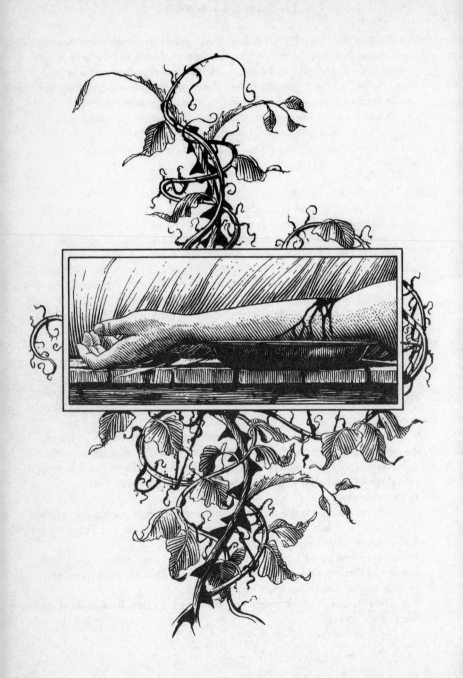

The master of my soul
May deliver me to destruction
Or to the gates of Paradise . . .
—Greek love song, 12th century

— XIV —

Achilles' cry went through Kelene like a well-honed blade. She reached out to take him in her arms as their last farewell; Dracula held her back. "This is my brother," she said, baffled by his interference.

"You have no brothers now, girl," said Dracula.

"I can say good-bye to her, can't I?" Achilles cried out.

"No," Dracula said very calmly. "There is no one's sister here, only my slave."

Kelene was stung. "You must not be so—"

"I will give you permission to speak when it suits my purpose," said Dracula. He turned to face Achilles. "She is mine."

The words stung and angered Kelene. How could her angel be so unfeeling?

"Mama's coming," Achilles called to her. "Mama and Alexander."

"They will be paid," said Dracula.

Achilles wailed, precariously near tears. "Kelene! Kelene! Don't go."

She looked at Dracula, uncertain what to do. "He is so young."

"So are you," said Dracula, then relented. "Very well." He lowered his arm and let her approach her brother. She knelt at the edge of the platform in front of Achilles, making sure the thin cloak was secured around her.

Achilles reached up and took her hands. "Oh, Kelene. I am going to miss you."

"You already miss Thalia. And Hector, and Pericles." She said the last two names softly, as if afraid to waken them.

"That's different." He did his best to grin. "So the Dragon Prince has bought you. It could have been much worse."

"Yes, it could." She shivered, telling herself she was cold. "And Zarrin will sell Orien back to the family. You can afford him."

"Yes," said Achilles, suddenly awkward. "If you hadn't . . . we couldn't . . ." He lost himself.

Dracula put his hand on her shoulder. "Come, girl. It is time we were gone."

"But Mama and Alexander—" Achilles demurred. "They will be here very soon."

"Come away," said Dracula. The strength in his grip made her gasp.

"Achilles. Tell them . . ." Kelene could not think of anything she wanted to say; she waved good-bye and let Dracula guide her to the rear of the platform, down a narrow flight of steps to the improvised courtyard where slaves were kept before being sold. A single, blowing torch barely lit their surroundings; she remembered that flimsy, undecorated wooden panels served to wall off the courtyard, but could summon no other details to mind as darkness enclosed her.

Dracula looked around in the darkness. "We'll wait here a short while longer. So you can hear what your mother says when she claims the money. The auctioneer will tell her you have left. She will not know you are listening." He was very close to her, his presence lying over her like a shroud.

"But why—?"

"Quiet," he ordered, his grip on her wrist tightening.

A short while later, Kelene heard Achilles call out to Alexander. She imagined him waving. He seemed very far away from her, as if she had gone leagues beyond the walls of Belgrade and not behind a flimsy wooden panel.

"Kelene is gone—the Dragon Prince bought her—he wouldn't wait for you and Mama to say good-bye—but there is so much money!" Achilles shouted, excitement overriding the tremor Kelene heard in his voice. "You won't believe how much! Hurry!"

"More than a hundred golden angels?" Alexander asked skeptically, his voice growing louder as he came up to the platform. "Has the auctioneer taken his commission yet? Will there be more than a hundred when he does?"

"Lots more," said Achilles. "We're *rich!*" He giggled in what might have been shock.

Kelene stood very still.

"Don't shout it out, then," said Melantha, her voice morose. "We don't want every thief in Belgrade to be after us."

"You needn't worry about that," said the auctioneer. "The Dragon Prince put all your family under his protection."

"If his protection is anything like the protection we have had from the Militant Angels, I would rather leave my fate in the hands of wolves," said Melantha.

"Mama!" Achilles protested. "The man is a prince. A Dragon Prince." His pride touched Kelene, who wished she could push aside the screen and embrace the brother who had always stood by her and her angel.

"Dragon Prince? Who is this Dragon Prince?" asked Melantha reluctantly. "I have never heard of him."

"He bought Kelene, Mama; he has chosen her," said Achilles before the auctioneer could speak again. "He is a very important lord."

Melantha paused. "Where is he from? Do you know that?"

The auctioneer answered carefully. "I have heard he comes from a fortress far to the east of here, in the Carpathian Mountains."

"So far; now I wonder why—?" mused Melantha. "What did he give for her?"

"Over five hundred golden angels!" Achilles exclaimed, unable to contain himself any longer. "Isn't it wonderful?"

"Strange, how quickly wealth can assuage grief," Dracula whispered in Kelene's ear. "Isn't it, girl?"

Kelene nodded once; she refused to feel the tears on her face.

"Impossible," said Melantha. "You can't be serious."

"See how highly she values you," Dracula murmured to Kelene. "She cannot imagine anyone being willing to pay such a price for you."

"She is worried about Papa," Kelene said.

"Lower your voice," Dracula ordered her.

"—crown and three brass lilies," the auctioneer was saying. "A remarkable sum."

"The wallet is very heavy, Mama," said Achilles. "Here."

"Put that down," Melantha said. "Alexander, you had better take the wallet. Make sure you do what you can to conceal it." She hesitated, then spoke to the auctioneer again. "Will he treat her well, do you think?"

"Why would he harm something he paid so much for?" said the auctioneer.

There was a brief silence on the auctioneer's platform.

"Have you heard enough?" Dracula asked Kelene.

"Not yet," she answered, smearing her tears across her cheeks. "Just a little longer. Please." She turned and looked up at him. "I'm not going to see them again. Am I?"

"No," he said. "Very well. Listen if you must."

"—Orien tomorrow morning," Achilles was declaring.

"No," Melantha said. "Tonight. Alexander, you must go to the Green Dog tonight." Her voice became agitated. "I want you to buy him back before we leave Belgrade. He must not remain in that awful place one moment longer than necessary."

"You are giving yourself pain for no reason," Dracula told Kelene.

She waved his remark away. "It's good about Orien," she said. "Mama's right."

The auctioneer coughed diplomatically. "You will not have long to reach Zarrin. The gates will be closed in an hour."

"This morning," said Melantha, "I was desperate for enough money to pay the physician, and the gold Zarrin gave seemed too small for my boy but barely enough for my purposes, and I was grateful for those few coins as I have been for few things in my life. Tonight I have so much gold that those ten angels seem paltry."

"And Kelene is gone," said Achilles.

"Orien will be grateful to her for saving him," said Alexander.

"Yes. We must be certain he knows of what she has done for us," said Melantha automatically. "I will tell him when we fetch him from Saint Nicholas Street."

"And Papa?" ventured Achilles; Kelene held her breath as she waited for her mother's answer.

"I will think of some way to explain it to him." She said nothing for two or three heartbeats. "She did insist."

"Come away," Dracula said to Kelene, pulling her back from the screen with an ease that was more dreamlike than anything she had experienced since she saw him striding across the market square toward her.

She followed after him willingly. He was not only her salvation, he was all the family she had left in the world.

The house Dracula had taken in Belgrade was in the most ancient part of the city. The building itself was about three hundred years old and had once been an establishment for monks. It huddled against a section of the first city walls as if trying to keep out of sight. None of the religious symbols remained, robbing the place of what little decoration it had once possessed; it was now as austere as the tomb.

"You will sleep in the room at the end of the corridor; Lajos will show you where in a short while," Dracula informed her. He led her into the central hall, which was wholly unfurnished but for an elaborate coffin set atop three trestle supports. Five torches sat in wall sconces, but their flames did not penetrate the darkness with much success. There was an abandoned air to the rooms, and the echoes lasted longer than they should have. No fire burned on the hearth, and the gaunt servant who greeted them said nothing as he closed the door against the night. "You will not leave the room until I give you permission."

"I'm hungry," said Kelene, then hurriedly added, "If you will permit me to eat."

"Someone will bring you food," said Dracula without interest.

Kelene lowered her head. She tried to think of her dreams, when Dracula had been her angel and not her owner. "What shall I say to you?"

He glanced down at her. "You need not speak." He gently touched her hair. "You know you must be ruled by me."

"As I have been," she said, feeling very brave for making this oblique reference to her visions of him.

His hand tightened on her hair and he pulled her head back. "That was nothing. You came in answer to my call, but you did not know what call you heard. You thought me a figure in a dream. Now you will learn how real I am."

"Yes," she said, hoping this was what he expected her to say.

He let go of her hair so abruptly that she staggered. "Never forget you are mine."

She murmured, "Yours," recalling the dreams she had had of him. Would they end now?

"While you are here, you will remain by yourself or with me. My servants and my soldiers will not speak to you. If you have anything to say, any questions to ask, you will address all to me and only to me."

"I understand," said Kelene, thinking she was hearing half-truths.

"No you don't. But you will."

The bed in which he lay had clean linen sheets with a horsehair mattress, but Diogenes was too far lost in fever to appreciate the change from a rough blanket on straw. Two beeswax candles cast light on his pasty features, and a basin of fresh water stood beside the candles. As Diogenes tossed in the bed, he called out for Kelene.

"What are we going to do, Mama?" Pallas asked, her voice high from fright and fatigue.

"The physician is coming again," said Melantha. "And now that we have secured this room, I know my husband will improve." She folded her arms. "At least we have Orien safe at last."

"Yes," said Pallas, who had been shocked to see her brother with carmined lips and a wreath in his hair. Orien would say nothing about it.

"Kelene! Kelene, where is Kelene?" Diogenes muttered as he worried at the sheets with shaking fingers. His face shone, the skin stretched tight and hot to the touch.

"What am I to say to him, Mama?" Pallas wailed quietly. "He keeps asking for her. I don't know what to tell him."

"I will attend to it," said Melantha. "But not before the physician has seen him. I don't want to upset him."

"But he—" Pallas stopped herself. "I will try to calm him, Mama."

"Good. And tomorrow we must find a reputable nurse for him; one who will tend him and follow the physician's instructions accurately," Melantha decided aloud. "The physician must know of one in all Belgrade who will not harm him with her care."

"I want Kelene!" Diogenes insisted, batting at shadows.

"Oh, dear; I had better . . ." Pallas indicated her father, going to his side as her mother nodded approval.

"Kelene . . . where is Kelene? . . . Something is wrong. Kelene! The Militant Angels are . . . Where is she?" This last was said lucidly enough as Diogenes recognized Pallas bending over him.

"She . . . isn't here, Papa." She pulled his sheet and blankets up high on his chest again. "You must not take a chill, Papa. Here. Let me fix your covers."

"Kelene," he repeated.

"Rest, Papa," said Pallas. "You are ill. You must get better. Especially now." She realized she should not have said so much. "We will need you to help us find a new place to live."

"Yes. Yes. The inn burned, didn't it? I'll talk to my Cousin Galatea. She will not refuse us a place to put up tents again." His eyes wandered and he grew fretful. "Why doesn't Kelene come?"

"She can't, Papa. Not now." Pallas dropped a cloth into the basin of water, preparing to bathe Diogenes' face with it.

"What do the Militant Angels say?" Diogenes burst out, trying to take hold of Pallas' elbow. "What warning have they given?"

"There is no warning that I know of, Papa," said Pallas as she wrung out the cloth.

"There must be," he said, sounding ill-used. "They must warn us. They always have before. Why would they desert us?"

"We have nothing to fear," said Pallas, glancing back at her mother as she wiped her father's brow. "Everything will be well."

"Does Kelene say so?" Diogenes asked in the voice of a child.

"Yes, husband," said Melantha, coming over to look down at him. "We would not have reason to rejoice but for her." She crossed herself.

"Well and good, well and good," said Diogenes, his febrile eyes half-closing as sleep overtook him.

"When are you going to tell him?" asked Pallas when she had put the cloth back in the basin and straightened Diogenes' covers again.

"You see how ill he is. It would not be wise to give him such a shock just now. I will explain it all: Orien and Kelene both. When he is improved, he will understand why—" She turned away and looked around the parlor. "We must thank the innkeeper for locating this place for us. It was a true kindness."

"Yes," said Pallas, her countenance troubled.

"It was a good thing for Alexander to agree to continue to help him; I would not like him to think that wealth made us callous to his situation. I think helping him shows how much we appreciate all he has done for us." Melantha was pacing the room. "Phaon is resting, isn't he?"

"In the next room, Mama," said Pallas, trying not to sound impatient. "I can look in on him again, if you like."

Melantha shook her head. "No. He must have his rest. Better to let him sleep now that Orien has returned. He may wake when the physician calls. He's had so much disturbance, poor boy."

Pallas sighed. "So have we all, Mama."

"But you are older. Phaon is little more than a baby, and in his short life he has known nothing but hardships and travail." Melantha daubed at her eyes. "If Pericles were alive, or Hector, Phaon would not be so alone. Having Orien back will make him less melancholy. He will have his brother to be his companion."

"Kelene is alone," said Pallas.

"But she is not dead," said Melantha, her mouth turning down. "And the man who bought her is a prince, a wealthy one."

"That does not make her any less lost to us," said Pallas. "With Thalia married, Kelene was my only sister remaining." She had to bite her lower lip to keep from crying.

"It is fitting that Kelene should be the means of our deliverance." Melantha turned away. "Stay here with your father. I'm going to wait for the physician, downstairs. It is time Alexander went to bed. He will have to rise early."

Pallas went back to her assigned duty. She noticed that her father had opened his eyes again, and she quickly took his hand in hers. "Papa, the physician is coming. Mother is waiting for him now."

"Pallas? Where are we?" Diogenes asked in a thready voice.

"We are at a travelers' guest house, Papa," said Pallas. "The Six-Horse Team. It is in Evangelist Square."

"Evangelist Square?" Diogenes repeated, astonishment serving to wake him fully. "In Belgrade? Where the wealthy merchants stop?"

"Yes," said Pallas, retrieving the cloth from the basin and wiping Diogenes' face with it. "Don't fuss, Papa."

"How long have we been here?"

"We came here this evening. It is approaching midnight." She saw how anxious he was and sought to alleviate the worst of his worries. "It is paid for, Papa."

Rather than reassuring him, this information served only to make him more uneasy. "How is it paid for?"

"Mama made the arrangements," said Pallas evasively.

"And Kelene? Did the Militant Angels offer any guidance?" His hand tightened on hers, his hold pitifully weak.

"I don't know," Pallas said, hating herself for this display of cowardice.

"What did she say? Kelene?" Diogenes pursued. "Tell me. Or send for her, and she can tell me herself."

"Mama won't allow anyone but me to tend you until the physician has seen you," said Pallas, hoping Diogenes would be satisfied with this answer.

"But why?" He waited for her to answer, then asked, "Am I so ill that it is unsafe for my children to be with me?"

"You may be," said Pallas. "Since I have been looking after you from the first, Mama thought it best that I continue to do it. To protect the others." For a thrown-together answer, she thought she had done fairly well.

"You're a good girl, Pallas," said Diogenes, his attention beginning to wander. "The Militant Angels have delivered us. They have guided us. Without Kelene's visions, where would we—"

"Kelene has delivered us," said Pallas with so much feeling that she recalled her father from his digression.

"Yes. She is our bastion against it all." He let go of Pallas' hand. "I'm very tired."

"I'll wake you when the physician comes," said Pallas. She sat beside her father, praying for his recovery as the night wore on. She was half asleep when the physician arrived—a self-important figure even at this late hour, his manner indignant and his attitude unsympathetic. Pallas stood up as he approached the bed. "Thank you for coming," she said softly.

"I was told his daughter was watching him," said the physician in a condemning tone. "Apparently she has retired."

"No," said Pallas, looking down at her ragged dress. "I am his daughter. I have sat with him since we arrived here."

The physician did not look at Pallas as he felt for Diogenes' pulse. "From a barn to this place in a night. No wonder his pulse is tumultuous."

"We were fortunate," Pallas said, hoping she was right.

"A daughter sold for fabulous sums. All Belgrade will be talking of nothing else tomorrow." The physician almost smacked his lips at the prospect.

"How sad that all Belgrade has nothing better to do," Pallas murmured demurely.

This remark did not please the physician, who ignored her completely until he demanded to see the contents of Diogenes' chamberpot.

"The servants took it away," said Pallas, aware that her mother had come into the room and waited near the door.

"Incompetents, every one of them," declared the physician. "I will have to see his urine to know how advanced the disease is. You will not allow the servants to take away his chamberpot in the morning—is that understood? In the meantime I will draw him, and if he remains feverish, I will have to bleed him as well. I will leave a poultice for the blisters. Have you sense enough to put it on the blisters three times a day until he has lost all trace of fever?"

"Yes," said Pallas.

Diogenes began to waken. His eyes opened blearily and he coughed. "Kelene?"

"It is the physician, Papa," said Pallas. "He has come to make you better."

"Have Kelene . . . come. Her Militant An . . . gels will know what . . . to do. They will . . . protect us." Each word came in a wheeze.

"The physician is here, husband," announced Melantha.

"Kelene! *Kele*—" More coughing silenced his cry.

"Perhaps, if it would calm him, it would be wise to send for this child," said the physician as he bent over Diogenes to smell his breath. "He is not wholly himself, and if she could assist him in some way . . ."

"It isn't possible," said Melantha quietly, trying to pull the physician away from the bedside.

"Has she taken ill?" the physician inquired, put upon. "I will not have time to treat both of them, I warn you."

"She is not here," said Melantha more quietly. "She cannot come."

The physician smiled, comprehension in his features. "She is the one—" His eyes narrowed. "You haven't told him."

"Not yet," said Melantha. "It would shock him, and since he is ill—"

"You may repose complete trust in my discretion," the physician interrupted. "I would have to advise sparing him. There will be time enough when he has recovered. You are wise, for a woman."

Melantha was struggling to find a response when the door burst open and Orien, fresh-scrubbed and wrapped in a borrowed Italian lucco, flung himself at his father's bed, sobbing loudly.

"Oh, Papa, Papa, Papa, Kelene's *gone!* They sold her to get me back! She's gone. We'll never see her again!" He buried his face in the covers.

At that the room was very quiet. Pallas put her hands to her mouth. Then Melantha went to Orien.

"You're tired. You've had a terrible day. It's extremely late. Your father is ill." She spoke in a low, persuasive voice, her hand on Orien's shoulder. "Come, Orien. We'll talk about this in the morning."

The physician came nearer to the bed again, craning his neck to watch.

Orien lifted his head. "I'm sorry, Papa! I'm sorry."

Diogenes gave his son a dazed stare. "Why?" he muttered.

"Woman," said the physician, sternly addressing Melantha, "get your son out of this room or I will not answer for what happens."

Melantha was already tugging at Orien's shoulders, dragging him off the side of the bed and struggling to get the resisting boy out the door. He dug in his heels.

"Papa!" Orien yelled, fighting to break free from his mother's grip. "I didn't mean to do it!"

"Do what?" Diogenes asked in bafflement. He looked at Pallas. "What is he talking about?" His voice was a little clearer now, and his attention was not so aimless. "What about Kelene?"

"He is overwrought, husband," said Metantha. "Seeing you ill has—" She had shouldered the door open and was about to shove Orien through it.

"He said . . . that Kelene was gone," Diogenes said with the odd lucidity of fever. "Where is she? What's become of her?"

"You will do yourself an injury if you persist in this," said the physician with a sharp glance at Melantha. "I will have to insist we be left alone, woman."

With a sudden tremendous effort, Diogenes levered himself onto his elbow. "Orien! Where is Kelene!" For that one moment, his voice was almost as splendid as it was when he was well, and it stopped Melantha in the open door; Orien shoved past her back to his father's bedside.

"Orien," Pallas warned, jarred out of her shocked stillness. "Do not. You don't know what—"

"Do not what?" Diogenes demanded, his cough returning. "Physician, I charge you: tell me what is happening."

"In the morning, when you are rested," the physician soothed as he made dismissing gestures to Orien.

The boy paid no attention. "I didn't bring enough when they sold me. So Kelene was auctioned. A prince paid hundreds of gold angels for her, because of me."

"You must not become agitated," the physician warned futilely.

"Sold?" Diogenes repeated in horror. "Kelene? Sold?" His coughing now seemed to wrench his ribs from his spine.

"Husband," said Melantha, rushing toward him, thrusting Orien out of the way. "Husband, I will explain it all. It was necessary to save you!

It was for you!" She reached out to him, only to be cuffed aside as Diogenes struggled to turn away from her. "Husband! Orien doesn't understand!"

Diogenes continued to cough, his shoulder drawn up as if to provide a barricade against what he had heard.

Pallas came nearer. "Papa?" she whispered, summoning up the courage to touch him.

He winced as if her hand burned him. "Go away," he muttered before a renewed bout of coughing claimed him.

The physician regarded her with somber eyes. "This is doing him no good. I will have to bleed him now."

"Yes," said Diogenes. "Bleed me. Bleed me dry." He struggled to keep from coughing. "Just tell my wife to stay out."

"Papa!" exclaimed Pallas. "You do not—"

"Tell her!" Diogenes insisted.

At the door, Melantha lowered her head and all but released her hold on Orien. Her voice was as subdued as her stance. "I heard him. I'll go."

The physician went to his case and brought out his knife and his cupping bowl. "You may have to help hold him," he warned Pallas as he reached under the blankets for Diogenes' arm.

Steeling herself for this task, Pallas approached the bed once again, half-expecting to be struck for her efforts. "I am ready," she told the physician.

Just before the physician lanced the vein in his left arm, Diogenes looked directly at Pallas. "Is she really gone?"

Mutely Pallas nodded.

"Then we are doomed," said Diogenes, and waited for the knife.

This time when he came to her, Kelene knew he was no dream, no angel, that his flesh was as real as hers. When she was offered the chalice, she knew she did not drink wine.

In love I am as conquered
As a city in flames.
—Greek lament, 15th century

⊢ XV ⊣

With an apologetic shrug the auctioneer told Melantha, "I do not know where the Dragon Prince stays in Belgrade. His fortress is many leagues to the east of here, in the mountains." He bowed to be polite. "I cannot help you."

"But someone must know," she persisted, her new shawl protecting her from the blowing snow.

The auctioneer shrugged. "I am sorry, woman. I must resume my work. With the storm coming, I will not have more than an hour to sell today."

"After yesterday, I would think you could lose one or two afternoons without sacrifice," said Melantha caustically. "My husband is ill, and he wants to see his daughter one last time. Do you think—"

"I think yesterday was the time for that," said the auctioneer, bowing as slightly as good conduct demanded; he left her at the edge of the platform and went to resume his auction of three stoic Egyptians.

"He wouldn't tell me anything," said Melantha to Alexander as she reached his side in the crowd.

"If he does not know, how could he?" Alexander asked reasonably. "Perhaps if we look around the market, someone will have seen him."

"Today?" Melantha asked, with a glance up into the snow. "In this?"

"It's possible," said Achilles as he tugged at his mother's hand. "We must try. For Papa's sake."

"May all the Saints protect us," Melantha cried out, making the sign of the cross as she rubbed at her eyes.

"We must hurry, Mama," said Alexander. "The storm is getting worse."

"And we promised Papa—" Achilles said, breaking off suddenly. "I know! I will ask the Watch at the gate. They will have to know."

"But will they tell you?" asked Melantha.

"They let us bring Papa into the city after the gates were closed for the night when they saw two golden angels to thank them for their charity," said Achilles, his cynicism out of place in one so youthful. "Four or five silver crowns should take care of their scruples."

"We must not let Kelene leave the city without seeing her father one last time. It would kill him, if she does." Melantha had been repeating this with liturgical piety since they had left the guest house that morning. "Very well. Go speak to the Watch. But hurry. Alexander and I will remain here, to ask the merchants."

"I'm going to the smithy. If the Dragon Prince has horses, some of them must need reshoeing. The farrier will know where he is staying, perhaps," said Alexander, and struck off across the square as Achilles ran off toward the main gate.

"We must find her. We must. We must. My husband will never forgive me if we do not," Melantha said to the sky.

Orien, who stood beside her, finally spoke up. "If we do not find her today, I promise I will, Mama. No matter how far I must go, or how long it will take me."

Melantha pulled him close to her side. "You must not say such things. You're not old enough to promise so much."

"But I will, Mama," said Orien. "Kelene saved me. I must do all that I can to save her. It is the only thing I can do."

"You don't know what you're saying," Melantha said fearfully. "When you are older we will discuss it. Until then, it is enough that we are all together."

"But Mama—" Orien began, only to be interrupted.

"No. In time you will see I am right." She clung to him as desolation swept through her. Dear God, was she to lose all her family because of Kelene? "Come with me, then, while I ask the people in the marketplace about the Dragon Prince."

"All right," said Orien. "But, Mama, I won't forget."

No one in the house spoke to her. Kelene wandered along the narrow, dim corridors, trying to find someone who would give her food. It was almost midday and she was very hungry. Occasionally she caught sight of a servant, but not one of them showed any indication of willingness to help her. Worse, Dracula was nowhere to be found. She had called out to him at first, but the eerie echoes of his name filled her with unease.

In one of the rooms, Kelene came upon a fire burning on the hearth and she went to it gratefully. The thin cloak she wore over her torn habit was woefully inadequate for keeping her warm; as she crouched in front of the blazing logs she began to rub her arms to speed heat through her veins once more. She would not allow herself to think of all that happened the day before. Better, she told herself, to dwell on what was to come, not what was past.

A footfall sounded behind her, and a scrape of wood on the floor.

She turned, expecting to see Dracula. The welcoming smile faded from her lips as she realized it was one of the servants carrying a small table and a camp stool. Rising, she saw that there were two bowls and a tankard set upon it. Recalling Dracula's admonition not to speak to his servants she decided the prohibition did not include acknowledgment of service, so she bobbed her head and said, "Thank you."

For an answer the servant scowled at her and hastened away, as if dreading what she would do next.

The meal was ample—a stew made with lamb, onions, and cabbage; a hearty broth of eels; and a plate of grilled liver strips covered in mustard sauce—and accompanied by a thick slice of black bread and hot plum wine. Kelene set to eating at once. When she was finished, she began to feel drowsy, as much from the food as the drink. After a moment's consideration, she decided to pull the stool as near to the fire as she could so that she could nap in the warmth of its glow. In a short while she dozed off.

She awakened some time later: the sun was low enough in the sky that its beams came in through the high, narrow window and left a pale smear of illumination on the wall by the door. The fire still burned, but most of the two logs had been consumed and the room was becoming uncomfortably cool. Kelene got to her feet, her head swimming with the suddenness of her movement. She listened, certain she had been startled by a noise.

Sounds, indistinguishable and distorted by echoes, rang in the corridor. Kelene listened at the door, trying to make out individual voices or words, but could not. She pulled the door wider, then stepped into the hall, frowning into the darkness that greeted her. Without any specific goal in mind, she began to walk, glancing into each room she passed, hoping to find the source of the echoes. The house proved larger than she had supposed it was, and her wandering took her in baffling directions.

When she came to the central hall—as much by accident as design—she paused beside the coffin, listening intently. She had had the oddest impression of movement within it. Telling herself she was being foolish, she leaned over, pressing her ear to the ornate carving on the lid.

"Nothing," she said aloud, as if hearing the word would make it more convincing. She studied the coffin with its elaborate dragon motif, wondering why Dracula had brought it. Who had died, that he had felt it necessary to carry the coffin on his travels, and place it so conspicuously in his house?

The echoes had faded some time before, but Kelene's curiosity was undampened. She continued to roam about the house, and since no one stopped her, she supposed she was not doing anything forbidden. When she came to a small inner courtyard with an old-fashioned gallery which must have served the monks as an ambulatory, she noticed half a dozen men-at-arms packing crates and chests, readying them for securing to pack saddles. A small carriage of Eastern design was already laden with cases. Kelene stared, trying to reckon the length of their coming journey based on what she saw being packed.

"You should not be here," said the servant Lajos as he came up to Kelene. How long he had been watching her, she did not know.

She blushed. "No one told me," she said, trying to sound contrite instead of resentful.

"I am telling you now," said Lajos, indicating yet another corridor. "If you will?"

It was tempting to defy him, just to see what he would do, but she realized this would be foolish.

"The master has given me permission to tell you that he will call upon you at dusk," said Lajos, following Kelene as she went away from the courtyard. "He will want you to receive him well."

"I am his slave," said Kelene. "How else would I receive him?"

Lajos only nodded, his face impassive. "Receive him well," he repeated, and left her in a room where another fire had been laid.

"But what—" she began, wanting to know what Dracula expected of her. Lajos was gone before she could finish her question.

She was glad to warm herself again. Her hands were very cold, she noticed; no matter how much she rubbed them, they did not become warmer.

Dracula found her there some time later, the twilight relieved only by the splendid fire in the hearth. He strode up to her, his face set in stern lines. "Your mother came here today," he said harshly, as if it were Kelene's fault.

"I . . . didn't know. I didn't see her." Had that been the source of the echoes that had so disturbed her earlier?

"Yes," said Dracula, dropping down on his knee beside her, his cloak falling around him in dark folds. "I know that. If you had summoned her, you would be torn and bleeding by now." His long hand twisting in her hair provided no comfort.

"You bought me; I am yours." She looked at her hands as she said this, as if by avoiding his eyes she preserved some necessary part of herself.

"You were mine long before I bought you," he corrected her, rising once more. "You must have better garments than that. You will freeze on our way through the mountains if you—"

"I have nothing else. All our clothing was destroyed in the fire at the inn. The habit was provided by the monks, for charity. And the cloak . . ." She fingered the rough-woven wool as if she found its texture objectionable for the first time.

"One of my servants will bring you new clothes tonight," said Dracula in the same offhanded way he had told her she would be fed. "This time, do not thank him."

Kelene blinked. "How did—?"

"Nothing happens within my domain that I do not know of," he said without any emphasis whatsoever. "Next time you thank a servant of mine, he will be beaten."

"But shouldn't I . . . If they perform a service . . ." She saw no change in his forbidding countenance.

"The service is not done for you, but for me. If you must say thank you, address me. The servants are only tools of my will." He waited while she thought this over. "They are as much mine as you are, girl."

"Very well," she said, displeased at having such limitations imposed upon her. She cocked her head. "What time tomorrow will we leave?"

"We will be on the road by noon. And we will travel after dark."

Kelene could not conceal her dismay. "But there are desperate men who prey on those caught on the roads at night," she said.

"No man is desperate enough to attack me," said Dracula. "You have nothing to fear, girl."

He stood and swung around on his heel, his cloak sweeping behind him. "You will want to sleep long tonight. Tomorrow you will not have the same opportunity."

"I will," she said, puzzled as to how she would accomplish it: she had never been able to sleep to order before.

"If you cannot rest tonight, you will be in a stupor by the time we stop tomorrow night." Dracula sounded faintly amused at the prospect.

Kelene watched him pace, thinking he reminded her of the wolves she had seen from time to time. He looked so feral, a creature more of nature than God. She wanted to ask him why he had given up his celestial realms for worldly ones. She let her gaze be held by the flicker of the fire, saying, "We have a long way to go."

"More than you can dream of, girl," said Dracula with an emotion very like pride.

Stung, she said, "My family has already come a very long way!"

"If distance were only a matter of leagues, that would be so."

Kelene did not look toward him. "If it is not leagues, then what is it?" Her palms were hot and her spine prickled.

He came close to her again. "The distance between life and death, girl, is greater than the broadest ocean. Until you traverse it, you will know nothing of distance."

"Will . . . will it be soon?" She continued resolutely to watch the flames.

"Not until I return to my native earth." He chuckled, the sound not unlike the rattle of falling rocks. "I did not come all this way to lose you so soon, girl."

Kelene folded her hands in her lap, trying to look humble. "I am your slave, my lord," she said, hoping it was what he wanted to hear.

"See you remember it. You have no one but me."

"I suppose not," she said sadly.

"Do not mourn for your family," Dracula said to her, his sternness less formidable than a moment before. "You are not as alone as you fear. I am here to be your family, and I will never leave you."

Mutely Kelene nodded.

Orien stood in the street just beyond the imposing gates to Dracula's house in Belgrade. He had been trying for the last hour to work up sufficient courage to knock on them, as his older brothers had done earlier in the day. Swallowing hard, he reminded himself he had sworn to find Kelene, to repay her for sparing him. Now that he almost had, his nerve deserted him. The armed, silent soldiers he had seen come and go from the house had frightened him. His hands were cold and chapped in spite of the luxurious new shuba he wore over his old clothes; he shoved them deep into the fleecy pockets, feeling guilty for enjoying the warmth. He did not know what he would tell his mother if he failed to reach Kelene. With the sun almost down, he was certain he ought to return to the Six-Horse Team; it was not safe on the streets alone.

Suddenly the gates swung open and four men-at-arms in black armor rode out on black horses, going at a brisk trot without regard for those in the street already. One of the soldiers nearly knocked Orien off his feet as they passed.

Scrambling up, Orien made a rush at the gate. A loose cobblestone caught his toe and sent him sprawling a short distance from it. He watched its inexorable closing as he stood up and tried to clean off the front of his shuba. Melantha would be furious to see how badly he had taken care of his fine new sheepskin coat.

He waited a short while, hoping the armed men would return and give him one more opportunity. But when he heard the bells sound for worship, he knew he dared not linger. Reluctantly he turned away from the dark house, saying as he did, "I will find you, Kelene. I promise you, in the name of the Militant Angels."

"Where have you been?" Pallas asked Orien in a tense voice as he climbed the stairs to their rooms. She stood at the door to her chamber. "Alexander was about to go in search of you." She seized his arm and dragged him inside, half-closing the door behind them. "Where were you?"

"I was trying to see Kelene," he said, puzzled by his sister's unusual tone of voice. "I said I would find her—"

"Mama's been beside herself with worry," said Pallas. "I'll go tell her you're here."

He shook his head. "I think I'd better."

"No," said Pallas firmly. "She'd probably break your jaw." Sighing suddenly, Pallas offered an explanation. "Father is worse again. We have sent for a pope to administer Final Rites."

She crossed herself.

Orien stared at her. "Papa? Papa's *dying?*"

"The physician says he can do nothing more," said Pallas. "Unless God wills he live, we will have to—" She broke off, unable to go on.

He should have gotten used to death, Orien told himself. There had been enough of it in the last two years. But it was different when Hector and Pericles died. It was sad, and he had prayed for them, but . . . "Papa can't die. He can't."

"I do not want it to happen, either," said Pallas as gently as she could. "And we must pray for him, that God may yet spare him for us."

Orien stamped his foot. "If Kelene were here, he would not die. Her angels would protect him." He was about to bolt for the door when Pallas grabbed the collar of his shuba. "Let go of me. I'll get her."

"Alexander and Achilles have already tried," said Pallas. "The servants would not let them see her." She began to weep without sobbing. "They probably didn't tell her anything about it." She took a deep breath to steady herself.

"But if we explained—" Orien began. "They'd let her know, wouldn't they?"

"I . . . I don't suppose they would. They're probably not allowed to," said Pallas quietly as she wiped her cheeks. "Go wash your face and put on something clean. You look a fright. How could you dirty that new shuba so quickly?" She stopped herself. "Never mind. Just make yourself neat. You will want to see Papa before the pope comes." She put her hands on his shoulders. "We have to be brave, for Mama."

Orien wriggled, his face screwed up with conflicting emotions. "I still think I should go find her," he insisted.

"It is more important to see Papa," Pallas said, her face wan in the candlelight. "The Militant Angels know what has happened here. We do not have to find Kelene for the angels to know." She shoved him gently toward the door. "I'll tell Mama you're here."

"Is Papa . . . going to die?" Orien asked quietly.

Pallas stared down at the floor. "He isn't trying not to."

"Then I will pray the Militant Angels will protect him." He crossed himself and folded his hands in prayer, saying as Pallas closed the door, "If you will save Papa, I will do everything I can to make up for what has happened."

A short while later Alexander came through the door, his expression thunderous though he spoke mildly enough. "Papa wants to see you, Orien."

"Is the pope here?"

"He is coming. Mama says we should all . . . see him before the pope begins the Rites." He did his best to favor Orien with a look of encouragement.

"We're supposed to say good-bye, aren't we?" Orien asked, knowing the answer already. He tried not to cry and very nearly succeeded.

"Yes," was the gentle response as Alexander led his brother into the hall. "It is what Mama wants us to do."

"I . . . I'll do it." He picked at the front of his clothes, removing the worst of the mud. "I thought it would be all right—"

"Papa won't mind," said Alexander. "Achilles is with him now. You can go in." He opened the door to the room where their father lay. "Don't say anything to upset him."

"You mean about Kelene," said Orien.

"Or anything else." Alexander moved aside so Orien could pass. "I'll come to get you when the pope arrives."

Three candles burned at the head of the bed, evoking the Trinity for protection of the ailing Diogenes. The covers were drawn up to his chin, making his face appear more waxen next to their pallor. A four-day growth of beard stubbled Diogenes' cheeks, the hair all but colorless. His lips were white and his half-closed eyes sunken in livid sockets. His shallow breath sounded rough as a saw.

Achilles knelt on the left side of the bed, his hands joined on the covers while he prayed. As Orien approached, he looked up, a hint of faith in his eyes. "Well? Did you find her?"

"No," Orien confessed as he came to the right side of the bed. As he went down on his knees, he said, "Papa, don't die. Please don't die."

"I don't think he can hear you," said Achilles. "I think Mama is the one who hears us."

Orien joined his hands and bowed his head. "May God heal you, Papa, and restore you to health as He has restored our fortunes." He thought it was what Melantha wanted to hear, and he considered his next statement carefully. "You have had the hardships; live to know the rewards."

"Kelene made the rewards," Achilles whispered.

"Ke . . . le . . ." Diogenes breathed.

The two boys exchanged looks, then Orien went on hurriedly. "God made you the center of our family. Do not leave us when we are not ready."

" . . . ne . . ." sighed Diogenes.

Achilles' hands tightened together into interlaced fists. "God, it isn't fair." His square face was a block of disapproval. "You have taken too much for what You have given," he muttered. "You drive a cruel bargain."

Impulsively Orien reached out and took his father's cold hand. "I will find her, Papa. Really I will."

Achilles shot a quick, irritated look at Orien. "You'll upset him," he warned.

"Only if he can hear me. You said he couldn't; so it doesn't matter," Orien reminded him, holding more tightly to his father's hand, hating it for the limpness of it, and the lack of warmth.

There were footfalls on the stairs and a hushed commotion in the corridor outside the door, followed by two discreet raps on the door.

"The pope is here," said Achilles, crossing himself and getting to his feet. "Come on, Orien. We have to leave."

But Orien could not bring himself to release his father's hand. "Papa," he said as he clambered to his feet, "I will find her. I promise you I will find her."

Achilles came around the foot of the bed and grabbed Orien's sleeve. "Come on." He tugged urgently, forcing him to drop Diogenes' nerveless hand.

"I will find Kelene, Papa," Orien said more loudly as Achilles dragged him toward the door.

" . . . Ke . . . le . . ." followed after them.

. . . And how my cries echo
In this loneliest of places!
—Greek song, 13th century

⊢ XVI ⊣

Kelene did not sleep well; all through the night the strange, ancient house echoed with the sounds of preparation for their departure. From time to time wheels rumbled through the inner courtyard, and once or twice mules brayed. She lay on her hard cot trying not to listen but unable to shut the sounds from her mind. The night rail one of the silent servants had provided for her was of luxurious silk, as pale as moonlight and soft as swan's down; she loved the delicious touch of it on her skin after the rasp of the habit. There were three other sorts of clothing waiting for her, laid out across the end of her cot in surprising contrast to the austerity of her chamber: a splendid, if a bit old-fashioned Italian gamurra with long, trailing sleeves was the most opulent, with gathered panels of wine-red and gold velvet. There was also a camisa of fine linen and a pair of elevated Venetian chiponei, with particolored leggings.

She regarded this finery with suspicion, thinking it more appropriate for a courtesan than a slave. Still, it was difficult not to get up and try them on, for she had never known such finery or such womanly things.

For once, she had not dreamed, and this time she was glad of it.

By the time the tall narrow window began to reveal a patch of tarnished-silver sky, Kelene was eager to be up. Even the thought of washing in cold water could not lessen her anticipation; her clothes were waiting, and it was nearly dawn. As she got out from under the heavy blankets, she fingered the silk of her night rail once more.

She found a pail of water outside her door. She exchanged it for her chamberpot, bringing the pail into the room and using it to wash her arms and legs, drying them on a corner of her sheet before reaching for the camisa; it almost floated as she put it on, light and gauzy as summer clouds; the neckline was embroidered with a pattern of lilies. The leggings came all the way up her thighs and tied around her waist with long braided cords. Last the gamurra, which was heavier than Kelene had expected as she wrestled her way into it. The velvet was soft and warm, like silken fur. She wished she had a mirror to see how she looked, but in all her wandering about the house she had not found one. She sighed, contenting herself with what she could see of the wide, tiered skirt and the long, fan-shaped sleeves. Then she worked her golden hair into braids and wrapped them around her head, securing them with the ornate tortoise-shell pins that had been given her the night before. Had she been married, she would have put a baizo-wreath of braided cloth around her braids, but being a slave, she was not entitled to such adornment.

For a moment, she longed for the chance to show her family how she was being treated, how well her Dragon Prince was caring for her, but the memory was so new and so painful that she quickly made herself concentrate on other things. "They left you to Dracula, girl; they took the gold," she said in stern imitation of her master. "They were willing to let you go. You are Dracula's slave. You have no family but him."

When she put them on, the chiponei proved awkward, the raised sole under the ball of her foot making it difficult to balance. She tottered around her little room for a short while, trying to master the clumsy footwear, wondering how the fine ladies of Venice were able to go any-where in such shoes as these. At least she was not expected to walk far in them, she thought, and longed briefly for the sturdy, wooden-soled boots with the high, fleece-lined tops she had worn on the long trek from Salonika to Sarajevo. Then she laughed aloud at her foolishness—who would prefer the ungainly merchants' boots over these elegant chiponei?

Unbidden, the answer came to her: *Anyone who wants to flee.*

She stopped still, listening intently. Nothing. She closed her eyes to enable herself to hear more keenly. Had she imagined it? Had those words been spoken? Had anyone heard them but her?

As the room grew slowly brighter with the coming of day, Kelene felt more oppressed instead of less. Day meant travel, and the rigors of the road. She paced, trying to get used to the chiponei. If only the sun would rise at last, she thought, then she would be less troubled.

When the door opened suddenly it was so unexpected that Kelene almost fell. She reached out her hand to steady herself and was caught in Dracula's grasp. She lowered her head in respect.

"I am pleased you are ready," he said as he released her. "It saves me having to wake you. " He was in the black armor she remembered so clearly from her dreams, and the cloak over his shoulders hung like black wings.

She could not tell if this was praise or rebuke, so she remained silent, not moving until he nodded in the direction of her cot. Gratefully she sat down, taking care to spread her magnificent skirts carefully so that the velvet would not be crushed.

"We will be leaving shortly, and this will be my last opportunity to speak to you before we leave." He stood in the corner farthest away from the window, making himself like a shadow. His voice was low and commanding, as she had heard it in her visions. She did her best to take comfort in it. "You will be brought your breakfast soon. I order you to eat it all without complaint. We will be traveling fast and hard, and I do not want you faltering for lack of strength."

"I will not falter," she said, hoping she sounded more fervent to him than she seemed to her own ears. "I have come a long way to get here."

"So you have," he said. "But the arduous part of your travels has not yet begun." He made a gesture that was at once imperative and forbidding. "While we travel, you will take orders from no one but me. My servants will not speak with you, nor will my soldiers. If you speak to them, they will pay the price." He folded his arms. "I depend upon you not to grow weak. If you fail me in this, I will have little use for you."

In spite of the warmth of her velvets, Kelene went cold. She huddled into her vast, colorful sleeves, trying to restore some heat to her flesh. Finally she said, "I will not fail you."

"No," Dracula said. "You will not. You will come to me whenever I call you, no matter what the hour or where we are."

"I want to serve you," she said. "I do not know how you have transformed yourself from my visions to the world, but—"

"From the first vision, you were mine," he said, his eyes like living embers. "Body and soul, you will be mine always."

"Yes."

"Do not think to defy me, girl," he warned. "I will not tolerate opposition, especially from the likes of you."

Kelene tried to appear compliant. "I am yours in all things," she said, doing her best to mean it; the first warm light of dawn brightened the narrow window as her Dragon Prince opened the door into the dark maw of the corridor.

Dracula chuckled just before he left her alone. "Not yet. But you will be. Or you will be nothing."

She no longer tried to get the servants to speak. Standing next to her cot she watched as two of them brought a camp table and stool, and a well-laden tray. When they had finished, they left her alone with a repast that seemed more like a banquet than a breakfast. Recalling the orders she had been given, she dutifully began with the crock of hot cheese and the new rolls. There were also a plate of blood sausage, a dish of yoghurt with raisins, and a bowl of eggs poached in broth. Surveying the whole made Kelene a bit queasy, but she did not dare to refuse any of the food.

When the servants returned, one of them brought her a small chest, indicating that she pack her night rail and her bedding in it. They took away her empty dishes and left her alone to make her last preparations for travel. Kelene found herself lingering over the work, as if by taking her time she could postpone the time of departure indefinitely.

But then the chest was filled and she had nothing to do but wait for one of the servants to summon her. She sat on the cot and tried to make herself be patient while she castigated herself for not learning more about her father's condition while she could. Surely the gold Dracula had paid for her would be enough to restore his health?

These gloomy reflections were brought to an end when one of the servants returned, taking up the chest and signaling her to follow him.

The inner courtyard was full of activity, the soldiers readying wagons, horses and mules. The harness-leathers creaking and the hooves of the animals on the paving stones were the loudest sounds Kelene heard. She looked about, hoping to catch sight of Dracula, if only to show him how readily she was doing his bidding; he was nowhere in sight. The servant pointed out an enclosed carriage drawn by four sturdy dark bay horses, clearly intending she should ride in it. With a sigh she complied, settling herself on the single seat as gracefully as she could.

It was annoying that the windows were covered with close-fitting leather blinds, but she knew better than to complain to the servants. She would tell her Dragon Prince that she would prefer to see where she was going when he summoned her that night. For the moment, she lifted the edge of one of them and saw that the ornate coffin was being loaded on the wagon-bed immediately behind her carriage; this equipage was drawn by six coal-black Hungarian Furiosos. Kelene shuddered and started to cross herself, then stopped as nausea roiled through her. She steadied herself on the seat, letting the blind fall shut.

A short while later, the carriage lurched into movement and the cavalcade began to pull out of the courtyard, into the streets of Belgrade. From nearby churches came the peal of bells announcing midday. The procession went at a brisk trot, slowing for nothing and no one; Kelene heard shouted protests and occasional screams of dismay as they continued through the streets unimpeded. Only when they reached the gates—Kelene assumed it had to be one of the two on the eastern side of the city—did they stop briefly. Then they were out of Belgrade, going along the busy road at the same steady trot.

In the artificial dusk of her carriage, Kelene tried to stave off boredom by identifying as many of the sounds she heard in the road as she could.

Shortly she was able to distinguish specific noises and smells in the general clamor. There was a pig farmer driving his stock to market; the piglets were squealing and the farmer had to pick up one of them, if the noises were any indication. Then a brewer went by, his cart laden with fragrant barrels of barley ale. Next they passed a family of gypsies; a few of them sang a mournful song in their own tongue. Then there was a group of soldiers—probably German, by the sound of them—arguing loudly. As they went over a bridge, the impact of hooves and the roll of wheels blotted out any other sounds around them. Only when they were on the far side did Kelene hear the warning call of a raven.

By midafternoon the horses had slowed to a walk, and the travel was less comfortable. Deep, frozen ruts in the roadway jarred and jolted Kelene's carriage; from time to time she could hear the coffin slide and bump on the wagon-bed behind her. She held on to the leather loops on the sides of her seat and tried not to get thrown about too badly as the soldiers guided them up a long, cold slope. Though her view was obscured by the leather blinds, she had the impression that the sky had once again clouded over; the wind had picked up and was unpleasantly icy, cutting through her velvets like a razor through flesh. She huddled against her seat, wishing she had something more to wrap around her.

Shortly after sunset the party halted briefly; the horses were watered and given two handfuls of grain and then they were underway once again. Kelene was startled to hear Dracula's voice shout as the soldiers resumed their travels. After hours of silence, his voice was a greater shock than she would have thought possible. She steadied herself as the carriage swayed, hoping that he would say something to her. But there was only the creak of harness, the jingle of spurs, the groaning of wheels, and the steady clop of hoofbeats. As darkness gathered, Kelene dozed.

She awoke some time later as the carriage bowled across a bridge. Along the edges of the blinds she could see the glare of torches. There were shouts and the noise of activity as the team pulling her carriage was halted. The crimp of chains and the shriek of metal gears filled her with anxiety.

Before she was prepared her door was flung open and two of the soldiers reached up to help her descend. She complied, shivering in the implacable chill that came over her as she stepped down onto the worn cobbles of what proved to be a large marshaling court. She smoothed the front of her gamurra and tried to make herself look neat; Dracula's men ignored her and the soldiers who had come to assist them did not stare.

"I will order a fur rug for you tomorrow," Dracula said as he walked up to her. "I had forgotten how cold you would be." He took her by the wrist and strode off.

After sitting for so long, Kelene was stiff, and the unfamiliar chiponei made her stumble as she struggled to keep up with him. Her attempts at apology were cut short with a gesture of his free hand. "I didn't—"

"This is Kodevna. We stop here until morning. You will have a supper brought to you. Eat it all. I will send for you when you are done." His brusque manner increased her unease as she did her best to keep up with his long stride.

They had entered a long corridor lined with torches. Ahead lay a Grand Hall ornamented with the devices of all the nobles who had defended the fortress. Kelene saw the elaborate dragon that matched the one on the coffin: Dracula was no stranger to this place.

Slaves rushed out to greet them, bowing deeply; Dracula paid no attention to them, continuing on to a small antechamber laid out in Turkish finery with hassocks and cushions covered in brocades, a wide brass platter set on legs for a table, and an elaborate water ewer on tall, carved legs.

"You will eat here. The slaves know what to do." He let go of her as abruptly as he had seized her. "There's no reason to speak to them. You don't know their language, in any case." He turned and strode away.

One of the slaves bowed tentatively to Kelene and pointed to the largest of the hassocks, saying something incomprehensible.

Kelene went where the slave pointed and dropped onto the hassock, taking no care to keep her skirts and sleeves from being wrinkled. Had she been alone, she might have cried; instead, she pinched her nose and bit the insides of her cheeks until the urge passed. *There is no reason to cry*, she told herself. *You have nothing to weep for.* She leaned back on the hassock, loving it for its comfort, letting it hold her, grateful for its stillness, and did her best not to think of Belgrade and the family she had left there.

A short while later she was brought a good-sized dinner, most of it rigorously simple food: soldiers' fare—cabbage, pork, cheese and bread— which she consumed without tasting. There was a goblet of wine as well; she drank it as if it were water and longed for sleep.

But Dracula had said he would send for her, and she would have to come when he summoned her. So she propped herself on her elbow and did her best to stay awake. It was a losing battle, and within an hour, she had drifted into a dream, a dream in which she rose and walked, unheeded, through the stone corridors, following a call only she could hear.

On the battlements, the Dragon Prince paced, his cloak spreading wide to carry him into the night sky. As Kelene watched, shivering in her silken night rail, he sailed over the countryside, circling like a gigantic hawk, his flight easy and so ordinary that

Kelene almost forgot to feel awe. Then he dove from the sky—her pulse hammered in her throat for fear—only to reemerge with the figure of a youngster in his hands.

At first, Kelene thought the child had been rescued, and she was about to shout her thanks when she saw Dracula take the boy and twist his head suddenly so that it hung against his shoulder. Kelene had seen enough chickens killed to know the boy was dead. What reason could her Dragon Prince have for doing this? She shuddered and tried to pray, all the while longing for a cloak to keep her warm and to offer its folds to hide in. As Dracula came nearer the ramparts with the young man still in his clutches, she tasted bile at the back of her throat. If he could kill that youth as indifferently as he would smash an insect, what might he do to her?

"It is the way of the hunter," said Dracula as he landed on the stones, letting his burden slump.

"Then he was damned? So young a boy?" she asked incredulously.

Dracula shrugged. "He is dead." He motioned to her to come closer. "Look. Is he so much different than a stag or a bear? You will not need the chalice much longer, girl. This is the fountain from where all life springs." He knelt and bent over the youngster. When he raised his head, there was blood on his mouth. Then he grabbed her hand and pulled her up next to him. "Do not look at him, girl. He is only fodder."

"He is a boy," she said, thinking of her brothers. "Achilles is much the same age."

"As are hundreds of others—thousands," Dracula said.

"I can't," she whispered.

"Communion wine is blood, so the popes tell you," said Dracula. "You have tasted it for yourself. Is it less repulsive for being in a golden cup?"

Kelene shook her head repeatedly.

He laughed, and it was not a congenial sound. "Christians are sustained by blood. They are not the only ones."

Shaking her head, Kelene tried to move away from him, but his grip was unbreakable. "You are not—" She did not know what she intended to say next; his shout silenced her before she could find out.

"Who are you to judge me? I have guided you and protected you since you were a child. You are my creature, and you will be like me!" He thrust her away.

She fell back, pain bludgeoning her senses as she struck the stones. Cringing, she drew herself into a protective ball, the pale silk a fragile cocoon around her, and did her best not to listen while Dracula finished his meal.

Finally Dracula rose and tossed the husk of the youngster over the battlements as if he were nothing more than a sack of grain. Then he turned around and addressed Kelene. "Be thankful for that boy, girl. If I were desperate, you would be in his place. Do not forget that." With that he bent down and brought her to her feet.

She was still with terror as he covered her mouth with his.

Kelene's head ached from lack of sleep and the unspeakable fragments of her dream that lingered into the morning; the taste of passion and metal remained on her tongue. When she rose not long after dawn, she had discovered smears of blood on the backs of her hands where she had tried to wipe Dracula's kisses away. There was a bruise on her thigh the size of a saddlepad and more on her arms.

As she dressed she had to accept at last that her dream was no dream at all. She had been summoned to Dracula's side and had watched him on the battlements. His flight and the youngster had all been real.

But those who fed on the living were pale and weak, wraiths, or so she had heard in the whispered tales in the marketplace. Dracula was none of those things. He had been her angel and now he was her master. What wraith could do that? These troubling ruminations were interrupted by the arrival of a servant with breakfast.

"Wait," she said, deliberately doing what she had been forbidden to do. "I have to ask you some questions."

The servant shook his head and made a gesture showing that he did not understand. He began to back out of the room.

"I need you to tell me about this place," Kelene persisted.

Again the servant gestured, ducked his head and went for the door, bowing as he let himself out.

It was tempting to refuse to eat, to smash the dishes and leave the food for the rats. But that impulse passed quickly as she recalled what Dracula had said to her the night before. Her life and her death were utterly in his hands. "Well," she said to the walls, "then I must shape myself to his wishes. For now." With that, she took the tray and began to eat, slowly and methodically.

An hour or so later, when she was summoned with gestures by two of Dracula's men to the marshaling court, she saw a pitiful figure huddled by the entrance to the keep. Kelene stopped and looked down at the whimpering servant. Shocked, she leaned over to see what had happened to him. Had Dracula truly punished this unfortunate for her defiance? She noticed there was blood on his chin, and she started to look away.

The servant made a garbled sound and grabbed the edge of her fan-shaped sleeve, forcing her to look back at him.

He rose on his knees, thrusting his face up to hers so she could see clearly: his tongue had been cut out.

Kelene gave a cry of horror and tried to pull away.

The servant spat blood on her, then released her sleeve in revulsion.

In the next moment, Dracula's men guided her past the coffin on the wagon to her own carriage. This morning Kelene did not look for her Dragon Prince among his men; before the door was shut on her, she gave a long, meaningful stare to the coffin.

*   *   *

Their next stop, reached well into the night, was a ruin. No guards opened the portcullis for their arrival; the arch gaped like a toothless mouth and the walls were breached in a dozen places. The keep was little more than a gigantic heap of stones, the doors long since rotted, the floors gone, the chimneys fallen in. Only half a dozen actual rooms remained, and they had rough new planking to serve as doors. There was no furniture in any of them but what the soldiers supplied from the goods they carried.

When the soldier brought her supper, Kelene remained resolutely silent, the memory of the mutilated servant strong enough to keep her from speaking a single word. She ate without attention and drank her wine quickly for the numbness it would impart.

When Dracula came to the inhospitable chamber Kelene had been given, he made no pretense of being a dream. He stood at the end of the makeshift cot, his cloak and armor discarded in favor of a long black Italian lucco with ermine lining the bag-sleeves. He looked down at her as if studying something that roused his curiosity.

"Did you have to do that to the servant?" she asked at last.

"You spoke to him. I told you there would be a price and that the servant would pay it." He reached out and touched her night rail.

"Did you hope I would beg you for mercy?" she challenged him, sitting up on her uncomfortable bed.

He laughed outright. "What is mercy to me?"

She watched him warily, doing her best to conceal her fear. "The man had done nothing wrong."

Dracula leaned over her. "He is nothing. You are my creature. You must learn to consider no one but me." He touched her neck, feeling the pulse.

"I will never be so callous."

"Never?" he taunted her. "At fourteen you are certain of this?"

"Yes," she declared, wishing she did not sound so foolish. "I am not going to allow you to turn me into—"

"Nosferatu," he finished for her.

"Whatever you are," she said, unable to say the other for the dread it filled her with. "I will resist you."

"How? I am in your visions, in your heart, in your flesh, in your soul. You are mine to do with as I will." He smiled at her. "One day, you will be glad of it."

"Not I," she declared. "I will never—" He suddenly drew her to him, confining her in his embrace while his mouth worked on hers. She nearly gagged.

"You will seek me out, girl," he told her as he bent to her throat. "You will not despise me."

Kelene felt pain and welcomed it. As long as she hurt, she had not lost all to him.

Fearing her lover would come
Fearing he would not come
Kept her from sleep . . .
—Greek lyric, 14th century

⊢ XVII ⊣

"There is a river we must get over, and I will have to be stronger than I am now. You will provide my strength," Dracula said to Kelene the following evening, not long after sunset; he had brought her into the armory of the ruined castle where a fire had been built in the old forge. All his soldiers were gone for the night, finding the best crossing of the Danube. "I trust you have not denied yourself food." He was dressed in the black lucco he had worn the night before, his lean, angular frame moving under the garment like sticks. He had nothing of the angel about him now: she wondered how she could have ever thought he had.

"No," she whispered. For a day in which she had done little, Kelene was exhausted. Her back ached and she felt as if her eyes had been boiled in her head. She did not want him to know how frightened she was.

"Excellent. Then I need not limit myself in what you can give me." He regarded her with a kind of indifference that made her want to scratch his face.

She shook her head. "You might as well take all my blood now. End it. You will have what you want, and so will I."

"So willing to die. As if dying made a difference." He cocked his head, his expression raptorlike. "Why would I want to do that, when I am so far from home, and you and I have finally—"

She spat at him. "You deceived me!"

"If anyone was deceived, it was not my doing," Dracula said. "You heard my call, and decided what you wanted to have calling you—you wanted an angel. Behold. I obliged you. The deception was as much yours as mine." He made a gesture of encouragement, showing her the kind of affection he might express to a dog or a horse. "You will understand, in

185

time. And you cannot tell me you were not pleased to see me when I came to claim you."

She stared down at her feet. "No."

"Your family was more gratified than you, but then, they had reason to be," Dracula went on, his voice smooth beyond cunning. He touched her golden hair. "You should have a chaplet of golden net, as the Italian ladies do. Then you would have a halo."

Kelene was not in the mood to be seduced. "What does that matter to you? I am your slave. Fine clothes make the prison less obvious, but—"

Dracula interrupted her. "What petulance. And for so little cause." He strode about the old armory, pointing to rusted hauberks and pikes, to an ancient length of chain with a spiked ball still attached to it. "Look at this place, girl. Look at what it was." He touched a shield where the device had been, now unrecognizable. "The Crusaders went this way, coming from Germany bound for the Holy Land. They made this their fortress. It was reinforced to withstand the fiercest soldiers of the Prophet, when the Kings of Europe went to reclaim Jerusalem from them. They intended it would be here when their Savior returns. Yet it fell, and hundreds died trying to save it. You think your sacrifice is so much greater than theirs, because I have given you velvet to wear?"

"You lied to me," Kelene said, but without the conviction she wanted to summon.

"Because it was what you wanted," said Dracula. "You were too young at first to know what moved you. You took what I offered and made no effort to do anything more than gain the approval of your father."

"You have corrupted me." Guilt all but overwhelmed Kelene.

"No more than any other," said Dracula without a trace of amusement. "All humanity is corrupt, in time."

She folded her arms, glaring at him. "You do not care if all the world perishes, do you?"

His eyes fixed on hers. "On the contrary, girl. I care very much. If all the world perishes, I starve." He reached out and touched her. "Some game is better sport than other, and some—"

"Animals?" she suggested, chilled to the very depths of her soul.

"Stock," he corrected, "is more valued than the rest. Please me well and you will be one with me."

"Risen from the dead?" she challenged with all the scorn she could summon up. "You, of all creatures, will give me resurrection."

"I have said so," Dracula replied. "By the time you rise, you will love the hunt as I do; you must, if you are to live. If you force me to end your life, you will die as the rest of humanity dies—to lie in the earth, turning to dust and less than dust."

"Better than preying on the living," she said, shaking with fear.

"Do you really think so?" Dracula asked without heat. "That is youth and ignorance speaking. You will change your mind."

"And if I do not?" she shouted. "How will you live?"

His answer came slowly and heavily. "You do not suppose I have never called another—that no one but you has heard my call?"

Kelene went white. "How can you . . . You are worse than the Turks."

"And the Huns and the Byzantines, and all the rest of the barbarians from the east," said Dracula with satisfaction. "And I have held my land against them all, since my Dragon Legion was posted there on the order of Caesar himself." He looked about the room, seeing something Kelene could not. "I gloried in my post, at being a Dux, a leader, instead of the hostage I had been when I first went to Rome. I was their vassal no more."

Kelene had heard tales of Rome, and all of them seemed to be more fable than substance. There had been more than one Caesar, at least she thought there had been. She knew better than to show her reservations outwardly, so she said, "It was long ago."

"Yes," Dracula agreed. "Rome was Rome then, the mightiest empire in the world, not a lickspittle servant to the Church. Rome was no petty tyrant but an Emperor before whom all the world trembled. Caesar favored me, trusted me with the protection of my homeland. I took what he gave me—a chance to return to the place I was born, to keep it secure, with the might of my Roman allies and the Dragon Legion to support me. He depended upon me to maintain the eastern borders against all mauraders; I accepted the task with pride, and swore I would never surrender to my foes. I thought as you did then, that it was best to die in honor. I knew nothing, girl, nothing. Had it not been for the woman who seduced me, I would be dust with my legionaires, and my homeland lost for all time. But she sought me out, called to me as I called to you, and I became hers." His eyes grew distant. "Some said she was a goddess, and worshiped her. I discovered otherwise."

"She was a goddess as you are an angel," Kelene said. She wanted to show a brave front, and very nearly succeeded.

Dracula regarded her almost with approval. "Yes. I withstood her as long as I could, but I could not prevail, nor did I want to, in the end. Oh, I postured for her, as you are doing for me, and I swore I would not surrender to her while my blood sang in my veins for her. But eventually I learned her ways, and if it were in me to feel gratitude, I would be grateful to her."

The coldness of his voice made Kelene shrink with dejection. Until this moment she had assumed she would find a way to remind him of his lost humanity. Her head throbbed with misery and the air in each breath cut at her lungs like sharp wires. "Don't you ever want . . . to go back?"

His laughter was empty as that of idiots. "To what?"

Kelene recalled her family, and at the same instant, their abandonment all but overcame her; she had nothing to say to him, so she tried to pray instead.

"Why bother?" he demanded. "Nothing can hear you."

She stopped, staring at him. "But God—"

"If there was one, would I not have found it out by now? I tell you faith is for children and the fainthearted. There is only silence when we are done. How could there be more?" he asked, and leaned forward so that his face was less than a handsbreadth from hers. "Say your words to the darkness, if you must. But remember that when you have done it before, only I have heard you."

It was useless to scream: Kelene was already awake and no one would come to help her, nor would her scream frighten him away. Screams, prayers, rebukes meant nothing to him. She felt him hover over her, his nearness making her flesh thrill, though there was no warmth in him at all.

Dawn was approaching, and Dracula was getting ready to rest through the day. He made no attempt to conceal his hunger, or to present it well disguised, as he had done so often before. His touch had no hint of tenderness, only demand; he did not bother to be gentle. His teeth seemed sharper, as if the keenness of his appetite had manifested in his bite. There was no pretense of wooing, no persuasive seduction, and when he was through with her, she felt weak and shaken.

"Tomorrow night we cross the Danube," he said to her as he prepared to leave her on the straw-stuffed mattress he had allotted for her use. "You can sleep through it all, if you prefer. There is no reason for you to be awake."

She tried to say something, but could not summon the strength or the concentration to make the words. The beat of her heart tripped rapidly in her ears, sound without substance. Her vision shimmered, and for an instant she thought he was once again her angel. Then she blinked and the illusion was gone.

"Do not chide me, girl," Dracula said to her as he reached the makeshift door. "It is not your place to judge me."

"I am your slave," she muttered, bitterness filling her. "How could I judge you?"

If she intended to injure him, she failed. "Never forget that." He turned and left her alone.

A short while later, she heard the dawn chorus and a counterpoint of hoofbeats as the soldiers came back from their night of scouting. As the birdcalls grew louder, the silence of Dracula's men became more troublesome to Kelene. Wolves hunting made more noise than they. Why did they not speak as other men did? Why were no orders issued, at least, and no outbursts of profanity when something went awry? Even their horses did not neigh or whicker. She rose unsteadily, one hand on the wall while her senses pitched like a boat in a storm. When she was certain she could move without mishap, she went to the door and looked out, holding her night rail close around her, the thin fabric woefully inadequate against the morning's chill.

The soldiers gathered in front of the smithy, their mounts tethered for feeding. They had improvised a spit over the forge and turned a small boar over the coals: the odor of the crackling meat jolted Kelene with hunger and nausea. She did not think she could bear to watch them eat.

Behind the forge, as if on an altar, the dragon-ornamented coffin lay, closed, massive, and more compelling than any of the armed men who stood near it. The men treated it with deference as they readied their meal.

As the first, tenuous rays of pallid light touched the stones of the ruined fortress, the soldiers moved uneasily, and Lajos, who served as coachman as well as general factotum, began his daily inspection of the harness and tack. They were like dark spectres, haunting the wreckage of the building. The soldiers moved closer to the spit over the forge, as if the increasing light had spurred their craving for meat. Now that the world grew brighter, the thing on the spit looked less like a boar and more like a misshapen child; the skin was blackened and cracked.

Kelene feared she might faint, although she was unable to say why. An ill-defined languor weighted her. Her rapid pulse thrummed without strength and her body ached. Suddenly she wanted to run away, to put leagues of mountain track between her and her Dragon Prince. The forests were less terrifying than he. She strove to animate herself, to rise and vanish into the forest, but her urgings were in vain. If only she were not so weak. If only she had the courage to take her things and go. If only she had some sensible wooden clogs instead of the embroidered chiponei. That last realization struck her with such impact that she fell back against the door of her room as if from a physical blow.

To her shame, Kelene began to weep, soft, hopeless sobs that drained away her will, doing Dracula's work in a way he had been unable to. She found her way to her mattress and flung herself down on it, her fist in her mouth so that she would make no more sound than the soldiers around the forge.

Nothing she had clung to, nothing she had taken pride in had sustained her. Her faith had betrayed her, her visions had been a lie, her

Militant Angel was malign, her sacrifice had brought her no honor. "What is to become of me?" she asked of the morning; the brilliant sunshine mocked her.

Halfway through the afternoon, the soldiers prepared to leave. Throughout the rubble-filled courtyard they readied their horses for the long night ahead. Two of the silent men assisted Lajos in harnessing the wagon carrying the coffin, then hitched up the horses to Kelene's carriage. The only noise was from the creak of leather, the clink of harness, the growl of the wheels over the flagging, and the muffled clamor of hooves.

Kelene wanted to ignore it all, to let herself drift in half-sleep. She supposed she would be put into her carriage awake or asleep, and might have tested the idea had not dread of Dracula's rebuke to the men made her reconsider. So she dressed herself and allowed two of the soldiers to escort her to the carriage, bearing herself with as much dignity as she could muster. She had been offered a plate of cold meat as she settled back on the seat, but she could not bring herself to eat any of it; the recollection of the charred body turning over the fire was too strong. Swallowing hard against the bile in her throat, she shoved the plate away and shook her head violently.

The soldier offering the plate bowed slightly and closed the door, returning her to the twilight she so ardently sought. Kelene no longer objected to the leather curtains, for as much as they shut out the world around her, they made it possible for her to forget what had become of her. She paid no attention to the last preparations, preferring to think of her family, imagining how they had prospered since she had left. By now her father must be well again, she thought, and Pallas could choose her husband as she wished with the dowry she would bring. The consolation of these reflections was fleeting, but it made her waiting more bearable. A short while later they were off, leaving the ruined castle behind to the rooks and bats that had claimed it for their own.

Not long after sunset, the party halted; there was a flurry of activity at the wagon behind her carriage. Kelene heard the coffin being opened, and one of the soldiers dismounted, surrendering his Furioso to Dracula and mounting postilion on the onside lead of the wagon carrying the coffin. Only Dracula spoke, issuing terse orders as he rode to the van of his troops.

The road grew more treacherous; once they were delayed when a wagon wheel wedged into a rut so deeply that the soldiers had to lever it out. Kelene listened, hearing the groan of the tortured metal as the wagon lurched free.

"Move on!" Dracula ordered as they set out again.

At the darkest hour of the night they reached the Danube, at an unexpected ford in an elbow of the river. Two low bridges crossed the deepest part of the water, meeting at a small island in the middle of the flood. A causeway of pebbles led up to the bridges and away from them, making the approaches possible for wagons, carts, coaches, carriages, and livestock. The soldiers halted the carriage and wagon, which surprised Kelene.

The door of her carriage opened; Dracula loomed in the opening. He climbed from the saddle into the carriage and pulled the door closed again. "This is where you prove your worth."

She wanted to ask how, but he was on her before she could, worrying her throat as the carriage rolled forward onto the first of the bridges. Much as she wanted to rage at this use, she did not. He lay over her, his weight pinning her to the seat while he drank with voracious greed. Everything about him demanded her wholly; she was feeding not only his hunger, but something far vaster.

The crossing seemed endless to her while Dracula took what he desired. Only when the river was behind them did he release her, kissing her mouth and leaving her blood on her lips. She did not move.

"Running water is destructive to me," he confessed. It was more than he had conceded to her in some time, and had she not been so weak it would have startled her. "You saved me from it."

She heard this as if from far away, over the roar of the river. Blackness hovered at the edge of her vision, and she seemed only tenuously attached to her body. She was distantly aware that he expected her to respond, but she could not.

"You should have eaten," he told her as he reached to open the door. "You must maintain your strength. I do not want to lose you yet."

"It doesn't matter," she whispered.

"It does to me," he said, and swung from the carriage onto his horse.

Through the rest of the night she dozed, no longer paying any attention to the road or the speed of their travels, or the condition of the road. Whether the carriage rocked or ran smoothly meant nothing to her; had she been less torpid she would have been alarmed. When they stopped at first light, she did not notice where they were, or what the place was like. Somnambulistically she allowed herself to be moved from the carriage to a wood-paneled, low-beamed room where a fire blazed in the hearth. Someone undressed her and put on her night rail, and someone else brought a tray of food. Kelene sat staring into the distance, her face pale and expressionless, her body nothing more than a puppet.

*   *   *

She woke, certain she had been wrapped in nettles. Every part of her was in agony. When the church bell chimed again, she winced as if the peal had struck a blow. Her hands were shaking and she had to press her lips together to keep from whimpering. She blinked, trying to remember where she was, and how she had come there. Vaguely she called to mind the river crossing, and Dracula in her carriage. He had used her, she decided, but she could not remember how, or anything that had come after. Lassitude kept her still in spite of the pain. A patch of sunlight on the wall suggested it was near midday, and as she turned on her bed, she saw windows, their shutters thrown open to the day. Another chime made her cringe. She put her hands over her ears to stop the next toll from hurting her, but it was to no avail: the sound burned like a brand.

Some little time later the door opened, and a portly, middle-aged woman came in, a tray in her hands, and a tentative smile on her face. "Good day to you, my lady," she said in a dialect Kelene could barely understand; beyond her Kelene could just make out a corridor of glossy polished wood, with carving along the molding.

Kelene was about to answer, then remembered Dracula's admonition. She nodded and did her best to look pleased.

"You can talk to me, my lady. He has said you may. The Dragon Prince. Dracula." She ducked her head to show respect. "He said you would be glad of a little conversation."

Now that the offer had been made, Kelene could hardly keep from speaking. Tears stood in her eyes but she resolutely held them back. "Where am I?" she asked.

The woman chuckled nervously. "That is not easy to explain; this stronghold is so remote, and its purpose so—" she said as she came up to the bed, making a clicking sound with her tongue at her own lack of information. She tried again. "This is not a place many know about." She held out the tray. "I was told I must watch you eat."

Kelene nodded, not knowing how much she ought to tell the woman. As she sat up in bed her skin seemed to be rasped. She sat very still until the worst of the agony passed, then she glanced at the tray. "What is it?"

"Meat and wine and cheese and bread and baked eggs," said the woman, eager to please Kelene. "The bread was made this morning."

In the past, this information would have triggered Kelene's hunger, but not now. She did her best to assume a degree of enthusiasm, but it was false, and she was ashamed of her deception. "I ought to eat," she said dutifully, vaguely surprised when she could not summon up any vestige of appetite.

"The food is good. The cook here is skilled," said the woman, fussing with the edge of her apron.

What should she say? Kelene wondered. The smell from the plates almost made her sick, but if she refused to eat, Dracula might punish her again. She broke off a piece of the bread and stuffed it in her mouth. She almost gagged.

The woman noticed Kelene's distress and moved quickly to hand her the flagon of wine. "If you will drink, it will go down easier. The wine is good. Sweet." She stood next to Kelene while she got down two sips of wine. "There, you see? It is pleasing, isn't it? The taste will make you hungry." There was a note of desperation in her voice, as if she were begging Kelene to agree.

Nodding, Kelene took another bite of bread. It lacked savor, but it no longer felt like matted straw in her mouth. She used more of the strong red wine to wash it down, then looked at the slab of meat. "What is it?"

"A roast," said the woman, looking away from Kelene toward the door.

The image of the thing on the spit returned and Kelene could not bring herself to slice off any of the roast on her plate. She started to shove it away; the woman flung up her hands.

"Oh, no. You mustn't. You are to eat every bite. If you do not—" She broke off abruptly.

"But I can't," Kelene protested. "I . . . I will vomit if I try." Her throat tightened. "Do not ask me."

"You must eat, eat all of it," she said, her voice dropping to a horrified whisper. "If you do not—"

"What will he do to you?" asked Kelene with sudden fatalism. She held up her hand as the woman began to shake her head. "No. Don't tell me." She did her best to imagine a meal she wanted—a breakfast of yoghurt, figs and cheese, with her mother fussing over them all. "I will eat this somehow." Staring down at the slices of cold, pinkish-brown meat, she was almost overwhelmed with dizziness. What about the food revolted her so? Or was it not the food, but what Dracula had done that left her so repelled by appetite? What had become of her, that she had let herself fall so far?

She picked up the knife and cut a sliver of the meat and put it in her mouth, thinking it would be disgusting. Instead, she was amazed at how savory it was. It was tender, and as she chewed, it became more delicious. She cut another slice and ate it eagerly.

The woman, watching her, sighed with relief. "There. You eat your food, and when you are done, I will show you what your duties will be while you remain here."

"Are we at his castle, then?" Kelene asked, surprised.

"No. But there is fighting not far away, and this party is to remain here until it is over." She rubbed her hands together.

"You mean they will aid the—" Kelene began, remembering how passionately Dracula had spoken of defending his homeland.

"No," said the woman. "I don't think so," she amended. "If they are, nothing has been said of it. And it may well be too late, in any case. Word came yesterday of a battle fourteen leagues from here. By the time they could reach it, the battle would be finished."

Kelene was shocked. "But surely—" she said, cutting another slice of the meat.

"He does not want to lose what few men he has to a battle that is already decided," said the woman decisively, but with the automatic assurance of one repeating instructions.

This appalled Kelene, who had not thought Dracula lacking in courage. "But what . . . suppose the victors were the enemy? What if they came here?"

"We are protected," said the woman, with confidence that made Kelene suspicious.

"How do you mean that?" she asked.

"There are . . . robbers in the forest. They guard this place, and our mistress does not summon the nobles to fight them off. She would rather remain in possession of her land than have it guarded by ambitious and rapacious nobles."

"Then why does she receive Dracula?" Kelene inquired, another slice of the delectable meat in her mouth.

"Dracula shares her opinion of the nobles in this region, and this is not his land." She folded her arms. "And there has long been an alliance between their two Houses."

When Kelene took the last slice of the meat, she was sorry there was no more. Perhaps she would be served it again before they left this place; she did not think it would be wise to ask for it, for it might be denied to remind her of her place. Turning her attention to the baked eggs, she discovered they lacked flavor after the meat, but she ate them anyway, washing them down with wine.

"I will return shortly," said the woman. "And then I will show you your duties for today."

"Duties?" Kelene repeated.

"Of course," said the woman with a show of impatience. "You are his slave, are you not? Did you think he would not expect some service of you?"

Kelene was about to point out that she had already performed her service to her Dragon Prince when he had drunk her blood, but she stopped herself. "I thought that, as we are traveling, I would not be assigned any yet." It was a lame explanation, and she knew it did not impress the woman.

"Then more fool you," said the woman.

"Yes; more fool I," Kelene said, and continued her breakfast.

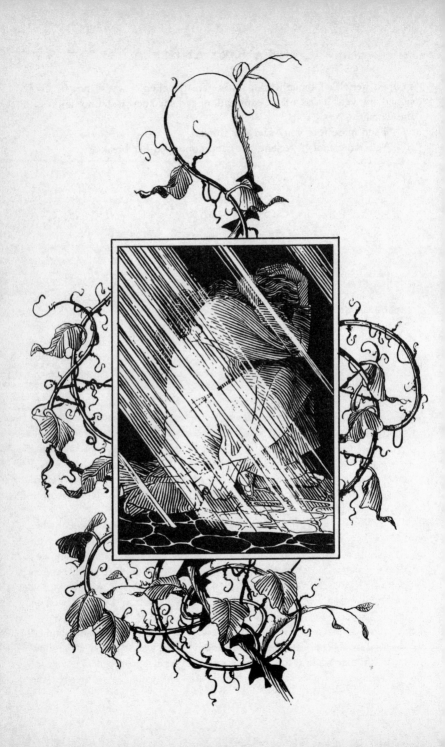

You bring me such grief
I fear my heart will break
Out of my breast . . .
—Greek lament, 12th century

⊢ XVIII ⊣

There were saddle pads—all of them worn and smelling of horses' sweat—
and blanket rolls to be packed in large chests for Dracula's soldiers. Kelene
could not guess why she had been ordered to do this, but she knew she
would not receive any explanation if she asked for one. The chests were
stacked in the tack room, and no one helped her wrestle them into place
for packing. The task was simple enough, but it took most of the afternoon
and left her worn out. The incongruity of doing this labor while dressed
in velvet splendor at first amused Kelene, but as her muscles began to
ache and stiffen, she no longer concerned herself with matters of style,
but concentrated on her chores, which quickly became drudgery. Tendrils
of golden hair escaped from the knot on the crown of her head, and she
felt sweat matting her camisa to her back. Within an hour she stepped
out of her chiponei, preferring the discomfort of bare feet to the hazard
of standing on elevated shoes. Never had she felt so isolated, not even
on the slave platform.

When she was called to supper by the woman who had brought her
breakfast, Kelene was more than ready to stop her work; she picked up
her chiponei and carried them rather than put them on again. "I am surprised," she said to the woman, enjoying the opportunity to talk to someone other than Dracula himself, "that Dracula should have so much stored
here. He must visit this place often." She paused so that the woman
could answer.

The woman's face revealed nothing. "He comes from time to time,"
she said as she indicated the long, poorly lit hallway. "If you will follow
me?" Without waiting for any response, she went out into it.

Kelene kept pace with her, hoping that she would say more, but the

woman remained silent. Kelene coughed, then said, "Will we leave here
tomorrow, do you know?"

"No; why would he tell me his plans?" the woman said, then pointed
to a thick oaken door reinforced with wide bands of black iron. "That is
where Dracula lies, in a place of honor. At sundown he will emerge again,
and you must be prepared to answer his summons. He is your master."

The prospect of another night being drained of blood to sustain Dracula made Kelene shudder. She lowered her head. "Where are we going?
Where are you taking me?" It was a safe question, and Kelene was grateful
to hear a voice other than her own, or Dracula's.

"There is a room set aside for Dracula's use, when he is not . . .
resting," said the woman in a tone that did not encourage further
conversation.

"Am I to wait there?"

"Until Dracula issues you other orders, you are to remain where you
are told to remain." The woman opened a carved door that groaned on
its massive hinges. "Your food will be brought to you directly. Eat it."
With that, she gave Kelene a gentle shove and closed the door behind her.

The room was not large, but its luxury was indisputable: four Ottoman
divans, each with its own hassock and all covered in Antioch silk, were
placed around a low table of brass and rosewood. That the silk was dusty
and the brass tarnished did little to distract from the astonishment Kelene
felt as she gazed about this gorgeous chamber. Four velvet banners hung
from the beams overhead, creating a room within a room. The banners
blocked out direct light from the windows behind them, making the fading
day into a kind of opulent dusk. The hearth was laid and the fire recently
lit; it was still taking hold of the logs. A cloying smell of decayed flowers
cut through the odor of wood smoke and made Kelene think of burials:
she shut the thought away as quickly as possible. She stepped onto a
magnificent carpet of Persian design, made of silken fibers so dense they
felt like fur under her feet. She wondered why Dracula would keep such
a room. "For seducing foolish girls, like you, Kelene," she said aloud.
Choosing the least dusty of the divans, she sank down on it and put her
feet up on the hassock before it. Much as she did not want to be caught
up in the place, she was unable to resist it entirely.

She was tempted to recline, to let the soreness of her body be eased
by the soft embrace of the silk, but she was afraid Dracula would be
displeased with her—he was so easily angered, and so capriciously—so
she remained sitting upright, her hands folded in her lap as she did her
best not to doze while she waited for what would come next. The room
darkened and was soon lit only by the glow of the fire.

Two servants came into the room with tall braziers, which they stood in front of the velvet banners and lit with brands from the fireplace. Incense as well as charcoal was ignited, adding its scent to the air—a pleasant, not-quite-sweet fragrance that became more pungent as it burned. The servants ignored her, departing as silently as they came. In spite of this, Kelene felt her spirits begin to lift, and not even a reminder of Dracula's presence could dash them entirely. She no longer felt as worn out as she had when she entered the room. The aromatic smoke seemed to have worked on her magically, and she smiled in appreciation; if incense had been this sweet in church, she might never have been tempted to answer the call of her angel. Stretching, she wiggled her toes and watched the door for what would happen next. All urgency left her as she waited.

A bit later—it was difficult to reckon time—another servant arrived bearing a tray with four covered dishes and a large chalice set on it. Without comment he put the tray on the table in front of Kelene, then left her alone. For all his notice of her, the room might have been empty.

Kelene lifted the lids of the plates one by one and was disappointed not to find any of the marvelous meat she had enjoyed that morning. But there were sausages with small dumplings in a thick gravy, a bowl of dried fruit in honey, a dark round loaf stuffed with spiced pork and onions, and a small platter of eels baked with butter and pine nuts. She savored it all, aware that only garlic was missing.

The chalice was nearly full to the brim with dark red Hungarian wine. In such a fine room, this lavish repast did not seem out of place, and Kelene was hungry enough to devour it all. She used the knife on the tray to spear one of the sausages—it was about the size of a finger, dark brown, and smelling of coriander—and popped it into her mouth. She had never relished food more.

The wine was heavy, heavier than any she had been given before, and so dark that it looked almost black against the gold of the chalice. Its sapidity filled all of her mouth and left an aftertaste of hazelnuts and something Kelene did not know. Had the incense influenced the flavor of the wine? Her scenes fused and melded. She alternated between the eels and stuffed bread, sipping at the wine to wash it down. By the time she began on the fruit-and-honey, her flesh tingled and she was slightly giddy.

Dracula did not want her asleep—she was convinced he did not. More than that, she did not want him to surprise her awake. She thought he might not like her so merry, either, but the wine had already done its work, and she could not be too concerned about it. Had the incense contributed to her strange intoxication? The odor was growing stronger, musty and grassy at once. She remembered that some popes would use incense to make their prayers more powerful. If their incense was like this, she thought in a distant way, it was no surprise that they might believe so. There was a sound in her head that was not quite music, fascinating, like chanting heard at a distance, so that the words were lost and only the cyclic melody remained, a helix of sound spiraling within her.

It was almost like her dreams had been, when he came to her at last. He was magnificent in black garments that shone like armor, as iridescent as an insect's wing. His cloak fell behind him, and once again she thought he flew. He came to her side, attentive and suitorlike, going on his knee and taking her hand to kiss before he spoke her name; she could not remember if he had ever used it before. This perturbed her in a far-off way, like seeing storm clouds on the horizon of a sunny day.

"You have done well today, girl," Dracula said, his voice as warm as she had ever heard it. "You are as excellent as I knew you would be. I am satisfied."

"Because I packed saddle pads and blankets? Anyone could have done it. There is no skill in the work." She wanted to silence herself for giving him this excuse to take back his praise—if praise it was.

"For doing as you were bid without cavil or question," he said, leaning toward her. "I know this is trying for you. You are not accustomed with my ways. It is difficult for me to remember that you are still very young, and not a soldier. You must forgive me for my brusqueness." His finger brushed her neck. "I have other clothes for you. They will be given to you in the morning."

She did not know if she ought to thank him. There was so much hidden meaning in everything he said. He might even be lying. She managed a few polite phrases, all the while wishing she did not yearn for him to touch her again. It was the wine, she thought, that made her so weak, the wine and being alone. The incense sapped her will. She could not speak; when she tried all that escaped her was a sigh.

"You are beautiful tonight," he said softly. "You should always be surrounded by things as beautiful as you."

The tribute took her aback. She stared at him. "What?"

He favored her with an amused half-smile; she was reminded of wolves. "You are turning into a very lovely woman, girl. It is a pity that the demands of this journey have not let me tell you this before now. In time I will remedy my neglect." He loosened her hair from the knot on her head and let it cascade through his fingers. "Better than all the gold I paid for you."

This was what Kelene had longed to hear, and she drank it in like rain on parched ground. "I want only to please you," she said, trusting he would want her to offer some part of herself in return for his admiration.

"And you do, girl, you do." He moved nearer still, blocking out the light from the hearth and holding out his cloak to wrap her in it.

"You are . . ." What should she say? Good? Kind? Neither was true, and she could not lie to him, for fear of what he would do. "Everything," she said.

"See that you remember it," he told her as he traced the shape of her breasts through the velvet of her gamurra, as if delineating territory.

"Oh, yes," she breathed, but whether to pledge her word or to encourage him in his explorations, even she did not know.

His eyes were hot as sparks in the night, and he turned them on her with such intensity that she was mildly startled that her skin was not burned by his gaze. "Kelene, you hold me in your power," he murmured to her, moving onto the divan beside her. "If you knew how much, you would be very dangerous to me." He tangled his hand in her hair and kissed the nape of her neck.

"Then why . . ." she began, asking herself why he would admit so much to her.

"Slave and master are bound together," he whispered, taking her face in his big, lean hands and turning her to him. He took his time about kissing her, parting her lips and tasting her mouth, holding her inexorably, not releasing her until she gasped and struck at his shoulder.

"I couldn't breathe," she said unsteadily as he broke his grip on her at last. "I . . ."

His face darkened and he moved back from her abruptly. "Never deny me, girl. Never."

She looked directly at him, and all hope fled. "I will not." How could she prove to him she had not meant to refuse him? She took his hand and put it over her small breast again. "They will grow bigger when I am older."

"Perhaps," he said, his tone still testy.

"But they will," she said, desperation making her protest shrill. "In a year, they will be bigger. And once I bear a child—" She hated the tears that stood in her eyes.

He removed his hand deliberately and paced away from her, his cloak hiding him from her in its ebon folds, creating its own shadow to conceal him. He remained with his back to her for a short while, and Kelene felt panic rising in her chest, making her ribs feel too tight. When he turned to her again his features were forbidding; he came toward her, splendid and ominous. "You work me well, for a girl so young—" He stopped in front of her, like a piece of a storm. "You have softened me, girl. You have made me forget why I bought you."

Had it been only moments ago that he had spoken to her so kindly? Had he touched her with more desire than hunger? Had she felt something aroused within her that promised more than her capitulation to his need?

She huddled on the divan, trying to identify the dreadful thing she had done. "I didn't mean to strike you. I had no air. I could not breathe. I had to—"

Dracula remained poised over her, his face set in imposing lines, his hands concealed in his cloak. "Do you think to play with me, girl? I am not some lovesick village lout, to fawn and flatter you. I am your master. You are my devoted slave, or you should be. I am your master in life and in death. I have been your master since you heard my call, and I will be your master when the world is gone and only we remain."

Kelene drew her knees up to her chin and hugged her legs to her chest. She rocked back and forth, back and forth, as if seeking to comfort herself with this small gesture. "What have I done?" she wailed to the air.

"Learn to obey me, girl, and you will not have cause to weep," he said, less heatedly than before. He trod across the gorgeous carpet to the hearth, saying to himself, "This will end. This will end," as he reached the polished stones.

Kelene held onto her legs more tightly and wished she could vanish utterly. She stared up at the ceiling, then shut her eyes, squinching them closed to blot out the fine room.

Dracula stood by the mantel for a short time, paying no attention to Kelene as he watched the flames devour the logs. When he turned back to her, a little of his graciousnesss had returned. "I should not have snapped at you."

Huddled on the divan, Kelene barely heard him. "I will do what you want," she told him dully.

"Most assuredly you shall." He walked back to her side and touched her hair once again. The gesture was more laying a claim than a benediction. "You will give me all I require of you, and you will not stint." He reached down and took her jaw in his hand, angling her face up to him so he could look directly at her. "Open your eyes, girl."

She obeyed promptly, trying not to flinch as his fingers tightened and he bent down. Her arms shivered, making her legs tremble. "I'm sorry," she muttered, resenting his attention as much as she longed for it.

"Yes." He did not release her. "Stand up."

Kelene's trembling increased. If she had been able to, she would have prayed. "I don't think I can," she said in a fading voice.

"*Stand up!*" he repeated, his voice no louder than before.

Very reluctantly Kelene managed to totter to her feet, swaying as Dracula continued to hold her jaw. She did her best not to appear resistant, but after a while she said, "You're hurting me."

"Yes, I am; I intend to." He bent and kissed her on the mouth as deliberately as he might order men into battle.

This time Kelene did not try to break away from him. You want his affection too much, she told herself, desperately clinging to a shard of her self-respect even as she leaned against his uncompromising strength. The more you depend upon him, the more truly you become his slave. The warmth of his arms around her, the protection of his cloak, the very power of his presence, all urged her to release her will to his. It seemed so foolish to continue to hold out against him, when he would make her life so much more endurable if she did as he wished. "I'm not a child anymore," she murmured without the conviction she had wanted to hear in her voice, or the defiance.

"Nor are you yet a woman," said Dracula, his tone becoming indulgent. "You are mine: girl, child, woman, or anything else."

"What else is there?" she asked.

"In time you will learn." He began to caress her, with more efficiency than ardor. "You will know what it is to hunt in the night, and to make your prey your sport. You will learn what pleasures come with terror." His hands went around her and cupped her buttocks. "You will discover the gratification of seduction, and the triumph of salaciousness. If you contravene my will, I will destroy you." His hands tightened and she stifled a shriek. "With me, you will be satisfied. Against me you will come to ruin." His mouth was ruthless on hers. She wanted to return the full force of her confusion so he would not blame her for any imagined rebellion.

She reached up, putting her hands on his shoulders, clinging to him for as long as the kiss lasted. Only when he released her did she draw her hands away. The glow of the wine had faded. "Do we leave tomorrow?" she ventured to ask after he had not spoken or moved for some while.

"In the evening. Yes," he said, as if grudging her so much. "Once we depart this place we will not return."

"Never?" Kelene asked.

He did not answer her. As if on impulse he clapped twice as he went to fetch the chalice standing empty on the brass table. "You are not to question me, girl." He held the chalice out to the servants who answered his summons, saying, "Another, for my slave. You know which to serve."

The servants bowed and went out of the room only to return almost instantly with the golden chalice held out reverently; the second servant bowed as much to the chalice as to Dracula. Without a word Dracula took the chalice and offered it to Kelene. "Drink. Drink it all, girl."

At the first taste of the dark liquid, Kelene had to force herself to swallow. But with Dracula watching her, she drank it down; after the second sip, it became easier to drink. She gave the empty chalice to Dracula with a trace of bravado, wiping her mouth with the back of her hand.

Dracula bowed to her, not deeply, but with enough approval that she began to aspire to greater success with him.

Kelene wakened late in the morning, still in the luxurious chamber. The divan which had served as her bed had been covered with a bearskin rug which she had wrapped around her while she slept, muffling herself in the soft fur. She could remember almost nothing after she had drained the chalice of wine. She put her hand to her head, wondering what had roused her; all she could see was a brilliant sliver of sunshine that had struck the back of her hands.

She peered around the room and noticed that new clothing had been set out for her: a gonella in the Genoese style of dark damask silk, in a color between deep blue and dull purple. To go under it, a cotta of saffron-washed linen. These clothes, like her velvet gamurra, were out of fashion, but to her the finery was enchanting, currently in style or not. She decided she could bear with the constraints placed upon her so long as she was shown respect and dressed as if she were a grand lady, and not an olive merchant's daughter from a vanquished city. She rose and drew off her night rail—which she had no memory of donning—and went to find a ewer and a basin so she could wash her hands and face before putting on these fine new garments.

When she was dressed, Kelene began to wonder why she had been left alone for so long. Always before she had been given breakfast soon after waking, and now she was ready to leave the chamber, but no one had come. She might have been in a deserted building for all the attention she was paid. She began to pace, her bare feet an odd contrast to the opulent fabric of the gonella, though the carpet was a pleasure to walk on. What should she do? she wondered. What did Dracula expect her to do? If he had given her instructions, she could not remember them. She was about to step into the corridor when the door opened from the other side and the woman from the day before nodded to her.

"Food is coming," said the woman, regarding Kelene's new raiment with a swiftly appraising eye.

Kelene felt embarrassed by her own inactivity, and so said, "I would have come to fetch you, but I had no idea where—"

"No matter. You have slept long, which is what your master ordered you were to do," the woman said with total neutrality. "The soldiers are under orders to leave tonight. You will have duties to perform today."

"What duties are those?" Kelene asked, thinking that she had packed as many chests as were waiting the day before. There could not be more.

"First you must eat. You will need your strength." The woman opened the door again, and a servant brought in a tray, put it on the table, and left, the woman following after.

Her fare was simple, with more of the delicious meat. She consumed this first, and rapidly. When she was done with the whole she set the plates aside, feeling strangely ashamed for bolting down her meal. She made herself wait patiently for whatever would come next.

"There are some cushions that need stitching," said the woman without preamble when she returned to Kelene. "How well can you sew?"

"Well enough," said Kelene.

"Plain or fancy?" the woman asked with a trace of interest.

"Plain," said Kelene, unable to keep from feeling oddly chagrined at this admission. "I have woven linen and wool. I can weave patterns; limited ones." She looked at the woman. Nothing in the woman's expression changed.

"Do what you can," the woman told her, preparing to withdraw.

"But where are these . . . cushions you wish me to mend?" Kelene asked.

"They will be brought. You will have enough to do," said the woman, bobbing her head as an automatic courtesy. "I must not linger." And with that she departed.

Alone again in this magnificent but neglected chamber, Kelene battled against her forlorn conviction that she was going to continue in silence until Dracula returned, when she would be delighted to have someone— anyone—to talk to. It was clear to her that Dracula was planning to make her wholly reliant on him for all her society; eventually she feared she would accept his bargain, little as she liked it, for to do otherwise would leave her as alone as a prisoner in the deepest dungeon.

Her headache, which had been nothing more than a blunt discomfort behind the eyes, now flared in her skull, making her forehead and neck smart. It spread through her shoulders and down her back, gripping at her spine with peppery fingers. She fought off a twinge of nausea; as she sat down she felt the sunlight on her face once more. She winced, sliding away from its heat.

When the servants brought the cushions, they found Kelene sitting in the corner, far from the warm patch of illumination on the superb carpet, its luminous colors almost as brilliant as stained glass. Her hands were pressed to her forehead as if to keep her skull from breaking.

Wasted by passion and restlessness
My flesh is consumed with suffering
And I mourn the loss of my strength.
—Romanian ballad, 14th century

⊢ XIX ⊣

Dracula entered Kelene's carriage halfway through the night. He took his seat beside her, saying, "You are awake."

"I cannot sleep," Kelene admitted. "I don't know why." She glanced at Dracula, doing her best to keep from staring. "I slept long into the morning. I think that if the sunlight had not touched me I might have slept the day through."

"Well enough," said Dracula. In the dim light of the carriage, lit as it was by a single lanthorn, his visage was preternaturally delineated, his eyes bright under his stern brows, his mouth hard and expressive at once.

"Will we travel far tonight?" Kelene asked, as much to hear him talk as to gain any useful information.

"Six or seven leagues, if we are not impeded," said Dracula. "We may go further if you will slake me."

"I am your slave," she replied, preparing to lean back. She knew now beyond all question that her value to him was her blood, her vitality. She had nothing more to offer him that he wanted. His plans had come to fruition. He had done all that he needed to in order to draw her to him, for her blood, not her visions. So, she told herself, your fine clothes are only a bribe, a badge of confinement. There is no escape.

"You will enjoy this, girl. You will delight in everything we do together, now, and all times." He laid his hand possessively on her thigh, ignoring her sudden stiffness. "You think you cannot learn to desire that—"

"That you drink my blood? That is what you want me for, isn't it?" She interrupted him petulantly, trying to brazen out her resistance with a stubborn tilt of her jaw.

Dracula did not laugh, but there was amusement in what he said next:

"If all I needed was blood, why would I come so far or take so long to claim you? It is not so simple, girl. Blood is easily come by in this world, as you should know as well as I." He flexed his hand on her leg. "As if only you could end my thirst! There are girls aplenty in Transylvania, if blood were all I wanted. There is more. Much more." He gave her a little time to consider this. "I want a bride who is like *me*, Kelene."

Kelene stared at him in horror. "But I am not like you," she protested, pronoucing each word with great precision. "You are a monster . . . an unnatural thing . . . a . . . a—"

"Vorlak? Nosferatu? Vampire?" he suggested in mocking dismay. "What if I am one of the Un-Dead? In your heart of hearts, wouldn't you rather rise than rot?" He leaned back and pulled her toward him. "You also take delight in causing others to follow you, to serve your bidding, to obey you. I am not your father, girl, to be swept up in your visions for my glory and the envy of others. I am your master."

"It wasn't like that. I . . . I offered my visions for the protection of the family. I served our welfare, to save us all," she said, no longer certain it was true. "I told them what the angel revealed to me, for our—"

"Not all of it. I know what you told your family. You did not reveal everything." Dracula reminded her as he began to stroke her through her garments, tracing the lines of her body. "You lied, girl."

"No," she said, troubled by her memories. "No, I did not truly lie."

"And you see what has become of you?" he challenged, as his hands became more demanding. He reached for her face and brought her around to him. "Keep the promise you made to me so long ago."

"I did not promise—" she began, only to be silenced by his kisses, disturbing and evocative. "I made no promise," she insisted when she could speak again.

"Of course you did."

"You keep telling me this is so. Do you think to convince me by repetition?" She resorted to insolence as a last bastion against him.

Dracula's caress was almost lazy. "Perhaps not tonight, or tomorrow, or a month from now, but you will come to own what is yours. And when you do, you will be joyful." His kiss was not so commanding this time and she was almost disappointed.

"Do what you will, say what you will, I will never be what you want." She did not have the courage to thrust him away, but she did not lean against him, no matter how tempting it was to bend to his will.

"Listen to you," he said. "You will hold me at bay with words, and I will relinquish my claim to you because of your eloquence."

"How dare you laugh?" She felt color rising in her face.

"Because my amusement offends you. It is almost too easy to prod you to recalcitrance." He took her hands in his. "You would do better to amuse me than annoy me," he said to her, his manner somber.

"You've threatened me before, and I am still alive," she said.

He released her hands. "But you would be wise not to press my concern for you too far."

Kelene lifted her hand to cross herself, but could not. She stared at the single snout of flame lighting the interior of the carriage. "Do what you will, then."

"And risk taking too much? Do you think I cannot tell when you are weakened?" He got to his feet in the swaying carriage, unable to straighten up. "I will not see you again until tomorrow night. You will not speak to anyone, or they will suffer the consequences."

"But where are you going?" she asked as she saw the door swing open and one of Dracula's soldiers riding alongside, keeping Dracula's horse ready for him to mount.

"Hunting," said Dracula. He swung from the door to the saddle, then closed the door on Kelene before he spurred away into the night.

The place where they stopped for the day was an old stone building whose original purpose was lost to time. The building was one with the mountains, stone and lichen, remote and isolated. There was no roof left over most of the structure; shelter was found in the underground chambers—large, vaulted, low-ceilinged rooms with evidence of occasional occupants, not all of them human. Dracula assigned soldiers to one of the rooms and Kelene to another, taking care to have his coffin placed in the chamber between them.

They had not traveled more than six leagues that day, for the road was poor and the going was hard. The next days promised no better prospects. The only one who did not seem exhausted by their journey was Dracula himself. The soldiers barely bothered to make more than a minimal camp before collapsing.

Kelene discovered that she had nothing to sleep on but the chests she had packed. They made a hard, uncompromising bed, but once she had spread her cloak upon them she slept readily enough, her fatigue all but overwhelming her.

As she had not done in days, she dreamed: *She stood outside a church; the pope in all his vestments waited in the doorway. When she tried to go in, he blocked her way. The pope pointed to the graveyard where five new graves scarred the earth, the newness of them like welts from a whip. Kelene could not read and so the markings on the crosses meant nothing to her, though the sight of the graves filled her with foreboding. While she huddled near them the pope came up behind her, intoning. "Your Great-great-aunt Iocasta. Your brother Hector. Your brother Pericles. Your father Diogenes—"*

"No!" Kelene burst out. "There was money for medicine and the physician. He is alive!"

"He is dead," the pope went on in the same declamatory style. "He is as much your victim as the others, for he followed you blindly to his ruin."

"He is not," she protested. "I saved him."

"You led him to his death."

"No," she said, her voice faint and unbelieving.

"You have brought devastation to your family. They only prosper now that you are gone and can no longer lead them astray."

"Then the gold has done good."

"At a high price."

"The last grave?" she asked.

"You have made it for yourself. You will not be fit to enter a church again until you are to be readied for burial. Your soul is already beyond the reach of the angels."

Kelene shook her head repeatedly. "Oh, no. No, that isn't possible. I am not so lost to God that I will not find—"

"You have turned from God to that which is dead and yet lives. You have accepted the resurrection of the vampire, not that of God. So be it." The pope raised his hand and made the sign of the cross over her, but in reverse, removing grace from her soul.

Kelene's despairing wail was so loud that it wakened her. She stared about in dismay at the underground room, her dream still with her, coloring her vision. For a short while she thought that perhaps she was indeed in the grave. Then she put her hands to her face and wept.

As the room grew darker and colder, one of the soldiers brought her four hard, dry sausages, a slice of cheese, and a cup of wine. He said nothing and left hastily.

Kelene sat down to eat. She had to chew diligently, for the sausages were dense. The cheese was dry and had a penetrating odor. She had consumed the wine before she was half-finished with this spartan meal. If only she knew whom to ask for more. Assuming there was more to be had, she reminded herself. She thought about trying to find the soldiers, but she would have to speak to one of them, and that could mean terrible consequences. She tried to eat the dry food and could not easily swallow. Had she not been famished she might have abandoned her attempts, but her hunger drove her to continue chewing.

They were underway once more not long after sunset, Kelene having been urged into her carriage by the soldiers. She cringed at the thought of being alone in the dark again. After two cups of wine, she might well fall into a doze, and if she did, she might dream. The afternoon's visions had been enough—more than enough. She sat as upright as she could, pinching her arms to ward off the least sign of sleep. The wheels of the carriage rolled along the uneven road, jerking and lumbering as the horses struggled to keep pace with the mounted soldiers.

It was going to be unendurable, this night. Kelene knew Dracula would no longer indulge her as he had—that he expected her to surrender to him unconditionally. She was ready to defy him. But she was afraid he had been right: that she was in his thrall. What made her most alarmed was his belief that she was in some way like him. Nothing would be further from the truth than that! She felt her indignation grow and took comfort from it. How could she have ever thought him an angel?

"I am not such a fool anymore," Kelene said aloud to the interior of her carriage. "I will not be taken in again." She folded her arms as if to prove that she was able to keep from being swayed by the coach or any blandishments Dracula might offer her.

Sometime during the night her head drooped, and then her shoulders slumped. Finally she slid onto her side, half-lying on the seat. She felt the coach moving forward and the motion rocked her into gentle oblivion.

When she awoke, it was midmorning and the party had arrived near a gypsy camp. The cries of children roused Kelene, blending with the last tatters of her dreams. She sat up on the seat and opened the leather curtains enough to look out, hoping she would not earn Dracula's ire for so innocent a gesture.

The gypsies had four wagons gathered into a kind of horseshoe-shaped formation, the cooking fires and women inside, the men and the horses at the opening. They studiously avoided paying any attention to the soldiers and the others in Dracula's entourage, as if they wanted to banish his presence by ignoring it.

Gypsies had always frightened her, but now they were a welcome contrast to the soldiers. She tried to think of some way she might speak with the tribe, but remembered how insubordination was punished among Dracula's servants. So she sat still, listening, hoping to learn much more as she waited.

A short while later one of the soldiers brought her a plate of food: hard sausages, cheese, flat bread, and some peppery cabbage pickles. Kelene was hungry enough not to quibble about the lack of utensils. She lit into her meal with the determination of a badger, and was finished almost before she had tasted anything. Her mouth was dry and she longed for wine, or even water, to wash down the food she had bolted. She licked her lips, attempting to have the illusion of moisture if not the reality.

At nightfall she was offered a cup of brackish water and two more sausages before they got underway, leaving the gypsies in their camp wailing over the loss of one of their old women. Kelene was afraid she knew what had become of her, but would say nothing.

"I am thirsty, and I want to wash," said Kelene as Dracula climbed into her carriage that night.

"And so you shall; water for bathing will be provided soon. I will order my soldiers to give you a drink, later," he told her. "We will be stopping for a day and a night to rest the horses. You may have a bath and your clothes will be brushed." He regarded her in silence for a while. "You said nothing to the gypsies."

"I was afraid of what you might do to them," she said as directly as she could. "You said you would punish them for my error."

"You went thirsty because of it," he said bluntly.

"You would have punished them if I asked for water or wine," she repeated. "You did before."

"Of course," he agreed without apology. "What does that matter to you?"

Kelene shook her head. "I do not want to be responsible for any more suffering. I would suffer with them." She remembered the accusations of her dream-pope.

"That is foolish," Dracula said in the same manner as he would discuss their accommodations. "If you were like them, you might have cause to have qualms. But you are like *me*, and you have no reason to think them anything more than fodder."

She lifted her chin, unaware of how much her demeanor mirrored his own. "You are wrong. I won't become—"

"I am not wrong. As you will discover before many more days pass." He reached out and touched her face. "I know those who are mine and those who are not." His fingers were light on her skin.

"I am not yours," she said.

"Aren't you? You do not shrink from me. That is the first step." His hawklike features were clear in the faint lamplight, as if he had fires within. "You will soon learn that your satisfaction is more important than theirs."

"How can I?" she demanded. "You are the one who has no regard for them. I can still know compassion."

"When you are thirsty enough, you will find out otherwise," he said. Then he leaned forward again. "I am thirsty now."

Kelene no longer winced at his bluntness. She sighed and stared at the lamp. "I am your slave."

"And my sustenance," he added as he bent his head to her neck.

His mouth grazed her neck and then there was a sharp pain that was less distressing than it had been; the metallic scent was no longer horrific. Kelene closed her eyes and wished she did not have to listen to the sounds of his feeding. That has nothing to do with me, she told herself as the lapping turned to sucking. I am not part of this. It is not my blood he drinks. It is not my flesh he has torn. It is not my life he is consuming.

He wiped his lips with the back of his hand, leaving a red smear along his jaw. "I've bloodied your camisa."

"You will give me another," she said listlessly. It was more than she could do to speak; the effort was too great. Absently she touched the place where her neck was cut, and flinched at the impact of her own fingers.

"You should rest, girl. You are tired." She might have mistaken this order for kindness.

"When do we reach—" she began, fighting the urge to sleep.

"We will be there before sunrise. You will rest all day and through the night if it pleases you," Dracula offered. He bent over her again. "One of my men will bring you a waterskin. You will need it, I think."

"How generous of you," she said.

"You are weak. Water now and food later will restore you," he said, with as much regard as he would show his horse.

"And when I have drunk and eaten, you will come again?"

"Yes. But do not fear. I will not end your life until you are within the walls of my own castle, where you can be safe." He prepared to leave the carriage again.

"Safe? With you?"

"Better with me than any other," he said, then swung out into the night.

They arrived at a fortress sprawled along the shoulder of a mountain. The gates were massive, hatched with iron, and formidable. They opened with a protesting groan and shut with the absolute finality of the coffin. Inside there was a marshaling court where soldiers practiced passages of arms and drilled against attack. Squires kept the soldiers supplied with weapons, and armed those readying for practice. Beyond this lay a second wall, less imposing, that enclosed a small jewel of a palace.

Kelene was half-awake as she was carried into this fine building, blinking at all she saw. It was difficult for her to believe she was not dreaming. Of all the places they had stopped, this one seemed the least likely in many ways, for it showed no signs of war or pillage, no scars of neglect or misuse. Its stones were red granite, those inside as polished as marble, with torches and lamps in such profusion that the palace shone like a precious stone. There were many windows glazed with expensive Venetian glass, as shiny as if they were new. Servants in dun-colored livery hurried to obey the sharp commands Dracula issued as the sky bleached with the dawn.

Her chamber was at the back of the palace, a high-beamed room that overlooked the kitchen garden. Even at this time of year, a faint odor of growing things rose on the morning air, spiking Kelene's appetite.

The bed was high and curtained, almost a second chamber within itself. The hangings were well made, embroidered linen from Austria. She looked at the bed as she stepped out of her clothes and climbed into it, too exhausted to miss the bath she had hoped to have. Her bloodstained camisa served as her night rail as she lifted the blankets. As she laid her head on the pillows, sleep overwhelmed her.

She awakened in darkness, achy and disoriented. The curtains had been pulled back so that she was not completely enclosed. She yawned and struggled to recall their arrival here, but could not separate her memories from the dreams that had followed. She sat up, her head pounding and her vision shimmering.

Someone had taken her clothes and put new ones in their place. She noticed the fine damask silk laid over the trunk opposite the hearth. Wasn't there something about blood on her camisa? Her recollection was fuzzy, but she was almost certain that garment was stained. She fingered her neck and found the punctures there—still sensitive but no longer feeling raw. She had not imagined it, then. She got to her feet with care, clinging to the hangings until she was confident she could walk without staggering. The torches in the hearth sconces blazed, making the room glow. There were two chairs, both upholstered, flanking the fireplace. She aimed for the nearer of them.

As she fell against the chair, she heard a noise at the door, and thought that once again a servant was bringing her food and once again she would be reminded of how utterly she was in Dracula's hands.

The person who came through the door was a soft-fleshed man of mountainous build and indeterminate age, with eyes like raisins in his wide, pleasant face. He wore the same dun-colored livery as the rest of the servants, but there was a turban on his head, and soft Turkish boots on his feet. When he saw Kelene, he bowed to her, saying in broken Greek, "I am Hamid, Select One. I am to take you to the bath." His voice was high, powerful and melodic.

Kelene had not expected to find a eunuch in this part of the world, away from the Turkish-held regions. She looked around for something to cover herself with—it was one thing for a eunuch to see her in nothing but her camisa, but she knew it was wrong for anyone else to. When nothing caught her eye, she asked Hamid, "What shall I wear?"

"Ah, allow this servant of you and the great ones to offer you this." He held out a long, loose robe made of heavy cotton. "It is modest enough for a Christian woman." He bowed again to show he meant no disrespect.

It was not easy to stand upright without holding onto the chair, but Kelene managed it as Hamid helped her don the robe over her camisa. A vague pain was forming behind her eyes and she thought that perhaps Dracula had fed more deeply than he had intended the night before. She could not bring herself to touch Hamid, not even to steady herself as she attempted to walk. After four steps, her knees buckled. She dropped in a tangle of her own limbs. There were bright spots spangling her vision as she strove to sit up. "I will be myself in a moment," she said to Hamid, who hovered over her like an enormous cloud.

"I will bear you, Select One," he said as he scooped her into his arms. "The bath is behind the garden. You will not want to walk so far."

Her lightheadedness began to fade as Hamid took her through the well-lit corridors, down wide staircases to the garden she had glimpsed from her room when they first arrived. Once Kelene caught sight of three of Dracula's soldiers, but other than that, she might have persuaded herself she had been abandoned.

The bath, when they reached it, was polished granite and wood, the main chamber dim and steamy. Hamid set Kelene on her feet, saying as he did, "I will attend you, Select One."

At another time Kelene might have been shocked. Now she nodded. "As you wish."

"The camisa is ruined," Hamid said as he helped her out of it. He sounded mildly disappointed. "The blood will not come out."

Kelene shrugged. "It doesn't matter."

Hamid shook his head as he tore the camisa in half. "No one should wear it after you," he explained as he indicated the shallow declivity in the granite floor filled with steaming water. "If you will sit there, I will wash you. Then you will lie on the bench and I will oil your skin."

"Like a goose for the roasting," said Kelene with a trace of a smile, and realized with a shock how long it had been since she had smiled. She was too worn out to question what Hamid said. As she stepped into the bath the hot water rose to her knees, uncomfortable for an instant, then intensely pleasureable; Kelene stretched out, the water embracing her. The sting on her neck as it lapped the bites there was fleeting.

When Hamid began to wash her with rough, soapy cloths, she felt like clay being molded by a master potter. Hamid then washed her hair with sandalwood-scented foaming oil. "The Select One wears a crown of gold," he murmured as he rinsed her hair.

Roused from her opulent torpor, Kelene remembered to ask something that had been bothering her. "Hamid? What place is this?"

"This?" His laughter was delighted as a child's. "This is the Palace of the Assassins."

Footsore and weary, I long
For the sight of my father's land . . .
—Moravian lament, 16th century

⊢ XX ⊣

Hamid brought Kelene her meal, saying, "You are to eat every bite. It is your lord who bids you do this." He put the tray down atop one of the chests in her chamber, then dragged a chair toward it. "This will do. You will eat, and then you will sleep. Tomorrow you will do the same again."

"Tomorrow?" Kelene asked in some surprise. "Aren't we leaving tomorrow?" She had dressed in the fine new clothes that had been provided for her; the new camisa had a suggestion of a ruff that almost covered the wounds on her neck.

"No, no. It is not what your lord said before he went hunting. You will rest tonight and tomorrow, and tomorrow night he will hunt again. The day after you will go." His smile was so automatic that it had no meaning. "There has been fighting east of here. Your lord is going to rearm his men while he can."

"Oh," said Kelene, finding the prospect of battle daunting. "I don't suppose there will be any real fighting . . . ?"

"Who can say?" answered Hamid, pointing out a plate of savory, dark gravy with collops of meat in it. "I am told you favor this."

She had tasted it, and relished the texture and flavor of the meat. "Yes. I do."

"Strange," said Hamid, pouring wine into her goblet.

"Why?" Kelene inquired as she drank the wine greedily. She attributed the odd sensation of buzzing at the base of her skull to the wine.

"Oh, it is not a dish most women like," said Hamid with elaborate nonchalance.

"How do you mean that?" she pursued, taking another mouthful.

"It is not what . . . suits the taste for women." He bowed. "I cannot tell you more."

"Cannot or will not?" she asked, more interested in her meal now than in what Hamid said. How odd it was, she thought as she ate, that the world could reduce itself to so few things. All her life was now defined by Dracula, travel, and nourishment. All the rest was becoming evanescent as morning mists. Her family—and she did her best to miss them—might have been in the deepest sea. Those enjoyments she had known had vanished, leaving her with this rigorously proscribed existence—in her way as cloistered as a nun.

"Will the Select One drink more wine?" Hamid inquired as he held up the amphora.

"Not yet. I would like some water." It was too easy to drink, she thought. By the time she went to bed, she would be fuddled if she continued as she had begun. "I'll have more wine later." She finished the meat and went on to the cabbage cooked in milk with pine nuts. "You said Dracula is hunting?"

"Yes," Hamid told her. "He and two others."

She looked a bit surprised. "Then the rest of the men are—"

"Here. Yes, Select One. They, too, are resting from their travels." He uncovered a basket of flat breads which he put near her plate. "Do not deny your hunger, Select One."

Kelene nodded in an absent way. "The men are resting?" She had to stifle a yawn, which she decided was absurd. How could she be sleepy? She had slept the day away, and now it was not far advanced into the night and she was already wanting to go to bed once more. She touched the wounds on her neck; they were hot under her fingers.

"Some of them," said Hamid, filling her goblet with wine once more.

"And some are on guard, while Dracula is hunting," she said, relieved to know she was still protected, at the same time chiding herself for relying in any way on Dracula to keep her safe.

"They have been given ale this evening. They will be drunk tonight, most of them," said Hamid patiently.

Kelene could not imagine Dracula's soldiers as anything other than silent and obedient, but she said, "They must be glad of the treat. When I was traveling with my family, we were always glad of—" She swallowed hard against the tightness in her throat.

"Soldiers are not like that, Select One," said Hamid, apparently unaware of her sudden pang of loneliness. "They are men whose work is death, and when they celebrate, they are as brutal as they are in battle."

Kelene tried to banish the misery that threatened to overcome her. She took a deep draught of the wine and forced herself to smile. "They are Dracula's men," she said, more to herself than Hamid. "They will surely obey him."

"He is gone hunting." Hamid bowed and removed the lid from a bowl of candied flowers. He put his hand to his waist as if to make his size important. "I will keep watch over your door tonight. Those men can roister as they like, you will have nothing to fear, Select One."

The title, which had pleased Kelene at first, now began to grate on her; she missed hearing her name. Recalling her family had made her more forlorn than she thought it would. "My name," she said, "is Kelene. If I call you Hamid, you will call me—"

"You are the Select One," Hamid interrupted her. "It would be more dangerous than it is worth for me to call you anything else." His features were suddenly pasty.

"But it is my name," she said, trying to sound persuasive. "We are alone here. Why should you not call me Kelene while we are alone?"

"I cannot," Hamid muttered.

"But why? Why can you not use my name? Why is it so unthinkable?"

"Your lord has made you his Select One, and I cannot—" He stopped, confused and distressed.

Kelene had an unwelcome thought. "Have there been other Select Ones?" she asked suspiciously. "Have there?"

"Not recently," said Hamid quietly. "I was very young when he brought the last one. I was told there had been others, but I never saw them." He coughed out of embarrassment. "I should say nothing of this. It is for your lord to tell you the whole of it."

"If he will," said Kelene. "He tells me very little, and I think that half the time he lies."

Hamid poured more wine into her goblet, offering it to her as a kind of apology. "Nothing should distress you, Select One."

She did not shake off her petulance. "Put it on the table by the bed. I'll drink it later."

Hamid almost bent double at the waist. "Select One, you must not . . . It is not fitting that you should despair."

"I do not despair," she said, her dignity making her seem more of a child instead of less. "I am *furious!*" She made an abrupt gesture to the dishes and trays from her meal. "Take this away. You will find those soldiers better company than I am."

"I doubt it," said Hamid. "They are not company I enjoy."

"I won't be, either," Kelene announced defiantly. "I am going to be very bad company tonight. I would like to . . . to—" She could not put her wrath into words.

"You will not be fighting with knives, or vomiting into your helmet," Hamid said to her with heartfelt sincerity. "You will not wrestle with the servants or urinate in the hearth."

Kelene shook her head. "Dracula's soldiers will never do that."

"Soldiers are soldiers, Select One, no matter who their master is. These men are no different. They live as what they are."

"And they are soldiers," said Kelene. "Very well. I will put the bolt on the door when you leave and I will not open the door again until you require it," she said, all the while wondering if it would not be exciting to provoke an incident. The trouble with that idea, she reminded herself, was that the soldiers might well pay for her actions, and if they resented her for it. . . .

"May God grant you many sons, Select One," said Hamid, bowing his relief. "The men are not to be trusted tonight, I fear."

"I don't imagine they will do anything to me."

"Of course not," said Hamid, though the apprehension never left his small, black eyes. He began to ready her room for the night. "I will put your wine on the table, as you asked. And I will leave the oil lamp by the door burning. The fire is banked and it will die without any danger to you." For all his bulk he moved gracefully through the room, making his words actions. "I will be just outside the door if you need anything. Call me and I will come. But do not open the door unless I tell you to, or your lord does." He bowed again and prepared to go, the last of her meal on the tray with the three extinguished torches. "Be sure to set the bolt."

"I will," she said, tagging after him to the door, feeling very small in his wake.

"May God send you sweet dreams and sound sleep, Select One," said Hamid as he went out into the corridor.

Dutifully Kelene slid the iron bolt through the two staples, then looked at her handiwork. "Nothing will come through this," she declared, as if reminding the bolt of its assigned task.

Lying in bed, she found herself listening to the sounds in the palace, trying to decide if they were louder or more worrisome than they had been earlier. She opened the hangings enough for her to see a small slice of the room, and this reassured her by its ordinariness. In such a well-guarded place, how could anything untoward happen to her?

Whatever wakened her sometime later, it was enough to bring her out of sleep with a gasp and a rush of fear that almost made her cry out. She stared out into the room, baffled that she saw no change but a lessening of light now that the fire in the hearth was nearly out. For her alarm, there should be something appalling—

A second blow on the door banished the questions and blasted the last of sleep from her mind. She got out of the bed, listening intently to the sounds of a scuffle on the other side of her door.

"Hamid?" she whispered.

Two more blows, as if from an ax, drubbed the thick wood. Harsh voices muffled by the door told her more than one man was trying to break through. A heavier weapon bludgeoned the door, and the wood sagged, nearly splintering along the grain.

The wide iron bolt suddenly looked woefully inadequate. Kelene began to look about for a weapon, something she could use to defend herself. The two upholstered chairs might slow down the men outside for a while, and that would give her more time to think of a better defense.

Another heavy blow left long cracks in the wood. The door would not hold much longer.

Kelene shoved one of the two chairs over against the door. It was heavy, hard to budge, but she had no illusions that it would withstand the onslaught from the corridor. She pushed the other chair against the first. She tried one of the chests, but could not get it to move.

The wedge-shaped blade of a Swiss halberd jammed into the grain of the wood, accompanied by a grunted oath of satisfaction.

Kelene did not know where to stand—behind the door might give a moment's protection, but it would also mean she would be trapped when discovered. If she waited on the other side of the door she might be able to bolt into the hall as the men rushed in. But what would she encounter and where would she go? She might have a moment to throw wine in their faces. But how would that would help her? There were no small logs by the fireplace she could use as clubs or could set alight to hold the men at bay.

The door began to break apart, splinters and chips flying inward as keen steel snouts poked through. Kelene moved back as the top of the chair against the door broke under another chop of the halberd.

Retreating to the bed, Kelene began to pull down the heavy hangings. It might make them stop their attack, or at least slow them down. She pulled more frantically as the crack in the door widened and finally an arm thrust through.

"He won't use her, we will," boasted one of the men pawing through the hole, trying to find the bolt.

"He can't keep her to himself." This new voice was slurred from ale and exertion. "It's time we had a share."

"We don't want her blood," sniggered a third.

Kelene gathered up the hanging she had pulled free and crossed the room to the second chair. Draping the hanging over the back of the chair, she moved it enough so that it would not be pushed when the door opened, then she took up the hanging once again. Struggling to hold the heavy cloth, she climbed onto the chair, hoping she would be high enough to cast the hanging over the men when the door finally opened.

"Keep working!" another man shouted.

"Holy Angels!" Kelene exclaimed softly. "How many are there?" She had supposed no more than two or three of the men would be bold enough to seek her out. It seemed that all the soldiers had come. She knew what they intended—she was not so much a child that she did not know what soldiers did to women.

She lifted the hanging high and held her arms forward, anticipating the instant when the men would break in.

A moment later the bolt was thrown and the men pushed inward. The other chair slammed into the wall, driven by the door.

Nine men struggled to get through the door all at once, each of them hitting and kicking to get through before the rest.

Kelene waited until the first of the men got free of the tangle; she tossed the hanging as she had seen fishermen in Salonika cast their nets. She was disappointed that it did not cover all the men, but it did land on more than half of them.

There were curses and confusion as the men tried to extricate themselves from the folds of the hanging. A few in the corridor fell back to avoid being caught up in the melee. If they had not been drunk, the soldiers would have sorted themselves out quickly; as it was, they became more muddled and confused as they tried to get out from under the engulfing cloth.

Kelene got down from the chair and ran to the far side of the bed. She wanted as many obstacles between her and the soldiers as she could manage. If only she were in her fine new clothes and not in her night rail. Her foot struck something under the bed.

The chamberpot! She reached down and retrieved it, then scrambled onto the bed in order to get near enough to smash this down on the first soldier's head. The heavy pottery struck with a gratifying thud; the soldier collapsed in an untidy heap. Jumping down from the bed, she made a grab for the oil lamp, swiping it off its hook with a single swing of her arm and sending it flying into the hanging, spraying oil as it went.

The thick cloth began to burn. Beneath the hanging, someone screamed.

Wails of pain from the trapped men changed everything: the soldiers outside the room now rushed forward, not to seize Kelene, but to drag the burning hanging off their fellows. Smoke filled the chamber, its acrid odor increasing the sense of urgency.

A man with his giaquetta aflame crawled from under the hanging and was at once seized and rolled until the fire was out. Three of the soldiers caught the hanging on their halberds and managed to lift it off the others.

"Get out. Get out! *Get out!*" she shouted. "All of you! Now!"

One of the men mumbled something belligerent, and was told to be quiet by the rest. Finally one of the men in the door said, "We didn't mean . . . what you might think." He nodded toward the man Kelene had brained with the chamberpot. "He said it was all right. That you were expecting us."

Kelene's fury rose anew. "Expecting you? It was *all right?*"

"We'll just carry him out, if you don't mind," said the soldier with an attempt at good conduct. His accent was rough and uneducated. "We won't bother you again."

"No," said Kelene.

The men who came to lift their unconscious comrade were now as sheepish as they had been ferocious. Few of them would look her in the face, and those who tried quickly turned away.

"We'll take care of the eunuch," the same spokesman told her as they lugged their former leader out into the hall.

"Hamid," said Kelene. "Is he—"

The soldier shrugged. "I think we cracked his skull. We'll make sure he's comfortable. They have hashish here. It will ease him out of the world." He stared down at the floor. "This won't happen again. You needn't worry."

"Hamid is going to die?" Kelene asked.

"Men with cracked heads do," said the soldier with more pragmatism than sympathy. "The Master Assassin won't like it, but worse has happened here." He ducked his head and backed out of the ruined door. "We'll make sure you are guarded."

"Send one of the servants," said Kelene. She was suddenly very cold; her teeth chattered as if she sat in snow.

"One of us would prefer the honor," said the soldier, lingering a step beyond the door.

"Get out," Kelene replied. She went back to her bed, moving like a crone, her whole body sore as if she had battled each man who came to her room. She sat down on the edge of the bed, but as much as she longed for the warmth it provided, she could not bring herself to get into it. With trembling hands she took the goblet in her hands and drank all the wine as quickly as she could. It seemed thick on her tongue, and the aftertaste was not as she remembered. Gradually she stopped shaking, and the worst of her chill left her. But she still could not get into bed. Finally she pulled the heavy quilt off it and pulled it to the one remaining chair.

There she sat with her knees drawn up and the quilt wadded around her until the sky lightened.

"The men will be punished," Dracula told her the next evening. "Would you like to watch?"

Kelene had been moved to another room, one with an antechamber. It was darker and more somber, with crossed war-axes over the inner doors, higher than Kelene could reach. The bed was high, needing steps to get into, with hangings of double-thickness. There was a long braided cord looped at the head of the bed, to keep invalids from falling out. She considered the offer. "What are you planning to do to them?"

Dracula fingered the quillons of his dagger. "The penalty for rape is castration," he told her.

After a short hesitation, Kelene said, "No. I have brothers."

"Do you worry so for them? Did fighting teach you nothing?" If he had regard for her qualms, he did not show it. "When you fought them, did you enjoy it?"

"No . . . No," she said, uncertain it was true.

"When you routed them, didn't you feel glad?" He came up to her. "You cannot tell me you wanted to save the men?"

"I . . . I didn't want them to hurt me," she admitted, unable to speak above a whisper.

"And so you hurt them first." His hand was heavy on her shoulder. "It would be best if you came to see your battle finished."

"You're hurting me," she said as his fingers tightened.

"You will watch," he insisted.

"Why must I?" she asked, tears welling in her eyes.

He bent down to look directly in her eyes. "If you let an enemy escape, he will have no respect for you and he will come again to—"

"They said they would not—"

He continued ruthlessly "—triumph over you. And you will deserve it." He shook her once. "You must conquer totally or fall. You cannot live with your enemies around you. Make them your slaves or be rid of them, but do not let them have any hope of prevailing over you."

The surge of satisfaction he evoked in her shamed Kelene. She tried to say what she meant and became lost in a jumble of half-phrases. Finally she gestured acquiescence. "I will watch. But I may be sick."

"Do not let them see it, if you are," he warned her. "They must know you are as hard as they are, or your weakness will undo you." As he straightened up, he dragged her to her feet. "Put on my cloak."

"Why should I do that?"

"So that if you are too troubled by what you see, you can hide beneath it," he answered, his voice light as if he found her distress amusing.

"I think what you are planning to do is . . . hideous."

"It is the law," said Dracula.

"It may be, but it is still hideous," she said.

Dracula dropped his cloak over her shoulders. The weight pulled at her. "Stand beside me, so they will know you and I are in accord."

"But we aren't in accord," she said, her blue eyes hot as the heart of fire.

"They had best believe we are," he warned her. "They are like wolves. Let them sense a leader's failing strength and they will dispatch him. Is that what you want? Would you betray me to them?"

"No," she said, a bit too hastily. She swung the cloak more closely around her, having a momentary impression that the cloak would spread and carry her off. Then she went to Dracula's side. "I am your slave. You are to command me."

"You remember at last," he said with an artificial little bow. "Do not forget it while I deal with these men."

"I will not," she said as he prodded her toward the door. "I only wish you had done this last night."

"The decision is still just. Would you spare them for killing the eunuch, too?"

"No," she said, not wanting to defend those who killed Hamid. "But they should be hanged for that, not castrated."

He propelled her through the antechamber and into the corridor and signaled one of the palace's guards to stand in front of her outer door. "But hanging is over very quickly. Castration lingers a lifetime, teaching an unforgettable lesson," he said to her. "Your humiliation would have lasted."

It was shocking to feel anger building in her. Kelene knew that every pope she had ever heard preach would have railed against her wrath as a great sin and unworthy of those presented in God's church. Her wrath sharpened, giving a new excitement. "I will try to watch," she said.

He strode ahead of her. "It will not take long. Then you and I will have the night to spend together."

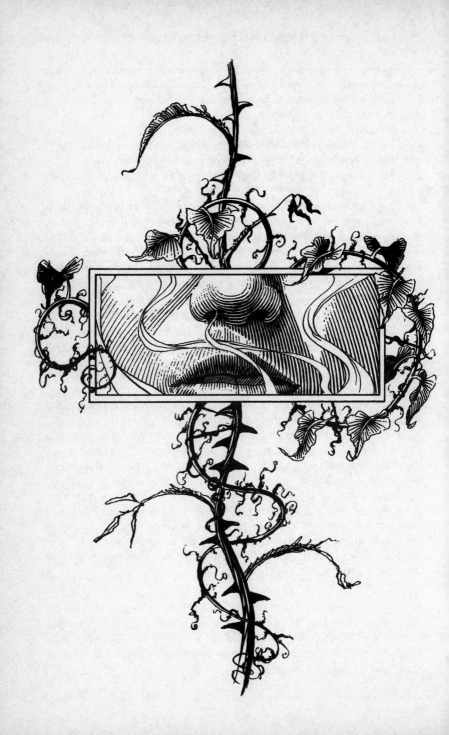

Smoke covers the sun
Flames blot out the moon
Grief shrouds my heart.
—Hungarian lament, 14th century

⊢ XXI ⊣

Kelene sat, dazed, in a small alcove overlooking the place where the sentences had been carried out. She had watched as Dracula sliced the testicles off six of his men, cauterizing the resulting wounds with red-hot irons. The smell hung in the air. All but one of the men had fainted from pain: the one who had not screamed obscenities through the whole ordeal. She wondered what had happened to the other three.

Was it possible that Dracula *was* right, had been right all along?—that she was the same sort of soulless creature he was? The intolerable idea, once considered, would not leave her. It circled in her mind like a vulture or a kite, seeking carrion. If only she dared to pray. But no words came. She could not beg for mercy when she knew that as much as she had been shocked and distressed by what she had seen, she had also exulted in seeing the men suffer for what they had tried to do to her. She folded her hands and lowered her head, so that she might at least give the appearance of piety.

Below her, the remaining soldiers made ready to travel, working in silence, their comrades tied over the backs of the horses pulling her carriage.

"The road will be hard tonight," Dracula said as he came up to her.

"It has not been easy before now," she said, refusing to turn toward him.

"This is worse than the rest," he told her. "The way is traveled by merchants with strings of mules, not carriages and wagons. It is narrow and not well marked. We will have to go slowly, or the wagon—or your carriage—could be damaged. The horses will have a difficult job ahead of them, and we have no farrier."

"Sometimes I think you care more for those horses than your men," she said.

"The men cannot pull the wagon or your carriage, and none of us want to walk all the way to Transylvania."

Kelene gave her full attention to the men below. "You will never be able to trust them again."

"They are sworn to me. They know my justice." Each statement was as final and grim as the words on tombstones.

"But you were the one who . . . you provided the opportunity for what they did." Without intending to, she turned to look at him. "If you had not ordered drink for them while you were hunting, it would not have—"

"Listen to me, girl," Dracula said sternly. "There will be many times when I am gone that only my soldiers or my gypsies will guard you. Of the gypsies I have no doubts—their loyalty is beyond any question. The soldiers are another matter."

"So it would seem," said Kelene.

Dracula touched her golden hair. "You have not yet learned to master them, and so they must remember that I will not permit any lapse in their devotion. I do not think they will forget it now."

"No, they will not forget. And they will blame *me!*" Kelene burst out.

"You did not wield the knife," said Dracula.

"That changes nothing." She wanted suddenly to get away from him, but he blocked her way into the corridor.

"You will find a cloak in your carriage tonight, a new one, of heavy Damascus silk. It is lined with marten. You will sleep warmly."

"Is this a reward for watching?"

He stood aside, his hawklike features set in mocking lines. "I will expect you to be ready at sunset."

She nodded to him, not wanting to be too willing. As she stepped into the hall, she said, "How much longer?"

"What?" he asked.

"Until we reach our destination?" She did not know how much more of this she could endure. "How much farther?"

"That will depend on my enemies," he said, a ferocious brilliance in his eyes.

"The Turks?"

"Among others." He hesitated. "It will be at least twelve days, if we encounter no fighting and the road is clear. If we do fight, or have to go around the fighting, it could take much longer. Without the carriage and wagon it might be ten days or so, but no less than that. It is a hard road for everyone."

"And yet you came all that way. For me." She wanted to sound skepti-
cal but knew she had not succeeded.

"You heard my call," he reminded her. "And Belgrade is nearer my
home than Salonika."

She would have liked to ask if the long, arduous and costly journey
her family had made had been for his benefit alone. Instead, she said,
"Was there fighting when you came?"

"Nothing more than skirmishes," said Draculas. "The Turks are very
active."

Kelene shuddered at the thought of battle. "What should I do?" she
asked quietly. "If there is fighting?"

"Avoid death and capture, of course. Take refuge in the forest, and
live any way you must." He shook his head. "You are not so young as
you like to think, girl."

"I suppose you expect me to be grateful to you," Kelene said to Dracula as he handed her up into her carriage as they prepared to leave.

His horse, a big, raw-boned bay so dark that he appeared almost
entirely black, pawed restlessly, eager to be off. Dracula gave a single,
sharp tug on the reins and the horse was still. "I expect you to be like
me," he said as she settled herself in the carriage.

"I am not like you," she said, her eyes downcast as she prepared to
close the door.

He arrested the action with his arm. "You rejoiced to see those men
beg and bleed. You were happy when they screamed," he said, releasing
the door and swinging into the saddle.

Kelene pulled the door closed and set the latch, telling herself she
had triumphed, and knowing she had not.

As the little party went away from the Palace of the Assassins, Kelene
again wished she knew how to write, for she was afraid that over time
her memory of the place would fade and distort if she did not record her
experiences while they were alive in her thoughts. It would not be long
until her memory of this place was like something out of a fable, and she
would find it hard to believe she had ever actually been here. Much as
she wished it, she did not think Dracula would teach her—if, she added
spitefully, he could read and write himself. She tried to review and memo-
rize as much of what had happened as she could, trying to keep all the
details accurate. She wished now she had done this with her family, for
already she was not entirely certain she could recall Orien's face precisely
as it was, or Pallas' voice.

Dracula rode with her in the later part of the night, performing a
kind of ritual upon her, making her body a kind of altar to his lust: he

laid her on the seat of her carriage and slowly stripped her of her clothes, casting them aside with deliberate neglect. The cold night air bit into her flesh, but her single complaint had brought her such resounding condemnation that she made no second attempt to stop him, no matter how marblelike she felt as the cold grew fiercer. She would give him no cause to punish her, not after what she had seen. His hands followed a ritual with the care of a priest, and though she knew she ought to feel defiled, instead she seemed to be truly consecrated.

When she was naked, he bent over her, staring down into her eyes with such intensity of purpose that Kelene was caught up in his command, though she had not intended to be. She had determined to keep one part of herself from him, sacrosanct. But it was not possible, not now. His need was paramount. Nothing was more apparent than that. She attempted to hold herself apart from him, but the power of his gaze with the grip of the cold worked on her so that she found the only spark of heat in the universe to be in Dracula, and living creature that she was, she was drawn to that one tantalizing heat in the immensity of cold around her.

"There is life, *my* life," he promised her as his long teeth grazed her neck. "And it can be everlasting."

In that instant she knew that the chalice she had drunk from so many times before had held the wine of her soul made his by his offering, and that what he drank from her now was his claiming her soul as his own even as her blood sustained him. She accepted this unholy sacrament, kissing his ensanguined mouth, tasting her blood on his lips, before he rose from her side

Only when he was gone did the blasphemy of what she had done overcome her, making her howl with despair as the carriage lumbered on into the night, the horses sweating from effort and fear.

Morning did not end their travels. Dracula took refuge in his coffin on the wagon and the men stopped for a short, simple meal of broth and cheese while the horses were given an hour to graze, and then they were back on the road, on a merchants' route that followed the crest and brow of a long chain of mountains.

Kelene, dazed and troubled by all that had happened the night before, did nothing but sit wrapped in her marten cloak, naked beneath it. She did not eat and could not bring herself to drink more than one or two sips of water when they were offered throughout the morning. She noticed the puddles in the ruts, and knew soon they would turn to churning morasses of mud. If there was more rain, they would surely have to stop until the road was drier. She could not bring herself to care. She began to hope the rain would come, that they would all be washed away, caught in a landslide or pulled under the mud. Then it would be over and she would be free.

Late in the afternoon the soldiers found an inn, a low, heavy-beamed building deep in a stand of larch and oak. There was a stable and a bathhouse, all better maintained than they seemed to be at first glance. The soldiers did not hesitate to stop, calling for the landlord in stern accents and demanding grain for the horses and food for themselves.

The landlord addressed them in a patois that was partly Hungarian, partly German, partly Greek, and partly Romanian. He was a man of middle years, with one shoulder higher than the other and an untrustworthy cast in his eye. He opened his doors wide, summoned his ostler, and urged the men to dismount. "We do not see many travelers at this time of year." He shrugged and glanced at the coffin on the wagon. "Returning the hero to his family, I see."

"To his native earth," said one of the soldiers without any humor. He indicated the carriage. "That is his woman."

Kelene, who had made a haphazard effort at dressing a little earlier, showed her wan face at the window.

"Pretty little thing," said the landlord with a speculative lift to a single brow.

"She will go to his home," said another soldier, getting ready to untie the men from the backs of the coach horses.

"Fallen comrades," said the landlord, nodding in approval.

"No," said the first soldier. "They disgraced themselves. They are still alive."

"Cowards? Never tell me a Christian soldier fled the enemy," said the landlord, trying to sound hearty. "Why, I cannot believe any—"

"These men attempted to rape the woman," said the second, as he eased one of the men over his shoulder. "Is there an empty stall where we can leave them for the night?"

"With her lord's coffin as witness?" The landlord took a moment to compose himself before answering their request. "I suppose you can use the donkey stalls at the back of the stable," he allowed, his voice lower than before. "They won't die, will they?"

The first soldier shrugged as two others carried the injured men over their shoulders toward the stable. "We will dine within the hour. The woman must have a private room. If you have a girl to serve her, see that it is done."

The landlord bowed, not quite respectfully, but with an attitude of caution that Kelene thought was prudent. "My daughter will tend her, if that suits."

"It will do," said the second soldier. "The horses will have to be brushed and rubbed down," he said to the ostler. "We will leave in the morning if the weather is clear." He paused, and added as if the answer were not important, "How is the hunting in this region?"

"At this time of year you do best with boar; they are dangerous, but not as dangerous as the Turks," said the landlord. "I have pork roasting even now." He again indicated his door. "The price, for good soldiers, is reasonable. If you provide another boar, I will reduce the rate still more." He said this with a sour smile. "What is the device on the coffin?"

"A dragon," said another of the soldiers, using the Latin word *draco*.

"Dracula?" The landlord looked shocked. "Surely not. They have gone over to the Turks, I was told; after Tepes they were afraid—"

"This is not Tepes, nor any of his. They are the cadet line of the House, the—" He used a word Kelene did not recognize, although the tone was condemning. "This lord is of the older line, much older, and truer," said the first soldier with what was clearly pride. "From the time of the Huns."

"Oh. The older line," said the landlord.

One of the soldiers returned from the stable and opened the carriage door for Kelene. He held out his hand but did not speak to her; she accepted his offer without a word.

Now she was glad to have the new cloak. It was too grand to let anyone think she was a slave. She saw the landlord stare at her hair and wondered why he made a sign to ward off the Evil Eye. Was blond hair so rare in this part of the world that it was regarded as dangerous?

"She will want to bathe. To wash away the blood," said the first soldier. "Your daughter will guard her."

"It will not be free," said the landlord, unable to stop himself. "It will not be a great sum, but it cannot be—" he amended with a look of chagrin.

"Two silver Roman popes," said the first soldier in a tone that made no opportunity for haggling. The landlord did not argue with the sum. "She will eat alone."

Kelene heard this last as if through the hum of bees. Wash away the blood? What blood? What had Dracula done to her? What did she look like? She hoped there might be a mirror in the bathhouse so she could look at herself before she washed. She allowed herself to be led in the direction of the inn, a little perplexed at what an effort such a short walk cost her.

"It is the grief that weighs her down," said one of the soldiers.

"She is so young," said another.

"She must rest, to restore her strength," said the first.

Kelene hated them for speaking as if she could not hear them.

The landlord took up their tone. "It must be very hard for her, being so near a child, to lose her lord."

"It is," said the first soldier.

Kelene wished she knew the soldiers' names, so she would not feel quite so much a captive. As it was they were soldiers and soldiers only. One might be older or stouter or more energetic than another, but it meant nothing without names. She felt the heat from the hearth of the inn's taproom and was mildly surprised that it did not kindle an answering warmth in her. She tugged her cloak about her shoulders.

"I will fetch my daughter," said the landlord, watching Kelene narrowly.

"Quickly," said the second soldier. "It will soon be dark."

"You are within doors—what does the dark mean to you?" the landlord asked as he left his taproom.

The men were silent as they waited for the landlord to return. Not one of them made a move to take a cup of beer or a wedge of cheese. Kelene stood surrounded by them, her head aching. She lowered her eyes and studied the rushes on the floor, thinking they were fresher than she had expected in such a place.

The landlord returned with his daughter in tow—a young woman with a long, untidy braid of dark hair down her back. The woman's clothes were worn but clean and her heavy felt boots were in good repair. She was nearing the end of her pregnancy, which made her clumsy and slow. She regarded the soldiers with apprehension, hanging back from them, staying near the entrance to the kitchen.

Kelene stared at her, thinking of Melantha. The memory of her mother was sharp enough to cause her to wince.

"Take her to the bathhouse and see she is cleaned up," said the first soldier, addressing the landlord. "Your daughter will attend her."

"Most certainly," said the landlord, signaling to his daughter to approach Kelene.

The young woman came and bowed as much as her swollen abdomen would permit. "I will take care of you," she said.

Kelene recognized the words with difficulty, but answered at once. "Thank you."

"See to her now," said the first soldier, as if annoyed at hearing Kelene speak. "Then serve her dinner in a room by herself."

"Of course. At once," said the landlord, making another sign to his daughter. "The bathhouse is hot enough, isn't it?"

"It is," she said, nodding in Kelene's direction. "I will show you the way."

"Thank you," Kelene repeated. She was about to shove her way

through the soldiers around her in order to follow the landlord's daughter
when the men stood aside for her as if they feared her touch. Holding
her head up, she followed the landlord's daughter.

The kitchen was large and amply stocked: ducks and rabbits hung
from hooks near the door; strings of onions and turnips lay on shelves
beside fresh-cut cabbages; dried branches of fragrant herbs were tied together and hung over the cooling new breads; the boar turned on the spit
over a high, banked log fire. There was food enough for a party three
times the size of Dracula's, for more than four days. The smell of the
place was rich and promising, but Kelene did not find it satisfying. She
supposed her exhaustion had once again robbed her of her appetite.

As they went out the back door and through the kitchen garden,
Kelene was struck by the incongruity of the inn, which seemed to be
nothing more than a remote hovel and yet was provisioned like a noble's
villa. For a landlord and one child and the ostler, there appeared to be
an inordinate amount of food being prepared. It was possible that some
company was expected, but if so, that party must have sent a messenger
ahead to arrange for a large supper. She had noticed no other person at
the inn. She was no longer willing to consider this evidence of plenty
simple good fortune, and put herself on the alert.

The bathhouse was large enough to accommodate a dozen people in
the main chamber. Warm steam rose from the four huge tubs, and the
smell of wet wood permeated the place. The furnace, a vast brick pile
with a bellows and thick leather hoses leading to each of the tubs, raged
away merrily. The landlord's daughter began to work the bellows, sweating
quickly and heavily.

"Which one?" Kelene asked, indicating the tubs.

"The largest," said the landlord's daughter, leaving off pumping to
point.

"And is there a mirror? A looking glass?"

"With the clothes." She pointed a second time to a row of small doors
like closets along the far wall.

"Where?" Kelene asked as she went to the line of doors.

"The third, I think. Or fourth," said the landlord's daughter, holding
up fingers for reinforcement.

Behind the third door there was a pile of clothes and leather hunting
armor; by the smell of them they had been worn recently. Kelene closed
the door quickly, hoping the landlord's daughter would not suspect she
had seen anything. She opened the fourth door and saw a small, pitted
mirror set in a wooden frame hung on the inside of the door; otherwise
the closet was empty.

The light in the bathhouse was dim, and the steam made much of the chamber seem insubstantial. As Kelene stared into the mirror, she blinked twice, seeing only a wraithlike paleness where her face should be. All that stood out was the ragged tear in the side of her neck, as sharply visible as the line of the doorframe of the closet. Four red smears along her jaw that almost glowed against her insubstantial flesh. In awe, Kelene touched the surface of the mirror, as if to reassure herself it was actually there. The glass felt hot under her touch and she drew her fingers back at once.

A moment later, Kelene peered into the mirror once more and realized with growing trepidation that it was no illusion: the ghostlike filminess in the mirror was her reflection.

PART

III

ARRIVING

March 1503–December 1511

In dreams are the realms
Of the soul . . .
—Greek lyric, 16th century

⊷ XXII ⊷

The landlord's daughter tossed her head; Kelene could not read her expression through the steam. "You're bloody, all right," the pregnant woman said, panting a little.

"I knew I was injured, but I never thought it was . . ." Words deserted Kelene. She began to undress, wondering what her body would reveal.

"I won't pick up your clothes," the young woman warned as she continued her labors.

"It doesn't matter," said Kelene.

"We have no soap. It harms the wood," the young woman went on. "You should use a brush. It's better."

"You don't have to keep working the bellows if it is too hard on you," said Kelene. "With your babe so near coming, you should rest."

The young woman shot Kelene a look of spite. "And have you say I was lax? I am not so foolish. You will not be able to complain of me." She pumped with renewed vigor.

"I would not," Kelene protested as she prepared to lower herself into the tub indicated. She slid out of her camisa, noting as she did that most of the neck was caked stiff with blood. What had possessed Dracula that he should use her so? Her hands trembled as she dropped it.

"So you tell me, but I know what you well-borns are like," said the landlord's daughter.

"Well-borns?" Kelene echoed. "I am hardly well-born."

"Your lord was well-born, and you are with his men," said the landlord's daughter, making no attempt to hide her contempt. She paused in her work and smiled. "But you may yet know what it is to beg your bread. And to spread your legs for a bed."

"So I might," said Kelene, wondering why the hot water suddenly felt so chilly, and the air smelled of mold and dankness the heat could not banish. Had Dracula left her so little blood that the mirror knew it?

"You have not earned your way as I have," said the landlord's daughter, in grim satisfaction. "But you will."

Kelene said only, "I suppose I may." She felt the frisson of danger, and could not tell if it came from within her or from the steam-filled room.

"Your lord doted on you, giving you fine clothes, but he could not keep you from hurt, and he will not now. You may scream, but it will mean nothing." She started toward the door, leaving Kelene alone.

The sound of the outside bolt being shot echoed dully in the hot gloom. The landlord and his daughter had captured her.

She got out of the tub and went to retrieve her marten cloak, paying no attention to the drafts that plucked at her skin, making it crinkle. She left her other clothes where they were and put her mind to getting out of the bathhouse without being discovered. At least, she thought, it was growing dark so she would be able to hide in the shadows.

There were a number of windows set high along the far wall, most of them blocked by shutters, though two were open enough to allow air to circulate. They were not easily reached, and Kelene was not certain she could climb out even if she succeeded in reaching one. Still, she thought, it was better than remaining in the bathhouse waiting for whomever was coming.

She poked about in the half-light and came upon a large wooden chest where wood was kept for the furnace. There were a dozen or so sectioned logs in it, and she at once began to lift them out so she could move the chest. They were heavy, but urgency gave her purpose and strength to work steadily. She made no effort to stack the wood, but instead let it fall where it might.

Outside someone coughed and someone else ordered silence. Kelene listened, unmoving, until she thought it would be safe to continue.

With the chest unloaded she struggled to push it across the room, doing her best to ignore the sounds she heard beyond the thick walls. At least, she thought, the sun was almost down and Dracula would waken soon. She shoved and dragged and jostled the chest, finding it less strenuous than she had expected. Perhaps, she told herself with mad amusement, the loss of her reflection was balanced by increasing strength.

Shouts came from the inn, and then the first tumult of fighting.

Climbing atop the chest, Kelene reached up for the half-open window just over her head. She hooked her forearm over the sill. Her feet proved useless, only scrabbling on the wood and nearly dislodging her hold. She began to pull herself upward with her arms and shoulders. The effort made her gasp for air, but she was getting somewhere at last.

By the time she was hanging half in and half out of the window, she could see a wedge of the battle. The men from the forest were pressing forward, most of them with swords and poignards, others with maces and crossbows. Suddenly she felt very exposed. If she were caught she would be easily dispatched. She had no weapon, and was all but helpless hanging out of the window like a trussed sheep. She wriggled and twisted and at last fell out, landing in a hawthorn thicket growing against the bathhouse which cushioned her fall with its spiny branches.

A man she did not recognize staggered toward her, his fingers clutching his shoulder where blood ran. He screamed, and Kelene realized he did not see her.

She got to her feet and slipped into the deepest part of the shadow of the bathhouse, preparing to wait until the man was gone.

Then he bellowed and lunged at her.

Kelene stepped aside, watching as the man blundered into the wall. She stood uncertainly for a few short breaths, then stepped toward him and gingerly pulled the dagger from his belt. Now she had a weapon. She was less afraid. She nudged the man with her toe. Relieved to discover he was solidly unconscious, she hunkered down beside him.

Only then did she realize she was free. She could run away and be free of Dracula.

To be an outlaw's whore, a farmer's drudge, or Dracula's slave. She held the dagger tightly.

Another of the attackers was fleeing, his crossbow no longer strung— worse than no weapon. He caught sight of Kelene and struck at her, using the stirrup as a club, missing her and cursing his bad swing.

Before she could think about it, Kelene was on him, her dagger raised in both hands. She hesitated only long enough to aim. She drove it down into his shoulder from above, the point penetrating deep behind the ribs. She let go of the hilt as the man cursed and flailed at her. He tottered away, his legs no longer working quite right. Then he fell, twitching as the blood surged out of him.

Kelene wanted the dagger back. But she would have to pull it out of the dying man, and she could not bring herself to do that. She glanced toward the inn and saw that the fighting had turned decisively; the men who had come so stealthily were now in chaotic retreat, driven off by Dracula's soldiers.

"Did you like killing him?" Dracula's voice from just behind her startled her more than anything she had witnessed that dying afternoon. He was wiping his sword on a corpse.

"Of course not," she said, moving nervously away from him.

"Not the least part?" he pursued, coming up to her again as he sheathed his sword. "You felt no pleasure in it? No?" He reached out and touched her. "Or are you afraid to own it?"

"I am not afraid," she said stubbornly, wrenching her hand from his.

"Not of your joy in killing? That does not frighten you, girl?" He stopped her before she could speak. "You should know. The landlord's daughter is dead."

"Dead?" She was pregnant. She could not be dead. "That's impos—"

"The leader of the outlaws cut her throat himself. I saw it." He laid his hand on her upper arm, his fingers closing around it possessively.

"Did you?" she found the courage to ask. "Or did you kill her?"

"Had I killed her, I would not have wasted her blood. Come." He led her back to the inn. "You had the chance to run and did not."

"Could I have escaped?" she asked bitterly.

"No."

"Did you expect me to try?" She held her head as high as she could, trying to ignore the inexorable grip on her arm.

"I do not expect you to be foolish. But you are very young."

Kelene's feet were cut and she was scraped and bruised, but she no longer felt so entirely in Dracula's thrall as she had been. Perhaps killing that outlaw had not been so terrible, after all. Perhaps knowing she could take a life if she had to would keep her from the despair that had haunted her. "I will need clothes," she was bold enough to remind him as they reached the rear entrance to the inn.

"And shoes, and a basin of water," he said. "And someone will go fetch your clothes." It was more concern than she had expected from him, and she felt tears well in her eyes.

"A basin of water," she seconded as she touched a scrape on her chin with her free hand. She willed her tears to be gone.

"But not a mirror," Dracula added as they entered the kitchen. Food was strewn everywhere, and two soldiers were carrying out the bodies of outlaws. The floor was sticky with blood.

"No," she said as she surveyed the destruction around her. "Not a mirror."

An hour before dawn Dracula returned with his men. He summoned Kelene from the small, ill-lit chamber where she had been sleeping.

"There are clothes for you in the trunk strapped to the back of your carriage. One of my soldiers will bring it up to you. You would do well to wear hunting clothes. Be prudent in what you choose." His vitality was as great as she had ever seen it, and she could not help but be drawn to him. Did battle and killing make him more vivid? She shied away from the answer.

"You will not choose for me?" she asked, wondering why she wanted so much to touch him.

"I am not a servant, girl," he said sharply. "You know what the road is like. Dress accordingly." He turned away, his cloak swinging to wrap him in shadows.

"You caught the outlaws," she said to his back.

"Yes." He did not look at her. He went out, adding before he closed the door, "We found their camp not long after midnight." Kelene saw then that the hem of his long cloak was heavy with blood.

One of the soldiers brought her chest to her, leaving Kelene to look through it. She saw the first clothes Dracula had given her, along with many other garments, most of them of fine fabrics and in dazzling colors. A few were so grand that she hardly dared to touch them.

Finally she chose a simarra of a deep brown with rolled epaulets, the bodice and apron trimmed with bands of embroidery in copper and gold worn over a gauze camisa with a narrow neck-band without frills or ruffs. It was the most practical selection, she decided. Felt boots finished her ensemble. She was just lacing these into place when Dracula came to her door again.

"Good," he said glancing over her. "We will be leaving shortly. Is the trunk ready?"

"Yes," she said, annoyed that he had not approved more enthusiastically of her clothing; she was wearing it to please him.

"Then go down and wait by the carriage. Do not speak to the soldiers." He waved her away, remaining in the room after she had gone.

The small innyard was filled with activity. Three soldiers were readying the coffin for Dracula while two others were hanging the bodies of the outlaws from the ends of the rafters. The sky was turning pale and in the distance birds were singing. Kelene went to the carriage and stood, reluctant to clamber in without help. One of the castrated soldiers stumbled out of the stable, his face stark and pale. He looked about dazedly, his eyes glazed with fever. Where were the others? Kelene wondered. She turned away from the soldier.

Dracula strode out of the inn, ordering one of his men to bring Kelene's trunk. He did not notice Kelene as he went to the coffin, lifted the lid, and lay down in it, then pulled the heavy carved lid closed.

About midday the carriage shuddered and jarred to a stop, the left rear wheel broken. Kelene got out of the carriage and stood on the narrow road while the soldiers labored to replace the wheel. It was a clear day, the promise of spring everywhere. In another time Kelene might have admired it, but now it seemed to her that all the budding trees were false,

that the blossoms only covered graves of the unknown dead. She walked
a short distance away from the carriage, curious about their isolation on
this remote track. How far did it wind through the fastness of the mountains and where did it lead? She shaded her eyes against the sun, and saw
in the distance dark birds circling.

She wanted to look away but could not turn her eyes from them.
Everywhere there were reminders of the brevity of life, mocking the spring.
How had she not seen it before?

One of the soldiers came to her and indicated it was time to get into
the carriage once more. She went with him without reluctance, for now
she began to understand him. Dracula commanded him and he obeyed. It
was the same with her.

They were underway again, going slowly to keep from damaging the
wheels of the carriage. Their pace slowed still more when they reached a
stretch of road that had been swept away. An unsteady, makeshift track
led around it. The soldiers ordered Kelene to get out of the carriage, and
put her on the back of one of the big bay horses, which a soldier led as
they undertook to cross the slide on the temporary road.

Rocks and pebbles slithered underfoot, and the carriage wallowed like
a ship in high seas. The wagon bearing the coffin skidded, its weight
dragging on the team; ahead of it, the carriage came to a halt. The soldiers
rushed to protect the coffin as it shifted on the bed. From her place in
the saddle, Kelene watched with growing apprehension as the rear of the
wagon swung slowly, the wheels groaning on the axle. The horses squealed
and crouched against the sliding weight of the wagon and its cargo. The
soldiers swarmed around the rear of the wagon, pushing, grasping. The
coffin continued to slide.

Kelene held her breath, dreading what would happen if the coffin
should fall out of the wagon. If the coffin was lost, what would she do?
What would the soldiers do to her?

Two of the men maneuvered their horses up against the rear of the
wagon and braced the coffin as other soldiers grappled with the wagon.
The panting of the horses and the groaning of the wagon were the only
sounds, punctuated by the clatter of small rocks falling.

Then the lower rear wheel jammed and the coffin teetered nearer the
end of the wagon bed. The soldiers began to shout. Belatedly the man
leading Kelene's mount tugged it away from the milling confusion.

"They should use the carriage horses," said Kelene in a quiet voice.

The soldier looked up at her, startled.

"The carriage can be taken to the edge of the slide, the soldiers tied
to them released, the team unhooked and added to the team pulling the
wagon. That would be enough to get the wagon clear." She was careful

not to address him directly, but out of the corner of her eye she saw the soldier nod. "I will stay where I am," she told him. "Save the coffin."

The soldier signaled Kelene to get down, helping her to alight before he swung up into the saddle, and spurred his horse up to the carriage. A moment later, the driver had the team in motion.

It was not enough. The heavy coffin dipped slowly and inexorably, to land on the loose soil where it began to shift and skid, so that the frightened horses around it sidled away from it.

Kelene did not realize she was running until she reached the wagon. She pushed her way through the mounted soldiers and reached the coffin. Without hesitation she flung herself atop it, holding onto the high relief carving of the dragon to secure herself, the length of her body pressed against the wood, her face atop the dragon's maw.

Two of the soldiers shouted for help, and a third roared for a chain to secure the coffin before it slipped any further. At the carriage, the soldiers worked more speedily to bring the team to the aid of the wagon.

Two of the soldiers carrying a chain between them kicked their horses into a plunge down the slope to a place just below where the coffin had slid. There they stretched the chain between them and waited, braced, for the impact.

The horses sat down on their haunches as the coffin careened into the chain. The soldiers grunted and swore in their struggle to hold the chain.

On the lid of the coffin, Kelene felt a cut open along her cheek where she was bounced against the wood. Her blood stained the open mouth of the dragon.

Finally the carriage team was hooked to the wagon team, and with the coffin off the wagon bed, the soldiers pulled the wagon free of the hidden obstruction. The soldiers did not quite cheer.

The carriage team was led back to the two soldiers holding the chain, and a hitch was improvised to pull the coffin off the slide.

During the whole of this, Kelene remained lying atop the coffin, maintaining her purchase with fingers that cramped and shoulders that shook. Only as the coffin reached the edge of the slide did she begin to wonder why she had done this thing. Very slowly she pushed herself into a sitting position; she was breathing quickly and she did not want to move from where she sat. She remained unmoving and undisturbed while the teams were reharnessed.

Then it was time to load the coffin aboard the wagon again. Kelene said, "No. I must stay with him." She held on, her fingers bleeding where she clung, her voice ragged with purpose.

Give yourself to me
Or be left to the beasts.
—Moldavian ballad, 13th century

— XXIII —

"Why did you do it?" Dracula asked her when he came into her carriage that night. Outside a freezing rain beat a steady tattoo, isolating the carriage from the night around them.

"Your soldiers told you?" Kelene's shoulders were sore and the cut on her cheek throbbed when she moved suddenly.

"They did not need to," he said, and repeated, "Why did you do it?"

She had been puzzling over that question since it happened. "I don't know," she said. "I could not stop myself." Admitting this made her tremble.

Dracula gave a single nod.

Kelene fingered the scab on her cheek. "I heard wolves earlier."

"Yes; there are wolves in these mountains," said Dracula, moving nearer to her on the narrow seat. "You spoke to my men. I should punish them for listening to you."

"Had they not listened, your coffin might be broken in pieces at the bottom of that slide," she countered. "Punish them for saving you? Punish me for what I said."

He said nothing for a short while. "The wolves are hungry. They want the horses."

"The soldiers ought to have scouts out, so that the horses won't be hunted." She realized that the soldiers did not need her to tell them this, but she had to speak of safe things—and how troubling it was when wolves were safer than men! She did not look at Dracula as she said, "Where will we stop?"

"There is a fort some leagues ahead. I am expected there." He put his hands on her shoulders. "You have not owned me yet, girl, but you will. By the time we reach my castle, you will."

"Why should that matter?" she asked. "You bought me, and that's the end of it."

"Buying you was nothing," said Dracula. "Any fool with a sack of gold could have done the same. But you must know that you are—"

She shrugged herself away from his hands. "I will not be what you are."

"You are already," he told her. This time his hands were not gentle. "You must sustain me again."

Kelene felt the now-familiar lassitude coming over her. How much easier it was to let Dracula command her. She looked up into the lambent glow of his eyes and made a gesture of acquiescence.

He stroked her neck before he struck.

He was not abrupt this time, but lingered over the sweetness of her body as he relished the savor of her blood.

As she felt his teeth, Kelene tried to recall how she had seen him in dreams. She understood now that he had fed on her then, but the dreams made it seem different. She missed them for their grandeur and her satisfaction. No more vistas of stars and eternity, no more chalices of dark wine. To be the earthly voice of an angel was so much more gratifying than being the slave of a vampire.

She sighed as Dracula embraced her, holding her as if to take heat as well as blood from her. "Not yet. Not yet," he murmured as he thrust her away from him. "We still have many leagues to go, and it will not do to end it before we reach the castle."

Kelene's eyes drifted open. "Why not end it?" she whispered.

"I have need of you alive," said Dracula. "Once you have risen, you will have to feed as I do." He kissed her wrist where the pulse fluttered just under the skin.

"I never will."

"But you will," said Dracula. "Think how it was to kill that man at the inn and you will want—"

"I will not want to kill, never in all my life," she said. How would it be, to bring down prey? Would it ease her restlessness or increase it?

"But after your life?" He brushed a tendril of blond hair back from her brow. "They will think you are an angel, with a halo, when you come."

"And they will be as deceived as I was," said Kelene.

He scrutinized her face. "You are worn out. I will not disturb you any longer."

"You have what you came for," she agreed.

"That is not the whole of it," he said, no trace of tenderness in his concern. "Sleep while you may, girl."

Kelene was drowsy, her head buzzing with the need for rest. She nodded to show she heard, and as Dracula went out into the rain, she put her hand up to staunch the wound he had made, noticing as she did that her blood felt cool on her fingers and that her other aches had faded to nothing.

The road leading to the fortress was old, Roman old, and like all Roman roads it was straight and built to last. The carriage rumbled over the ancient stones without mishap, the wagon following behind. The soldiers, all but two riding in pairs, escorted the vehicles as if on parade, and when the portcullis rose, they lifted their swords hilt-uppermost to show respect for the place. The two soldiers still recovering from bandit-wounds lifted their arms in salute.

This fortress was square, with watchtowers at all four corners. The thick walls showed the ravages of time and war with stoic indifference. Arriving as they did at sunset, they saw the gray stones warmed by the ruddy light, as if the walls were hot. No flags flew above the ramparts, and no heraldic device surmounted the gate. The men who manned the fortress spoke a kind of Czech, and wore surcotes with the device of a star in its detriment. For a moment Kelene was amused that their device and her name had the same meaning—dark star. They were nearly as silent as Dracula's soldiers, sounding but one call on their trumpet when the wagon with the coffin was safely within the courtyard at the center.

Kelene looked at the fortress without emotion. It was only another stop on her journey, no more significant than any other place Dracula decided to stop for the night. She hoped she could maintain her disinterest once she had to face Dracula himself. Her body had not warmed during the day.

Servants with the black star device opened the carriage door for her, and although they spoke to her kindly, she did not know any of the words they used.

Obediently Kelene followed two female servants along a stone gallery, wondering as she went if these servants knew who they entertained in the coffin. If they did, would it trouble them? Kelene looked about for signs of a chapel or church and found none. Nor did crosses stand on the highest peaks of the fortress to guard against perils the walls could not keep out. Kelene knew this ought to worry her, but with the blood of the man she had killed on her hands, she did not know if anyone would permit her to enter a chapel. She wanted to weep but even that was too much effort.

The room to which she was taken was simple as a nun's cell; there was a small fireplace, but that was the chamber's one luxury. Kelene looked around her, at the simple narrow bed and the one plain chest with a ewer of water atop it. If there had been a crucifix over the bed, she would have thought it appropriate for so austere a chamber, but nothing adorned the walls, neither of religion or war. Kelene sighed as she sat down on the bed. She was distantly aware of hunger, but it was like a memory of a need, not the need itself. Before she was aware of it, she was dozing, drifting in dreams.

The place had to be Belgrade, for she recognized the walls of the city and the spires of the churches. There was the platform where she had stood, where Dracula had come and paid for her, turning from the angel of her dreams to her master in life. She had not thought the city so remote.

There was the market square where the farmers brought their produce and poultry for sale, and there it was that she saw Pallas, bargaining for a brace of fine geese. But this Pallas was dressed in fine cloth cut in the Austrian fashion, with a chaplet on her dark hair that had pearls worked into its fretwork. She had two servants behind her, one carrying baskets, the other acting as a guard. She had not remembered Pallas being so pretty, or so tall. She wanted to bring the faces of her family to mind, but the dream was obstinate and would reveal only Pallas.

How her sister had prospered, thought Kelene, and knew it had come about because of her sale. It was what she had wanted, but now that she saw the prosperity, she could not stifle the resentment that came with it. It was one thing to be doing well in the world, it was something else again to be so pleased about it. Kelene wondered if Pallas ever thought of her.

As she watched the purchase of the geese and then three shoats, Kelene saw that for a moment Pallas frowned, not in annoyance but sadness. The happiness of her sister was not untrammeled. That made Kelene feel less slighted. But it was still difficult to remember leaving her mother and brothers forever. Kelene wanted to see how Melantha was, and wanted to hurry Pallas at her tasks, for she did not know where to look for her family in that city she had left so far behind. She noticed that Pallas was known in the market, and those who greeted her did so with respect, and a trace of friendliness not always found in the marketplace.

What would Melantha look like now? Would she recognize her? Kelene wanted to conjure her mother's face, and could not. She was certain Melantha had dark hair and rich brown eyes. That much seemed right. But her oldest sister, who married in Sarajevo—what had she looked like? And what was her name? It would come to her. Thalia. That was it. Thalia.

How very ordinary it all looked: the marketplace with its throngs of people, the farmers crying their wares and prices. It was hard to imagine that war could shatter it all in hours. How to tell them, how to alert them? There must be soldiers in the city— why weren't they more apparent? Had they left the gates unguarded? Kelene wished she could warn her sister, so that Pallas might give the alarm, reminding them all they were not safe. But much as she strove to touch her sister, nothing happened.

At last Pallas reached the stall where onions and herbs were sold. She purchased dried fennel and a string of onions, remarking to the old woman selling the herbs that she would be glad of spring with all the fresh savor it would bring. The old woman agreed, and took the money Pallas' servant gave her.

Then Pallas asked for garlic.

Kelene stirred on her bed and tried to waken, to break away from what she could not tell. The dream had her, though, and she could not escape. *Pallas had the servant carry the garlic, which was marginally better for Kelene as she watched. Her shopping done, Pallas ordered the servants to accompany her back to the inn. This surprised Kelene, who thought with so much money her family must surely own a house by now.*

The inn was large, of high quality, catering to those with wealth and position. Pallas went in the side door, which puzzled Kelene, for there was no reason Pallas should approach that place or any house as a servant.

In the kitchen Pallas was met by the staff with prompt acknowledgment, the cook bowing to her. Pallas had her purchases handed over and issued instructions which Kelene watched with increasing interest, for apparently the servants regarded Pallas as their mistress. The cook asked questions and relayed information, which Pallas heard with a nod of encouragement and an indication that a lamb turning on a spit should be put on a large pewter platter for serving. Kelene wished she could smell the odors in the kitchen, could delight in Pallas' skills once more.

Then Achilles came into the kitchen. He was dressed very well, in Italian fashions, his hair neatly cut and a velvet cap on his head. He grinned at Pallas, remarking that all but two rooms were full, and the wine kegs had been delivered.

Pallas asked after their mother and was told she was in her private chambers.

Better and better, thought Kelene. They had claimed the best the inn had to offer. Then she realized that her family had purchased the inn.

Kelene's satisfaction was short-lived. Achilles made a remark about their father's grave, and Kelene wanted to shout to him not to say such things.

Pallas responded that the next morning they would attend services for his soul, but that she didn't intend to spend the whole day in church—there was far too much to do, with new guests arriving in the afternoon.

Alexander came to the inner kitchen door and called out that new guests were drawing up in the courtyard; this created a flurry of activity in the kitchen, and all mention of Diogenes ended.

So it was true, Kelene realized as she woke abruptly. Diogenes was dead. It was as if all her joy was gone in a breath. Why had she been sold, if not to save her father? It was good to know that her family would not go hungry again, but that was not the same as having her father alive. And none of her family seemed to care that Diogenes had died, or that she was gone. Only then did she realize how much she had clung to the hope that some day she would see her family again.

Putting her dream behind her, she tried to make some order of her dress and her hair. She could not imagine she would be left unattended all through the night, and she did not want to look wholly bedraggled when she was brought her evening meal. It would be presented soon, she was sure of it. It was the company more than the food that she longed for.

But the day faded and night came on and Kelene remained alone in her cell, the fire diminishing as the logs burned down, so that eventually she was left alone in the dark, with only her memories to comfort her.

Eventually, Kelene lay down on the bed fully clothed and fell into an uneasy sleep.

By dawn, hunger wakened her, and she rose, annoyed and apprehensive. Had Dracula forbidden the servants to wait on her? After all she had done for him, he could not fully neglect her, could he? Her trunk had not been carried to her cell, and so she improvised, cleaning her face with clear water from the ewer on the single chest. That done, she worked on her hair again, trying to keep the braids from coming wholly snarled like untended yarn. She was aware that with all her efforts she presented a very forlorn appearance, and she could not improve it without help. Dissatisfied, she tried the door and found it barred on the outside, so she began dejectedly to pace her cell.

Finally a single blare of a trumpet announced the beginning of morning within the fortress. At once eager footsteps were heard in the hall, and crisp orders rang out in the courtyard. It was as if the place had awakened from a sorcerous daze.

A young woman in maid's clothing let Kelene out of her cell, and led the way along the gallery to a large room where many women had gathered around a high table where lavish viands had been set out. Reminded of her dream, Kelene was eager to eat, but when she approached the table, only the lamb, with pinkish rare flesh exposed, struck her fancy, and she refused the sweet cheese in dates that was clearly the favorite dish here.

Taking an empty seat near the window, Kelene tore at the meat as if to pull it from the bone. She did not bother to chew the meat very much, bolting it down in mouthfuls. She lowered her eyes to her plate and was astonished to discover she had consumed every scrap of meat and was still hungry for more. She went back to the high table and chose more of the lamb and four small round sausages covered in a dark sauce. This time she managed not to wolf down her food, and when she was through, she was no longer sharp-set, though some remnant of hunger remained with her—small but intense.

None of the other women looked at her; they spoke infrequently and went about their meals with the floating manner of somnambulists. Kelene looked around to see if she could determine the cause, and noticed that most of them drank from the tall brass samovarlike container at the end of the high table. Three of the women had dark weals on their necks, wounds which they ignored as surely as they ignored the others around them and the brilliance of the morning light. While Kelene watched, one of the injured women filled her cup from the brass container and drank from it eagerly.

Curious, Kelene approached this object, and as she did, she smelled a sharp, resiny odor that was so unpleasant that she sneezed. Embarrassed, she went down the high table as if looking for one last bite, but the brass samovar held a part of her attention. What did it contain that these women became so lethargic that they floated when they moved, their eyes fixed on vistas far beyond the walls of the fortress?

Somewhat later as Kelene prepared to get into the carriage again, she caught sight of one of the women at a window above the courtyard; her ferocious gaze was fixed directly on Kelene. Then the woman shook her head once and turned away, leaving Kelene to ponder what she had done to earn the woman's hatred as the carriage moved out of the courtyard and onto the wide military road once more.

"Why did she look at me that way?" Kelene asked Dracula that night as they continued to travel under a cloudy sky.

"Why should it matter how a woman looks at you, girl?" he responded. Tonight he was being gallant. It was almost possible for Kelene to forget she was a slave.

"I have never seen such an expression of . . . loathing." Kelene raised her hand as if to shield herself from the recalled look.

"Do not be troubled," Dracula recommended, fingering the neck-band of her camisa. "She is nothing."

"But to have such feelings—" She interrupted herself. "I don't know why it should bother me. But it does."

"You do not yet understand," said Dracula soothingly. "In time you will, girl. In time you will." He had taken his place beside her in the carriage and had put his arm around her shoulder, as gently as her father might have done.

The thought of Diogenes saddened Kelene. "I dreamed about my family." She made this a confession.

Dracula said nothing; his long fingers closed on her shoulder as he waited for her to go on.

"My sister was buying food in the market. Such an ordinary thing to do! And when she went back to the inn, I realized the family owned it." She made a forlorn attempt at a smile. "They will do well. That is something. But they spoke about my father. They said he was dead."

"You knew he was," said Dracula, his hand still hard on her.

"I didn't want to know it. I thought there had been a mistake, or . . . or a misunderstanding." She stared at the little lamp flame. "I hoped it wasn't so."

The carriage swung as the road turned, pressing the two inside more closely together.

"I never make mistakes about death," said Dracula, his voice as cold as her hands.

She tried to nod, but his fingers gripped her too tightly. "I do not doubt."

"Very good," said Dracula, and released her, his eyes boring into hers as he turned her face to his. "I will not lie to you about death, girl."

She swallowed hard. "Yes."

His kiss was abrupt, without tenderness.

He released her at last, saying as he did, "You're changing, girl."

Kelene could think of nothing to say. She leaned on his shoulder, letting the carriage rock her.

A short while later, Dracula kissed her again, more persuasively than before. He kept her close to him. "You have nothing to fear from me tonight," he said as he caressed her body through her clothes.

"What do you mean?" she asked, anticipating his answer.

He continued to stroke her, speaking quietly and without the ring of command that so often accompanied his words. "I need nothing from you tonight, girl. I am sated—"

"Those women?" she interrupted. "You drank from them and not from me?" She shoved herself away from him, feeling heat mount in her face. "How *dare* you?"

He regarded her with stern amusement. "I did not know you would be jealous."

"I am not jealous," she declared. "I am offended. You have used me unkindly and I am vexed." Her head was held very high, her neck stiff. "I am your slave. Those other women are not."

"You are getting very weak, girl," said Dracula. He looked at her with piercing eyes. "You would not last all the way to my castle if I took all I need of you as we travel."

"You should have said something. You ought to have explained it all."

"To my slave?" he countered. "You can make no demands of me, girl. It is for me to make demands, and for you to answer them. If I choose to take what I need from anyone it is nothing to you, and you will not question what I do."

"No. Certainly not. I have nothing to do but give my veins to you until they are empty. I have no value beyond the blood in my body, which you own. You can discard me like refuse when it pleases you, and I will have no reason to complain."

"Yes. I own you, and I may do whatever I want with you, now and any time. You ought to remember these things before you take me to task again," he said, no trace of conciliation in his demeanor. "You think yourself slighted. You are not. You are jealous. If you were not, I would beat you."

"I am not jealous," she said at last.

"You are." He took her hair and held it tightly, making her face him. "You do not want me to live through any other, but you disdain what I seek. What if I have my gratification of you and no other? You will be dust before a month passes. Once my castle is reached, all this will change and I will honor you as you wish. It is the claim you make on me, as I have made mine on you. Until you know this is true, you will not live the life I will give you."

"I am not like you," she said through clenched teeth.

The carriage swayed heavily, its motion tugging at Kelene, but Dracula did not release her; his grip was unbroken and his stare relentless. "You are jealous of the women. They had more cause than you. They are lost, abandoned, for they could not hear my call."

"They are your slaves?" Kelene asked, shocked at this revelation.

"No. They are less than slaves to me, because they are not like me. You, girl, you are like me." He finally let go of her. "You will know the pleasure of those Un-Dead, which none of those women ever will. They will not rise from death as you will. They will not be my companions, as you will. They will not live in my castle, as you will. They will have no claim upon me, as you will." He said this slowly. "You think nothing of what your life will be. You are young and the young are foolish. You must not remain so foolish, girl."

"I will grow older."

"No," he told her with flat conviction. "You will lie in your coffin before the summer is gone. If you are to learn, you must do it quickly. When you rise it will be too late to prepare for your life." He prepared to leave the carriage, reaching for the door latch to let himself out. "Think of what I have told you while we travel. Your life is nearing its end. What will happen beyond that you must decide." He opened the door and swung to the outside of the carriage, waiting for one of his soldiers to bring up his bay. "Do you want to die and remain dead?"

"Death would end my slavery."

"And begin your punishment, a punishment beyond anything you could endure at my hands. The Militant Angels do not permit God's honor to be slighted," Dracula said calmly. "You can expect no kindness in death."

"Then I can hope that my father will welcome me," she said without conviction.

"Do you think so? You are my creature, and God will not look kindly on what you have become. It is useless to repent, for you have embraced me and I have taken your life into me, as you would take communion from the popes." He was about to vault into the saddle when he added, "Your father would not like what you are now, girl. You cannot appeal to him and find mercy, any more than you can call upon God."

What travail passion brings:
I would spurn it
But for my erring heart.
—Hungarian lyric, 14th century

⊢ XXIV ⊣

All the day before vultures and other carrion birds had circled in the distance, their numbers small at first, then massing as the afternoon came on. This morning the birds' numbers were greater still. They no longer dozed lazily on the wind, but dropped down the sky with the deadliness of quarrels and arrows, squabbling when one of the birds arose from its feast with some morsel unfinished.

"There has been a battle since we passed this way," one of the soldiers remarked to another as the company paused at a stream where horses and men could drink.

"Not so long ago," the second soldier agreed. "By the look of it, the fighting ended two or three days ago."

"Scavengers," said the first, disgust making him terse.

"At least we will not have to bury the dead," the second remarked. "They'll be nothing but bones by the time we get there."

The first soldier swore and then said nothing more.

Kelene overheard this from inside the carriage. She was interested in spite of her increasing exhaustion; even Dracula's use of her the previous night had not dulled her mind. She had been caught up in thought for the last three days and was dismayed at where her ruminations had led her. If Dracula were right, she had nowhere to turn but to him. It did not comfort her to know that he had not lied. She would have much rather been able to console herself with the knowledge that he was as mendacious as the foes of God were said to be.

When they began moving again, Kelene thought she sensed a reluctance on the part of the soldiers, a slight resistance that expressed itself in a slower pace and periodic halts to examine the sky to the east of them. As the day darkened Kelene listened for the sound of the wagon stopping and the groan of the coffin lid as it was ponderously opened, but evening came and Dracula did not emerge. Kelene let herself fade into a semiwakeful state. It was pleasant not to have to think, and better not to dream.

The horses whinnied, and one of the men exclaimed aloud. The wind had shifted and for the first time it brought the stench of the distant battlefield. More penetrating than overwhelming, the smell of corruption lingered enough that when the wind shifted again, the horses remained uneasy and the soldiers acted testier.

They stopped for the night at a hastily deserted farm. Chickens scratched in the yard and a pig squealed for food, but the rest of the barns and pens were empty. When Kelene was escorted from the carriage, she noticed that there were no carts or wagons about; the farmer and his family had had time enough to pack most of their possessions before fleeing. She remembered how carefully they had prepared when they left Salonika, and then how much they had abandoned in Sarajevo.

Dracula met her in the cavernous kitchen of the farmhouse. His soldiers were still in the yard, putting up the horses for the night. "You are tired," he said by way of greeting.

"I suppose so."

"Then you must sleep well tonight. Tomorrow will be demanding of us all." His black cloak rustled on his shoulders, moving with him.

"I . . . I dream when I sleep," she said uneasily.

"You do not want to dream. You used to revel in your visions. Why not now?" He came up to her, haughty and dangerous as any hunter in the wilderness. "Do not be afraid of your visions, girl. They cannot hurt you."

"They make me sad," she admitted, not wanting to tell him how painful it was to see her family. She rubbed her face and felt a fine, gritty dust on her skin.

"Sadness does nothing. It is not worth your attention." He stood over her, not so much threatening her as encompassing her in his shadow.

She could not meet his stare. "I cannot stop my dreams."

"You will, in time," he promised her, moving back.

Kelene took a deep breath as if he had been robbing her of air. "But not yet." She cocked her head to the side. "You know about the kites and the vultures, don't you?"

"I know there is a ruined town ahead, one where a battle was fought recently. I know our road goes through the place." He folded his arms. "You will discover what maddened dogs men can be."

"I have seen a village after soldiers destroyed it," said Kelene. How long ago that had been. She recalled herself then as nothing more than an ignorant child, striving to earn her father's praise and caught in the enchantment of Dracula's summons. She would not be so easily manipulated now, she told herself, and hoped it was so.

"A small village is not the same as a town. There will be more than a few houses burned, and there will be many bodies in the streets." Hot sparks burned in his eyes.

"And birds to eat them," said Kelene before he could.

"More than birds, my girl. Dogs, pigs, even cats will eat the dead when there is nothing else to eat. So will men." His teeth showed, but he did not smile.

She looked at the cold hearth, thinking that she would go hungry again that night. "You have seen more than I," she whispered.

"Vastly more," he agreed, and swept past her out of the kitchen.

Righting an overturned stool, Kelene sank down on it. As she did, she thought back to the long hours her Great-great-aunt Iocasta had kept to her place near the hearth, her blighted eyes turned toward the flames, which she claimed she could see as dim, bright smears. Now Kelene sat by a cold hearth, her memories fading as Iocasta's eyes had. Filled with a shame she could not understand, Kelene remained where she was for half the night.

All through the morning the smell grew worse, sweetly cloying and rotten. Overhead the birds continued to flock, their shrill cries cutting through the corruption-laden wind. The soldiers kept tighter holds on their reins; the drivers held the teams in firmer grips, for the horses shied and minced along, their nostrils large, sweat on their flanks, heads carried high on stiff necks, the whites of their eyes showing. From time to time one would buck or try to back up and have to be spurred into obedience. Although no smoke rose from the destruction ahead, the odor of charring mixed with the stronger presence of decay.

Finally, at midday, the sawtooth wreckage of the town walls appeared, the thick boards blackened and leaning crazily, held up by a half-shattered gate. Beyond were houses with fallen roofs and crumbling walls. In the carriage, Kelene peered out, lifting the corner of the blind to see a narrow portion of what lay ahead. She would not shield herself from carnage again.

At their approach, birds took to the sky in vast, noisy clouds, shrieking their protests at the intrusion.

Swaths of dried blood kept the streets from throwing up dust as Dracula's soldiers escorted the carriage and the wagon bearing the ornate coffin into the center of the town through streets made narrow by sprawled bodies, now collections of exposed bone. The stench was now as real as a wall, and as obdurate. Every breath was painful, and Kelene's eyes watered from the smell.

None of the corpses Kelene saw had eyes left. Many had open abdomens, the organs torn out, but whether by men or birds it was impossible to tell. Incomplete skeletons of children were spitted on pikes, left exposed like offerings to the birds. Discarded and broken weapons were everywhere, some still clutched in dead hands, most cast away.

In the town square, an Orthodox church lay in ruins, the remains of the popes crucified to the doors. Bodies of women were piled inside the narthex, tossed aside in death. Beyond them children sprawled, the marks of teeth in their rotting flesh, their small bones already smashed and gnawed.

There were bodies of soldiers among the fallen as well as townspeople, some of them more intact, preserved by their armor. Insects had come in their endless ranks, invading the metal carapaces of the dead soldiers. The soldiers stank more hideously than those without armor, and their bodies wriggled and writhed with life. Half a dozen corpses hung from the stone front of the town hall.

A number of the birds had come back to their feeding, watching the new arrivals warily as they resumed tearing flesh from bone then cracking bone for marrow. As a large vulture floated down over the town square, one of the horses reared and tried to bolt, causing the rest to whinny and sidle until the rebel was brought under control.

Kelene remained in her carriage, filled with revulsion and excitement at what they had found. She wanted to scream or weep or pray, but she remained as silent as the soldiers, making no sound. She caught her hands together, unable to contain the enormity of her reaction.

"We cannot be stopping here," she said as one of the soldiers opened the door for her and extended a hand to help her descend.

Although the soldier said nothing, he remained waiting for her, and eventually Kelene laid her hand on his and climbed down, holding her skirts as high as she could.

The soldiers gathered in the center of the marketplace, drawing into a tight group as if to defend themselves from ghosts. The horses continued to fret, stamping and nickering in distress, refusing to be calmed by their riders. The stark shadows of midday lent harsh light to the scene, making it more forbidding in its very clarity. Kelene, surrounded by armed men, could not rid herself of the sense that she was wholly unprotected.

"I cannot eat here," Kelene told the soldiers, for once not caring how they would suffer for her speaking to them. "And I cannot sleep here, either."

The soldier who had opened the door for her regarded her with a mixture of bafflement and reverence. He indicated the town hall directly ahead of them.

"I will not go into that place," Kelene announced. "You cannot compel me to go in there."

The soldier bowed to her, and turned away from the carriage.

Four of the soldiers entered the building. A short while later one emerged, white-faced, and vomited onto the bloody flagstones of the market square. Another of the soldiers went to support him.

The soldiers looked about, trying not to appear embarrassed by the distress of their fellow, and one of them still in the saddle lowered his head to his knee.

Kelene was mildly astonished that she had no desire to be ill; the town was ghastly to see and the death was inescapable, but she could not make herself feel overwhelmed by it. Horrible though it might be, it was only death. Now that the fighting was finished, the town had achieved a terrible peace. She looked up into the brassy sky and watched the birds hovering, like so many scraps of Dracula's cloak.

Eventually the other three soldiers came out of the town hall wreckage, one of them carrying a massive ledger under his arm.

As the soldiers came across the open square, a loud sound of rats came behind them. A moment later a deluge of the rodents poured from the front of the town hall, as if they had been released from captivity. The soldiers moved hastily to get away from the noisy, determined rats, knowing that the animals could eat their way through living flesh and bone when desperate enough. The undulating carpet of rats spread out across the marketplace, almost liquid in its movement, the high, chittering cries seeming unnaturally sharp. The scrabble of their claws grated on the worn flagstones.

The horses neighed, trotting in place to keep the furry creatures from biting at them as they rushed into the streets and the broken buildings. The soldiers swore and struck out at the rats with swords and lances. In the sky the birds protested shrilly.

Kelene stepped back onto the carriage, getting away from the rats. The sea of shiny, red-eyed animals was more repellent to her than even the vultures circling overhead. As she watched them, she swallowed convulsively to keep bile from rising in her throat. Only when the last of the rats was gone did she descend once more, shaken and pale.

The soldiers were more skilled at concealing their discomposure, but it was apparent that they had been as much upset by the rats as Kelene. One of them attempted to laugh, but ended in coughing.

"Where are they going?" one of the soldiers called out when it was clear the rats were going in some direction away from the market square.

"I can't see," one of the others complained, his arm up to shield his eyes. "They're moving fast."

"So long as they go, what does it matter?" the driver of the carriage shouted with feigned indifference. It was as if they were speaking to hear voices of the living in this place of destruction and death.

"At least they do not want our horses," the soldier who had helped Kelene step down pointed out to the rest.

"Or us," added the carriage driver.

"We will go around the hill road. It is longer but the valley is—" The soldier now at the head of the party did not quite hold his breath, but the rest understood him.

"It's all like this," said the carriage driver, Kelene supposed as an explanation to her.

"The bodies will be hacked into pieces and piled," said one of the men.

"And worse things done than the birds do," said a third.

Listening, Kelene wondered if Dracula would punish them for speaking aloud. He had not harmed any of his soldiers after she had climbed on his sliding coffin, and she had spoken then. Perhaps this would have the same significance to him, and he would allow the men this opportunity to speak without having to face his wrath.

"No food left," said one of the soldiers as if answering a question.

"Did you expect any?" another asked as he dismounted, taking care to keep tight hold on his horse's reins.

"No," the other admitted, then hefted his short sword with a purpose. "If anyone is left alive, they will—" To Kelene he seemed truly frightened instead of posturing for her benefit, which held her attention.

"Worry about dogs, not people," said the carriage driver. "They will fight. Anyone left will not. Those who could fight are dead or gone away."

"How could the Turks be so cruel?" Kelene wondered aloud.

"Turks didn't do this," said the driver of the wagon. He spat. "This was Christians, against their Christian brothers."

A few of the soldiers chuckled nastily, and one of them said, "Orthodox against Orthodox, not even Catholics. Only Christians crucify their popes. The Turks would have flayed them."

Kelene was certain they spoke for her benefit, making her aware of what they already knew. She wanted to know why they did this, but did not want to ask them. If they were to be punished, she did not want to be the reason for it, not after what she was seeing. She held her skirts, lifting them higher as she walked a short way through the soldiers toward the wagon where Dracula's coffin lay.

"Do we have to remain here much longer?" another of the soldiers asked as the soldier with the ledger handed it to the driver of the wagon.

"Not now," he replied. "There is nothing else we can do. We have what we came for."

In spite of her intention to say nothing more, Kelene could not keep from adding, "You could bury them."

The soldier who had spoken rounded on her, his face set and revealing nothing of his emotions. "Bury them? There are hundreds of bodies. If we worked for a week we could not find them all, let alone make graves for them. The birds will do a better job in any case. And the insects." He signaled for his horse, mounted up, and gestured to the others to follow him.

Kelene got back into the carriage, at once grateful for its protection and fearful of confinement in something so small and dark, like a moving sepulcher. She kept her leather blinds up as the soldiers escorted her carriage and the wagon out the eastern side of the city. It was important to her to discover the depravity of war, as if by knowing that, she would accept Dracula as less savage than she had thought him.

Then the town was behind them and lost to sight around the curve of the hill, and only the birds hanging in the sky served to mark the place.

By the time they stopped for the night, Kelene was so tired that her body felt wooden when she moved. The moon was halfway up the sky and for once not obscured by clouds or hidden by trees. Had she not been so worn out, Kelene might have taken pleasure at the sight, for it was nearly full and shone as if it were made of fine silver.

The place they halted was a small, simple hunters' lodge. A narrow balcony ran the length of the upper floor, giving a view of the hill rising to the north and east.

"In the first light of morning, you will see the mist rise from the lake," Dracula said as he stepped out on the balcony where Kelene stood, waiting to be called to her meal. She had begun to fear she would fall asleep before she had eaten, and that she would drowse even while he was with her. He would not look kindly on that, and she could not bear his anger tonight. In a day or so, when she had put the town and the death and the feasting birds behind her, she could endure his ire, but not yet.

"I can't see a lake," she told him.

He strode up to her. "You spoke to my men."

"It was so . . . hideous, I had to say something. I wanted to be sure we were all still alive." She touched her forehead, aware now that her temples were throbbing. "You should understand that."

"You know they will answer for it, and so do they. You did not begin it, they did. They will accept their flogging without protest." He stood next to her, not quite touching her. "You have nothing to fear tonight. I will hunt elsewhere."

"Oh." She was disappointed to hear this, for she had been looking forward to his nearness to distract her and keep her from having night-mares of the town. She assumed he would need her blood. She shook her head once, noticing how the moonlight limned his features, making him appear paler than he was, and his features even more severe than before. "What game is there in the woods?"

"There is always game." She was astonished that he could sound so remote and at the same time so anguished. Why should he, of all creatures in creation, be dismayed at hunting?

Leaning on the railing, she turned toward him. "Why did we stop in that town?"

At first he did not answer her, and when he spoke his quiet, unin-flected words held her as shouts and oration would not. "Long ago that town made a stand against the Huns. They fought valiantly, and were triumphant, at high cost. It was my Dragon Legion that held the old walls for Rome."

"It was your home?"

"No," he said. "But my soldiers and I fought the Huns for it, on the orders of Caesar Honorius, who had released me from ransom so long as I would fight against the enemies of Rome. All of those of us who served under the Dragon fought the Huns for Rome to preserve our homelands. Rome could spare no more legions to aid us, with the Visigoths at their gates. We were the last of their allies in the east by then." He folded his arms. "We fought the Huns everywhere in these mountains. Sometimes, I think I can see them still, galloping on their ponies, wild as wolves." He moved abruptly away from her, his bearing proud.

"You did not want the town to fall," she said, beginning to understand what he was telling her. She still wondered if she had failed Salonika by not remaining there, no matter how futile that would have been.

Dracula took hold of the railing and leaned out into the deepening night, his cloak lifting on his shoulders. "You will know, one day, perhaps."

"What?" She did not want him to leave until he had answered her. "What do you want me to learn? Why won't you tell me?"

"Because it cannot be told," he said, his face now nothing more than a pale outline against blackness. He turned suddenly.

Without meaning to she reached out and touched his cloak. "Don't go."

"Release my cloak." He said it calmly, the tone low.

The night was very still. Kelene managed to make her fingers work

enough to let go of his cloak. She withdrew to the door to her small
bedroom, moving backward, watching him as she went in case he should
strike out at her. When she could pull the door closed, she said, "I meant
no harm," before seeking the sanctuary of the room; she did not see him
leave, but when she made herself brave enough to look out on the balcony
again, Dracula was gone.

The next night Dracula ordered her to come to him. They had arrived
at a village so lost in the fastness of the mountains that the people who
lived there spoke a language only their fellow villagers could readily understand. Dracula had been accorded the best house inside the walls, one
with high, narrow windows that archers could use to shoot at attackers.

Dracula's chamber was warmed with a blaze in a fireplace as high as
he was tall. The two logs burning there were of tremendous girth, and
from time to time, sparks jumped out onto the stone floor. There was an
enclosed bed, a pair of Ottomite sofas, and a large table with three chairs
drawn up to it. Four braziers gave the corners of the room an uncertain
illumination, and the odor of an incense Kelene had not encountered
before.

"Come in, girl," he told her as a villager left her at the door.

"Where are we?" she asked as she obeyed.

"It is the border of my homeland," said Dracula, with a gesture of
possession and welcome that Kelene had to admire; she had missed the
grandeur of his presence in her dreams; now he had achieved it again. "In
four days we will reach my castle. We would be there in two if we could
fly." His laughter was harsh and unfamiliar.

She hesitated, not knowing what his expansiveness might portend.

"I said come in. Be welcome, girl." He indicated the table. "You will
have your meal here, with me." He swept about the room, his cloak
rustling as if wings folded down his back.

She remained where she was, her mind alert to his changing manner.
Her gonella was one she had not worn before, a fine Florentine brocade
in deep russet and rich peach that made her hair seem like burnished gold
under its chaplet. She thought now she would have been wiser to choose
familiar garments. In strange clothing, she felt more perplexed by Dracula's
demeanor than she would have been had she worn one of the other gowns
she knew better. Uncomfortably she watched him approach her. Kelene
put her hands behind her back.

"You will come in, Kelene," he ordered her with an assumption of
courtesy she did not find convincing.

Hearing him speak her name startled her to movement. Once over
the threshold, Kelene felt foolish for having faltered. She realized Dracula

appeared to be trying to offer her the hospitality of his country; this was the border and he intended to treat her as a good host would receive a guest. Her only reservation was her awareness that she was not a guest. She made her way to the table and drew out a chair. "I am yours to command," she said, so he would know she had not lost sight of her station.

"So you are," he said, remaining at her side, saying a third time, "Come, girl. Sit down. I know you are famished; you ate little yesterday." He watched while she seated herself. "I am finally in my native land; you are leagues and leagues away from yours. I know what it is to be so far from the place of your birth."

This graciousness would not deceive her, Kelene vowed inwardly. She would not be put off her guard. "We have traveled fast."

"I have been eager to be here. I gain my strength here, with the earth of my blood under my feet." He took a cruse of hammered gold and offered it to her. "Drink with me."

Her fingers closed around the chalice; carefully she tasted the contents, making herself swallow. "I have drunk, lord."

He took the cruse from her and drank deeply, apparently unaware of her staring at him. "It is the wine of my homeland."

"It is blood." Admitting this aloud should have disgusted her more than it did; Kelene kept her eyes on the cruse.

"Yes." He leaned down and kissed her on the mouth. "The savor is sweet."

"Blood," she said again. Yet she had to admit it warmed her as the fire in the hearth did not.

"You will come to know its virtues, girl; you have some sense of them already," Dracula said. He took another long draught, his eyes alight with malice and pleasure. "At my castle, you will develop a taste for it."

"How?"

"You already hunger for it," he said. "You have yearned for it." He came up behind her chair and, reaching around her, put the cruse in front of her. "I have left the last for you."

"You show me too much favor," she made herself say; she would not touch the gold cruse.

"So fastidious," Dracula said as he laid his hands on her shoulders. "That meat you so prefer is not pork, girl. It is not veal, or venison."

Her body, already cool, now was seized with a cold that began in her bones. "You lie."

Dracula bent over her. "And yet you eat human flesh eagerly enough," he whispered softly.

Kelene could not move. "I do not."

On the hearth one of the massive logs broke, sending a shower of sparks into the room in a brilliant, brief cascade.

He kissed her shining halo of braids. "You want to believe so, but—" He shrugged and picked up the cruse.

She could hardly breathe as she listened to him drink. "At least that is the last of it."

"Oh, there is more, girl," he said as he put the cruse down once again, empty. "There is always more."

The grip of winter and the grave
Are less stringent than my sorrow . . .
—Romanian ballad, 13th century

⊢ XXV ⊣

Her first realization when she woke was that the sunlight burned her but did not make her warm. Kelene rose and went to close the shutters so that she could continue to rest. But now that she was awake, she felt the first pangs of hunger, and shame washed through her, robbing her of any satisfaction she had felt at refusing her supper the night before. She told herself again that Dracula was lying, that he had to be. How could she eat human flesh and not be revolted by it? She would never enjoy it, she insisted to herself as she began to put her hair in order, using the wooden comb Dracula had given her the night before. She looked about for a mirror, and then stopped.

There was a rap at the door and a woman of middle years let herself in without waiting for a call. She had the look of all the villagers: tall, angular, with dark hair, pale skin, and eyes of a blue so light they were almost silver. She carried a tray with food on it—dates and bread, along with six sausages.

At the first sniff, Kelene's mouth watered. She made herself eat only the bread and dates, but she could not keep from looking at the sausages, hoping the intensity of her gaze could capture their goodness without staining her soul more deeply. She ate standing, prepared to run if she were tempted to forget her oath.

The woman smiled carefully, as if she feared her skin might crack. She said something to Kelene while pointing to the sausages, making a gesture of encouragement.

"No," Kelene told her, doing her best not to speak too sharply. There was no point in making the servant angry. She went over to the window to get away from the lure of the meat.

The woman sighed heavily and picked up the tray with great reluctance. As she went toward the door she paused and made a last attempt to get Kelene to change her mind. When Kelene shook her head, the woman departed as if she were about to attend a funeral.

"It will be soon," Dracula said as he wrapped his arms around her, the moon dappling them with white leprous patches where the leaves let the light through. He had risen at sunset and had vanished almost at once. By the time he returned, red splashes on the front of his black leather giaquetta, the night was more than half gone and Kelene was so hungry that she could not sleep.

Kelene had been assigned a tent, but had not gone into it. Instead she paced the little clearing, hating her famished desire for the meat she now wanted to despise. Her need to resist the hunger was weakening as the night lengthened toward morning. By sunup, she thought, she would be faint, and then her determination would fail her.

"You are my slave. You cannot be held to answer for what I bid you do."

"But I cannot . . ." She hesitated. What he said was true enough. As long as she was his slave, she had to answer only to him. The argument was sophistry, and she knew it, but she was so hungry.

"I command you," said Dracula, his voice deep and smooth. "You cannot refuse me, girl." His arms tightened.

"But I cannot eat human flesh." She said this so softly that she hardly heard it herself.

"Because you know what it is," he pointed out, pressing her face to his shoulder. "Before you knew, you ate it heartily and asked for more."

"And for that I am mortified," she said, the words muffled.

Dracula swung his cloak around her. "You might as well fear the ghosts of all the lambs you have eaten."

"But . . . everyone would loathe me," she said.

"I do not loathe you, girl," said Dracula. He lifted his head as an owl, huge and silent, floated overhead, disappearing among the trees almost at once.

"No," she said, half in relief, half in accusation.

"And if I do not, what would the rest matter?" He lifted her chin with his hand. "Do it because I wish it, if you will not do it for yourself."

"But . . . I can't abide what I want most," she said, and made an effort to break free of his arms.

"Then you will have to follow my orders and eat because I require you to eat," he told her, maintaining his embrace.

"I am your slave," she said.

"See you do not forget it, girl," he said as he swept her up into his arms like the child she no longer was.

She was at once gratified and miffed that he would treat her so. She wiggled, but not enough to force him to release her, for she had no desire to be dropped. Her exhaustion was so draining now that she decided to let him carry her. When she was more composed she could challenge him. He was all that stood between her and a life of unthinkable hardship and abandonment. She would be idiotic to forget that. "When we reach your castle, what will happen to me?" It was hard to imagine what it would be like, being in his company and not traveling.

He carried her to her tent, setting her down on the narrow bed before he answered. "You will come to love it."

She stared at him as he sank down beside her. "What is it like?"

"The castle is high in the mountains. Standing on the battlements, you will be able to see for many leagues." He caressed her face. "No one will show you disrespect."

"Respect? For a slave?"

"You are Dracula's slave." He could not banish the hunger in his stare. "Once you are one with me, you will know what it is to be feared."

She wanted to tell him she wanted no one to fear her, but in her heart, she knew this was no longer entirely true. "I will try to sleep now; you are back and I am safe."

"From everything but your desires," he said, stroking her hair. "Very well. Sleep, girl. Go into your visions, to the heart of your dreams and remember what you find there." His touch was light. As he lured her into sleep, she felt one instant of dismay, and then the dreams had her.

She rose above the trees, lifted on invisible wings, and hovered on the slow night wind. Around her the woods were still but alive, the hush caused by her passing. She liked the ease of sailing along the sky, her flight effortless. The tents in the clearing disappeared behind her as she ventured to the south and east. Some time later—the time reckoned in the measurements of dreams—she noticed a small cluster of houses, a hamlet in the middle of the forest where peasants made their best of sheep and goats. There was a sound of a fiddle played with more energy than talent; the melody was spritely, but it circled around a mournful center, with more tears than laughter in it. Kelene followed the sound and found herself standing at the edge of the clearing where the hamlet stood. She moved toward the scraping strings, wanting the company of another human being, though it was only a figment of her dream.

She had almost reached the thatch-roofed stone house when the playing stopped and a man's voice called out. Kelene rounded the end of the house and saw the man, fiddle in his left hand, bow in his right, standing in the open door of his cottage. "Your playing caught my notice. I—" She got no further.

"Demon! Devil! Creature of the night! Go! In the Name of God! You took Radu

but you will not take me!" He made the sign of the cross and stepped back into his house, slamming the door as Kelene rushed forward.

"No," she cried out. "No. I am nothing like that. Let me in. I will show you." She had reached one of the windows and was looking into the central room of the cottage when the peasant slammed the shutters in her face.

"Go away! Go back to your grave and leave decent Christians alone! You've had your prey for the night! Hunt somewhere else, can't you?" He went from window to window securing the shutters.

"I only wanted to hear you play," Kelene said sadly, her dream already pulling her away, drifting her up into the air away from the hamlet. As she passed over the last house in the clearing, she could see a newly dug grave in the little graveyard beside the domed chapel. No wonder the man had been frightened, she thought. One of his neighbors had just died.

This did not make her feel less lonely, but the hurt of having the shutters closed against her faded a bit as she realized the cause. The man would have been suspicious of anyone coming out of the forest in the night. She did her best not to be downcast as she traveled over the treetops toward the rising slope of the mountains.

Campfires glowed where gypsies were drawn up for the night. These had trough-bedded wagons and not the enclosed wagons Kelene had seen before. There were makeshift tents attached to the wagon beds, making them into sleeping quarters for the night. Six horses grazed in hobbles, two of them piebald and spotted, making them look like painted dolls instead of carthorses. She noticed one of the wagons stood apart from the others. It was stacked with large crates that were secured in place with heavy ropes. Looking back at the horses, Kelene was amused by the animals her vision had conjured, less sinister than the crate-laden wagon. Her melancholy faded as she went up the mountains, sometimes skimming the tops of the trees, other times soaring high above the rocky shoulders of the peaks, as the creatures below shrank to the size of ants and the trees were nothing more that fuzzy swaths.

There had been high peaks in her visions before, when she still believed Dracula was a Militant Angel. She assumed she was remembering the place she had dreamed before—the high crag with great peaks rising around it, a vast, forbidding realm of mountains. She felt herself falling toward a high stone tower, circling down until her feet touched the platform.

"Well," said Dracula's voice out of the darkness. "Do you know where you are?"

"You brought me here before," she replied, half-afraid he would offer her another filled chalice. She looked about, unable to see him.

"I am with you," said Dracula.

She did not question him as she made her way around the top of the tower. The highest peaks glistened with snow; the wind off them was like a steel blade, and although this was a dream, she shivered.

"Look around you, girl," Dracula said, as close as if he spoke in her ear. "Look and do not forget."

Kelene stared into the night. Was it his order or her dream that showed her the majestic peaks and the wide stone steps leading down from the tower? Look at it, she thought. Look at what? Was it the tower or the mountains he was commanding her to see? She scowled, wanting to soar again, to go into the vast night and to escape, at least for the last of the night, the world around her. The tower fell away beneath her and she reached upward toward the distant stars.

Dracula's voice pursued her. "You will return. And when you do, you will know."

"Know what?" she asked.

But he did not answer her, and in an instant she was looking again at the walls of the ruined town, where stealthy men made their way through the destruction, pausing now and again to claim some lost trophy. She saw the knives they held and knew they would fight any foe—human or not—for the pitiful remnants of the dead. She was certain what she saw was real, as real as the Ottomites advancing through the Balkans, and as merciless.

Then she was nearing the gates of Belgrade, where she knew she would see her family again. For once she faltered, for much as she missed them, watching them this way made her feel immensely alone. She remained outside the walls, listening to the calls of the Guard as they patrolled their posts. Belgrade was safe; that should be enough, she told herself. Why go through the torment of seeing them?

The inn looked as prosperous as she recalled from her previous vision. The woodwork was glossy with beeswax and the front room was in good order, with benches for the travelers and a settle by the hearth. The main staircase bent twice reaching the floor above; the carpet on it was new, with no trace of wear. All the guest rooms but one were occupied, and the servants' dormitories had more than half the beds filled. The rooms for Kelene's family were over the kitchen, good-sized chambers with sturdy beds and standing chests for clothes. Kelene looked in at them in turn.

"Kelene?" Orien rubbed his eyes and pushed onto his elbows.

She was so startled to hear him speak that she stopped where she was.

"Kelene? Is that you?" The question did not come from her dream, but from her brother who was awake.

The sound of his voice jarred her, goading her into action. In less than half a heartbeat she was gone, rushing away into the night.

Dracula was still beside her when she woke, her sudden wakefulness making her blink and shake her head.

"Orien saw me," she blurted out.

"Orien will think he dreamed, and so will the rest of your family."

"If he tells them," she said cautiously. "He might not say anything."

"He will, you may be sure of it. You are his rescuer and they know you have dreams that are not like other dreams." Dracula rose, gesturing to the door of the tent. "Dawn is coming. I cannot stay." He bent and kissed her mouth. "You are mine now, body and soul."

"You bought me," she said, wanting to go back to sleep.

"I called you. The gold is nothing." He touched her hair and then left her alone.

Kelene lay awake, longing for sleep but afraid of her dreams. She invented ways to stay awake; she knotted her fist and put it under her side, hoping she would be too uncomfortable to drift off. When she began to doze, she threw back the heavy woolen rug that had been laid over her and let the morning cold keep her awake. She listened to the soldiers as they rose, and she wished she could be like them, answering only to duty. The soldiers knew their obligations and the penalties for disobedience, and otherwise they were left to themselves. Dreams did not bring them anguish.

A wedge of cheese and a hard round loaf of black bread was all the breakfast she was offered. It was the same as the soldiers ate. She was grateful that she did not have to refuse the sausages, for she doubted she would be able to.

Not long after midday they stopped to water the horses at a ford in a rushing stream swollen by melting snow. The soldiers passed around more bread and cheese while the horses drank, and one of them remembered to cut slices for Kelene. It was warm in the sunlight, but Kelene kept to the shade of the trees while she was out of the carriage. Some while after Dracula's soldiers had stopped, the sounds of goats indicated someone was approaching, possibly bound for the ford as well. Kelene listened to their cries, more strident than those of sheep, and was enjoying the ordinariness of the sound when another joined it and brought her pleasure to an end: there was a tune being played on a fiddle, a kind of circular melody twisting brightly around a lamenting core. She had heard it the night before in her dream, and the sound of it now dashed all her cheer; she climbed back into the carriage at once in a futile attempt to shut out the fiddler's tune.

At sunset they were still traveling, and made no provision to stop. Kelene supposed Dracula intended to press on as long as the horses held up, for he was clearly eager to reach his castle. It would mean another long, fatiguing night, but she was certain riding in a swaying carriage she would not sleep well enough to dream.

Dracula entered Kelene's carriage not long after he rose. His clubbed black hair was glossy, all trace of gray gone. His eyes were unusually bright, as if fires were glowing within them. "Tonight you are to stay in your carriage, girl," he told her without preamble. "Do not leave it, no matter how tempted you may be."

"Then we are not going to travel until dawn," she said. "We are trotting still; you must have some place you intend to arrive. Is it far away? Is it your castle?"

"No; neither far nor my castle. Remember what I have said." He prepared to get out again, but was stopped when she made herself ask him, "That goatherd, the one with the fiddle? Did you—?"

"I fed on a peasant; it may have been one from that hamlet." She had no immediate response to give him.

He was preparing to sling his leg over his horse when Kelene found her voice. "He cursed me, for what you did."

"One day you will do the same, girl, and earn the curses honestly," he said as he leaped onto his mount.

"I will not," she insisted as he rode away from the carriage. It was infuriating, she thought, to have him speak so to her and then ride off before she could respond. He would have to listen to her eventually.

Why, she wondered, did he want her to remain in the carriage when they stopped for the night? Was it only the exercise of his mastery, or was it something more? What was there about the place he planned to stop—for surely he knew what the place would be, or why would he issue the orders he had?—that he did not want her to be seen there? Or what did he want her not to see? She puzzled on the question until the carriage began to slow and shouts greeted the arrival of Dracula's company.

The language was vaguely familiar. Kelene heard the greetings with curiosity and the certainty that she recognized a few of the words. It might be nothing more than tone of voice, but she was well aware that Dracula was being welcomed with respect that bordered on reverence. She heard the laughter of children and thought they might be in a small village, or perhaps a peasants' hamlet, though she noticed no barnyard odors and no sounds beyond a braying mule and the whinny of horses.

There was also the distinct odor of lamb cooking over an open fire. For once she knew she could eat without hating herself for her hunger. She was ready to eat, hoping food would be brought soon. Someone laughed and someone else began to pick out a tune on a lute. One of the soldiers shouted approval.

All Dracula's soldiers had halted, and in a short while, Kelene heard and felt the team being unhitched from her carriage. She heard the thud of blocks placed behind the carriage's front wheels. There were exchanges in the tongue that was tantalizingly familiar but not quite recognizable, and then a man called out Dracula's name. Kelene listened as his name was repeated until it became a chant. This continued a short while, and the soldiers seemed to join in. Kelene was tempted to shout his name with the rest, but did not.

The welcoming noises straggled to a stop; the lute began to play

again and a woman started to sing. Kelene knew the song; she had heard
gypsies sing it in the marketplace in Sarajevo. This must be a gypsy camp,
she thought, and she had an uneasy recollection of the one in her vision,
with the spotted, piebald horses. Not that this was the same place. It
could not be.

As if to confirm this assumption, the door to the carriage opened and
Kelene was handed a bowl of fresh-carved lamb, a section of pickled
cabbage, and a slab of bread with a serving of butter to accompany it.
There was a knife and a spoon for eating, and a goblet of rough new
wine for drinking. Kelene began to thank the woman who gave it to her,
only to have the carriage door slammed in her face.

At another time Kelene might have found the lamb delicious, but her
overriding hunger for the detestable meat she had been given before inter-
fered with her enjoyment, making her cringe with every morsel of food
she consumed. Nothing she could say to herself mitigated her hunger.
How could she prefer human flesh to this? Was she truly becoming like
Dracula, and was this the proof of it? That she drank blood knowingly
and ate human flesh? She had no answer she found acceptable, and she
was unable to do more than pick at her meal. Blood and flesh, blood and
flesh, she could not rid her thoughts of their savor. She made herself wash
down as much of the food as she could, though the wine was far from
the best and it overwhelmed all the other flavors in her supper.

A shawm was playing with the lute now, its plaintive tones making it
sound almost like a human cry, and not the result of air blown past two
reeds and fingers on stops. The gypsies did not sing with the musicians,
and Kelene listened, caught in strong emotions as the sad little tune went
on. While she listened, she invented her own lyrics for the melody.

When at last the musicians were silent, a shout went up from many
voices, and again they began to chant "*Dracula, Dracula, Dracula, Dracula,*"
this time adding force to their adulation with the beating of drums. Then
Dracula addressed them, speaking in their language as if inspiring them
to do battle. His voice rang with purpose and command; the gypsies
answered him with shouts and the trilling of tongues, as the Ottomites
did.

For Kelene it was like hearing her angel speak to her again, and she
was quick to summon up all the strength she could to resist the powerful
effect he exercised on her. Dracula was no angel—she had been a fool to
think he was—and what he brought was not the protection of God but
something no Christian should seek.

When Dracula finished the chanting resumed, and went on for almost
as long as he had addressed them. Then a man with a deep, age-cracked
voice began a harangue. Listening, Kelene wished she knew what he was

saying, for the sound of his words was so mellifluous that she supposed understanding more than his tone and delivery would reveal great eloquence.

In time, that, too, ended and music began again. This time there were more instruments, and from what Kelene could hear, the gypsies were dancing to the energetic tunes. It was horrid to have to sit in her carriage, able only to listen to the sounds. She put the bowl that had held her supper on the floor of the carriage, thinking it would provide her an excuse to delay the person sent to fetch it for a moment or so longer than if she simply handed the bowl over. She was disgusted with herself for having to use so degrading a ploy for such a small advantage, but she felt so alone.

The celebration was becoming more frenetic, with whoops and abrupt exclamations. A few of the voices were slurred and aggressive.

Kelene decided she would wait a while, until the festivities were at their height, and then she would slip out of the carriage to watch. She realized she would have to cover her head: drunken or not, the gypsies would notice a blonde in their camp. She lifted the flap of the leather shade and peered out, looking to see what had become of her guard. She could not see him. Then she noticed a figure next to the carriage, propped up but seeming to drowse. She looked for other soldiers and saw none. For a moment Kelene questioned the wisdom of her intentions, but her loneliness weighed too heavily upon her. What would the gypsies do that would be so terrible?

Vigorous, rhythmic clapping suggested to Kelene that the celebration was nearing its height. There were shouts and applause. One of the soldiers brayed out a marching song, joined in the chorus by his fellows. She would have to move soon or abandon her plan entirely. Picking up the bowl from the floor of the carriage, she decided that if she carried it she might explain her presence outside of the carriage—if it was discovered—as her wish to return the bowl. She knew it was flimsy, but it was better than no means to account for her actions. She took the lap rug from under the seat in the carriage and threw it around her head and shoulders as if it were a shawl. Satisfied that she was as prepared as she could ever be, she put her hand on the door latch and let herself out of the carriage.

Fate is writ on running water,
Fortune rides on storms . . .
—Greek ballad, 16th century

⊢ XXVI ⊣

As she lowered herself down to the ground, Kelene saw a soldier leaning against the rear wheel of the carriage, a wooden goblet dangling from nerveless fingers. She supposed he had been posted to guard her. She stood uncertainly, holding the door of the carriage open, prepared to retreat if he noticed her. But he was deeply asleep, his jaw slack and his legs splayed out in front of him like a discarded toy. Kelene stared down at him, in case he should waken, but the soldier slept on.

Kelene did not hesitate; she clutched her improvised shawl tightly, held onto the bowl, and looked around her, deciding to keep the gypsy wagons between her and the central fire where the tribe was gathered for the evening. As she came around one of the wagons, she saw the gypsies' horses hobbled and grazing at the edge of the clearing: two of them were spotted with piebald faces. She recognized them—who could fail to remember such ridiculous spots and faces?

"You can't steal them," said a voice behind her.

Alarmed, Kelene jumped at the sound and turned around to face the rear of one of the wagons. An old woman sat in the back of it, her legs dangling over the end. She smoked a long, tubular pipe like the Ottomites used. Her face was indistinct in the shadows, but Kelene had the impression of wrinkles and deep-sunk eyes. She was surprised to be addressed in Greek. The woman's accent was strange, but Kelene could understand her. "I wasn't intending to steal one."

"Just as well," said the old woman, sucking on her pipe and blowing out acrid smoke. "They would fight you if you touched them." She continued to watch Kelene. "You have come far."

"You speak to me in Greek. Why?"

"You are Greek, aren't you?" the old woman asked.

"Yes. But why did you think so?" She came nearer to the back of the wagon, as much to keep her voice low as to see the old woman more clearly.

The woman shrugged and took another long draw on her pipe.

Kelene was nonplussed, and could think of nothing to say for a long moment; the old woman was content to smoke her pipe. Finally Kelene put down the bowl and said, "They are having a fine time."

"Why do you think so?" the old woman asked, a spark of interest in her eyes.

"They are singing and dancing," Kelene answered.

"That does not mean they are doing it from happiness or joy," the old woman said, smoking more. "They are under obligation to Dracula. Not as stringent as yours, but they are showing him they have not forgotten." She regarded Kelene in silence, her eyes squinted against the smoke wreathing her head.

"But in such a way?" Kelene gestured toward the bonfire. "They do not seem displeased."

"I did not say they were, only that they are not happy." Her mouth widened in the suggestion of a smile. "You will learn."

"Learn what?" Kelene asked.

"Everything that Dracula wants you to know," she replied as if there could be nothing else to learn.

Kelene came the last few steps to the back of the wagon. "He told me to stay in the carriage."

"You have disobeyed him," said the woman with satisfaction. "He will not overlook your actions."

"That doesn't trouble me," said Kelene with more bravado than truth. "He has ignored me for everything but his need. It should not surprise him that I would do this."

The old woman regarded her narrowly. "You are fourteen?"

Kelene stared. "He told you?"

"He tells me nothing. I know things." She leaned down toward her pipe. "I may not have visions like yours, but I know things." Her expression became less remote as Kelene stared at her in amazement. "Your visions have not blessed you, though they have saved you more than once. That is because you have belonged to Dracula all your life, and he gives no blessing but some protection to those who are his. When he bought you it was only the end of what started before you could speak." She cocked her head as if listening to more than the music.

"Yes?" Kelene urged. "What more?"

"This journey is not over. You have farther to go than you think. You have not finished with your family yet," said the old woman slowly.

"There I fear you are wrong," Kelene said quietly, not willing to volunteer anything more. She was about to turn away.

"Your brother will seek you out. The last one who spoke to you, he will come, not this winter or the next, or the one after, but he will come, and when he comes, he will sustain you." Her chuckle was harsh and ended on a cough.

Kelene shook her head. "Your knowledge has failed you, Grandmother," she said respectfully. "My family has seen me for the last time." She could not imagine Achilles coming after her, and she had seen him, the last of her brothers, as she left Belgrade; that seemed a lifetime away from her now.

"But for the one brother." The old woman gave Kelene another long stare. "You will remember when the time comes."

"I will never see him, whichever one he is," she said with conviction.

"You will," the woman repeated firmly. She glanced toward the bonfire. "The men are getting very drunk. When they are drunk they are quick to claim women."

Kelene shivered. "I only wanted to be among people," she admitted.

"And you have been. So it is best now that you do not remain here." She smoked her pipe, a distant look in her ancient eyes. "You are not so unthinking as you want him to believe you are. But he is not deceived. He knows you are his."

"So he has told me," said Kelene, suddenly eager to leave the old woman alone. She did not like the things the woman said.

"He will punish you," the old woman said a bit louder as Kelene started away from the back of the wagon.

"He has already warned me," said Kelene. She glanced back toward the carriage and saw that two of Dracula's soldiers were trying to get the soldier sleeping beside it onto his feet. Kelene moved more hastily.

"Believe him," the old woman called after her.

Kelene increased her speed, holding her skirts up as she ran.

The soldier who had fallen asleep drunk was trying to walk unaided by his comrades, and he gestured impatiently as one of them struggled to hold him upright. The rest of the camp, soldiers and gypsies alike, were by the bonfire, raucously entertaining themselves in an atmosphere of increasing confusion. The songs being sung were less coherent now than they had been earlier, and the musicians' playing had become chaotic.

Kelene waited until the soldiers had turned away from the carriage toward the bonfire to approach and let herself back into it. She had to pull herself up, dragging herself by holding onto the doorframe. She felt her skirt snag and she kicked it loose, hauled herself onto her feet and turned around as if she had just opened the door to look out. This was forbidden, but not so great a trespass as getting out of the carriage.

Another soldier had joined the three, his face severe though he walked awkwardly. He shouted to the drunken soldier, his reprimand delivered in overly precise phrases.

"What are you doing?" Kelene demanded, as if she had been disturbed by the soldiers.

"Not supposed to . . . to talk to you," the soldier who had been upbraiding his fellow said as he peered at the carriage.

"And I am not supposed to talk to you, either," said Kelene without apology. "But there is so much noise that I had to find out what was happening out here."

"It's all right," said the soldier. "Nothing to worry about."

"Do you think so?" Kelene challenged, thinking that she would protect herself best by not allowing the soldiers to question her. "My guard was asleep at the wheel of my carriage, lost in drink, and you think I have no cause to concern." She realized as soon as she said it that she had revealed too much. She was certain they would catch her in this admission that she had at least looked out of her carriage before this moment, or how would she have known where he had fallen asleep. "He was snoring," she improvised.

The soldier who had failed to guard her went white. "I didn't mean—"

"Be quiet," said the one who had put himself in charge. "Come away. We'll have to find out the whole." He motioned to the others with him to move away from the wagon. "Find someone to take over the duty." He looked sharply at Kelene. "Close the door. Don't look out again."

It was difficult not to smile as Kelene followed his orders. She sat down on the padded seat and sighed heavily once, congratulating herself on getting through the potential disaster with nothing more than a little discomfort. She leaned back, beginning to be pleased with herself. She had managed to elude her captor without discovery. Perhaps she would succeed in eluding Dracula's anger as well. The thought of that made her smile, and she decided she would sleep well, without any dreams to disturb her. She shook her skirt impatiently, then settled herself on the seat.

She awoke late in the night, when the music had stopped and the glow of the bonfire had become nothing more than a few winking embers. She put her hand to her eyes as she stared into the blackness to determine what had brought her so abruptly out of sleep.

A moment later Dracula climbed into the carriage. He stared at her, and although it was too dark to see him, she could feel his ire.

"You thought I would not know?" he asked. "These people are loyal to me. They would not do anything against my wishes. Do you understand me, girl?"

"My name," she said slowly, "is Kelene."

"Do you understand me, *girl?*"

She levered herself upright, determined to brazen it out. "What have they said I did? Other than speak to your soldiers?"

There was something of a smile about his mouth. "I am not so easily deceived as you want to think, *girl*," he said emphatically. "I know that my soldiers failed in their duty." His voice was cold now.

"They were celebrating, as all the rest were. As you were," she said, keeping the dread out of her voice but not the tremor.

"It is my right. They had their duties to attend to. Including watching you. Had your guard not been lax, you would not have been able to get out." He held out something to her; she took it from him, puzzled.

"It is from your skirt. I found it on the ground outside the carriage," he said, so calmly that she was startled by what he revealed. "It would not have been outside the carriage if you had not been."

She fingered the fabric, recalling how she had had to kick her skirt free of a snag as she got back into the carriage. "That should not have happened," she said, speaking more to herself than to him. She forced her eyes upward to meet his. "Yes. I had the chance to get out, and I took it. There was so much going on, everyone sounded happy and I wanted to . . . to be a part of it, if only by watching."

Dracula shook his head. "You deliberately went against my orders."

"Yes," she said again, now fully erect on her seat. She would not plead with him this time, she decided. She was done with begging.

"You know what becomes of rebellious slaves," he said quietly.

"If you are going to kill me, then do it," she said.

"I am going to kill you, girl, but not yet. Killing is an easy thing. With your death so near, what terror can it hold for you now?" He reached out and brushed her cheek with the backs of his fingers.

"What are you waiting for?" she asked, doing all she could to hang onto her fading courage. "You can kill me tonight, or tomorrow, or whenever you please. It is your right."

"And you want to be a martyr to my rage?" He did not quite laugh. "Would that make you proud of yourself?"

Heat mounted in her face. She glared at him. "Very well; you frighten me. Is that what you want?"

"I want you to accept what you are, what I am going to make you," he said. "It would serve my purposes—and yours—better if you will not fight me at every turn."

"I am sure you would prefer capitulation," she said resentfully.

"I would prefer you embrace what I know you to be. The longer you refuse to know what you are the longer you will give yourself pain, and all to no benefit." He took her hands in his. "My call is rarely heard, and not all those who hear it answer it as you did."

"More shame to me," she said, with a pang of guilt for how proud she had been of her visions.

"No shame at all, if you will only open your eyes, girl," he said. "You are determined to remain blind, and you think that this is virtuous."

"I am not blind," she insisted, trying to pull her hands away without success. "I do not want to be a vampire. Why can't you believe this?"

"You answered my call," he said simply.

"I thought I was visited by the Militant Angels," she said.

"Your father wanted you to think that. If he had not made you want to believe, you would have known me as I am. Your angel had my face."

She sighed. "I think so." She put her hands to her face. "Was I wrong about all of it?"

"You were right to flee," said Dracula, his voice low. "Not I, and not the Militant Angels would have been able to save you if you had stayed in Salonika, or Sarajevo."

She pulled her hands away and laced them together in her lap. "I did hear you, but I did not understand," she said after a long silence.

"And now you will not let yourself understand, no matter what I say to you. When it is over and you are one with me, you will find out I have not lied." He took a long breath. "You will remain in this carriage until I tell you otherwise. If you try to leave, I will give orders that you are not to be fed. The soldiers who failed in their duty will answer for it, and you will watch. Each of them will lose one eye."

Kelene could not swallow hard enough or fast enough. She went pale, and her throat constricted. "It isn't right," she said in alarm.

"What has right to do with it? They were given orders that they failed to fulfill. You will have to watch it. That, my girl, is your punishment. At dawn, just before we leave the gypsies."

"Won't the gypsies object?" Kelene asked.

"Why should they?" Dracula bowed over her hand. "You are my slave, and my men did not protect you as I ordered. The gypsies will see nothing unfair in what I demand in recompense. They would think it odd if I did not make such a claim." He went to the door. "If you speak again, the person to whom you speak will lose a hand or an eye for it."

Kelene nodded mutely.

"We will reach my castle soon. When we do, your ordeal will end." He stepped out of the carriage. "Remember, you must watch at dawn."

"All your soldiers have suffered on my account," she said. "They must despise me. Or you."

"It hardly matters, girl. They have their sworn duty." He indicated the stars overhead. "It will be dawn in a while. Sleep now, if you can, and waken to see these men pay." With a gesture that was a dismissal, he strode away through the camp, pausing once as three sleepy gypsy voices called his name in homage. Kelene listened as if to her own condemnation.

The morning came unkindly to the camp. A slight drizzle was in the process of turning to a steady downpour.

Kelene had wanted to don the russet-and-gold ensemble but had not wanted to undress so completely in the gypsy camp, and so remained in the garments she had been wearing for the last two days. She combed and rebraided her hair. Only her certainty that they would be punished more harshly if she refused made her continue to ready herself.

Those soldiers who came to her carriage were silent and drawn up in two columns with all the formality of troops parading for the rulers of the world. They opened the door and helped her descend, no one looking directly at her.

The gypsies had come to the remnants of the bonfire, their manner that of abashed children. They did not speak. The rain had doused more than their fires, making them all look bedraggled and tawdry in the morning light. They remained in their places as if they had been ordered to remain there.

At a sign from one of the soldiers, three of their numbers were brought forward; Kelene recognized one as the soldier who had fallen asleep by her carriage. He was quite composed, but his lower lip trembled. There were two men behind him, resolute and resigned to their fate.

Kelene was shown to a place across from the spot where the men waited. She saw the gypsy farrier come forward with his tools in his hands and a large bucket of coals. She thought he looked a bit ashamed of himself as he set about preparing for his work; he did not look at any of the soldiers, but he gave Kelene one uneasy glance as he began to work the bellows on his bucket of coals until they came to life. The soldiers remained where they were as the coals glowed.

Without any signal Kelene ever saw, soldiers came forward to hold the condemned, one of the three offering his arms as if for martyrdom. Then the farrier looked at the nearest of the men. Taking a tool used to trim the hooves of horses and mules, he put it into the coals and then lifted it, thrusting it into the left eye socket of the nearest soldier, its jaws open to pluck out the eye.

The soldier fainted without a sound. Kelene thought she was perilously near fainting.

As the first soldier was lugged away by his comrades, the second one was brought up. Again the farrier performed his task, leaving Kelene as weak as the half-blinded soldier. As the third was brought, she bit her tongue to keep from screaming. She put her fist in her mouth as the third collapsed between the two soldiers holding him.

The farrier made a gesture of resignation as he completed his assigned tasks. Then he left his position, leaving the soldiers to tend to their fellows.

Through this all the gypsies said nothing. Now, however, one of them pointed at Kelene and proclaimed something. She was not certain what the import of the words were, but they were pronounced passionately, and Kelene recognized the force behind them. She shook her head, then looked toward the men. She saw the soldiers drag them away toward her carriage.

Had the men not just been blinded, she might have called out in protest; as it was, she gestured emphatically, not wanting the men near her. No one paid any attention to her until one of the soldiers came and led her back to the carriage and helped her to get into it.

The three men had been piled in on the floor of her carriage; two were unconscious, while the third moaned loudly. All three had a sheen of sweat on their faces and a smell of fear about them. Kelene stared at them in horror. She realized her protestations were useless when the door was firmly closed on her and her helpless companions.

The horses were brought and harnessed to the wagon, the soldiers working in their customary silence. Then the men saddled and bridled their own horses, mounting up while the gypsies came to the wagon where Dracula's coffin was secured in place with strong ropes, the precaution they had used since the coffin had almost been lost down the mountainside.

Kelene lifted her feet onto the seat so that she would not have to touch the soldiers as the company moved off, leaving the evidence of their passing in the newly sodden road.

They had traveled most of the morning when one of the soldiers began to ask for water. His voice was cracked; shortly he became delirious. Kelene leaned down, using the lap rug to wipe his face, flinching at every sound he made. She could see the bloody ooze on his face but found it difficult to touch it. The soldier was breathing more rapidly and shallowly than the other two on the floor of her carriage. His skin was clammy and he was sweating as the other two were not.

Kelene shifted her position so that she could give that soldier more attention; she was troubled that she did not know his name.

When the company paused at midday, Kelene was given a waterskin along with cheese and bread; she took these and made herself try to eat a portion of the food, but quickly discovered that she could not. Her hands shook as she held the cheese, and when she tried to swallow the bread she could not force it down her throat. The water she saved for the soldier who was getting worse. By the time the company was underway again the soldier was only semiconscious; the other two were awake enough to move as far from their comrade as the narrow well in the carriage permitted; they watched Kelene tend the soldier, their faces revealing nothing of their thoughts.

By late afternoon the stricken soldier had fallen into an unresponsive sleep. He would not swallow when Kelene put water on his lips, and he was unable to balance himself so that when the carriage pitched and swung, he lolled, increasing his injuries. At last one of the two soldiers who were improving opened the leather shade and called out, "There's a dead man in here."

Kelene looked up sharply. She had been trying to clean the worst of the blood and milky fluid off the soldier's face. Her hand hovered over him, and she regarded him, doing her best to keep her feelings to herself.

The carriage was pulled to a stop and in a few moments one of the soldiers opened the door; he held the reins of his horse as he inspected the body on the floor of the carriage. "Dead, right enough," he said as he prepared to pull the corpse out of the carriage.

"Stand clear!" someone outside the carriage shouted.

The door was held wide as the dismounted soldier took his place at the head of the body and hooked his hands in the soldier's padded leather giaquetta.

Overhead the rainclouds were unraveling, showing patches of blue through their flimsy gray. Ordinarily this might have cheered Kelene; now it seemed a mocking reminder of indifference. She offered to hand the waterskin back to the soldier at the door; he ignored it as he dragged the dead man from her carriage.

She wanted to know where they would bury him, and what they would do for the repose of his soul. She assumed it would take time to bestow the soldier, and prepared herself to wait. So Kelene was doubly astonished when, a short while later, the soldiers remounted and the company moved off again, leaving the soldier's body behind under a hawthorn bush.

Two of the soldiers remained sitting on the floor of her carriage, stoic to the point of apathy. Kelene did her best not to look at them, and wondered why it was she did not weep.

Do the mountains forget?
Do the seas?
Or only fickle men?
—Greek song, 11th century

⸺ XXVII ⸺

Their last night on the road was spent at a house tucked into a fold of the mountain. The house looked old, but not ancient, its carved wooden interior the product of the industry of artisans dead two or three hundred years. Half a dozen servants greeted Dracula as he emerged from his coffin at sundown, their reverence for him so striking that Kelene supposed they must worship him. After all she had endured, she found this cruelly amusing.

By the time someone showed her to her chamber she was ready to demand that someone take care of the two remaining soldiers. One of them was developing an infection in his eye-socket. But the servants said nothing to her and she was afraid to speak.

Now her silence made her furious. The door had barely closed when she burst out, exclaiming to the walls, "How *could* he let that soldier die that way? He's a monster." She stared around at the lavish carving of faces wreathed in or half-hidden by leaves. "If you can hear me, I think you're a monster. You might as well have strangled him and spared him a day of agony!" She had not ordered the soldier's eye put out—that was Dracula's doing, and though he said it was her fault, she would not accept it. "You *killed* him!" she shrieked.

"He was mine to kill," Dracula answered from outside her window.

She swung around, her long, ornate sleeves catching on the edge of the small table where a single lamp burned. The lamp went flying as the table crashed to the floor. Kelene went completely still. Dracula had reached her window from the outside of the building. Her chamber was on the second floor. She flung up her hands. "What are you doing here?" she demanded; it was the first question that came into her mind.

"I am watching you, my slave." He pointed to where an edge of the woven carpet was smoldering. "Put it out."

She had already picked up the heavy coverlet from the bed and had raised it to beat out the flames when she became aware of his fear. She stopped the swing of the coverlet and let it hang limp in her grasp. "Why?" she asked, trying not to show how much the fire alarmed her.

"Put it out, I said," he repeated more urgently as he clung to the outside of her window.

"I will if you will swear to me that you will not punish your soldiers again as you have done. You will not make them ride with me when they are in such pain and hate me so much." She gave the coverlet a suggestive swing, making no attempt to conceal the delight she felt at his discomposure. "The fire could spread at any moment."

"All right," Dracula said, his eyes fixed on the brightening flames. "I swear. Now put that out."

Kelene did not take long to beat the fire to ashes. The acrid smoke left behind a malign incense of charring, but she tried her best not to be troubled by it. Finally she turned back to the window. "You had better come in," she said, wondering if he would honor his oath to her. "How did you get up there?"

He swung the window open and stepped inside. "I climbed," he said, recovering himself as he pulled the window shut.

"Tomorrow," he said with deliberation, "we will arrive at my castle. You will be received by my servants. They know who you are and why you have come, and you are not to act in any contrary way when dealing with them." He began to pace. "The gypsies will bring the crates of your earth and your coffin, but they will not travel as quickly as I do."

"They say the dead travel fast," Kelene heard herself respond.

"Not while they are in the company of the living. I have made plans for your death. But you will live until I am back in my castle." He kicked at a burned fragment of carpet almost as if it were alive.

"I will live until tomorrow?" She asked it calmly.

"Perhaps two or three days beyond. It depends on how quickly your provisions are in place." He watched her carefully for a brief while.

Kelene made a gesture ambiguous enough to satisfy them both. She was aware that the fear she had seen in him while the fire burned was now gone and he was once again master of the moment. She was aware of a grue up her spine as the significance of what he was saying struck home. Without asking his permission, she sat down on the nearest chair a heartbeat before her knees gave way. "In two or three days."

"As soon as everything is ready. Then you will not be able to lie to yourself about how you are like me." He halted in his circuit of the room, studying her intently for a short while—hunger, need and something more predatory in his expression. "You may want to deny this, but once you leave your coffin you will know all that you have refused to comprehend." He strode up to her, the feral light glowing in his eyes with such brilliance that she had to look away from him. "You do not know how much you tempt me now."

"To kill me?" she inquired, achieving a false self-possession that was almost good enough to convince him.

"If you die here, the death is eternal." Some of the rapacity faded from his gaze, but not enough to give Kelene any sense of reassurance. He still kept his distance, as if wary of his impulses as much as she was.

"You are depraved," she said, speaking without heat.

"I am Un-Dead," he corrected her. "For most, that is my depravity."

"They do not know you," said Kelene, her recklessness making her feel slightly drunk. Why prod him this way now? she asked herself, then answered the question for herself aloud. "As you say, you can kill me."

"Ah, no," said Dracula, going near the hearth as if to show his fright had been an aberration. "I have not brought you so far to lose you now." He folded his arms, his cloak hanging wider from his posture. His face, lit from beneath by the fire, was demonic.

"But you have no right to make me a . . . an Un-Dead," said Kelene, her determination lifting her spirits as she confronted him.

"I do, you know," he said, his ferocity banked more than the fire. "When you answered my call, I gained the right. I come where I am invited." He came across the room to her, looking down at her. "You will learn not to deny me."

She shook her head. "I won't."

Instead of arguing, he walked away from her. "You will change your mind." At the far side of the room he swung around again. "It is useless to protest. Until you waken in your coffin . . . When you awaken, I will not need to explain it."

"If that is so, why do you persist?"

"To make you less frightened. Some vampires madden with fright and must be destroyed. Those who raven like mad dogs I leave to the peasants. They know how to deal with vampires." His face was set.

"And you abandon your own kind?" she demanded. "After they have come to you in trust?"

"As you have?" he countered, his voice dropping to a potent whisper.

"What reason would I have to trust you?"

Dracula read something of her consternation in her eyes. "Yes. Why trust me, though I have not lied to you. The lie was yours alone." He made no more effort to perpetuate their disagreement. "Tonight dine well. You will need strength."

"If you order me, I must. I am your sl—"

"My slave, little as you act like one." He shrugged, his cloak moving as if to resettle down his back. "It is my order that you dine well tonight, on whatever is served you." He held up his hand. "In exchange I will permit the herb woman to treat the two soldiers. You know which two."

Kelene stared at him. "No matter what I do, I am damned," she said.

"You would be damned no matter what you do," he said silkily. "This way you may salve your conscience for a day or two more."

She knew it was useless to attempt to cross herself, so she put her hands into her lap and stared down at them.

He nodded. "The woman serving you will bring you new clothes. Wear them tomorrow for your arrival at my castle."

Had she not been weary of her other garments, she might have considered refusing, but she had longed for other clothes for days—she, who had rarely owned more than three changes of clothes was now disappointed with five elegant dresses with camisas to go with each! She murmured a few words of thanks.

"You will be ready to leave in the morning, early, for the journey is nearly ten leagues and the road is steep. We will not arrive much before midnight." He went to the window. "I will not return tonight. Rest well."

She did her best to look impervious as he opened the window and climbed out.

A while later two women brought her a large supper, served on plates of fine Venetian glass and in fluted blown goblets that revealed the dark color of the drink that was brought for her. Kelene smelled the aroma of the meat first, and she did her utmost not to accept the watering of her mouth and the surge of appetite that was a physical force inside her.

One of the women set the plates on the table and motioned Kelene to come and eat, indicating the lavish fare set out, with fine breads and cabbage with pine nuts to accompany a platter of carved meat.

Kelene wanted to fire a resistance within her soul, but her hunger was stronger. When she began—with a broth in which floated small, aromatic dumplings—she told herself she would fill up on the broth and on bread and would not want so much of the pinkish meat that was tantalizingly revealed through a dark sauce studded with mushrooms. Certain that her good intentions would be worth nothing, she had her first taste of the broth and at once recognized the flavor for what it was. Her shoulders drooped and she abandoned herself to intense enjoyment. As she drank the dark wine that was not wine, she was grateful that death would soon deliver her from this hideous desire.

For she was determined to remain dead and never rise from her coffin. She could do that much, she told herself. Perhaps it would expiate some part of her many sins and recommend her to the Militant Angels—the real ones, who would enforce God's Will on her soul, whatever that might be. She hoped there was still some humility in her soul where penitence might begin.

It may have been the angles of the peaks or the long shadows of the pines on the rising slope, but the light possessed an undertone of darkness that Kelene found at once fascinating and sinister. In the morning as they set out she decided to leave one blind up; almost at once she became aware of the quality of the light, unlike any she had ever noticed before— it was the way in which the sun's rising shine went through the mountain passes, or so she thought at first. But as the day wore on and the light grew higher, the darkness did not dissipate, but seemed to infuse the light with a shadow that permeated everything.

She had dressed in the gamurra of Antioch silk that she had been given. It was a shade between green and blue, but so dark that its folds looked black. The wide, elaborate sleeves were edged in gold braid and the lacing in the corsage was also gold. The camisa was embroidered in gold. Had Kelene seen this splendid dress when Dracula first claimed her, she would have been overwhelmed by its finery, but now she paid little attention to it, thinking of it as one more bribe meant to buy her capitulation, as his gold had purchased her body.

The road was old and barely wide enough for her carriage and the wagon. The soldiers rode single file. They kept their horses climbing until the animals were panting and lathered; the soldiers allowed their mounts a little water from the freshets spattering down from the melting snows above them, then started them going upward again.

In a few places there were peasants' houses, all with their doors facing to the south, and all with elaborate crosses on the peaks of their roofs. In the small fields the peasants paused in their work to watch the company pass. A few of them crossed themselves, but most bowed, bareheaded, to the wagon carrying the coffin.

At noon the soldiers tethered the lathered horses beside a pond and began to eat. When one of them offered Kelene sausages, she did not refuse. As she ate her midday meal on one of the last days of her life, she could not shake off her memories of her father. If he had known what she would become, he would never have taken pride in her as he had done. A traitorous notion intruded: what if he had known but did not care? Surely Great-great-aunt Iocasta must have spoken to him about her concerns. Just as surely, Diogenes had not been swayed by anything she said. At the time Kelene had felt vindicated. Now she felt manipulated.

When the company mounted up again, Kelene tied all her blinds up, doing her best to ignore the discomfort of the sunlight. She wanted to know where she was going, if it was to be her final resting place.

As the company made its way higher up into the mountains, they encountered offerings beside the road. At first there were only a few, and they were small things—a runt puppy, three goslings—left next to piles of stones. By midafternoon the offerings were more generous—two lambs, both bleating and fretting at the ropes that held them to a dead tree with stones piled against its ancient trunk—and more frequent.

The road now twisted up the side of a mountain, past waterfalls that descended to the river far beneath them in the increasingly narrow gorge. The turns grew sharper and the horses had to scramble for purchase on the old stones. As dusk came on, the roadway became more and more indistinct in the gloom and the soldiers went more slowly. Finally they passed a massive outcropping boulder; Kelene could see an offering on the side of the stone, blood still running from the animal. She could not see clearly what it was, though it was large enough to be a foal or calf. Then the boulder was behind them and they were on the narrow track running along the crest of the mountain, the tremendous mountains spread out around them in the gathering night, encroaching on the spring sky.

Tired though they were, the horses walked faster, and one or two had to be pulled in from the trot. Kelene knew they sensed the nearness of their own stable, and she became more alert; Castle Dracula could not be far off now. She might not want to arrive there, but, perversely, she wanted to see it. Leaning forward on her seat, she stared out the window.

There was a single, brief pause not long after nightfall when Dracula emerged from his coffin and took his place at the head of the company. Three of the soldiers unfurled banners with his dragon device on them, and they became a procession in the remoteness of the Carpathians.

Not far away, wolves bayed, their wails undulating like a madman's song. Their howls followed the company for almost a league along the ridge—staying below the travelers in the trees, but keeping up their cries as if in salutation.

The moon began to rise, its pale shine doing little to dispel the shadows. Washed in that bloodless gleam, the road ahead looked insubstantial. Although in its third quarter, the moon seemed unnaturally large and its lume was white as bleached bone. The mountains loomed against the edge of the sky; snow cast back the pallid light as if taunting the moon. Kelene wanted to see more clearly but could not make out the shapes in the night. She held onto the straps in the carriage as the team pulling it went faster. Her pulse was strong in her ears, and when she put her hand to her throat the beating of her heart was there under her fingers.

Eventually the company passed a long stretch of crumbling stone wall and started up a causeway to the huge stone-fronted building that surmounted the highest peak on the long spine of mountains. The drop to the river was sheer and long, making the echoes of the horses' hooves eerily repetitious. A single trumpet-call signaled their arrival at the cavernous gates. Torches appeared on the battlements overhead as the gates began to gape.

Kelene sat straighter on her seat, wanting to show Dracula that she could behave as the occasion demanded. As her carriage passed through the gates she had the impression of more silent soldiers standing at their posts, their weapons at the ready. Who were they fighting? she asked herself. What foe would come against such a castle as this one?

There was a flurry of activity around Dracula as he dismounted, and a ragged kind of shout went up, very like the cries of the wolves that had accompanied the latter part of their journey. The dragon banners were furled and stowed before anyone opened the door of Kelene's carriage. She began to fret as the soldiers tended to their duties without any notice of her.

Then Dracula himself swung the door wide and held out his hand to help her descend. "The gamurra becomes you," he said as she alighted.

"You can't see it," she responded, in no mood to be catered to by the man who had vowed to kill her.

"I can," he told her sharply, and snapped an order in a language she did not recognize. A path opened through his soldiers, leading to a second massive door going inside the keep. He led her toward it, stopping once to issue another order before the inner door swallowed them up.

Kelene found herself in a long, stone corridor lit by braziers and occasional branching oil lamps with half a dozen wicks for brightness. Aside from the two of them, the hallway seemed deserted. Dracula walked with clean strides that she had to run to match; her sense of the rooms that they passed was cursory as she did her best to keep up. She felt as if they were winding into the bowels of the mountain, for occasionally there were groups of steps set into the corridor, all of them leading down; she was afraid to breathe in such a place.

"Stop," he said without warning.

She stumbled a few steps then halted, breathing deeply as much from excitement as this sudden exertion. She had not realized the skirts of her gamurra could weigh her down so much or would tangle about her ankles as if attempting to trip her. Standing in place, she still felt she must be moving; the long hours in the carriage and the rapid descent into the castle gave her the sensation of ongoing motion.

"You will come with me," he said.

"What else would I do?" she asked, the sharpness gone out of her words with panting.

He rounded on her. "This is my castle, girl. You will remember that."

She nodded once, too disoriented to resist longer. "I am your slave."

"See that you do not forget." He pointed to an arched doorway. "That is the main hall. Coming in from the western gate we had to enter through the soldiers' court. Had we come in the south gate, you would not have to traverse the corridors." He all but thrust her into the room, keeping hold of her arm just above her elbow as if he feared she might bolt.

The main hall was high, of stone like the rest of the castle. There were few ornaments, either in carving, or paintings, or armorial displays. A single staircase connected the hall with a small gallery above. A fireplace of heroic proportions blazed with the trunk of a good-sized pine denuded of branches. A number of smaller doors opened onto the main hall. Furnishings were as sparse as the decoration: half a dozen chairs of various styles and ages, two tall chests with locks on them, plain shelves near the larger central door where items of clothing could be left. A long, simple table was set up in front of the fire with plates that appeared to be gold set out upon it; of particular note was a jeweled, golden chalice that Kelene had seen before in her dreams. This held her attention while Dracula clapped twice, saying, "Sit down, girl. It is time to eat."

She gave a half-hearted and incoherent protest as he guided her forcefully to the table. "I am not hungry."

"Of course you are," he said in rallying tones. "If you worry that you will not rise early, no matter. You may sleep into the afternoon, if it pleases you. It will help prepare you for your life here." He drew out the chair—an Italian courtesy that took her by surprise—and helped her to be seated. "This is an old castle—as old as I am. It has been rebuilt twice since the first stones were laid." He went to the hearth and stared down into the fire. "The cadet lines have other castles, but this, six leagues west of the Borgo Pass, is the only true Castle Dracula." He shed his cloak, tossing it casually over a cross-shaped chair.

Gone were the wings that had made him so angelic in her eyes. In the place of the angel was a tall, lean man with powerful shoulders and a long, lean body that she found disturbing, as if by looking more human he became more monstrous. All semblance of the angel was gone now, and she was left with this predatory creature who looked too much like a man. She was about to speak when two servants came into the hall, both holding trays. As Kelene watched, they bowed to Dracula as if to a king, and then went to the table. The men took no notice of Kelene as they set out the plates and platters; I might as well be invisible, she thought, for all the notice they pay.

When everything on the trays had been set out, the servants bowed to Dracula and left the hall again, as silently as they had come.

"Well, girl, eat," said Dracula, as if he had lost all interest in her. He moved to one of the chests. Taking a key from someplace Kelene had not noticed, he opened the lock to look within.

"You are not eating." He turned toward her, a bent-bladed kukri knife in his hand.

Kelene stared at it, immediately aware of his vow to kill her. "But—" She could not imagine him insisting she eat now, unless it was the Roman tradition of granting those condemned a last meal. She started to shake her head when Dracula put the knife aside.

"Eat. You have nothing to fear tonight." There was something very like affection in his countenance, which was more unnerving to Kelene than the knife had been. "This is my home, girl. You are welcome here."

She rubbed her face as if that might make her believe more of what she saw. Slowly she picked up a spoon and began on the soup. She did not attempt to convince herself that its deep red color came from beets. When she had finished the soup, she next ate the rough wheaten porridge with a cream sauce, all topped with baked cheese. She knew she could swallow this without hazard. But there was meat, this time cooked in a stew with cabbage and onions, so redolent that all other odors were banished by it. "It is very good," she said—because she had to say something, and because it was true.

"The cooks know they must do well or they will answer to me."

"But you don't eat," she pointed out, as if he might be unaware of it.

"I am master here. Those who live here are mine." He closed the weapons chest and went to one of the chairs, a square-backed one of black wood, with a leather-padded seat and armrests carved with fierce animal faces. His long hands caressed the open jaws of these beasts. "When you are done, I will take you to your chamber."

"You? Not a servant?" She could not keep from blurting out the questions.

"You will have a servant to help you, girl." He sounded as if he had indulged her beyond any expectation. "You will be bathed and cosseted for tonight and tomorrow and possibly one night more."

"Until you kill me," she said flatly.

"Yes." He looked directly at her, the shine of the firelight making his eyes glisten with flames. "Until I kill you."

Light has fled the sky completely,
Only endless night remains.
—Greek lament, 11th century

⊢ XXVIII ⊣

Her chamber was on the floor above the main hall, one of a suite of five, opening from a hexagonal common anteroom onto the gallery. The only difference between this chamber and the other four was that hers over-looked the south courtyard; the others did not. There was a small locked door on the far wall which Dracula did not mention.

"Who else lives here?" Kelene asked as Dracula paused on the threshold.

"No one; not now." He indicated the antechamber. "The gallery door can be closed and locked during times of trouble. This part of the castle was considered the last place of defense."

"But it can also be a prison, can't it?"

"Yes," he said without excuse. "I will leave you and summon a maid to assist you. You will not be able to undress easily without help."

Kelene knew this was true because it had been an effort to dress in the beautiful gamurra. The heavy, clinging silk reminded her uncomfortably of cerements. "That will be useful," she said, certain she ought to say something.

"When you waken, you will be bathed and I will show you the prepa-rations that are being made." He was at the door already, preparing to go.

"For my death," she said, trying to sound as if this did not trouble her; she knew she had failed.

"For your death," Dracula agreed. "Your death will be memorable."

Kelene wanted to answer him with pointed phrases to show she was not willing to be intimidated. But her tongue felt like wool in her mouth and she could not frame a retort that expressed any part of her emotions. "Let me sleep," she made herself say so that she would not be as silent as the servants in the castle.

"As long as the sun shines tomorrow, you may sleep," he said, and left her chamber, closing both the inner and outer door behind him.

Kelene covered her eyes with her hands as if to shut out the room and all knowledge of where she was. Why had she thought she could make him change his mind? What possessed her to imagine he would want her to remain alive? She sat on the edge of the high bed allocated for her use, where she rocked back and forth. She had had chances to run away and she had not taken them because she had thought it would not be safe. Now she was at Castle Dracula, which would surely be her grave. What had she saved herself from? Dracula was going to kill her. And she had been idiotic enough to let him have her as a willing victim. What in her visions had made her think she could be saved by him? Why did he want to have her with him? Why had he prolonged the inevitable?

Kelene's thoughts were interrupted by the arrival of the servant whom Dracula had sent. She was past her first youth, but not old; she had haggard features and the kind of stolid hopelessness that Kelene had often seen in refugees fleeing the Turks. The woman's expression mirrored her own.

"I am to help you prepare for sleep," said the woman in passable Greek. "In days to come, I will teach you Hungarian and Romanian."

"Days to come," Kelene echoed in a hollow voice. She stood up and began to unfasten the lacings on the corsage of her gamurra, all the while unable to stop the tears that welled in her eyes.

"There is a night rail under the coverlet," said the woman. "I am Magda."

"I am Kelene," she said at once, all but overcome to know someone's name other than Dracula's. She would have welcomed any gesture of friendship or cordiality, but this was not offered. Magda stood waiting while Kelene finished with the lacing.

"I will pull it off if you will bend over," said Magda. "I will take the shoulders."

"Fine," said Kelene, resenting the coldness of the servant. She almost stumbled as Magda pulled the gamurra off in a single, energetic tug. Now Kelene stood in her shift, thinking she ought to be cold.

As Magda folded the gamurra and prepared to put it in the clothes-press at the foot of the bed, she said, "I will bring you another camisa when you wake."

Perhaps, Kelene thought, the woman was too tired to be friendly. It was past midnight and she may have been up since dawn. That would be enough to make anyone sullen. Keeping this notion as a consolation, Kelene pulled out the night rail, slipped out of her camisa and into the night rail while Magda closed the clothespress and pulled back the coverlet. "Thank you," Kelene said as she slid between the covers.

"You have no reason to thank me. I am only doing my duty." She watched while Kelene adjusted the coverlet, then went to let herself out. "When you wake, go to the anteroom and ring the bell there,"

"I will," said Kelene, trying not to feel too sorry for herself. She could have died as Hector had, consumed by fever and unable to fight any longer. She was not the only girl to face death before she had a husband. Chiding herself for her self-indulgent tears, she did her best to relax and sleep.

The visions of her dreams pursued her as the night lengthened into dawn: *Not Belgrade now, but Sarajevo, at the home of her uncle, now reduced to ashes and rubble by the Ottomite soldiers who had Markos surrounded. A small man with a ledger was accusing Markos of withholding money from them.*

Markos stood in his one remaining garment, pleading with the man with the ledger, claiming the monies were for an investment that would bring riches to the city and to the Ottoman rulers. He was so terrified that his face looked like tallow. He kept repeating that he was not a thief, that he was only trying to make enough money to support his family. Kelene watched him, remembering the warning she had given and wondering if her failures had brought about his ruin. He might well think so. She watched while a wooden block was brought and a stout soldier in the sultan's livery came, an ax over his shoulder.

Screaming, Markos was dragged to the block and his arm was ruthlessly pulled down. The ax fell and he screamed like a woman in labor. His arm was bound up in a mechanical way. When his left arm was put on the block, he was unable to fight any longer. She stared at him in the dream, thinking he would not live much longer than she would.

Then she slipped away from the burned house and the calamity that had carried away that part of her family. She drifted over Sarajevo, then into a simple monastery where the cloistered monks prayed in their whitewashed cells. All was quiet, but for one cell, where Brother Iraneus—he had not hanged himself as Markos had said, then— was confined, weeping and muttering scraps of prayers. He had gnawed the flesh off the backs of his hands; the raw wounds were putrescent. He kept telling God he would not touch another child, not ever.

He seemed to become aware of Kelene's presence in the room, for he looked about wildly, his matted hair and beard showing flecks of ruddy foam from his lips. "Sorceress! Damned thing!" he screamed. "I can never atone as long as you haunt me!" He began his prayers again, and a moment later chewed more flesh from his knuckles, his screams turning to laughter that was more distressing than the screams had been.

Kelene felt herself slipping away from Brother Iraneus' cell, hoping that this was indeed only a dream and not a true vision. She would not like to have Brother Iraneus' madness on her soul along with all the other sins she would have to answer for.

Then she saw the magnificent bay at Salonika and the homesickness that went through her was so keen that she thought it might be enough to kill her right now. The vision showed her the house where they had lived. She recognized it by the bay view, for the house itself was much changed. The Ottomite residents had altered it, making it larger and changing the garden entirely. Kelene could hardly bear to look at it.

Near the gate there was a blind beggar holding out a begging bowl, the beggar's arm was so emaciated that it seemed the beggar must be dead already; surely this was a spectre and not a living—Kelene recognized Great-great-aunt Iocasta with difficulty. She heard the old woman call her name, and fled the dream and the vision, though it seemed she was swimming in melted pitch for all the progress she made.

She wanted to wake up, but could not no matter how hard she tried.

All at once Dracula was before her in the darkness. "Well? Is it so much better to be with your family, to remain in the life you had before?"

"You mock me," she said, her emotions in turmoil.

"What you see would have befallen you and all your family if you had not used your visions to protect them. Girl, few gifts are truly without price." He came down out of the sky, his cloak spread out around him. "Your father demanded your visions and you gave them. That is all."

"And you called me," she said. "What of Brother Iraneus? Why do you show him to me?"

"Do you know what is done to sorceresses who drive priests mad?" His voice was even, and then he told her. "Their breasts are pulled off with hot pincers, their legs are smashed in the boot, and their wombs are ruptured with the pear. If they are still alive, they are burned." He watched her from his place above her. "Would you have preferred that to what I will give you?"

She was pale and shaking. "I must wake up," she muttered. "I must wake up now."

"Not yet," Dracula said in a serene voice. "There are more things you must see." He held out the chalice to her. "Drink. You will be fortified."

"Fortified at what cost? You have shown me that nothing I have done has spared any of them." She could not move; the chalice hung before her, alive with golden light.

"Would you have done better to become slaves of the Ottomites?" He waited for her to answer, coming lower in the sky to hear her reply.

"Would that have happened?" she asked softly.

"Your visions saved you, and your family. You see what has become of your aunt; would you want all your family to suffer as she does?" He was almost beside her.

"She has visions, too," Kelene said, troubled by his questions.

"And she did nothing about what she saw. So now she has to pay the price for her stubbornness." He caught her in his arms. "Don't you think this is better than dying, begging, outside the wall of your own house? Don't you think I provide safety that nothing else in your life has done?" He did not kiss her, though his arms tightened.

"I want to wake up." She could not breathe.

"Soon, girl, soon. There is one other thing you must see." He released her at once *and vanished up into the air. She followed his progress until he was a black speck against the night sky.*

"No more. No more," she pleaded. "No more. Please." She hated to beg him for peace, but she could do nothing else.

"Time is short, girl," he admonished her from the vast emptiness of the sky.

She resigned herself to what he would show her, for she could not escape him, no matter how desperately she wanted to. For a long moment she hung in space, the earth falling away beneath them.

Then she saw Alexander at the inn, an elderly woman beside him. She was telling him something that made him frown, nodding thoughtfully. Kelene wanted to hear what they were discussing, but the words eluded her.

Pallas came from the kitchen, her face rosy from working over the hearth. She came to her brother when he called to her. "What is it?"

Hearing her speak made Kelene want to weep again. In so little time all this would be gone for her. She made herself listen.

"There is an offer for you. A man with a child of two is seeking a wife. He has money and could help us at the inn."

"A man. What man?" Pallas asked, the color fading from her cheeks.

"He is a worthy man," said the elderly woman, who was acting as the matchmaker. "He is twenty-four. His wife and second child died together a year ago. He has some money, as I've said. He wants to come to Belgrade to live and not just to sell his work. He is a carpenter. He makes chairs and cabinets and tables. All things the inn would need. He has his own tools, as well."

Pallas nodded as if bowing to the inevitable. "I will see him."

"Very good," said the woman. "He will be delighted to hear this. A carpenter with a cook for a wife may go far in this world." Kelene saw brother and sister exchange nods. "A meeting will be arranged. Next week?"

"Yes, unless my sister changes her mind," said Alexander, glancing at Pallas.

The woman said all the correct things and left them alone.

"Are you really willing to see this man?" he asked when the hallway was empty.

"I will have to marry someday," said Pallas. "This man might do as well as any." She smiled at Alexander. "I will be guided by what you recommend. I do not want to see disruption in the family after all we endured . . . ." The words straggled off.

"Our father would be proud," said Alexander.

"Of our inn, I think so. But our selling Kelene?" She crossed herself.

Alexander copied the gesture. "It was her sacrifice," he said.

"Yes. And our prayers will thank her every day," said Pallas. She turned away from Alexander. "Well, this carpenter will be a useful addition," she said with uneasy brightness. "If he does not stink, or sleep with his shoes on, I will have to consider him."

"Oh, he will have to be better than that," said Alexander. "For my sister, he must be noble and honest and treat her like a duchess."

"At least," she responded, laughing as Kelene had not heard her laugh in more than a year.

"And name your first girl Kelene," added Alexander, doing his best to match her tone.

She was awake. The sun was high overhead and the wind had come up, making the stones of the castle moan with its passing. Kelene sat up in bed, feeling more worn out than when she went to sleep.

As she opened the curtains around the bed she had the strange notion that someone had been in her room and had fled as soon as she came out of sleep. She dismissed the idea as the last fading scrap of her dream; she did not want to think of it as a vision. That would be too final. For a short while she remained seated, the curtains pulled aside. Then she slowly got down, her feet touching the cold flagstones without discomfort. She walked around the room, seeing clearly for the first time.

The bed was comfortable enough, though the bedding was plainer than what Kelene thought she would find in this place. There were two chairs, three chests—one of them standing—and a clothespress. There were no mirrors. Kelene noticed her felt boots had been put next to the bed, and she might have put them on before she went out into the anteroom but she changed her mind. She wanted to find out how far she could get in the castle before the servants noticed she was out of her chamber.

The anteroom was as stark in the daytime as it had seemed at night: the stones were blackened with smoke and age, so that the lamps hanging lit did little to dispel the gloom of the place.

Kelene put her hand on the latch of the door to the gallery—she realized it had to be the right one because it was banded with iron and the others were not. She was easing it open when it was tugged out of her hand. A moment later Magda came through the door, bearing a vast drying sheet. She looked at Kelene with an expression of annoyance. "I didn't know you were—" Kelene began.

"You didn't know you were watched over?" Magda was incredulous.

"Why should I?"

"This is Dracula's castle and you are here on his invitation—"

"He bought me in a slave market. That is not an invitation," said Kelene. "Why should he have anyone watch his slave?"

Magda made no immediate response. When she spoke again it was as if nothing of their exchange had taken place. "You are to bathe and dress. Then you will have your meal. At sundown Dracula will show you about the castle."

"They brought his coffin in from the wagon, did they?" She intended to find out if she could shock Magda, but the woman merely nodded and pointed to the door.

"You will want to put on a house robe before you go out. The bathhouse is behind the kitchen. It was heated at midmorning and kept hot ever since." She pointed in the direction of the room Kelene had just left. "The house robe is in the clothespress."

"I am not a child," Kelene said. "You cannot give me orders as if I were a child. I am fourteen. Girls often marry at my age, when there is enough for a dowry."

"So they do," was all Magda would say as she followed Kelene back into the bedroom. "But so long as you are a stranger here, you may want to have me tell you about the place rather than having to discover it all for yourself."

Kelene gathered what dignity she could and attempted to be better-behaved toward Magda. "Since I will not be here long, I suppose it would be sensible to let you—"

But now Magda did look surprised. "You will not be here long? What are you saying?"

"What?" Kelene was puzzled. "Surely you know that Dracula will . . . drain me of blood tonight or tomorrow night."

"But you will not leave," said Magda with apparent relief. "You will remain here, of course. You will not be able to go far unless he"—it was clear from the way she said *he* that she meant Dracula—"provides you with your coffin."

"Not more of this rising from the dead?" Kelene said incredulously. "He may have risen, as he claims, but how can anyone else?" She paused as something occurred to her. "If this happened, if those he preys upon survive, wouldn't half the world be vampires by this time?"

"Most die and remain dead," said Magda with a primness of manner that was at odds with her words. "But where Dracula chooses it to happen, the dead rise in his name. He does not often call them to him, but when he does, they are his forever. You will see." She opened the clothespress and took out a house robe. "Put this on. I will take you to the bathhouse."

"If I must, then I must," said Kelene, preoccupied with her thoughts. Kelene allowed Magda to remove her night rail and wrap the robe around her. "Why would he . . . ?"

"Why would he what?" Magda asked when Kelene did not go on. "Why would he bring you here? He will tell you himself if he has not already. Why would he bother with a young woman like you? I cannot tell. Why does he want you to be like him? He must know something that convinces him; I cannot guess what it is. He does not confide in me." She indicated the door. "The bathhouse is ready."

"And he expects me to do this for him. To make myself obedient." Kelene sighed as she went through the anteroom again. "What a dismal little room."

"You would not think so if there were enemy soldiers on the other side," said Magda as she led Kelene out onto the gallery.

"Has that ever happened? Have enemy soldiers gotten into this place?" She could not believe it possible.

"Not in my time," said Magda, pointing the way to the rear stairs.

"Have you been here long?" It was as much a ploy to keep Magda talking as expressing real interest, but Kelene listened to the answer with growing understanding as they went down the stairs.

It took Magda a short time to answer, as if she were ordering her response. "I was not quite your age when I was brought here. I was not prepared for . . . It was supposed to be to my benefit as well as . . . My parents were indebted to Dracula—he had saved them from brigands on the road when they attacked our merchant camp." Her voice fell into a sing-song as if she were reciting a litany. "My parents were certain the brigands would have killed us all but for Dracula. They also hoped he would want to . . . to make me his . . . concubine, for they had four other daughters to find places for, and I was thought to be the most promising." She pointed to a window that revealed a drop into the river chasm. "Sometimes I think I would like to jump."

"Jump?" Kelene repeated, not following her change in thought. "Jump where?"

"Down there," said Magda. "When I know I am nothing but fodder and will always be nothing but fodder." Her face changed; her mouth smiled but her eyes were cunning. "I might push you down, but he would make me pay for it. You aren't worth what he would do to me."

This casual ferocity struck Kelene with great force. She half-turned on the stairs, ready to defend herself from Magda, all the while unable to accept that this colorless woman would be so jealous of her, and for such a reason! To want to be drained of blood by a vampire—the longing was inconceivable. If only Magda knew how she had been deceived with visions of an angel. "I would gladly trade places with you," she ventured, carefully feeling her way down two more stairs.

"If I thought it was—" Magda broke off. "You say that readily enough now, but you will change your mind. When he wants, it is his." Kelene saw the impassive mask return.

"I did not seek him," said Kelene, hoping it was as much the truth as she wanted it to be. "He . . . seduced me."

Magda laughed aloud, no amusement in the sound. "He? He is no seducer. He commands and he is obeyed. You cannot refuse him. No one can, when he wants the things he wants."

By the smell they were nearing the kitchen. Kelene supposed there would be cooks about, and perhaps a scullion or two; she thought she would be safe. Unless the rest of the servants harbored the same emotions as Magda did—then she would be in a nest of asps. With this distasteful insight accompanying her, she reached the level of the kitchen. "Which way do I go?" She did not like having to rely on Magda. But there was no one else she had reason to trust.

"To the right," said Magda. She poked Kelene with her thumb to propel her in the direction. "Go."

Kelene was wary, not knowing what else might be in store for her. She made her way down the corridor and out into the shattering light of the kitchen yard. Bringing her hand up to shield her eyes, she was relieved to see that the sun had a debilitating impact on Magda, who seemed to wither as she escorted Kelene to the stout wooden door around the corner from the kitchen, facing northeast, as if in defiance of winter storms which came from that direction.

"The bath has two compartments, one hot, one cool. You may use whichever suits you," said Magda as she held the door open for Kelene. "You need not rush. I will return when you are finished."

It was a relief to know she would be left alone; Kelene did not know if Magda meant to harm her while she bathed, but had she remained with her, the possibility would have haunted her the whole time. As it was, she fixed the bolt in place before she began her exploration of the small, dark bathhouse. The more northerly room was where the tepid bath was; the pool was deep and carved out of the rock on which the castle stood. There were weathered and cracked mosaics on the floor around the pool. The hot bath was nearer the kitchen, the ovens and hearths heating the bath through a system of exhaust channels from the kitchen. The bath here was smaller, unornamented, the walls damp with steam and the odor of old mortar. Kelene decided that the heat would restore warmth to her body, and so shed her house robe and got into the hot bath.

Lying back in the pool, she let her thoughts drift. She had come so far to end up like this. Why, she wondered, did she have to heed the angel who was not an angel? She banished these ruminations, deciding instead to remember pleasant things. There was a song Melantha had sung when Kelene was a child, a song about a woman who loved a spectre. Most of the words eluded her, but a few of the verses remained, along with the weird, wandering melody:

> "No man who lives has found my heart
> No man who lives has wooed my soul,

No man who lives has claimed my hand,
No man who lives has brought me joy;
*   For I have such delight*
*   In my spectre's sweet night*
*   That no living man's right*
Can turn me from his loving touch.
Or call me from his happy grave."

She realized what she had been half-singing and silenced herself. What made her recall that, when there had been other songs? She hurried her bathing and got out of the steaming water, noticing as she did that she was still cold.

At sunset Dracula came into the main hall, very grand in a black satin dogaline over a long giaquetta of deep purple Bolognese brocade. Somber as his clothing was, it was also magnificent. He greeted Kelene perfunctorily, his manner that of a tutor with a recalcitrant pupil.

She waited, wondering what he would do next. She did not want to begin anything herself, knowing that a misstep with him could banish his cordiality in an instant. She watched him as he went to the main door that led to the southern courtyard. It was nerve-wracking to remain silent, but she managed it.

"The gypsies will not arrive until tomorrow. You have one more night." This announcement almost seemed to embarrass him. "I will use it to show you what is coming." He held out his hand to her, "Come, girl. I will take you to your—"

"Final resting place?" she suggested sweetly. "I might as well see it." She went to him and laid her arm on his as if she were a great lady and not his slave. "I am at your service. Take me where you wish."

"You would have ended up a harlot," Dracula said as he led her down yet another of the descending stone corridors which seemed to be everywhere in the castle.

She could feel a flush spread over her face and neck. "What do you mean?"

"If you had stayed with your family, you would have had to turn harlot in order to eat, and I would have had you for far less than I paid for you." He gave a single nod.

The cold Kelene felt now reached through every fiber of her being. "I had no chance, did I, to escape you?"

"No, girl, you did not," he said as he took a torch from its sconce on the wall to light the last part of their descent.

They emerged in the deepest part of the castle, in the vaults where two coffins lay atop stone catafalques. Four other catafalques stood empty, all of them dusty with neglect. The vaults extended far beyond the range of the torchlight; the flickering light made the area seem vast, its shadows encroaching, the catafalques and coffins isolated in terrible majesty. Heavy pillars with heraldic capitals loomed over the biers. The vaults echoed with whispers of wind and other things—she did not like to guess what. One of the coffins Kelene recognized: she had lain atop it as it slid on the side of the mountain. The second one was unfinished, its lid not yet in place; the wood was as polished as the wood on Dracula's coffin, and the purple lining was of Milanese silk.

In spite of herself, Kelene was fascinated with the unfinished coffin. She went to it, fingering the silk and stroking the wood as if it were alive. As Dracula came up to her, she heard him say, "It is yours, Kelene."

Impulsively she asked, "Do you have to close it? Ever?"

He answered quickly. "Yes. Yes. It will preserve you in the daylight hours only if it is closed." He kissed the nape of her neck. "But during the night you may leave it open, if that pleases you."

She gave a distracted little nod. "There are no others?"

He glanced at the empty catafalques as if they were new to him. "Not now."

"But there have been?" she asked.

"And may be again," he said in the same detached manner, as if Kelene could have no reason to know about it. "But this is all you need concern yourself with. This is yours as long as this castle survives."

She found his assurance comforting but his nonchalance upsetting and could not fathom why. "Tomorrow night? You are certain it will be tomorrow night?"

He put the torch in a sconce on the pillar between the coffins. "Yes," he said as if swearing an oath.

Very distantly she heard herself say, "I will be ready."

No sailor lost on the wide sea
Is more lost than I . . .
—Croatian lyric, 14th century

⊢ XXIX ⊣

As soon as these words were spoken, she nearly collapsed. Her pulse thrummed in her neck.

"You will be," said Dracula in the same fatalistic tone. His hands went around her under her breasts and he pulled her back against him. "You will be with me forever."

The thrill that went through Kelene was as passionate as it was unexpected. Here, in this place, the revulsion she had expected to feel vanished and was replaced by this intense anticipation. What was it about this terrible vault that so fired her emotions?

"You are mine, Kelene," he whispered to her. "Here you know it."

She shivered, unable to speak her desires aloud. She attempted to turn in his arms, to face him, but his hold would not permit it. "You . . . you will be with me when I die?"

"Yes, and when you rise," he said.

How much she wanted to see his face, to endeavor to read his face while he said these things to her. "But death—" She stopped, unable to put into words the finite dread that consumed her.

"It will not have you long," said Dracula, stepping back from her so abruptly that she had to grab the edge of the coffin to steady herself.

To Dracula, was that hours or days or years? She did not want to imagine. She gazed into the dark of the vault, trying to envision what it would be like arising in this place. "What will I—"

"You will be with me, one with me," Dracula said, forestalling her questions. "You will not be alone, so long as I am walking. I will be with you."

"And I?" she asked quietly. "If I will be like you, and Un-Dead, will I also be a vampire?"

"Yes. As you have been seeking to be since you were a child." There was no approval in his words, and no condemnation. She heard him out as she stared into the darkness.

"How far does this go?" she asked suddenly, unwilling to listen to him tell her again how he regarded her.

"The vault is under the whole of the castle," said Dracula with a hint of pride. "It is as old as the oldest stones."

She nodded to show she had heard. "And what lies here?"

"Not the bones of my victims, if that is what you are thinking."

"I thought you knew what I was thinking," she said, turning to look at him. "You claim you can."

"This is not worth the effort." He approached her. "Would you like me to leave you alone here, so that you can discover for yourself what is here? Or would you rather explore the rest of the castle?"

"Must it be one or the other?" she asked.

"No, but if you remain down here, I will stay with you. If you want to explore the castle's higher levels, I will call Magda to guide you." His fine garments ought to have been out of place in the vault, but, Kelene decided, they were part of the funereal splendor of the coffins and catafalques.

The air swirled around her, as if from a suddenly open door, and she shivered, though not from cold. There was something about the way of the place—the thrill she had felt surged through her again. She cocked her head as if listening to something being whispered.

"You see?" said Dracula. "You know this place. You do not shrink from it as most would do. You know it is the haven you have longed for."

She said nothing in response, unwilling to concede that to him.

But he would not relent. "This is your home, the home of your soul. This is where you can be safe, without fear of anything but me. Death will not hold you, the world will not impose on you. You will remain young and lovely. So long as you please me."

"Yes. I have grasped that," she said. Even if his promises were true she would be someone—something—other than she was when she woke in her coffin.

"You will be more truly Kelene," he said as he once again came up behind her. "You will be what you are, not what your family wanted you to be."

"I will be what you want me to be," she said in a small voice that nonetheless echoed in the vault. "Whether or not I live again, I will still be your slave. Won't I?"

"Forever."

Without speaking, Kelene walked away from Dracula to stand at the head of the two coffins. For quite some time she remained still, her mind deliberately blank. She wanted to know how it might feel to be dead.

"It will not last long," said Dracula when she had not ventured a word or movement for some little time. "The sun will go down and your death will end."

"I do not know if I can believe what you say. To be one of the Un-Dead . . ." She lifted her hands in resignation mixed with supplication. "How will I—?" She could not go on.

"You will drink blood. You've done that already." He came up to her; she had the impression that in spite of the soft words and courteous conduct he was hunting her as relentlessly as he had ever hunted anyone.

"But where will I find it?" This question hung on the air between them. "Your servants surely cannot . . . And your soldiers should not . . ."

"My servants will supply you until you are ready to hunt with me," he told her, taking her by the shoulders and pulling her against him. "You have fed me. You will be fed thus."

A sensation of nausea came over her. "How?" She could not make herself recall all that had passed between them during their long journey. That she would have to do the same thing was unthinkable.

"You knew it would come to this," said Dracula in a low voice.

"But I thought . . ." She shook her head. "I don't know what I thought, but I did not suppose I would . . . be what you are."

"How did you suppose you would be different?" He turned her around so he could look directly into her eyes.

"I don't know," she confessed.

He stepped back from her and turned away. "When the gypsies come, we will finish this." He held up his hand in what might have been a benediction. "Remain here or come with me, girl."

She looked around the vault, wanting to recapture the sense of protection she had felt, but could not. With a wistful sigh she trailed after him up the long twisting stairs and long corridors to the main hall.

Much later that night she stumbled upon the library for the castle. It was an enormous room, dark and smelling of leather and dust. There were stacks and shelves of books bound in leather, some of it stiff and cracked with age. There were pressed pages of ancient parchment, a few with older texts faintly visible beneath the black writing. Kelene touched these with awe and wished again that she could read. A place like this was clearly a treasure, a neglected one. If she knew how to read, she would have a use beyond her service to Dracula. The servants would respect her if she could read, or at least they would not disdain her as they did now. All these books! In a place like this she would flourish, if she could read.

She remained in the library until the high, alabaster windows began to lighten, their shine opalescent, when she realized that she would have to return to her room. It was hard to go; she had only just gotten started with her explorations. To have to give this up for her bed seemed a hardship. A few of the books were falling apart, their spines glutinous, their pages matted and foxed. These were the hardest to leave, for they were the most fragile. But she needed rest. She would not get rest while these books were all around her. It struck her that she would not sleep there again, that the coffin on the catafalque in the vaults would be her bed once Dracula returned her to life.

It was difficult for her to leave the library. She told herself she would have years and years and years to explore it, but with the looming hour of her death coming, she could not rid herself of the conviction that she would never see it again. Holding these two contradictory thoughts as her uneasy companions, she closed the door and found her way with difficulty to the gallery.

Magda was waiting in her room, looking ill-used and out of patience. "Where have you been?"

"That does not concern you," said Kelene. "I was given permission to look about."

"With me to guide you," Magda countered. "You could have got lost in this place. You don't know the castle yet." She had the sullen gaze of one who is struggling to conceal anger without success.

"I did not get lost, as you see," said Kelene, her own temper ragged. The experiences of the night were bearing in on her; she wanted time to herself, and not with this servant who looked at Kelene as if she were an interloper.

"You will be wakened before sunset," said Magda. "You will be made ready for Dracula."

"Fine," said Kelene, her head coming up.

"You should not have gone off that way," Magda said, unwilling to let it go. "If anything had happened, I would have been held accountable."

"Nothing happened," Kelene reminded her. "I found my way. I am not wandering in the corridors like a ghost. You did not have to go looking for me." She was unfastening her lacings, wondering if there would be new clothes for her to wear for her death. "Help me out of this. I am tired."

"You should deal with this yourself," said Magda as she grabbed the shoulders of the gamurra and helped to pull it off. "You can manage the camisa yourself. You have before."

Kelene did not make any comment as she finished undressing. Her hands were cold and moved like twigs as her apprehension became worse. She reached for the night rail under the coverlet and heard Magda laugh.

"If this were my last day of life, I would not sleep it away like an infant. I would be up and doing. You will not see the day again."

"If I had not been up all night, I would agree. But since night will be my day, I had best get used to it." She was even able to offer a kind of smile as she pulled on the night rail. "You will be far more useful to Dracula than I will."

"Because I have blood in my veins and you will not have?" Magda challenged her. "Is that all you think he wants?"

"What else is there?" As soon as Kelene asked the question she realized it was the crux of her worry: why did Dracula want to waken her from death if all she would be was another creature like him, needing the same blood he sought? Wouldn't he prefer to have no other mouths to feed than his own? She started to shake, so violently that she felt she had been taken with a palsy.

"He does not like to feel old. And he is old," said Magda. "You will keep him young." She laughed harshly, making no excuse for insubordination.

"How can I do that?" Kelene hugged her arms around herself but her shivering continued and grew worse.

"By remaining as you are now. He will measure himself by you." She spat and made a sign with her hands that Kelene knew was not flattering. "Do you think he is without vanity because he is a vampire?"

"But what difference will I make?" Kelene climbed into the bed, huddling deep in the coverlet. "I am—"

"You are young and that pleases him. You belong to him, and that is the most—" She rounded on Kelene as she flung down the gamurra. "How could he choose you? You are an ignorant child!"

"Are you so certain that if he had not found me, you would have been the one he selected to make a vampire?" Kelene asked sweetly.

Magda thrust the gamurra into the clothespress and slammed the door, her face hard with rage. "I do not—" Her indignation did not allow her to finish.

Kelene settled back in the bed, her shivering reduced to occasional trembling. She did not watch Magda leave the room, but heard the inner and outer door close. Satisfied that she was alone, she let the first wave of sleep lap at her consciousness and begin to carry her off.

Kelene wakened out of dreamless sleep with a tingle of danger; the back of her neck felt as if she had broken out in a rash, and she was tense. She lay very still, hoping to give the impression she was still asleep. Who had come into her room? And for what purpose?

The sky, glimpsed out the window, showed the last ragged streamers of sunset, gloriously golden fading to slate. Was it possible the day was already gone and she was being summoned to Dracula? Why had Magda not spoken, if she was in the room? Every sense fired, Kelene waited.

"You are awake, girl," said Dracula from somewhere near the door.

"Is it time?" asked Kelene, her head coming up. Why was she so glad that it was he who had come into the room?

"Shortly," he answered. "The gypsies are finishing your coffin. They have brought earth from Salonika for you to lie upon, and carved the lid of the coffin from the trunks of olive trees your father used to own." He had come nearer to her. He was still in the black-and-purple garments she had seen him in the night before. "I have just awakened."

"The sun is still up," said Kelene. "I thought you could not—"

"The sun is always up somewhere. Now it is far away from us and I can move about." He was now standing at the foot of her bed, blocking out the light from the window and imposing his darkness on her. "It is time you prepared."

"Where is Magda?" Kelene asked, uncertain of what he expected.

"She is with the rest, making the main hall ready." His stern features softened a little.

He glanced toward the window. "When it is full night, we will begin. The whole of the night will be yours."

"Is there a ceremony? Will you give me Final Rites?" She did her best to laugh at these suggestions, but beneath her lightness there was grief.

"You might call it a ceremony. And you have no need of Final Rites," Dracula responded and strode to the door. "Do not think to delay overlong with dressing. You have until the light fades and then I will expect you to come to me." He paused a moment. "I came a far greater distance for you."

When she heard the outer door close, she flung back the coverlet and got out of the bed, casting aside her night rail as she did. Hastily she undid her braids and ran her comb through her hair, trying to make it right by feel alone. She did not work long before she rebraided her hair and wrapped it into place. Without a mirror or Magda it was the best she could do, and she did not bother more about it. When she opened the clothespress she found a camisa of silk gauze the color of new cream set out, the gamurra beneath it. She pulled it on slowly, the sensuous fabric sliding over her flesh like a long trail of kisses. It would have been more enjoyable had she not remembered she was dressing for the tomb. Now she knew that she would not be able to escape what Dracula intended for her, that her hope that this was nothing more than an illusion or a game was false. So as she dressed in everything but shoes, she planned.

There were oil lamps all along the gallery when she emerged from her chamber not long after, bright winking eyes of flame that moved as she went past. All the main hall glowed; hundreds of oil lamps had been hung from pillars and sconces throughout the big room, and they burnished the stones to Florentine gold. Where the dining table had been there was now a platform that was partly a bed and partly an altar, covered by a single sheet of pale silk that glimmered as if lit from beneath. Four of Dracula's soldiers were putting a series of wide, carpeted steps into place at the side of this structure; they did not look up from their labor as Kelene came down the stairs, nor did the servants setting out the two jeweled goblets on the mantel.

Magda was among the servants, but aside from one fulminating glance, she paid no more heed to Kelene than the rest did. Once again Kelene felt she had been rendered invisible, as if she were a ghost already, no more substantial than her reflection and no more real. There was no sign of Dracula anywhere. Kelene walked around the platform, feeling the textures under the soles of her feet, wanting to find things to make herself more real. Then she took stock of the platform, trying to imagine how it would be used between now and dawn.

The servants and the soldiers departed from the main hall, going their ways without speaking, leaving Kelene by herself. Not knowing if she would be allowed to sit, she began to pace, making the rounds of the room until it blurred before her eyes in a smear of lamplight.

"So you haven't run," said Dracula from an alcove near the fireplace. He was part of the darkness and brought it with him when he emerged into the light.

"How long have you been watching me?" she asked, hearing the accusation in her voice. "And where would I run?"

"If you were frightened enough, it would not matter," he said as he came down to her. He was wearing a high-necked Hungarian shuba cut of twilight-purple velvet; beneath he had a bag-sleeved lucco in black silk. "You would run for the sake of running."

"And you would hunt me down," she said.

"Yes." He went to the fireplace and took one of the two goblets placed there. "Here. It is yours."

"No. I mustn't—"

"You will want it tonight. And you will want it later." He took her hand and closed the fingers around the shining metal. "There."

"It's heavy," she said as she secured it with both hands.

"And it is still empty," he said.

Kelene went pale. "You will fill it?" she whispered.

"No. You will." He caught her up in his arms, the chalice between them, an unyielding reminder of the purpose of their evening.

Kelene did not struggle against him; she thought it was too late for anything so futile. Her skin ached and her eyes were flooded with tears which she wanted to dash away but could not. "Do not make it too . . . hideous. I will not oppose you if it is not hideous."

"It will not be," Dracula told her, before his mouth closed on hers. At first all she felt was the pressure of the chalice against her hands, but then, gradually, she began to respond to the kiss, letting it take hold of her as Dracula had, making her want to gain more from him, to fire him with passion beyond his iron control.

This time it was Dracula who moved back, and who had to recover himself; Kelene watched him as she tugged the chalice from between them, setting it down on one of the carpeted steps leading up to the bed on the platform. "Do I drink your blood? If you drink mine?"

He looked as if he might strike her, then he answered, "It is too late for that."

"Why?" She held him off for a moment, not expecting him to answer. Then she let him embrace her again.

"You are mine," he told her. "You are like me."

She did not like to hear this, but Kelene did not resist; it would not help her plan if she gave him reason to chastise her. With a smile that did not light her eyes, she encouraged his caresses, sighing as he began to unfasten the gold lacing of her corsage. She tried to recall how he had courted her when she had thought he was an angel in her visions, and she could not. Since he had put aside his winglike cloak, Dracula had ceased to be her supernatural guardian and was now the Un-Dead man who could not bear to be old and alone. If he sought her as an anodyne for his loneliness, Kelene could understand it; she could even find some sympathy for him in her heart.

"You will like how we live. You will," he said, his fingers on the cream-colored silk, unfastening the ties that secured it. His whole body was taut with wanting her. For the first time, Kelene had a renewed hope that she might have some power with him. It was no longer inconceivable that his need for her might extend beyond blood and visions. She was going to find out; it was the heart of her plan.

She looked up at him as he opened the neck of her camisa. "Does this please you? If I were older, I would know what to do, but . . . you must show me."

He did not hesitate. "You will learn all," he said as he slid back her camisa and gamurra from her shoulder, exposing her body to the small swelling of her breasts. His hands were on her, more demanding than they had been before, and she did her best not to wince as he closed them over her breasts.

As her gamurra slid down her body, the sleeves alone held it up. Kelene felt his breath quicken; so far her plan was going well. If she could continue to anticipate his desires, she would not have to capitulate completely. She could maintain her soul no matter what he demanded of her body. He would be the slave of his passion as she was his slave. She tugged one arm out of the double sleeve of gamurra and camisa, so that the garments hung lopsidedly along her body. She could not free her other arm to be rid of her clothes entirely. She did not want him to decide when she was to be naked, for that would surrender too much to him. She stood on tiptoe, glad now she had left her felt boots back in her room; she initiated the kiss, taking pride in her daring. Capricious it might be, but she began to think he might want her to show him encouragement; he certainly did nothing to hinder her attempts. As he held her more tightly, Kelene realized she had played into his hands again, that he had instigated the whole. But she did not want him to stop, or to be subject to his anger again. So long as he showed her passion, she knew she had not disappeared from the earth entirely. She no longer thought about her plan to captivate him—that was slipping away from her as she began to feel the power of his will.

Holding Kelene in a powerful embrace, Dracula bent swiftly and nipped at her throat. As she stifled a shriek, he stood back and watched while a ribbon of blood ran down from her neck, between her breasts and slid down her belly to the blond-tufted cleft between her legs, then began to make its way along the insides of her thighs; a fold of the cream-colored camisa tangled around her ankle turned red.

She put her hand to the wound; he pulled it away. "But—" she protested.

"The hurt doesn't matter. Let it run," he said, and very deliberately removed her other arm from her clothes, tugged the garments free of her feet, then knelt down before her and began to lick the blood from her body, starting at her ankles and rising to meet the brilliant stream.

Fascination warred with repugnance within Kelene as Dracula worked his way from her calves to her knees, then to her thighs; her neck twinged whenever she moved, but was increasingly less noticeable as Dracula continued to feast upon her. The sensations Kelene felt dismayed her. The worst of it was that it was so pleasant.

When he arrived at her neck again, her breathing was deep and her eyes slightly unfocused. She was limp and unprotesting. He murmured before he took a second bite at her, this one larger. The dark blood flowed from the wound more freely, and he drank it more eagerly.

Lightheaded, she staggered against him, holding his hair as he worked his way down her body. Each beat of her heart made a warning pang where he had bitten her, but the warning did not seem important. She could no longer remember her plan for subjugating him, or hold herself upright as his mouth touched her, finding the places where her pulse hopped and biting tiny cuts in those places to sweeten what came from her neck. Her body stirred, excited and confused. She began to feel cold again despite the fire in her flesh. Her head went back and the breath caught in her throat. All the mastery she had both abhorred and sought worked upon her as he fed until she felt her knees about to give way.

"Not yet, girl," he said as he rose and swung her up into his arms, carrying her up the carpeted steps to the bed on the platform. He laid her out on the silken sheets so that she was beneath him, his shadow lying over her as he picked up the chalice. Then he was on her, bending to her throat. Blood welled into his mouth and streamed off his face. He lifted the chalice to catch every precious drop of it while he swallowed greedily.

She was marble-cold but that hardly mattered. For the first time in more than a year, perhaps for the first time in her life, Kelene knew she was real. No longer a manifestation of her father's pride, no longer the tool of her visions, Kelene felt she was back on that high peak she had been shown in her dreams, when Dracula had first offered her his chalice to drink from.

"Too soon," he said, tugging at her to make her sit up.

Her body responded disjointedly as if controlled from a distance. All that she could do was gasp out a few words as Dracula held her sitting, the half-full chalice pressed against the rise of her breast.

"In a little while, girl. Not much longer. You are doing very well. Your life is strong within me. Just a little more." He crooned the words, lifting the chalice before her eyes and draining it while the glory of the main hall faded in her sight until only the shine of the chalice jewels remained; then that, too, winked out.

Paler than her discarded camisa, Kelene was lowered back against the silken sheet. Dracula made sure she would not roll or slip, then he set the emptied chalice on the mantel next to its mate. Then he came back and half-knelt on the carpeted steps in order to work the cream-colored silken camisa over Kelene's head and down her body. She lolled in his arms, no more animation in her than if she had been a puppet. Dracula worked quickly, paying no attention to the dying flames of the oil lamps. By the time he had her dressed again half the lamps were out and the main hall was lost in shadows.

Dracula swung her body up into his arms, and carrying her as if she weighed no more than a sack of meal, he bore her through the long, descending corridor, down into the vault where her coffin waited, its new lid in place and the catafalque filled with the earth from Salonika the gypsies had brought. He took his time laying her out, crossing her hands on her breast and adjusting the neck of her camisa so that the wounds he had inflicted were not immediately visible. He made sure her golden braids were neat and that her bare feet were tucked under the lining of the coffin. Then he swung the lid of the coffin closed. As he did, he admired the pattern of a Byzantine angel carved there, the wood still showing the marks of the chisels and smelling faintly of olives.

She was so young, and very fair
That Death could not resist her.
—Hungarian ballad, 15th century

⊢ XXX ⊣

Kelene opened her eyes but found no light. She tried to move, but discovered that she was imprisoned in a space scarcely larger than she. She opened her mouth to scream when the lid of the coffin lifted and the light of a torch flared in her vision.

"You thought you had him," Magda exclaimed as she lifted the torch higher, waving it so that the flame danced. "I will not allow it!"

It was an effort to try to move. Kelene had almost no strength as she tried to pull herself erect. Before she could manage it, she was thrust back into her coffin. "What . . . ?" she managed to say, making an effort to gather her thoughts. What had happened to her that she should be lying here? Why was Magda threatening her with a torch?

"Do not play the fool with me," Magda said, her features distorted by the torchlight. "You will not have him!"

"Get back," Kelene muttered.

"It isn't sunset yet and you are weak. You cannot fight me. You don't know how!" She swung the torch around so that the heat flicked over Kelene's face. "When he rises, you will be ashes."

"And he will turn to you?" Kelene said, all the while knowing that the fire would be her death—that even Dracula feared it. And here was Magda with a torch, ready to burn her where she lay.

Magda let the flames singe the edge of the lining of Kelene's coffin.

Kelene kicked, her bare foot scraping on the coffin lid, but without force, and Magda easily avoided her.

"So! You think you can fight me? You, in your coffin? You should be in your grave." She bent down, her face a handsbreadth from Kelene's. "He cannot save you. This time there is no reprieve. You will die, as you should have done already."

Kelene's thoughts were suddenly very clear. She spoke with no trace of fright. "He will not come to you if you kill me. You will die if you burn me." She was able to work her left arm under her, securing a little leverage for movement.

"He will need blood. He has taken it from me before. When you are gone, he will again. He will forget you." She smiled.

Kelene took a risk. "You know you are not young enough. You've lost half your teeth and there is already white in your hair. Why should he seek anything from you beyond what he has had?" She had her hand flat against the bottom of the coffin now.

At that Magda struck out with the base of the torch, her fist and the wood striking Kelene on the side of the jaw. She screamed in rage as she reached for the lid of the coffin to close it once more.

Kelene took her chance. She sat up, propelled by her left arm. Magda was not prepared for Kelene's movement; she let go of the lid and nearly dropped the torch. "Wretched child!" she yelled. The sound echoed through the vault.

The torchlight, unsteady to begin with, now became another distortion, revealing and obscuring at once. The lid of the coffin swung back from full open. Magda swung the torch like a club; the flames hissed and almost went out as Kelene scrambled over the side of her coffin to land crouched at the foot of the catafalque. Magda flung herself on Kelene, biting and scratching and trying to bludgeon her with the torch.

Weak as she was, Kelene realized she had more strength than Magda; she felt her strength increasing. She seized Magda by the shoulders, fell back, then pulled Magda over her. Using the impetus of the other woman's wrath, Kelene slammed her into the side of Dracula's catafalque. Magda struck with a gratifying thud, and lay, moving fitfully. A fretwork of blood spread over her forehead and began to run down her face as the torch finally went out.

In the dark, Magda's pooled blood looked like embers, with light enough to draw Kelene's eyes. With an emotion she did not recognize, she fell on Magda, her mouth to the stunned woman's bleeding forehead. She drank eagerly, savoring the sweetness of it, and relinquishing her prize only when Magda slumped, falling on her side, lost in unconsciousness.

Aghast at what she had just done, Kelene straightened up, wiping her mouth with the back of her hand. She had actually drunk Magda's blood! It was unbearable to have such a hunger. To drink the blood of the living was despicable. And yet—how much the blood had restored her! She could feel the strength of it in every fiber. And finally she was almost warm, the blood igniting a heat she had thought she would never know again. It was all she could do not to return to Magda and drink more. It was too horrible to think about. She leaned back against the side of her coffin, trying to decide what to do. It was not simply a matter of her thirst for blood. Magda would waken eventually, and would more deeply resent Kelene than she had before. For during the day Kelene would be in a stupor, and Magda would be able to do . . . anything.

The lid of Dracula's coffin began to open; Kelene could just make out the shape of his hand as he raised it, the hinges moaning softly as Dracula emerged, his purple lucco unrumpled. He looked around as if the dim light was more than sufficient. "You have risen already." He made a gesture of approval. "No matter."

"No matter?" Kelene exclaimed. She pointed to the unconscious woman, suddenly so enraged that it was an effort to speak. "She was going to burn me in my coffin. She had her torch ready, but she had to gloat first."

"Gloat—why should she gloat?" Dracula asked.

"She would have you to herself. You would have to . . . to survive through her." Her anger was like a fist inside her, pounding on her bones.

"Did you argue with her?"

"In a manner of speaking," she responded.

Dracula nodded.

"But if I had not?" She waited a moment for him to say something. When he did not she resumed. "We fought—"

"And you prevailed," said Dracula, his certainty infuriating to Kelene.

"I am here. But had I not . . ." She did not go on; she thought she detected a glint in his eyes. "You are the author of this, aren't you?"

"She did not hurt you," Dracula pointed out.

"She intended to. What if she had succeeded? She had a torch." Kelene heard her voice echo in the vaults, too high and too petty to restore her pride.

"I would never expose you to such danger," he said, going to Kelene's side. He laid his hand on her head as if blessing her. "But I rejoice that you triumphed when the danger came."

"I don't believe you," she muttered.

"I have no reason to lie," he said. "Why should I, when I have been at such pains to find you and bring you here? After so many years, why would I let anything happen to you?" The questions were so reasonable that she had no answer for them, but the sensation of a cold fist in the center of her chest. She rubbed her mouth again, very surreptitiously, wanting to remove all traces of Magda's blood without drawing attention to the act. Her hope that Dracula had not noticed this vanished when he said to her, "It is good to taste."

Kelene gagged. The wind sneaking through the vaults was more important to her than Magda, or her blood. "I should not have—"

"You should. It was necessary. When vampires are new-made they are very weak, and if they do not get sustenance they soon go mad." He studied her face. "I would not like you to be mad, Kelene."

"Mad? No." What she had done sane was bad enough; to become prey to her own overwhelming impulses was unthinkable. She coughed once, as if she had to get the last of the blood from her throat.

"You will need to drink again before morning," Dracula told her, apparently unaware of her increasing reservations. "There is a boy with the gypsies. He is not a gypsy, but a foundling. He has a clubfoot. Go to him and you may have your fill. He is strong and he will not fight you."

Kelene wanted to be shocked, to be able to ignore the spurt of excitement that this information gave her. She made herself nod in response, and then she began to tremble. "What have you done to me?"

He put his arm around her to steady her. "You want me to tell you that you will not have to live the way vampires live, but that isn't possible. So you want me to tell you it is all right for you to live this way."

It was the kindest thing he had ever said to her and she was struck by that if nothing else. "I suppose so," she conceded.

"It is the way I have lived since the time of Honorius. If I thought it was wrong, I would be dust by now, and you would be a slave of the Ottomites in Salonika." He tightened his hand and shook her. "You do not think it wrong. You know that the hunger and its satisfaction is all that is real; the rest is amusement. And hunting."

"Amusement and hunting," she said slowly, finding a resonance within herself that was too powerful to be disregarded. She wished he would let go of her and was about to tell him so when he released her.

"The boy will be rewarded by the gypsies for what he does for you." Dracula paid no heed to the shock in her eyes. "You will not be making him suffer."

Wincing, Kelene started to turn away. "Why should they allow me to . . . to use him?"

"They do not want to be vampires when they die. It is hard enough being gypsies. This tribe has long traditions of serving me; I reward their fealty well." He bent and picked up Magda, slinging her over his shoulder. "The boy was abandoned by his family—probably because of his clubfoot—and the gypsies took him in. He is not part of the tribe and he will not be allowed to rise when he dies." He started to the stairs out of the vault. "You will not kill him, any more than you have killed Magda."

"I'm grateful for that," said Kelene, her sarcasm lost on Dracula.

"In time that will fade," he said, and left her alone.

The south courtyard was not as imposing as the western one, for it was designed to receive carriages instead of men-at-arms. Its gates were

hung on tremendous ornate hinges and kept closed with a wooden bolt
as thick as a blacksmith's thigh. The flagstones were set with care to ensure
that the wheels of vehicles would not break, nor would the occupants of
carriages be tossed about. Wide, shallow steps led to the door, making
that part of the castle appear welcoming. An old rosebush climbed up the
tower at the side of the gate. By starlight the place had a soft glow that
Kelene thought enchanting. But she was not out simply to walk under the
stars. She was on her way to the gypsy camp. She was just curious, she
insisted, to see how the gypsies made allowances for Dracula while saving
themselves from him. She had donned a filmy Milanese giornea the color
of fresh apricots, with trailing sleeves knotted at the bottom; even fifty
years out of fashion, she looked glorious. She had left her felt boots and
her shoes back in her room in the castle.

The lich-gate was rusty and its hinges screamed as Kelene shoved it
open. She went out quickly, as if she was afraid she would be watched,
though she did not know why she feared she might be. The grass outside
the castle wall was not very high yet, and dew had settled on it, so that
the hem of her giornea was soon drenched and her bare feet soaked. None
of this bothered her as she ran merrily on.

The meadow just outside the south gate of Castle Dracula sloped to
the southeast and was rimmed with pines. The gypsies had set up their
camp a short distance from the gate, near the spring at the edge of the
trees. Their stock were tethered where the animals could graze and drink,
their wagons providing a loose enclosure for the gypsies to pile their
bonfire and to keep watch on their tribe.

The clubfooted boy, dark-haired and Slavic-featured, sat on the rear
step of the covered wagon. He was no older than Kelene. His face promised great beauty in another two or three years. He wore a shawl wrapped
over his smock and breeks, for the night was cold.

Kelene paused before he saw her, and took a moment to watch him.
She pressed her hands together, trying to contain the confusing impressions that almost consumed her. She enjoyed admiring him, and her admiration was no longer as innocent as it had been just a day ago. But she
would have to do more than look at him.

The boy turned as if attracted by a sound. He caught sight of Kelene
and an expression that was part obsequious, part encouraging came over
his wonderful face. "They said you would come," he said in clumsy Greek.
"You're really beautiful."

She was too pale to blush, but she felt as if fever spots were in her
cheeks. "I was told you would be here." She went a few steps nearer. It
would be pleasant to touch him—just touch him—she thought. She extended her hands. "I am glad you are here."

The boy was able to smile now, but he was not so practiced that it was completely unconvincing. "I am glad, too." He closed the distance between them, laying his hands in hers. "Tell them you like me. When all this is over, tell them you like me."

His words startled her; this plea was too much of an intrusion from the world and not enough of an assurance that she was not so dangerous that he would fight her off. "All right. I will. If I like you."

"Good enough," he said, and began to kiss her. These were not the beginning efforts of a youngster, but a skilled demonstration of practiced expertise. His soft lips opened hers.

Startled, Kelene pushed his shoulder, not certain she was ready for what he seemed to be offering. "I . . . It will take me a little time."

He would not release her. "Please. Let me do this. I know how."

This abrupt change from seducer to penitent was perplexing. Kelene considered him. "All right," she said again.

The boy resumed his expert kissing, using imagination and variety in what he did. From feather-light brushes of her eyelids to nibbles at her ears to long, slow, wet explorations of her tongue, he made every nuance of what he did arousing.

Kelene gasped as he opened her giornea and began to excite her more; his mouth knew just where to go and what to do. A still part of her mind wondered how a boy so young should have learned so much. Would the same thing have happened to Orien, had he remained with the man who bought him? This dashed the pleasure from her; she started to pull away, saying "No. No. This isn't right. No."

The boy held onto her. "You can't. Please. If . . . if you don't like me, they'll beat me." This last came out in a rush. He put his hand to her mouth, his voice dropping to a whisper. "Let me, please let me."

"They would really beat you?"

"Yes. They have before." He took her face in his hands and kissed her with persuasive desperation. "Oh, please."

She hated to admit it, but with the arousal of her flesh, her hunger was growing as well. The ache she felt for him was not for his body, but his blood. With a sigh she put her hands on his shoulders. "You know what I will do. They told you, didn't they?"

"Oh, yes. You will drink some of my blood." He smiled, knowing he had won. "The gypsies will look for the marks."

She closed her eyes. "Do what you—" She got no further; his mouth was on hers again, his hands slid inside her giornea, and the tingling he gave began again and redoubled as he strove to please her. As he lay down and pulled her atop him, she had a moment of dismay as she realized her virginity was lost. But then it did not matter.

"Now," he panted as he moved beneath her. "Now. Now. Now."

Kelene bent forward, lying against his chest to reach his throat. It took three attempts to pierce his skin, and as she sucked at the small wounds she had made, she felt him tremble and spasm. His blood was delicious. She kissed his chin, and got off him, taking care to wipe her mouth on her sleeve before she looked directly at him. "You may tell them I am pleased with you."

The boy nodded, murmuring a few words of thanks as he sat up slowly, one hand to his head. "I'm dizzy."

"You will be better when you've eaten and slept," she said, feeling concern for him that troubled her more than she liked to admit.

"You will tell them—" he began.

"That you satisfied me, yes, I will. And the marks are on your neck. They will not beat you." She knew her golden braids were in disorder, but that no longer seemed important. She fussed with her clothing enough to make it look not quite so disheveled. "I will tell the servants and they will tell the gypsies. I . . . I must rest . . ." Her words faltered.

"Yes. And you will come again?" He asked this eagerly enough to almost persuade Kelene that he, too, had found some pleasure in what they had done.

"I . . . I will try," she said softly, as if imparting a secret. She would far rather live off this beautiful boy than drink the blood of the stolid servants in the castle. She touched his cheek, thinking how soft his skin was, and how much his dark lashes were like wings.

Somewhere in the woods, a bird called, the first, earliest herald of morning.

Kelene heard it with the same alarm that she would have heard can- non-fire. She started away from the boy, looking back once to wave at him, and then rushing to the lich-gate. She pulled it open, and tugged it closed behind her, racing across the flagstones, her feet still damp from the dewy grass in the meadow beyond the castle walls; she left small, damp impressions of her passing.

An ancient servant, with gnarled fingers and a bent back, opened the door to her. "Can you find the way?"

"I think so," said Kelene. "Tell the gypsies the boy was to my liking." She felt better for having done as she had promised. "Not tomorrow night, but sometime soon I would like to . . . to . . ."

"Yes. I will let them know." The servant ducked his head as Kelene rushed on through the main hall and into the corridor leading to the vault.

Dracula was there, preparing to get into his coffin. He watched her as she came rushing to her own coffin. "Well?"

"I know I waited too long," she said as she got up into the coffin. "You don't need to punish me."

"Not that. The boy."

She answered slowly, searching for the words to tell him, aware that there was more at stake here than kisses. "He was wonderful. He did such things that I. . . . He was so . . . much . . . kinder than you." She flung this at him and was disappointed when he laughed aloud.

"And suppose I had been . . . kind. What then?" he said as he swung his leg into the coffin; the purple lucco rippled and shone in the dull lamplight.

"I would have . . . liked you better." The words were barely audible, but they echoed through the vault.

"Why should I need your liking, when you are mine? What I have is greater than liking; the call you answered is eternal." He waited a moment. "Suppose you did like me? Suppose you were devoted to me, enraptured by me. What then? Would you have been willing to forsake me and prey on that boy, or any other?"

"Prey upon him?"

"Use him, then, if you prefer. Had you found such joy in me, would you be willing to go elsewhere?" He was sitting in his coffin now, the lid up, preparing for the long repose of the day.

"You treat me as you do to help me?" she said incredulously.

"And me. I must hunt as you must hunt. It is foolish to pretend otherwise, girl." He looked at her. "You do not want to believe me, do you?"

She shook her head, feeling guilty for no reason she could understand.

"Kelene, listen to me. You are a vampire. You live on the blood of humans. They are your sustenance. If you intend to live, you must learn to hunt them. You will have to learn to be what I am. Most of those you hunt, you will not remain with long, for too many will die if you do."

"Why should I not?" she asked as she settled down in her coffin.

"You cannot remain with any prey too long, unless you want to kill them. And they notice if you linger." He looked at her as he lay back. "If you grow fond of them, you will lose them to death. And all passion dies, except the lust for living." He reached for the lid. "Amuse yourself with the boy. What you learn from him will be useful to you when he is gone." He did not give her a chance to ask any more questions but pulled the coffin lid closed with a final, hollow thud.

This time her dreams were fragmentary, some of them nothing more than quick visions, like the world seen in a flash of lightning, maddeningly incomplete: *Her family's inn, a woman in a grand dress with jewels on her fingers, standing on the stairs, her servants behind her, speaking to Alexander—*

Achilles with a basket filled with breads and cheeses over his shoulder, going among the soldiers camped outside Belgrade, selling the food for silver and copper coins, trudging through the camp without hurrying. He reached the largest tents, familiar enough there to be hailed. Then he was smiling and joking with one of the officers, but showed him the hilt of a dagger before he continued on with his wares—

Pallas talking to a man somewhat older than she, a diffident fellow with broad shoulders and an unremarkable face, he leaned forward to help her purchase a large sack of barley. Pallas looked tired as she paid for the grain—

Orien with Melantha, selecting cloth for window coverings, Orien hanging back, his young face thoughtful. Mother and son both appeared to be deep in an argument of long standing. Each had that fixed posture that indicated there was no resolution possible. They maintained their truce while the mercer showed his wares, but it was certain their dispute would continue—

A bridge over a wide river, endangered by floods, the road leading to it already lapped by the rising river. At one end the boards supporting the span were loose enough to flap against the roadway of the bridge, each blow promising destruction. Great trunks of fallen trees careened into the bridge as the waters carried them down from their places higher in the mountains. On the far side of the river a company of Ottomite soldiers, thwarted by the loss of the crossing, turned north rather than west—

Three haggard men in rough clothes, all of them unable to walk, dragging themselves along the narrow road, their hands bleeding. They pressed on with the brutish determination of starving cattle, without fellowship. When they came upon a small chapel, they fought among themselves for the few scraps of food the pope was able to offer them—

The razed city, the birds gone now that all the bodies were nothing but bones. Some of the buildings that had been partially intact had now fallen to rubble. Already dust was blowing down the streets, covering everything there, obliterating it from the face of the world. A skull on the step of the collapsed church grinned up at the empty sky—

The foundling boy in a town with the gypsy tribe, being taken to a merchant's house, to the side door where a soft, plump woman in prosperous-looking garments seized his hand and pulled him into the empty servants' hall, reaching for his smock as she did. She stroked his smooth, hairless chest and lay back on the dining table, lifting her wide skirts and spreading her legs, coaxing him while she fondled the front of his breeks. Behind the door, two gypsies went silently into the house as the boy bent to distract the woman—

Magda seated on the edge of her narrow bed, a bandage around her brow, a dull look in her eyes. Fresh bruises showed on her shoulders and arms. She was muttering while she sat, though no words were audible. She gnawed at her lower lip, letting it bleed when she ripped the skin—

And then Kelene was awake—and hungry.

The face of my mother is hidden
In shadows, my brother has become
A stranger with passing years . . .
—Greek lament, 15th century

⊢ XXXI ⊣

By early summer the gypsies were gone. They would return at the end of winter. Kelene looked forward to their coming, since the boy Piro would be back. In spite of what she had been learning to do, she could not rid herself of her fondness for him. The nights were short, but there were travelers abroad and hunting was easy; Kelene had quickly learned to use all Piro taught her to deal with the men she sought out. Dracula said nothing about this, but encouraged her to seek her prey among strangers in the region.

"The peasants all carry crucifixes and put garlic at their windows. Strangers do not do this," he said. "Travelers are not quickly missed if they are on these roads, so when questions come, the time is long past when anyone will recall them." He gave an approving nod to Kelene's gamurra worn half unlaced and without a camisa beneath, revealing the swell of her young breasts. "What man would not welcome you?"

Magda continued to serve Kelene, resentful and wary most of the time, occasionally impertinent and surly. She was the one who told Kelene about Dracula's previous women, eking out the details over many weeks.

"There was one before I came; perhaps fifty years ago, perhaps a hundred. She was called Ileanna. She came from the plains to the south, or so everyone believed. My mother's mother saw her. They say she was very beautiful." She continued to mend a tear in Kelene's filmy giornea.

Some days later, she said, "Ileanna—the one I told you about—she was brought here to be a servant. Or it may be that Dracula chose her as he chose you. But she was put to work here for years. She was used as we all are used, but Dracula raised her above the rest, and made her one with him—or that is what everyone recalls." She resumed braiding Kelene's golden hair. "They say he adored her."

One night after Kelene returned from hunting men in a pilgrim's train, Magda warned her, "You don't want Prioska's fate to befall you."

"Prioska now, not Ileanna?" Kelene said as she shrugged out of her loosened gamurra.

"Prioska came after Ileanna. I saw her once when I was very young. She was Hungarian; she came from a village near Brasov. They say Dracula brought her here to keep her as his own."

"They might say that about any woman he brought here," said Kelene, unwilling to be jealous of the long-vanished Prioska. "In time they may say it about me."

Magda blinked slowly, like a lizard, and after a while, she picked up the bloodstained gamurra from where Kelene had stepped out of it.

Shortly before the gypsies were to return, when a blizzard blew out of the north, driving snow and ice through the mountains like a conquering army, Magda revealed more to Kelene. "Those catafalques in the vault. You don't suppose they were always empty, do you? You did not think you were the only one."

"Aside from Ileanna and Prioska?" Kelene answered coolly, not allowing herself to be goaded into a hasty retort as she had done in the past.

"Yes. Aside from those I have told you about. I thought you would want to know."

"All right," said Kelene, bored from long nights roaming the castle, feeding on placid servants. "You are determined to tell me. Go ahead."

Magda spat, and said, "All the catafalques have had coffins. All of them. Sometimes there is more than one woman here. From the stories they tell in the villages around here, there have been as many as five."

"Five," said Kelene as if the number had no significance. "And what is this to me?"

"Only that he will want more women. In time he will have them." She laughed.

"I suppose he will," said Kelene with feigned unconcern.

"They say he sometimes lets his women fight for him," said Magda, smirking.

"Why should they?" Kelene could not stop herself asking.

"Why, to have his favor. To be his nourishment," said Magda, taken aback by so obvious a question.

"But, if the women are in coffins, they must surely be like him. What reason would they fight for him?" She saw that she had Magda at a disadvantage and she put her thoughts to work more fiercely. "When others come—if they come—I will deal with them."

At the Nativity, when Dracula and all his servants did not leave the castle, Kelene found him in the library, a huge parchment volume open on the high desk before him. He was studying the page intently, frowning from time to time as he encountered a phrase that he did not immediately understand. He wore an ermine huque over his black-and-purple brocade garnache. The garnache's wing-cut sleeves reminded Kelene of his cloak. His hair was clubbed back and he wore an embossed ring on his right-hand Jupiter finger.

"Have you read them all?" she asked.

"Yes," he answered.

"Will you teach me?"

He thought about it for a short while before he answered.

"No. It isn't fitting." He closed the book. "If it distresses you, I will not continue while you are here."

"I would like to learn to read," she said, the wistfulness in her voice honest but a shade too practiced now.

"It isn't fitting," Dracula told her a second time. "It would not be suitable for you."

"You sound like my father," she said. "He said so long as I could recognize—" she could not say Christos and Kyrios "—holy names, I would know all it was becoming for a female to know."

"And can you? Do you know the holy names?" He leaned forward on his stool, his sleeve fanning out as if preparing for flight.

"Oh, yes. All of us were taught that. But only my brothers could read. And only Achilles did it well." She shrugged as if to deny her interest. "It's just with these long nights, I thought it would be interesting to read."

"It might," he said. "But you have other skills you can use to fill the hours. You embroider and weave, don't you?"

"Your servants do that," she said sharply.

"That does not mean you cannot," he pointed out.

Without intending to, she said, "Did Ileanna or Prioska weave?"

He studied her. "So you have heard of them." He straightened up on his stool. "No. Nor did Yasmine, nor did Lujuba, nor did Tatya, nor did Milova, nor any of the rest of them."

"How many have there been?" she asked, holding her breath for his answer.

"Sometimes as many as five in a century," he said calmly. "A few times more."

"Five in a century." She knew her sums well enough to challenge him. "A new woman every twenty years?"

"Some fewer, some more. I have been careful. I do not take too many, or those so high-born that the Church would care. It suits my purpose best to find the ones who hear my call, as you did," said Dracula. "You knew you were not the first. Why should you be the last?"

"What happened to them?" She did not want to speak about these women but could not keep herself from asking now that she had begun. "You said I would be with you forever."

"And so you will," said Dracula with an automatic note in his words.

"The others were not with you forever." Her head was up, her chin at an angle. "Did you promise them forever?"

"They died. Some willingly, some unwillingly, but they died." He folded his arms. "Prioska kept returning to her home village for prey; the people were not willing to give up all their young men to her, so they trapped her and beheaded her and buried her at a crossroad, her body turned downward, her head set between her feet, with garlic in her mouth." He went on. "Ileanna became despondent. Some vampires do. In her greatest melancholy she lit herself afire. Lujuba threw herself off the parapet into the river gorge; we never found all her bones. They say it was for love, but it was not. Milova was apprehended by a band of monks who drove a wooden stake through her heart and left her exposed to sunlight. Tatya, as I recall, was drowned in a pool of holy water. The local popes had sworn to stop her depredations, and they did. Would you like to know the rest?"

"No," said Kelene in a small voice.

"That is why I have told you to take your prey from among strangers— travelers and others who have no connections to this place. If you will be sensible—" He got no farther.

"It is winter. The passes are blocked with snow. Where will I find any travelers now?" She met his eyes steadily. "You can make do with the servants, but can I?"

"If you are sensible, you can," he told her in a tone that permitted no opposition. "If you become greedy, or try to practice your arts on them, it will turn out badly for everyone. You will have to kill any servant you seduce. We cannot have vampire servants." He regarded her narrowly. "The peasants in this region know what they are facing; they have killed vampires for ages and ages, longer than I have been here."

"But you are still here," Kelene said. "How is it that they die and you do not? You say they know how to kill you. Have they never tried?"

"I am stronger than they are. And I am not stupid. They used to try often. In the last three hundred years they have left me undisturbed." He swung around on his stool. "Let me tell you about Mnisku. She was here for more than three centuries. There were other women during that time, but she managed better than they did. She hunted well beyond the villages here, and when enemies were abroad in the land, she attacked them first, for the peasants would not mind if she rid them of a danger greater than herself. She was clever, and did not disobey me. When she was dragged into the sunlight, I mourned her as I have never mourned anyone." He cocked his head to the side. "Bryeis lived for over a century, but she was killed by a wooden crossbow quarrel long ago."

Kelene considered this. "And you do not think I will endure as long, do you?"

Dracula studied her before he said, "It would surprise me."

"Then when you said forever, you meant until I was killed." She stared directly at him.

"I meant forever." He saw she was about to make another demand, and he added, "Alive, dead, Un-Dead, you are mine. You are all mine."

Accepting this, Kelene nodded once before she turned to leave the library. "I will hunt tomorrow night, but not in the villages around the castle. I will not intrude on the servants."

Kelene dreamed only rarely now, and what she dreamed she did not readily recall when her coffin lid was raised at sundown. But now and again she would catch a fleeting sight of her family, and realize with a start that she had not thought of them for days or weeks. Kelene decided it was her hunting that had robbed her of her visions, for she hunted at night. Her visions came at night; now that she was Un-Dead, night was her time, and she did not sleep then, even when she did not hunt. She had come to think it was possible that the visions were also a part of the night, and that she would need to sleep then to regain them.

Magda knew something was troubling her, and took advantage of Kelene's unacknowledged worry to tweak her. "You have not kept him as you thought you would, have you? He takes blood from me and four of the others. Why should he keep all the servants to himself?"

"The servants are his," said Kelene as she continued her embroidery on her giornea. She had become used to Magda, and paid her little mind.

"You are not the chosen one any longer." Magda pointed at the window where icicles hung in the fluttering torchlight. "He can go nowhere and he still does not come to you."

"He sleeps in a vault next to mine," said Kelene. "None of you can do that."

"Because we are still alive." Magda made a gesture of finality. When this earned no response from Kelene, she said, "The gypsies are coming. They will be here at the end of the month, when the passes open again."

"It is a hard time of year to travel." Kelene continued to stitch the minute pattern of roses and apple blossoms on the front of the giornea.

"You should be glad they are coming back. That clubfooted boy will be back." The lascivious roll of Magda's eyes was almost comical. "You will have reason to be happy to see them here again."

"So will everyone at the castle," said Kelene, unwilling to say more.

"You will have your lover again. You will not have to hunt like a wolf through the night." She got to her feet, her weathered features creasing with malevolent delight. "And you will not spare him. You will kill him and the gypsies will bury him with a hawthorn bush planted in him, to keep him in his grave."

"Why such spite for a young man who has never harmed you?"

"Because it will make you miserable to kill him." Magda glared at Kelene.

Kelene pretended not to hear.

Piro had the first dark hint of a mustache on his upper lip, and there was a slyness in his smile Kelene had not seen before. His stance was confident and faintly taunting. He grinned as she came up to him, his gaze directed to where her gonella was open at the corsage. Despite the cold she wore no camisa, and her feet were shod in kidskin Turkish slippers. She smiled back, and felt a yearning for him.

"Did you miss me?" he whispered before he wrapped her in his arms.

The rest of the gypsy camp was silent; frost imparted sparkle to the grass and patches of snow made the night shine. It was like something out of a fable, a place where everything was possible.

"I missed you," she said, not at all certain she had—not as she thought he meant.

"And now I'm back." He began to kiss her, slowly at first, his intensity growing as she returned his passion. He drew back and took a long breath. "Waiting has sharpened your appetite."

"Yes," she admitted, not happy about it.

"Then we shouldn't keep you from your desires any longer." He had learned more in his travels, things to do to make women more ardent. He demonstrated them all now, with a pride that Kelene thought was not as deserved as he did. Unfastening the lacing of her gonella, he kissed her neck. "I don't want you to be cold."

"I won't be." Over the last months she had become increasingly impervious to cold and heat.

"If you say you won't, so be it." His hands went to work more expertly than before, like a musician testing a new instrument. He had his mouth at her breast when she became aware that he was paying attention to her in a self-congratulatory way. Other men she had sought out had been less proficient, but a few had shown this same faintly contemptuous ease with her body. He stopped what he was doing. "What's the matter?"

"I . . . I don't know," she lied.

"Doesn't this please you?" He worked his tongue around her nipple, watching her face from the corner of his eye.

"It pleases me very much," she admitted, thinking it pleased her too much, too readily, too impersonally.

"Well, then." He went on, kneeling in the opening of her gonella. "I can tell you like this."

"I like it," she said, not wanting to try to deny what her body made obvious.

"You are tense," he said as he tried to part her thighs. "You've been without me too long. You have become caught up in wanting." He nodded to himself. "It will take a little longer, but you will like it better," he said to her, preparing to slip his fingers inside her. "In a short while, you will be like butter, all warm and sweet and slippery."

Kelene wondered where the frightened boy of last spring was. Was she actually more stirred by the sound of his pulse than the savor of his kisses?

Piro stroked and touched. Sweat stood out on his brow in spite of the cold. He panted, making ghosts on the air with each breath. He reached up with one hand and caressed her breasts, occasionally pinching her nipples.

Finally Kelene pretended she was ready for him, lying back against the loading ramp of the wagon, letting him get atop her as soon as she was in position. Since his need was now urgent, he was trembling with effort not to release too quickly. She slipped one hand over his buttock, the other around his back, and whispered, "Go ahead." Then, as he sighed and bucked, she put her mouth to his throat.

The glorious red fountain was sweeter than anything he had done to her; the wonder of it filled her as she continued to drink.

Piro collapsed on top of Kelene, his breathing still deep as he tried to recover himself. He was not yet aware that she had not stopped sucking the bite in his neck. He tried to turn his head, but she had not yet released him. He ran his hands down her flanks as if to show he was complimented.

Kelene was shocked at how much she had wanted to drain him. She had not understood until this night what Dracula had meant about the thrill of draining prey. Now she knew. She had barely stopped herself before Piro was dead. Her hands trembled as she put them to her face, as much to cover the stain on her mouth as to seem ashamed of what she had done.

"You really needed me," Piro said boastfully. "I could feel it."

"So could I," said Kelene, her voice subdued.

"Next time you'll enjoy it more," he said, his confidence restored.

"I hope you will, as well," said Kelene, her doubts greater than his. "I have to get back."

"Will you return tomorrow night?" he asked as he got off her, and held out his hand to help her up.

"No. Not so soon. The next night, perhaps, or the night after." She knew he would not have recovered enough until two nights passed. "One of the servants will inform you."

He winked. "I hate to waste time. We won't be here forever."

Kelene shook her head. "No; not forever." She let him kiss her once only, and very lightly, so he would not taste what was in her mouth.

"Do you want me to walk with you . . ." he offered, although the words sounded automatic.

"No," she said abruptly. "I know the way." She slipped away from him, hurrying back across the frosty grass.

A little more than a year later she killed him, draining all his blood as he lay beneath her. His impaling flesh shrunk away as she took his life into her, as she had taken his body.

She got off his corpse and closed up her new dark red gamurra before taking the time to lay him out for the gypsies to tend to in the morning. Her grief was slight, much less than she thought it would be. Perhaps in a day or a week she would feel something, but now there was only the profound satisfaction of a body replete.

When she went down into the vault, she found Dracula waiting for her, his gamache slightly stained in the front, the stain still wet and red. "The gypsies will want gold from you," she told him as she lifted her coffin lid.

"The boy?" Dracula asked. He nodded his approval.

"I know I killed a boy who gave me pleasure," she said, the first twinges of misery making her less content with what she had done.

"You would have done it eventually." He had gotten into his coffin and watched while she hesitated. "Do you suppose you could have continued to spare him?"

"I . . . I don't know."

"Or that the gypsies thought you would? They know what you are, and they serve me as devotedly as you do." He paused before closing himself in. "You said he had become cocksure. Would you have wanted him much longer?"

"His blood was sweet," she said by way of an answer.

"Sweeter than he had been, I'd wager," said Dracula. "Rest well, Kelene. You have pleased me very much."

She watched as his coffin lid dropped into place. It was time for her to do the same, but this time she had an irrational desire to watch the sunrise. How simple it would be. And there would be one more legend for the castle.

If only some of the women who had preceded her had not remained with Dracula so long, she would be able to give up this Un-Dead life, at least she told herself she could. But others had sustained themselves much longer, and she could not stand the failure her death would be; if one of them had lived for three centuries she would achieve four, or five. For a short while she remained undecided; then she lay down and closed herself in her coffin.

That autumn Magda tried to kill Kelene again. This time she waited in the corridor to the vaults, two torches in her hands. She met Kelene at a sharp bend in the passageway, stepping out to brandish the torches, laughing as she did. "This time you will not survive!" she crowed. "This time you perish!"

Kelene was more annoyed than frightened. "Put those down!" she ordered.

"Oh, no. I will not let you have the chance to hurt me." She thrust the torches ahead like fiery mauls. "You think you will keep him, don't you? You think he will defend you. But he gets no blood from you. I am more precious to him." She came a few steps closer and chuckled as Kelene retreated.

Kelene did not waste time or thought arguing with Magda. She continued to back up, holding her skirts up behind her with one hand, waiting for a chance to catch Magda off-guard, a moment when the servant over-reached herself or took an unwary step.

Magda continued to press what she thought was her advantage. "He has no use for you. I am what he needs. You are nothing."

"Then why bother to kill me?" Kelene asked, her tone as calm as if they sat together with their sewing.

"I do not like the regard he has for you," she confessed, swinging the two torches as if to light the hem of Kelene's new giornea. "You still look little more than a child, and you are anything but that. You're unnatural. You're an abomination."

Kelene moved backward more quickly, hoping that Magda would not realize how near they were to the main hall. If she could get out of the corridor she could face Magda with very little risk. She pictured the two curves that came before the main hall. One was near, the other a dozen strides beyond. She took care to count her steps.

"They'll bury you. With your head between your feet." Magda was getting reckless.

"Do you think that Dracula will not punish you if you kill me?" Kelene asked in the same steady tone as before.

"Why should he?" Magda demanded, then seemed to realize what Kelene was attempting to do. "Oh, no. You're not getting away from me, you wanton."

With only a breath in which to act, Kelene fell back as if she had tripped on her giornea and was helpless at Magda's feet. As Kelene hoped, Magda uttered a shrill cry and ran at her, torches at the ready, only to run into Kelene's upraised feet. An instant later she was flying over Kelene, torches lighting her own clothing as she went. Then she slammed into the corridor wall. The torches, beneath her, burned a moment longer then went out.

Kelene got to her feet and went to Magda. The woman was profoundly unconscious and the color of whey. Kelene knelt down next to her and tugged the front of her bodice open. She had almost finished feeding when Dracula appeared in the corridor.

"You have had trouble?" he ventured.

"Not any longer," said Kelene, finishing without apology.

The traveler was a middle-aged fellow in scholar's robes. He and his mule were making a bed in a peasant's barn almost three leagues from Dracula's castle; he had not noticed that the crucifix on the roof of the barn had fallen, nor had the peasant. He had an oil lamp for light and a journal to write in. He had settled down to record his day's observations after his frugal meal of cheese and smoked bacon when he noticed the barn door opening. This startled him, for he recalled hearing the peasant's family bolting the shutters over their windows shortly after sundown. He looked up, half-expecting the peasant to demand another silver duke for the lodging. Instead, he saw a ravishing, fair-haired girl on the edge of womanhood. She wore an old-fashioned gamurra—probably the gift of some landholder's wife—without a camisa. Her feet were bare and she smiled a welcome that was unmistakable.

"You must be lonely," she said as she came through the door and closed it again.

"I . . . . I don't think about it," said the scholar, who recently had thought of very little else. He could not imagine why this magnificent creature had come into the barn. What did a traveling scholar have that a lovely child would want?

"Then you would rather I go?" Kelene asked, pouting a little.

"No. No," said the scholar, getting up from his nest in the straw and wiping his hands on his stuff robe. In the next stall his mule munched contentedly on new hay. The scholar felt no alarm. He approached her tentatively. "Why did you come here?" He cursed himself for asking, for giving her an excuse to leave.

"I came because I am lonely, too." She held out her hands to him. "This place is so isolated. No one ever comes here."

He could easily believe that. He nodded. "And you want to know about the world beyond this place?"

"Among other things." She put her hands on his shoulders. "This place is not only isolated, it is boring." Her voice dropped. "You aren't boring, are you?"

Boring the scholar could well imagine. He had come from a hamlet in Bohemia and he could not remember it without an acute sense of wasted days and years. "Yes, places like this can stifle the mind, but the world exacts its own price. The world is not what you think," he began, as if preparing to lecture her.

"I know that," she said. "I would like to know other things. Worldly things." She slipped one hand inside his robe and unfastened the ruff at his neck. "I know a man like you has learned many things. You would rather show me those things than tell me about distant cities, wouldn't you?" She stopped her exploration as she encountered a chain around his neck. "What is this?"

"Saint Jerome," said the scholar, his breath coming faster. Nothing like this had ever happened to him; he could not believe it was happening now, but that he felt her hands and saw the lamplight glint in her blue eyes.

"This is not the sort of thing a saint should see," Kelene said. "Don't you think it would be best to—"

The scholar began to unfasten the chain. "Yes. Saint Jerome would not want to see what—" He tossed the medal aside, taking care to let it fall beside his journal so he would not lose it in the straw.

Kelene locked her hands behind his neck and tried to kiss him. He pulled back slightly. "Don't you want?" She was growing impatient as he drew back from her.

"You are an eager child, aren't you?" he said, making it almost a rebuke. He brushed her loose golden hair back from her face to take the sting out of what he had said. "Do not rush when there is no reason to."

His fingers made their way down her neck to the half-open corsage. "Let me have a little time, and we will both be happier for it."

She let him make a place in the straw, and as he began to recline, she went to his side. "Tell me what to do," she said, letting her clothes fall open.

The scholar stared. This child with her budding woman's body was offering him enjoyment beyond anything he had known since his student days. What was such a treasure doing here in the mountains of Transylvania? He did his best not to look too long, or if he stared, not to do it too hungrily. "Come here beside me. There's plenty of room." He patted the straw and had a moment's terror that she might change her mind and deny him, even accuse him of forcing her. "I won't hurt you."

"Mine!" Kelene exclaimed as she pulled him forward into a kiss that lasted until the scholar had to breathe. "It's been so long," she whispered, running her tongue over his lips, down his jaw to his neck. Then she began to open his clothes, all the while displaying a skill at pleasure that left the scholar astounded when he could feel anything more than the chaos of his senses.

His last thoughts before she went for his throat were that if he were to die now, he would die happy.

"You've fed well," said Dracula when Kelene met him in the main hall toward the end of the night. He was in his deep purple lucco, and there was a golden fillet around his brow, making him as regal as he was sinister.

"The peasants will find him in the morning. They will put a stake through him, to be sure he doesn't waken at sunset." She wanted to sound indifferent to this fate, but was unable to manage it.

"It will not matter to him, Kelene. He is lost already. Nothing they can do to his body will change anything." Dracula watched her for a moment. "Where are you going to hunt again?"

She had thought about it on the way back to the castle. "To the west this time, tomorrow night, or the night after. There is a shrine on the road that the people of the region call a saint, but is not. Travelers shelter there, thinking it is—"

"Safe. I know the place. The ancient god who protected that place has been forgotten." He indicated the windows two floors above them. "It is time you and I were asleep," he declared.

"So it is." She did her best to match his tone. When he was pleased with her she was not wholly alone.

He laid his hand on her shoulder. "Come." As they continued down the corridor, he said, "I have heard that there is a party of travelers from

Hungary bound for the east who will reach here in a night or so. I think we must make them welcome."

"Yes, if there are not too many of them," Kelene answered.

"Four men and their escort. The escort can be dealt with. The men will be the prey." He nodded in the direction of the vault. "Rest well."

Kelene felt a coldness go through her that was new. It was one thing to hunt away from the castle, but quite another to lure— "Why not meet them on the road?"

Dracula regarded her with a look of disappointment. "Think, girl. There are four of them. They will be noticed, as will any visitors they might receive. If they are here, we will not be at risk, and they will not be able to escape." He halted and made her turn to him. "We need not drain them all at once. We can keep them for a while, and use them many times. We will not have to hunt as long as they still live." He showed his teeth, but he did not smile.

Something deep within Kelene shattered as she heard this; from the first Dracula had been guiding her to such compliance. Nothing would change it, if it could be changed. She ducked her head. "I didn't understand," she said very quietly.

No night ever as dark as this one
No soul as damned . . .
—Greek lament, 16th century

⊢ XXXII ⊣

Over the next few years, Kelene became proficient at seduction; in time she began to enjoy the satisfaction she gained from deceit as much as the blood she drank. She learned that her fourteen-year-old body and face made her alluring to many men, who did not reckon on the fierceness of her soul. She never had visions anymore; at times she had difficulty recalling she had ever had a family.

Two servants replaced Magda: Donje, who was not yet eleven and served as a chambermaid, and Syna, who was mad enough to see armies in the air but whose needlework was flawless. These women became the nearest thing Kelene had to companions. The servants, the soldiers, and, for the end of winter and start of spring, the gypsies were all the society Dracula allowed Kelene to have.

"You are calling again, aren't you?" Kelene demanded one night when they had returned from their hunting. "You are trying to find a new—"

"Another," he corrected her. "You are alone. You would be happier if you had someone else to—"

"Share you with?" she challenged. "That is what you intend, isn't it?" She had not known this could frighten her so much. She was certain of what her place was with him so long as there were no others to claim any obligation from him.

"Are you defying me, girl?" He gave her some little time to answer; when she said nothing, he folded his arms. "You will not defy me."

"And you will not demean me by putting another in my place!" She could feel his betrayal as surely as she had felt the heat of Magda's torches. "How can you do this?"

"You do not rule here, girl. I do," he reminded her sharply, and strode off without looking back.

Kelene had not been able to weep for some years. Instead she tore her latest embroidery to shreds and draped these over the furniture in the main hall. It gave her a sense of striking back that evaporated almost as quickly as she experienced it. How dare he bring another— She could not think of it without fury. Then something happened to calm her: a cohesion of impressions deep within her provided a key to her problem. She sat down in the tallest chair, her hands in her lap; the lamplight on her face showed features serenely unexpressive, like those of a saint in an ikon. When she rose a little later, she was untroubled. She had found her answer. "Syna," she called as she looked up toward the gallery where the madwoman usually spent her empty hours.

"My lady?" Syna answered, her voice thick with sleep. She thrust her head over the gallery railing and blinked at the rent fabric hanging from the furniture. "Ghosts!" she cried out, and hid behind the nearest pillar in the gallery.

"No. No," said Kelene, trying to keep her from becoming lost in her delusions. "I have . . . done something with my sewing. That is all."

Syna peeked out. "Your sewing? My lady? Is that what I see?" The trusting, cautious question almost made Kelene change her mind, but then she steeled herself, unwilling to give up her tenuous place in Dracula's realm.

"I have something I must tell you," she said, and motioned to Syna to come to her. "Nothing will hurt you while I am here." It took some time to coax Syna down from the gallery, and then Kelene had to remove all her torn sewing from where she had draped it before the haunted look left Syna's eyes.

"What do you want, my lady?" Syna inquired with a respectful nod of her head.

"I want you to watch for me." Kelene managed a conspiratorial smile. "I want you to keep alert for intruders." She turned Syna's face to hers. "Not like the travelers who come here from time to time, or like the soldiers, but something worse. If Dracula brings a new woman here, she will be dangerous. We will have to protect him from her so that we will not all perish." She leaned forward. "She must not be allowed to live. She will have to be burned in her coffin if any of us are to survive." Now she patted Syna's hand solicitously. "If we are reduced to beggary, I will try to make sure you do not starve."

"Why would we be beggars?" Syna asked, her voice rising in fear.

"Because the woman Dracula brings is dangerous and she will ruin everything." Kelene glared at the oil lamps near the hearth. "If we do not destroy her, she will destroy us." Nothing was more certain to her than that.

"I will watch," Syna promised.

"Very good. We will take care of Dracula if he will not take care of himself," Kelene said, the fear which had gnawed at her entrails retreating.

Dracula departed for Cernovcy at the end of the harvest, swearing to return before the gypsies did. Kelene watched him go with black wrath in her heart. While he was gone she lured a merchant from Poland to the castle and kept him alive for more than two weeks, dispatching him reluctantly when he fell into a stupor.

When Dracula returned he brought with him a nun, a woman of about twenty with the unmarked face of piety and a full measure of denied desires that made her willing to devote herself to Dracula instead of plaster statues. Her coffin, a plain oaken box, accompanied her from Cernovcy, removed along with her from the convent. Her name was Euphrosia, for the saint martyred at Jerusalem, and she had spent all her life from age seven in her convent. She bore herself with habitual humility that made Kelene long to pull the wimple from her head.

"You will learn to like her, girl," Dracula told her; this was an order.

"But how? She thinks I am a harlot," said Kelene.

"She is like you were when I brought you: she does not know who she is. It will take her longer than you to throw off the shackles of her training. You had endured enough to know that there will always be change. She has not learned that yet." He put his hand on Kelene's shoulder, resting it heavily.

Kelene made a gesture of consent and sent for Syna at once.

"But she is a holy woman," Syna objected, when Kelene reminded her of what they had to do.

"She *looks* like a holy woman," Kelene corrected her. "You know that holy clothing often conceals great evil." She looked deep into Syna's eyes. "If we let such a woman stay with Dracula, she will bring destruction."

Syna trembled and fixed her gaze on a blank place in the air. "They see her. They see her."

Kelene knew better than to ask whom. She laid her hand on Syna's. "You must watch her."

On the night Dracula took Euphrosia's life—with less ceremony than he had given Kelene—Syna and Kelene watched from the gallery, the madwoman whimpering occasionally for no reason Kelene could discern.

"Before she wakes, you must burn her coffin," said Kelene when Dracula had carried Euphrosia from the main hall toward the vaults. "Take the torch from the wall and burn the coffin while she is sleeping." She was not certain that Syna understood her. "You have to burn her while she is in her coffin asleep," she insisted.

"Before sundown," said Syna, her expression distant.

"Yes. Before sundown. If you do not do this, Dracula will suffer and so will I." She wanted to be sure that Syna grasped the importance of what she required. "This will save us all."

"Burned in her coffin," Syna muttered.

"Yes," Kelene said emphatically, encouraging Syna. "Before she can harm us, we must—"

"Burn her in her coffin." This time Syna spoke with as much conviction as Kelene had ever heard. "Burn in her coffin. Before sundown." Her face had the shine of fanaticism as she put her hands over her heart and said once more, "Burn in her coffin."

Kelene smiled. "I will be grateful to you, Syna. Always."

"Before sundown," Syna chanted, not quite hearing anything Kelene said.

She woke to the odor of charring and fading screams. She seized the latch that opened the coffin lid and swung it open, making herself move swiftly as if in fright.

"What has happened?" she asked loudly as she got out of her coffin with alacrity.

Household servants stood around the ashes on the catafalque on the other side of Dracula's coffin; four of them held buckets and there were puddles of water on the uneven stone floor. Two blackened planks were all that remained of Euphrosia's coffin.

The steward looked at Kelene as if startled to see her. "One of the servants . . . She claimed she knew . . ." He indicated the ashes in a helpless shrug.

"You mean, the burning was deliberate?" Kelene asked, glancing nervously at Dracula's coffin. "How could that happen?"

"The servant took a torch from the corridor. She came down here. She . . . she served you, and she must have thought . . ." Again the steward shrugged.

"Served me? What are you talking about?" Kelene was now genuinely worried. She looked from one servant to another. "Who did this?"

"Syna," said one of the others. "Well, you know she did not . . . she was addled. You know she was."

Kelene knew this was an excuse for inaction, but she let it pass. Dracula might say more later, but she would not speak against any of them. "You say was?"

"Efran, there," said the steward, pointing to the most strapping of the servants, "smelled the smoke and raised the alarm. When he came down, he saw Syna with her torch standing at the foot of the master's coffin.

The new one was already burning. He fought with the woman and in their struggle he broke her neck." He made another motion to show he had played no part in it. "She is lying outside in the courtyard."

"I want to see her," said Kelene, thinking rapidly, trying to avoid the encroaching sense of guilt that took all the pleasure from Euphrosia's death. She thought she must owe Syna an apology, although she could not help but be relieved that the madwoman could no longer talk.

"There was nothing else he could do," said the steward.

"I still want to see her," said Kelene.

Again the steward looked upset. "There will be light in the sky for a while. The sun is down, but it isn't night yet." His demeanor became even more self-effacing. "It would not be right to bring her inside again."

"Yes, I understand," said Kelene, a bit more briskly. "If the sun is down I should not suffer too much." She went past the gathered servants and the last of the wreckage of the coffin, not realizing how much her demonstration of concern for her servant impressed the rest of the household.

The northern courtyard was deep in shadow, but Kelene could see the supine form of Syna laid out not far from the small gate that led out of the courtyard and onto a narrow breastwork walkway over the river gorge. She went over to her servant's body. "You deserved better," she said, with sorrow in her voice.

"And you deserved worse," said Dracula out of the shadows. "If I did not think I have some part in what you did, you should be as cold as that poor demented creature who did your will." He stopped an arm's length from her. He was very straight and grand, with his cloak hanging behind him as she remembered him from her visions. "I will not trust you again, not after you instigated this." He nudged Syna's body with his booted foot.

Kelene had no defense to offer and she knew it. "I could not endure a rival."

"She was not a rival," said Dracula.

"Not to you," Kelene said in an undervoice. "You—"

"You are mine. You do my will," said Dracula. "And you must show me that you do not oppose me." He touched her fair hair. "Until you do, you are forbidden to leave the castle—"

"But—but how will I—" To remain at the castle was to be deprived of all opportunity for variety in sustenance.

"Any traveler reaching the castle will be yours. You may use the travelers as you wish. And when the gypsies return, they will take mercy on you—perhaps." He turned away from her. "Your coffin will be moved to a different part of the vault. It will be up to you to find it." Then the shadows swallowed him up.

"But who— If you are not with me, I am alone," Kelene called after him, her words a plea so heartfelt that she was certain he must turn.

"That you are," came his voice out of the darkness.

Kelene stood next to Syna for half the night, unable to return to the castle, afraid of what the servants might do to her. When she finally went inside again, Donje met her with the news that her kindness to poor, mad Syna had moved the other servants to look on her with new respect. Kelene heard this without responding, afraid anything she would say would show her for the traitor she was.

More than two years later, Kelene at last had the chance to vindicate herself. By that time she had become desperate, her body plagued by hunger, her mind searching for new experiences. The exile Dracula imposed upon her seemed complete. She often wandered by the library, longing for the ability to read. If she had the chance to use the books, she would not be so wretched, or so she told herself. There was so little to do. Sewing palled, and she had long since learned her way through the confusing levels and corridors of the castle. She was coming to understand how women like Syna might go mad.

It was late in the year and an icy rain was falling, promising sleet and snow in the next few days. The servants had begun to ready the castle for the inaction of the Nativity, and Dracula was often gone all night in preparation for the week he would remain inside the walls.

Kelene had been pacing the gallery over the main hall when one of the servants came hurrying to find her. She had put on her wine-red velvet gamurra the gypsies had brought on their last visit. The waist was higher than her others, and the skirts had stiffening to hold them out. She had decided it was not very comfortable, though it looked very grand with huge slashed sleeves edged in gold, with the inserted sleeves pulled out through the slashes. She paused as the servant signaled her. "A traveler has come," he announced with some trepidation.

"A traveler? At this time of year?" Kelene asked. She was famished. "Alone?"

"So it seems," said the servant. "He has a donkey, but no escort."

"Is he lost?" she wondered aloud.

"It would seem so," the servant replied. He waited, his head bowed, while Kelene thought.

"Dracula is gone for the night." She knew the answer.

"Yes." The servant coughed. "We can bring food to the main hall."

It had been two months since Kelene had had a traveler to entertain. Her hunger was a constant demand. "Yes. Do that. Something very nice. Whatever is in the pantry. Pork and . . . oh, whatever the cook does well." She began to pace, not with restless constraint this time, but with exhilaration. "If he needs a bath, see he has one."

"The bathhouse is hot," the servant told her.

"Good. That will give you a little time to make the main hall more . . . comfortable." Her smile was practiced, a combination of innocence and lasciviousness that had captivated more than one unfortunate man. She clapped her hands at the servant. "Well, get to it. And tell Donje to bring the ermine rug. He might as well see the best we have to offer." She thought of one more thing. "Tell me what you learn about him as soon as he goes to bathe."

"At once," said the servant and hurried away to receive the traveler.

Kelene went down to the main hall quickly, and called for more oil lamps to be hung and lit. She had no intention of letting the new arrival have his first meeting with her in a room as dark as a cave. She ordered another whole section of log for the fireplace and called for a pair of jeweled chalices, and the huge, overstuffed Turkish hassocks for reclining upon when the traveler had finished his supper. The servants made haste to do as she commanded.

In a short while the first servant was back. "He is from the west, a young man, perhaps eighteen or so, with light brown hair; fair, but not golden like yours. He has a short beard, the kind the men from Austria wear, full around the chin and jaw but not very long. He wears good clothing and his boots are first quality."

"What weapons?" Kelene hoped he was not a young mercenary looking for work; that could be trouble.

"He has only the arms a prudent man carries: a short sword and a dagger."

"Is he Austrian, do you think? Swiss? They're fair, aren't they? Bohemian? German? Hungarian? Polish? Serbian?" Kelene asked, wanting to know how to address him when he was led to her.

"He speaks Hungarian but with a Greek accent," said the servant.

Kelene's smile faltered. "A Greek accent? Are you sure?"

"Greek or something similar," said the servant. "It is much fainter than your accent, hardly more than a trace."

"Ah," said Kelene, her anticipation increasing, for fellowship, no matter how fleeting, she treasured beyond anything but blood; she might even have the pleasure of speaking Greek again for a few nights. "Then I should plan something remarkable for him, something that he will never forget."

"What more can we do?" the servant asked. "The food is being prepared. Is there anything else you want done?"

"You can make sure the setting is the best. Gold plates, everything on covered platters, the best we can give him. Oh, and make sure he has at least two goblets of wine before you bring him in here; make it the Bull's Blood. I want him ready for—"

The servant bowed and went away; the hassocks were put in place, close to the hearth but not so near the dining table to be too obvious. Kelene continued her efforts, ordering Donje to put sandalwood in the braziers at the far end of the main hall. She was sorry she had lost her reflection, for she wanted to know she was as attractive as possible. This man would have to supply her needs for at least two weeks if she were not to be reduced to the most severe pangs of hunger before the gypsies returned. If Donje were a little older, she would be tempted to ask her opinion, but Donje was still more child than woman and thought anything in velvet was beautiful.

By the time the main hall was ready, the servants said the traveler was almost finished with his bath.

"Give him a guarnacca to wear, one with loose sleeves so he will not have to fight his clothes," Kelene ordered, filled with seductive plans.

Donje said she would tend to it; she wanted to see this man who had so excited Kelene. "He will be tripping over his own feet in his eagerness to be with you. You will enjoy him as much as he enjoys you."

"So long as he wants what he finds, he need not trip; I will be certain that his enjoyment is assured," said Kelene as she put the finishing touch on her ensemble—a long strand of pearls that hung down between her breasts, emphasizing their smallness and the smoothness of her skin. She wore no camisa. With her gamurra lacings all but undone, she was a most enticing figure, or so she hoped.

"He will be ready shortly," said Donje. "They are giving him wine, to preserve the warmth from the bath."

"Very good." Kelene readied herself to meet the newcomer.

Donje glanced down the corridor leading to the kitchen. "I hear voices."

Kelene did as well, but she did not mean to seem anxious. It wasn't as if this were the first time she had ever seduced an unwary traveler.

The young man was escorted by the steward. He was in the guarnacca Kelene had requested; it was one that Dracula had worn years ago and then discarded. It dragged around the feet of the traveler as he made his way carefully down the hall, his hand still holding a pewter goblet. In the lamplight, Kelene saw that his hair was indeed light brown, and he had the stalwart handsomeness of youth; his beard was full enough to make his jaw appear wide and firm whether it was or not. He was not completely steady on his feet, and when he said something to the steward, his words slurred; his voice was low and musical. His cheeks were rosy from wine and the bath, and as he glanced ahead, he fell silent.

"Good evening, traveler," Kelene said in Hungarian, lowering her head in a gesture of counterfeit modesty. "On behalf of the lord of this castle, I welcome you."

"Happy . . . happy to be . . . be here," he said as he drained the contents of the goblet and handed it to the steward. "Excel . . . cellent wine. Don't know . . . when I've had better." Despite his efforts his speech was not crisp. He looked around the main hall, his eyes slightly glazed in the lamplight. "Quite . . . beaut . . . utiful. You're hospit . . . able to strangers." He laughed, and had to grab for the top of a high-backed chair to keep upright. "Sorry. Didn't intend . . . tend." He swayed and steadied himself. "So much wine . . . I probably . . . ably shouldn't have . . . have had that third . . . cup." He belched heartily. "Empty stomach. Sorry."

"We have been remiss," said Kelene. "Bring in food for our guest. He is hungry." For Kelene, just speaking the word aloud was painful, a reminder that she was famished.

"Thank you," said the traveler. He leaned a little nearer to Kelene. "Such hair. Like spun gold."

"Thank *you*." She gave him a hesitant look, but one intended to encourage him. "Here is the table laid for your feast," she went on, gesturing to indicate the dinner waiting for him. The arm movement pulled her loosely fastened gamurra lacings open slightly and gave him a fleeting glimpse of her flat young belly. "I will do myself the honor of serving you."

He looked at her in diffuse shock. "You? But you're . . . you're . . ."

"The lord of this castle has not yet returned tonight," she said. His accent reminded her a little of her father. "I will be host in his stead." The tip of her tongue flicked over her lips. "Sit down. You will not have to starve any longer." With that she held out the chair for him, and lifted the lid on the tureen. The fragrance of onions flooded through the main hall. "There is bread in the basket. Let me ladle this out for you." She had her hand on the utensil before the traveler sat down. "This soup is very sustaining."

A cold wind went through the main hall, making the traveler shiver as he reached for the bread. Kelene looked up into the gallery but saw nothing to account for it. An instant later it stopped.

Collecting her thoughts, Kelene poured out the soup into the large, gold bowl. "It is very good."

He blinked twice. "You aren't having any?" he asked, watching her pour wine into one of the two jeweled chalices.

"It is my custom to have my meal when my guest is done," she said smoothly, putting the chalice within easy reach. Then she drew up a chair and sat on its arm, letting the folds of her gamurra fall so as to reveal glimpses of her leg. The swell of her small breast showed enticingly through the gamurra lacings. "Do not think about me. I will be satisfied."

The traveler was just drunk enough to be willing to let this pass. He reached for the bread and broke off a chunk to eat the soup. "Good," he approved. "My own sister . . . sister couldn't do better." He let the bread soak in the soup as he had a taste of the new wine.

Kelene played with the open lacing of her gamurra, then fingered the rope of pearls. "What do you think?"

Taking a larger swallow of wine than he had intended, the traveler said, "Lovely. Just . . . lov . . . ely."

"Do you like—" She ended this with a rearrangement of the gamurra's velvet skirts, revealing more of her leg to provide him another temptation.

He had the soup-soaked bread halfway to his mouth. "I like," he said, then bit down eagerly on the bread, so that the soup ran through his fingers and he had to lick them quickly. He gave a soft, self-conscious laugh.

This was very promising, thought Kelene; she saw his face flush. In a short while he would be more ravenous for her than for the food he was being served. She lifted the lid on the largest platter, revealing a roast goose stuffed with raisins, mushrooms, and rice. "This is next. There is pork after," she said, recognizing the odor from the other good-sized platter.

"Wonderful," said the traveler, and reached out negligently to touch her pearls where they fell down her front. "Pretty."

Kelene poured more wine in the chalice, giving him another opportunity to touch her pearls. She shivered as his hand brushed the curve of her waist. "You have come far?"

He blinked at her. "Far? Today? No. Not today. Not in such weather." He busied himself finishing the soup while Kelene began to cut meat off the goose. "Started two months ago." He drank the last of the soup and washed it down with wine. "Fine. Fine. Fine, fine, fine."

"Have you much further to go?" Kelene asked, transferring the slices of goose to the edge of the platter so he could more easily reach it.

"I . . . I don't quite . . . know," he confessed as he stuck his fork into the goose.

"Why?" she pursued, edging nearer to him. "Are you so far from the main road?"

"I . . . don't know," he said a second time, dutifully chewing on the goose she had cut for him. His eyes kept straying to her.

"The pork," she announced, lifting the lid. "Shall I slice some for you?"

He nodded several times, trying to swallow the goose. He drank more wine to wash it down. "Very good," he said.

As she sliced she leaned over the table so that the opening of her gamurra revealed her breast; her pearls swung forward and seemed in danger of being dragged through the tangy sauce covering the pork. The traveler reached out to grab them, and as he did, he slid his hand inside her corsage and cupped her breast. Kelene held very still. Finally as he started to withdraw his hand, she said, "You don't have to."

The flush that stole over his cheeks made her suspect he was not quite so old as she had thought at first; either that, or he had been raised by monks and popes and had had little experience of women. "I . . . I . . . you . . ." In his confusion and embarrassment, he downed the last of the wine in the chalice.

Kelene refilled it, then took his hand and returned it to her breast. "If it pleases you, I am pleased."

Quickly he licked his other fingers clean and reached out for her, resting his head between her breasts. He sighed deeply. "God." Kelene winced and he started to draw back.

"No," she told him. "Just let me move a little." She came a step nearer to him, trusting he would not use holy names again for a while. "Isn't this more comfortable?"

He nodded, his face against her body. "If I weren't . . . en't drunk, I could . . . keep my hands . . . off . . . off you."

"Then I am thankful you are drunk."

"So'm I," he admitted, nuzzling her breast and fumbling with the folds of her gamurra to secure a better purchase on her.

Kelene allowed him to stroke her clumsily for a little while, but as his breathing deepened, she moved back a step, holding out her hand to him as he looked at her in dismay. "Come," she said, preparing to help him get up. "You and I will be more comfortable in front of the fire."

He did not at first understand her; then he mumbled something about liking his supper cold. He staggered to his feet and let Kelene guide him to the hassocks. He dropped onto them without grace, and flopped back against the huge cushions, his eyes too shiny in the lamp- and firelight. He held his arms up to her.

Kelene knelt down beside him, opening his guarnacca, then slowly licking him from his navel to his chin.

Breath hissed in through his teeth. He murmured something in Greek as she pushed his clothing aside and straddled him while he could still respond. She was on him in a single, sinuous movement. As he moved slowly beneath her, she bent forward to nip at his throat.

His blood filled her mouth as his seed filled her barren womb.

Almost at once he was asleep, snoring gently while Kelene lay beside him, gently licking away the last trickle of blood.

He wakened well into the night. He tried to say something, but she waved his remarks away.

"We will have many nights to share delights," she said as she leaned forward to kiss his brow.

He shook his head. "No. No, I must continue my journey tomorrow." He looked shamefaced as he admitted this. "I told your servants—"

"The roads will be impassable tomorrow," she said steadily. "Your journey can wait until you may travel without freezing." She leaned near enough to press her body to his.

He sighed. "I wish I could." He reached out and fingered the golden tendrils around her face, a distant expression in his eyes. "She was about your age, with yellow hair."

Kelene had been trying to think of other ways to persuade him to remain with her, since she would keep him until she drained him of life and blood. She did not at first hear what he had said. "Who?"

He propped himself on his elbows. "My sister. She was taken away from us, oh, more than seven years now. I swore I would find her and bring her back."

Kelene nodded, half-thinking of how to keep him at the castle, half-listening.

He rubbed his beard. "I wanted to try sooner, but until my mother married again, she needed me to help her at the inn. She told me it was useless to look for my sister after so long, and made me promise that if I have not found her in a year I will return to Belgrade and admit she is gone."

"And when will that be?" Kelene's voice was high and strange.

"On the Feast of Saint Nicephorus of Antioch; I have a little more than a month left." He yawned, stretching, and then put his hand to his head. "The wine."

It was an effort for Kelene to speak. "Your mother—what is her name?"

He answered without hesitation. "Melantha. We came from—"

"Salonika," said Kelene, wanting to embrace him and run from him at once. "You can't be Achilles."

He stared at her. "Achilles? How do you—" Then his face went white. "I am Orien."

"Orien? But they sold you! You were just a child." She rose and backed away from him, beginning to shake all over.

"Kelene?" He stared at her. *"Kelene?"* He was sitting upright now, pulling his guarnacca closed. "But you're . . . you're . . . You're twenty-one, or twenty-two. You can't be Kelene. You *can't!"* Somehow he scrambled to his feet, panic in his face.

"I know how I look," Kelene said, trying to keep him from bolting.

"Well, to speak truth, I do not know how I look. That is why I am no older than what you remember." She continued to talk as he started to back away from her, horror showing in every nuance of movement, every shift of expression. "I wouldn't have done . . . this, if I had. . . . But I didn't. Nor did you. It was a mistake, Orien. A *mistake*." She was on her feet going after him. "Please Orien. Don't look at me like that."

"What are you? God and the angels, what has become of you?" He reached for his neck where his medals and crucifix would be, but they were gone. His eyes widened in fear.

Kelene did little more than flinch at the holy names. "Orien. You don't understand." She stepped closer and tried to gently touch his arm, but he managed to elude her.

"Get away from me. Don't come *near* me!" He continued to retreat from her toward the dining table, his clothing clutched tightly closed. "Dear God, Mother was right to warn me. She said you were not—" He reached for a chair with his free hand and shoved it between them. His retreat put the table in Kelene's path. "Oh, no. Oh, no. Sweet Savior, how can I tell them? How can I *go back*?"

"You cannot go back," Kelene cried. "You—"

Her answer was interrupted by laughter, soft and cruel, from the gallery above them. Dracula moved into the light. "No, you cannot go back. You cannot leave."

She looked at her brother, whose stricken eyes were filled with loathing, and then at Dracula.

Then she rounded on Orien. "You came to save me, little brother, and so you shall." With a power she had never felt before she sprang at him, leaping onto the dining table and scattering the remnants of the meal. The chalice overturned and spilled wine across the table and floor. Platters and tureen crashed, goose and pork and bread and soup mingling as one.

Then she fell on him, his pleas unheard, his struggles in vain, his curses and cries of *"Monster! Devil!"* cut off without hesitation.

She rose sated, stronger than she had ever been and free from the burden of false hope. She went to Dracula's side, leaving Orien's body where it lay like so much discarded rubbish. "I am your sl—" she began.

"Yes. You are mine," he said, and very slowly kissed her brother's blood from her mouth.